Once There Was Fire

Once There Was Fire

A Novel of Old Hawaii

Stephen Shender

Pai'ea Press
Aptos, California

Maps courtesy of Lahaina Printsellers, Maui, Hawaii

Cover: Kamehameha Landing at O'ahu, 1795; Copyright Herbert K. Kane, LLC
By permission of the artist's estate

Publisher imprint design: Linda Pope

ISBN: 0692771336
ISBN 9780692771334
Library of Congress Control Number: 2016917974
Pai'ea Press, APTOS, CALIFORNIA

With love, for Lisa, Melanie, Troy, and Jane

Table of Contents

Ka'ahumanu

Kalanimālokuloku, son of Keoua Kalanikupuapa'ikalaninui. Keoua was the *ali'i moku*—high chief—of the Kohala District on the *moku nui*—the "Big Island"—of Hawai'i. His father was Kalanike'eaumoku, and his father—my great-great grandfather—was Keawe II, who ruled Hawai'i in the days when the haole monarchs King James II and Queen Mary II sat on the English throne. My grandmother's forbears ruled the island when Queen Elizabeth wore the crown. By mo'olelo reckoning, I can trace my high-born lineage back nearly seven hundred years to the days of Pili, the first great *mō'ī* of all Hawai'i, who boldly sailed here from distant Samoa, at a time when the haoles' ancestors still believed that the waters' horizon marked the end of the earth.

What haole missionary, merchant, or whaler can say the same? Who are they but descendants of the flotsam and jetsam of Europe—of ne'er-do-wells, religious outcasts, and common criminals? They immigrate to our islands in ever-increasing numbers, with little respect for us and less understanding. They would have us forget our own people's ways and adopt theirs. I have adopted many of their customs, in outward manner at least. But I never forget that I am *Hawaiian*, and I am resolved that future generations will not forget. This mo'olelo will be my legacy to them.

The haoles consider our people indolent. We were never thus before they came. We were industrious people. We wrested a living from the land with implements of wood and stone and with our bare hands. We reshaped whole mountainsides into terraced fields, irrigated them, and farmed every inch of arable soil. We bred and cultivated *taro* for wetland planting and dry-land planting. We grew sweet potatoes, breadfruit, yam, banana, coconut, and sugarcane. We raised pigs, ducks, and geese. From plant fibers and bones we made fishing line and hooks; we wove nets, constructed traps, transformed trees into canoes, and harvested the bounty of the sea.

Occasionally, the sea also delivered a bounty of a different sort than the accustomed fish, octopus, and squid—strange pieces of wood with long, narrow, sharp-pointed objects of an unknown material embedded in them that we would sometimes find washed up on our beaches. These we sometimes called *koa li'ili'i*, or little koa, after the hard wood of the koa trees, from which we fashioned our canoes. Other times, our people called them *pahoa*, because they were sharp, like our wooden daggers of old. We treasured them as rare gifts from Kanaloa, the god of the sea, and we sometimes affixed them to our clubs to enhance their deadliness. We knew nothing of the haoles' iron in those days.

We were disciplined people. Our old ways were often hard. Our society was well ordered and our *kapus*—our laws—were unforgiving.

Over everyone were the ali'i, the chiefs who kept order among our people. Next were the *kāhuna*, our priests. The kāhuna guided the chiefs in their decisions. They prayed to the gods, divined their intentions, interceded with them for the chiefs and the common people with sacrifices of animals—and, yes, even human sacrifices—as events demanded or the seasons warranted, and maintained the *heiaus*, the temples of the gods. In this way, they ensured—as much as they could—that the gods would not become angry with the people and would bless them with abundance.

Other priests tended to our people in times of illness. Still others were expert in the meaning of weather patterns, in astronomy and navigation. They were our high masters of various practical pursuits such as farming, canoe building, and carving.

Below the kāhuna were the *maka'āinana*, the "people of the land." They farmed, fished, and plied crafts as their parents had done before them. The maka'āinana were hard-working folk upon whom the ali'i and the kāhuna depended almost entirely for clothing, material goods, and sustenance. They were free people who could come and go as they pleased. Nevertheless, many ali'i persisted in calling them *kānaka*—their servants.

Last were the *kauwa-maoli*, the defiled ones. The kauwa were either born to their low estate or they tumbled into it by defeat in battle. Once kauwa, a person could not hope to rise to a higher state. It was his fate to labor for the maka'āinana, who in turn accepted their own lot.

The ali'i, however, were never satisfied with theirs, constantly contending among themselves for power and land. Throughout our history, this contention—between island chieftains and island kingdoms—was ceaseless. Disputes were often settled by war. The ali'i went to war without consulting the commoners under their protection, calling upon them to take up arms on their behalf whenever they deemed it necessary. The maka'āinana obeyed their chieftains' orders without question. To do anything else was forbidden—*kapu.*

The ali'i enforced the kapus. The penalty for transgressions was most often death. For example, a commoner could be executed for failing to prostrate himself before a chief, or even for touching the shadow of certain ali'i. In the haoles' eyes, and in the eyes of our young people today, these old laws are repugnant. In the old days, however, our chiefs believed that such severe penalties were required to enforce respect for themselves and for their authority, which they believed was essential to preserve order.

As severe as they were, our old laws were tempered by mercy. The laws of the gods—*kapu akua*—bestowed absolution upon those who ran afoul of *kapu ali'i,* the laws of the chiefs. Any person who violated a kapu ali'i had the right to seek asylum in a sacred place of refuge. If this unfortunate could attain such a place before a chief's punishment could fall upon him, he was deemed under the gods' protection. After a time, a kahuna would pardon him and he could then return home, unmolested.

Our gods were many and they invested every aspect of our lives. Our greatest gods were Kāne, Kū, Lono, and Kanaloa. Kāne was the first mover, the creator of all we see. Kū was the god of male strength and plentiful harvests. Kū was also the god of war. Lono was the god of wind, clouds, and rain, and fertility. We looked to Kanaloa, the god of the sea, for bounteous fishing. We had many lesser gods and goddesses. Laka, the goddess of hula, and her sister, Pele, goddess of the volcano, were foremost among them. There were gods of plants and of animals, gods of streams and pools, gods of mist, and gods of fog. Each family had its own guardian god, its *'aumakua.* Truly, everything around us was spiritual. The most important gods required offerings, and Kāne and Kū frequently demanded human sacrifices. But Lono only rarely required human flesh.

Unlike the haoles, we took joy in our bodies. We were people of nature, and sexual pleasure was part of nature's order, and part of our harmony with nature. For us it was a matter of delight, not denial. Our men could partner with many women, and our women could partner with many men, as love or simple attraction dictated. Still, lifelong unions were common among our people, and for clarity's sake, I will often speak of "marriage," "husbands" and "wives," and even "in-laws." But in truth, marriage in the haole sense was unknown to our people before the Christian missionaries' arrival. Thus, no one's circumstance of birth could ever be a cause for shame among us.

Thus we lived for centuries—secure in our rank, mindful of our laws, and in harmony with our gods and their creation. We had much *aloha* in our lives, but we did not live tranquilly. We were violent when necessary, as bloodthirsty in war-making as we were lusty in lovemaking. Bloody conflict was a constant among us as our chiefs contended for dominion. But in this respect, we were no worse than the haoles themselves.

We persisted in our intramural bloodletting for hundreds of years, until one man put an end to it by subduing all the islands. That man was my late uncle, Kamehameha. This is his story, as I mostly learned it from his favorite brother—my late father, Kalanimālokuloku, better remembered these days as Keli'imaika'i.

Alapa'i

ʻA ʻohe puʻu kiʻekiʻe ke hoʻāʻo ʻia e piʻi
No cliff is so tall that it cannot be scaled

threw herself into Keoua's arms, crying. He broke free of her des-
and held her at arm's length. "Where is our child?" he demanded.
‹eoua," she replied through her tears, "someone or something
e night and took him from me as I slept." With this, she collapsed
wailing inconsolably.
s true?" Keoua asked, directing his question to his sister-in-law,
Our son…was stolen?"
rother," Kamaka replied. "Keku'i gave birth to a fine boy in the
when we awoke this morning, he was gone." She bowed her head
d her eyes.
was too distraught over the loss of her infant son to mention the
rusion of Alapa'i's soldiers, and Kamaka said nothing. Keoua and
'u were about to go to war in Alapa'i's service and they might
ghting alongside the very men Alapa'i had sent to murder the
aka did not want to jeopardize the brothers' lives with knowledge
poison their thoughts and distract them in the heat of the coming
Nae'ole, she would say nothing to Keoua and Keku'i until the
ght. Better to let them truly mourn their son's supposed loss than
to despair and possibly give Alapa'i cause to doubt them and his
sified report.
er," Keoua said to Kalani'ōpu'u, "we must find my son."
ōpu'u hesitated. "We do not have time," he said. "The fleet will
soon. Our uncle will be angry with us if we delay him."
w time is short, Kalani," Keoua said, "But I must use whatever
ve to find our child."
Kamaka guiding them and the still-sobbing Keku'i trailing be-
wo brothers set off for the birthing house, where they searched
gn of the baby's abductor. But Alapa'i's soldiers had trampled the
Nae'ole had been careful to leave no trace of his passage through
foliage, and the brothers' search proved fruitless.
n was halfway to its zenith when they first heard the calls of conch
the direction of the coast. "It is time, brother," Kalani'ōpu'u said.

Waipi'o Valley, 1748-1753

Kamehameha—"the one set apart"—began life in near isolation, taken from his sleeping mother's side within hours of his birth and spirited away to a remote farm at the head of the Big Island's Waipi'o Valley. This abduction, in the dead of night, almost certainly saved my uncle's life.

Late in her pregnancy with Kamehameha, it is said that his mother—my grandmother—Keku'iapoiwa, dreamed she hungered for the eyeball of a chief. Word of Keku'i's strange dream-craving reached the ears of Alapa'i'nui, the reigning *mō'ī* of Hawai'i. Alapa'i, then preparing for war against his father-in-law and rival, Kekaulike, the mō'ī of Maui, was not pleased.

Keku'i was the wife of Alapa'i's nephew, Keoua. She was also Alapa'i's own niece. She had lived for several years at Kekaulike's court on Maui, having returned to Hawai'i just within the past year to become Keoua's wife. It was common knowledge that during her recent stay on Maui, she had pleasured herself with one of the king's sons, Kahekili. Now, despite her declaration that my grandfather, Keoua, was the father of her baby, and Keoua's public acceptance of the child in Keku'i's swollen belly as his own, rumor-mongers at Alapa'i's court whispered that the baby's father was in fact Kahekili.

Mindful of these rumors, Alapa'i consulted his kāhuna on the significance of Keku'i's bizarre yearning. "It means that this woman's child will grow up to become a slayer of chiefs," they said. One young priest, Ka'akau, advised Alapa'i to slay the infant. "*E 'aki maka o ka lauhue*," he counseled. "Nip off the bud of the poison gourd." The mō'ī resolved on the spot to kill Keku'i's baby as soon as it was born.

My uncle Kamehameha was born in a secluded *hale*—a thatched grass house—at Kokoiki, in northern Kohala, where Alapa'i was then gathering his army and fleet for the coming invasion of neighboring Maui. He came into this world in the midst of a raging storm. Attended only by her sister Kamaka, Keku'i ground her teeth and cried out as she strained in labor. Outside, the rain fell in near-solid sheets and the wind howled, drowning out the sounds of both Keku'i's screams and Kamehameha's birth cries.

Learning that Keku'i was about to give birth, the king had dispatched a party of soldiers to kill the infant. "Find her; find her child and slay it—and tell no one," he said. The soldiers had set out at once, but the intense storm frustrated and slowed their search.

Alapa'i's plans had meanwhile come to the attention of Nae'ole, chief of Hālawa, who was a cousin of Keku'i's father. The childless Nae'ole was about fifteen years older than Keku'i and regarded her as the daughter he never had. Nae'ole began to make plans of his own.

Nae'ole had gone to Kamaka with news of the murder plot against Keku'i's unborn child. Now, as Keku'i lay deep in slumber alongside her newborn son, Nae'ole slipped into the hale through an opening Kamaka had fashioned in one of the thatched walls. Moving quietly to Keku'i's side, he knelt and gently picked up the infant. The baby opened his eyes and whimpered softly. "Hush, little one," Nae'ole whispered. "Your life depends on it." In the hale's dark interior, the newborn would have seen little more than Nae'ole's shadowy form and Nae'ole would have barely made out the baby's features. Yet years later, he swore to my father that the baby Kamehameha had regarded him with a profoundly serious stare and then, without another sound, closed his eyes.

Swaddling the baby in bark cloth against the driving rain outside, Nae'ole stole away. Keku'i, exhausted from her birth ordeal, did not stir. Nearby, Kamaka watched through hooded eyelids as she pretended to sleep.

Daybreak brought clearing skies and a commotion outside the hale. After a long night's search in the rain, Alapa'i's soldiers had at last found Keku'i's birthing place. Their captain, a hulking warrior brandishing a club, burst in upon the sleeping women. "Wake up! Where is the child?" he demanded.

Keku'i's eyes flew open and she reached fo
Ignoring the club-wielding soldier looming ov
my son? He is gone!"

Kamaka feigned surprise. "Keku'i, what h
baby?" she cried.

The king's officer stood slightly stooped o
to the other in confusion. His eyes fell upon K
the thin trickle of milk oozing from her nippl
knew there would be further proof of nativity:
bark cloth for ritual burial. But there was no b

The captain clenched his war club, turne
way out of the hale through a knot of men tryi
baby. This woman has miscarried," he told th
fleet's departure almost at hand, he and his s
time searching for the missing infant, but ne
Alapa'i admitting to failure. "Come with me,"
to the fleet. We have a war to fight." The o
Behind them, Keku'i fell sobbing into her sist

By this time, Nae'ole—with Keku'i's ba
miles to the east, making toward Kauhola Poi

After burying the afterbirth under a *hala*
Keku'i and her sister returned to Alapa
band Keoua and his half-brother Kalani'ōpu'u
with the invasion fleet. Keku'i and her sister
shore, amid ranks of double-hulled war canc
eye could see in each direction. The blue-gre
the shore glistened in the light of the new da
sharp focus in the storm-cleansed morning ai
the 'Alenuihāhā Channel.

Kek
perate h
"Oh
came in
at his fee
"Is t
Kamaka.
"Yes,
night. A
and aver
Keku
sudden i
Kalani'ōp
soon be
child. Ka
that coul
battles. C
time was
to preten
soldiers' f
"Bro
Kalan
be leavin
"I kn
time we k
With
hind, the
for some
ground a
the nearb
The s
shells fro

"We have had no luck here and the war fleet will leave soon. We must go back now."

Keoua sighed. His shoulders sagging, he turned toward the two women, who were huddled together on the ground near the hale. "Alapa'i will be looking for us," he said.

"But what of our son?" Keku'i cried.

Keoua gently raised Keku'iapoiwa to her feet and held her close. "If our son is still alive, our families' 'aumakua will watch after him," he said. "The child's fate is in their hands now."

Kamaka kept her silence.

As my grandparents forlornly made their way back to the coast, Nae'ole—with my infant uncle swaddled in bark cloth and tied securely to his back—reached the sandy beach at Kauhola, where two young men from his village were waiting by a single-hull outrigger canoe resting in the shallows. A wet nurse, already seated in the canoe, waited with them. Nae'ole shifted his precious burden from his back and handed the baby to the woman, who put the child immediately to her breast. Then, without a word among them, Nae'ole and the younger men pushed the canoe into deeper water, jumped in, and set off down the coast in the direction of Hilo.

With all three men paddling, the small canoe made swift progress, reaching Waipi'o Bay as the sun was settling toward the weatherworn summit of Mt. Kohala to the west. Nae'ole's goal was the far end of the narrow Waipi'o Valley, where he held administrative title to an *ili kūpono*—a subdivision of land within the larger boundaries of the Waipi'o *ahupua'a*. The sunlight was already cut off by Waipi'o's high walls, and deep shadows were falling on the valley floor as Nae'ole and the wet nurse disembarked from the canoe. Nae'ole took the sleeping baby from the woman, strapped him to his back once more, and slipped away into the gathering darkness. Nae'ole went unseen and unheard by the inhabitants of the night-cloaked valley, just as he had planned. And so the infant Kamehameha—who was destined to unite these islands into one nation for the first time in our people's long history—arrived in stealthy anonymity in Waipiʻo, which was to be his place of refuge for the next five years.

Naeʻole left Kamehameha with a *makaʻāinana* couple—tenant farmers who worked a plot of land in the Hālawa chief's valley domain. Their names and the names of their children are lost to memory now. They were commoners, after all, and beneath the notice of the aliʻi. For this reason, Naeʻole was confident that Kamehameha would be safe in their keeping. Should Alapaʻi send spies in search of the child, they would never think to look for a kapu aliʻi prince among mere *kānaka*.

"Guard this child well," he told the couple as they prostrated themselves before him. "He is precious in Kāne's sight. You must keep him close at all times, and he must never leave this farm. As far as anyone else here is concerned, he is your own son. I will return to visit him from time to time."

Naeʻole handed the baby over to the woman, who trembled slightly as she took the infant from him. Little Kamehameha began to cry. It was his first sound of complaint in a day and a half. "Even then," Naeʻole later told my father, Keliʻimaikaʻi, "your brother Kameha was as hard as a koa trunk." The farmer's wife, who was almost never without a baby of her own, guided my uncle Kameha's mouth to a milk-engorged nipple. Kameha drank lustily.

The Waipiʻo Valley climbs the rainy, windward side of Mt. Kohala on the Big Island's Hāmākua Coast. Waipiʻo's walls are high and its floor is almost flat. In its formation, it is like a deep war-club wound in the side of the mountain. But this wound runs with clear, sweet water from the rains that fall daily as Lono sends his clouds scudding against the mountain's eastern flanks. The rain falls on the mountainside and cascades down the valley's thousand-foot-high walls in myriad waterfalls that shimmer as they catch the rising sun's early light. The water from the falls runs into the Waipiʻo Stream, which courses down the valley's three-mile length, emptying into the ocean at a black-sand beach. The air of Waipi'o Valley is always filled with the soothing sounds of falling, rushing water and the musical calls of birds. The soil of the valley's floor is the richest on the island. Anything will grow readily there—coconut, banana, breadfruit, yams, and especially taro. It is even said that the valley's pigs are the most succulent on the island.

It was in this paradise on earth that Kamehameha passed his earliest years. Kameha never questioned the constant attention that the farmer and his wife lavished upon him, accepting it as his natural due. He hardly noticed how the couple tensed when he became angry over some small thing, dropped whatever they were doing that moment, and rushed to soothe and placate him—attending to him in a way they rarely would to their other children. The farmer and his wife were affectionate toward my uncle Kamehameha after a fashion. But mostly what they felt toward him was trepidation. Kameha was, after all, ali'i. His very person was ordinarily kapu for commoners. The couple knew without question that their lives would be forfeit to Nae'ole if even the slightest harm should befall Kameha while he was in their care. This unspoken understanding passed between the farmer and his wife in anxious glances whenever the little boy seemed ill disposed. It colored their demeanor toward him with reserve even in the happiest of times, and Kameha undoubtedly sensed it.

Ignorant of his royal forebears and his kapu status, Kameha could only have been mystified by this odd coolness from his supposed mother and father. "It must have had a bad effect on him," my father told me many years later. "When he first came to Alapa'i's court, your uncle Kameha was very quiet and serious beyond his years."

Kamehameha looked forward to the infrequent visits of his "uncle" Nae'ole, who would journey from Hālawa to see him, on the pretext of superintending his land holdings in the valley. In Nae'ole's embrace, Kameha found the warmth that was missing in the arms of his Waipi'o Valley "parents." Nae'ole would joke and play with the little boy in a way the farmer and his wife never did. It was only in Nae'ole's presence that Kamehameha knew the release of unbridled laughter.

Late one morning early in Kamehameha's sixth year, Nae'ole arrived at the farm. Knowing that Kameha loved the Waipi'o Stream and often played along its banks, Nae'ole went there first and called out to him. Kameha, who had been playing with two of his foster brothers at the stream's edge, ran to Nae'ole, his bare feet fairly flying over the grass, still glistening from the morning's rain. Kameha's whole body glinted in the sunlight as well. After the fashion of small children in those days, he wore no clothing. "Uncle," he cried. Then, instead of throwing himself at Nae'ole, he pulled up short. The old man was different. Rather than greeting Kameha with a broad smile and open arms as he usually did, this day Nae'ole kept his arms to his side and his expression was serious. In one hand he held a narrow length of kapa—bark cloth.

"Boy," he said, extending the strip of kapa to Kameha, "you must put this on."

Instead of taking the cloth from Nae'ole, Kameha tilted his head and looked quizzically at him. "Why must I wear that, Uncle?" he asked.

"Just do as I say," Nae'ole answered, in a hard tone Kameha had never heard from him—or any adult—before. Kameha's large brown eyes widened with surprise. "Come here," Nae'ole said, more kindly now. "Let me help you."

Nae'ole tucked one end of the bark-cloth strip under Kameha's chin, gently tilted his head forward until the cloth was pinned between his chin and his neck and instructed the boy to hold it there. Then, Nae'ole passed the kapa through Kameha's sturdy brown legs, wound it around his small waist and hooked the cloth back on itself at the first turn at Kameha's back. "You can let go of the kapa now," Nae'ole told Kameha, who lifted his chin. The remaining length of bark cloth dropped in front of Kameha, extending to his knees and covering his thighs like an apron. "That is how you tie a malo," Nae'ole said.

Kameha wriggled uncomfortably in the unfamiliar loincloth. "I don't like it, Uncle," he complained. "It itches."

"Nevertheless, you must wear it now," said Nae'ole. How ironic little Kamehameha's reaction to this minimal stitch of clothing now seems in view of the eagerness with which he and our people later adopted the stifling manner of haole dress.

"Why must I wear it?" Kameha demanded.

"Because it is unfitting for a young ali'i prince such as you to run around naked like a kanaka child," Nae'ole said.

"I am a prince?" Kameha asked, dumbfounded.

"Yes," said Nae'ole. "And now it is time for you to return to the court of King Alapa'i'nui and meet your true father and mother."

"I had been living a fiction," Kamehameha told my father years later. "Nothing was as it seemed."

"Come boy," said Nae'ole. Turning away from Kameha, he started down the trail that followed the burbling stream to the mouth of the Waipi'o Valley. And without a word of farewell to the man and woman who had cared for him for the past five years, Kameha followed Nae'ole down the valley to the sail canoe that was waiting for them at the black-sand beach.

The farmer and his wife, who had kept to their modest hale during Nae'ole's last visit to the farm, got no words of thanks from the old chief. But they required none. After all, they still had their lives.

Much had transpired in the world outside Waipi'o during the five years Kamehameha had lived there in unwitting exile.

The morning after his birth, King Alapa'i's fleet had crossed the 'Alenuihāhā Channel to Maui for a preemptive strike. Kekaulike, the king of Maui, had earlier invaded Hawai'i, inflicting great havoc along the Kona Coast, where his troops had pillaged and burned numerous villages. Alapa'i had only just consolidated his hold on the Big Island and Kekaulike supposed that Alapa'i was weak and vulnerable after bloody struggles for power with his half-brother, Kalanike'eaumoku, and then Mokulani, the chief of Hilo. But Kekaulike had miscalculated. Alapa'i assembled a fleet of canoes and intercepted Kekaulike's forces at sea, defeating the Maui fleet in the ensuing naval battle.

Later discovering that Kekaulike was gathering a larger fleet of war canoes for a second invasion attempt, Alapa'i had set sail for Maui.

As it turned out, the gods took the king of Maui before Alapa'i could put a spear through him. Landing first at Kaupō on Maui's south coast, Alapa'i learned that Kekaulike had died. Maui was now ruled by Kekaulike's son, Kamehameha'nui, whose mother was Alapa'i's half-sister. Sailing up the coast to Kīhei, Alapa'i met with his sister and the new king. Instead of making war, Alapa'i concluded a peace treaty; instead of fighting, feasting ensued.

Peace at Maui did not mean a return home for Alapa'i's people. Instead, their mō'ī invaded neighboring Molokai, to do battle with the king of O'ahu, who had occupied that island. By making common cause with the chiefs of Molokai, Alapa'i aimed to defeat the O'ahu king there so that he could then seize O'ahu for himself. My grandfather Keoua and his older brother Kalani'ōpu'u distinguished themselves in this fight, cornering the O'ahu ruler after a five-day fray and slaying him as he tried to flee the battlefield.

Alapa'i's designs on O'ahu, however, were foiled by the slain king's brother, Peleiōhōlani, the mō'ī of Kaua'i, who now ruled O'ahu as regent for his late brother's infant son. Peleiōhōlani inflicted costly defeats on the invading forces when Alapa'i tried to land at Waikiki and later at Kailua. Unlike Alapa'i, Peleiōhōlani had no taste for further bloodshed at this time, and sent an emissary to Alapa'i with an offer of peace. Embarrassed by his failure to score a quick victory on O'ahu, Alapa'i accepted and returned at last to Hawai'i.

It was customary among the ali'i for wives to accompany their husbands to war. But because she was exhausted and weakened after giving birth to Kamehameha, Keku'i did not follow Keoua to Maui, and Alapa'i's

saw before him was still in his prime, but already in decline. Prolonged peace was softening Alapa'i, both in body and intellect. Where Alapa'i's skin had once been taut over a warrior's hard muscles, now it was soft over an idle man's mantle of fat. Once his eyes had been hard as stones; now they were turning rheumy from too much 'awa drinking. Alapa'i's mind had once been occupied with plans of conquest and stratagems of war. Now he was preoccupied with placating his various chieftains while he played one against another to maintain his power. Kameha, of course, could not have grasped all this at his young age, but he must have sensed some of it, for he later told my father, "There was nothing much remarkable about old King Alapa'i when I first met him."

Alapa'i suspected that Kameha was somehow taking his measure. "Am I so strange to look at, boy?" he asked. Startled, Kameha looked away. His eyes settled on a carved wooden figure atop a pole directly behind the king. From its feet to its shoulders, the carving was a man. Its legs, arms and torso were thick and powerful. Its manhood was unmistakable. The figure's hands, held at its sides, were open but tensed as if ready to reach out suddenly. Above the carving's squared shoulders all resemblance to a human being ceased. The head was hugely disproportionate to the body, and grotesque. Elongated nostrils flared above a gaping, tooth-filled mouth that overran the figure's cheeks with a cruel grimace. Eyes that seemed to meet at the bridge of the thing's nose and wrap around its head to where its ears should have been cast a baleful stare, its fierceness heightened by the stone lamps' wavering light.

Kamehameha could not take his eyes off it. "What is that?" he blurted.

Alapa'i laughed, and now his smile was genuine again. "Ah, that is Kūkā'ilimoku, our war god," he replied. "He protects me here in my *hale*. Are you not afraid of him boy?"

Kamehameha regarded the king very seriously. "If he protects you, I do not fear him." Kameha said.

Alapa'i sat up and clapped his hands. "Well spoken, boy," he said. "One day, perhaps, Kūkā'ilimoku will protect you as well."

Now Alapa'i looked back over his shoulder toward the rear of the hale. "Nephew, niece," he said, "come here and welcome your son to court."

A man and woman whom Kameha had not previously noticed stepped forward into the light. The man was tall and muscular. The woman was shapely, but beginning to thicken about the waist. "Boy, this is your father, Keoua Kalanikupuapa'ikalaninui," Alapa'i said. "And this is your mother, Keku'iapoiwa."

Keku'i held out her arms. Kameha hesitated and looked back at Nae'ole, who nodded to him. Slowly, he stepped forward into his mother's waiting embrace. Keku'i bent low to hug Kameha and pulled him to her breast, sobbing softly. Kameha held himself stiffly as Keku'i's warm tears fell on his shoulder. Keoua, at Keku'i's side, placed one hand on Kameha's head. Kameha stood very still.

"What is the boy's name?" Alapa'i asked.

Keku'i released Kameha and an awkward silence settled on the group. The little boy had never been formally named. In the old days, we named our children during a ritual cutting of the umbilical cord. But on the tumultuous night of Kameha's birth, the ritual had been overlooked.

Kameha himself had never wondered about his name. Observing how sturdy he was, even as a baby, his Waipi'o foster parents had taken to calling him *Pai'ea*, after the hard-shelled crab. Nae'ole, on the other hand, had never addressed him by anything other than "boy." Now Kameha looked confusedly from one adult to the other. "All at once I realized that even my name was not real," he would later recount to my father.

Keku'i broke the silence. "His name," she said, "is Kamehameha."

"Ah, 'the lonely one,'" said Alapa'i. "That is a fitting name for one who has spent his first years so far removed from his parents and estranged from his mō'ī's court." Keku'i looked away. Keoua continued to rest his palm lightly on Kameha's head.

"My lord," Keoua said, without looking at Keku'i, "since our son has been so long away from your court, perhaps he should remain with you now for his education in the ways of the ali'i and the warrior. Please take him in hanai to raise."

"That is wise," Alapa'i responded. "Your first-born son, Kamehameha, shall stay here with us for the time being. Nae'ole will continue as his tutor and Keakaka'uhiwa will be his foster mother." Keaka was one of Alapa'i's wives, and the mother of his oldest son, Keawe'ōpala. Keoua nodded his assent. Keku'i said nothing.

And so it came about that my uncle Kamehameha, reunited with his parents at long last, was immediately given over by them to the care of King Alapa'i, who had once plotted to murder him at his mother's breast. Kameha, who would not come to understand Keoua's reasoning until much later in life, only felt the sting of rejection.

"At the time, I did not understand why our mother and father did not want to keep me close to them," he told my father years afterward. "But later, I realized that Keoua meant to reassure Alapa'i that he bore him no grudge for his plot against my life—and he believed that by entrusting me to Alapa'i's keeping, he would forestall any further plots against me."

"*Wohi*!" The older boy hurled the insult at Kamehameha like a short *ihe* spear. He pressed close to Kameha, towering over him. "Prostrate yourself before me, wohi!" the boy demanded. The older boy was Kameha's cousin, Kiwala'ō, the son of his uncle, Kalani'ōpu'u.

By this time, Kameha had lived at Alapa'i's court long enough—several years—to know that coming from Kiwala'ō, "wohi" could not be an insult. If anything, Kiwala'ō was lower-born ali'i than Kameha. While Kamehameha's parents were second cousins, and their grandparents were half-brother and half-sister, Kiwala'ō's parents were not even distant cousins. Furthermore, young Kameha understood by now that even as a lower-ranked wohi, he need not prostrate himself before any other ali'i, not even his mō'ī. For months afterward, other boys at court had teased him about the way he had thrown himself to the ground like a worthless kanaka before Alapaʻi.

Now, instead of lying down before Kiwalaʻō, Kameha bulled into him. "Lower-than-wohi," Kameha challenged him. "Make me!"

Kiwalaʻō hesitated. For though Kiwalaʻō was a head taller than Kameha, the younger boy was solidly built, and he had already won a reputation among the other boys as a fearless wrestler and boxer.

"Make me!" Kameha repeated, shoving Kiwalaʻō hard in the chest and glaring up into his startled eyes.

Kiwalaʻō was debating whether he should shove back when Kameha's *kahu*—his tutor, Naeʻole—approached. "Kamehameha," Naeʻole called out, "come away now. It is time for your instruction."

Kameha stepped away, keeping his eyes fixed on Kiwalaʻō's. "Perhaps you can make me prostrate myself before you later, Kiwalaʻō."

"What was that about?" Naeʻole asked Kameha as they walked away.

"That *kuhaulua* wanted me to prostrate myself before him." Kuhaulua were the lowest-ranking aliʻi.

"That *kuhaulua* is your own *ʻohana*, Kamehameha," Naeʻole replied. "You would do better to make him your friend, rather than your enemy."

"I will try, Naeʻole," Kamehameha said, "but family or not, Kiwalaʻō would do better to stop irritating me."

By his twelfth birthday, three years later, Kameha was more than a match for the older Kiwalaʻō in size and strength. Abandoning whatever thoughts he had about besting Kamehameha physically, Kiwalaʻō no longer taunted him. For his part, Kameha was careful to avoid giving offense to his cousin. But neither tried to make a friend of the other.

With his acceptance into Alapaʻi's household, Kamehameha plunged into a tangled ancestral web woven of generations of "marital" unions and less formal partnerships of both political convenience and

In fact, Kamehameha was already becoming quite skilled with the ihe spear and the longer pololu javelin. War—preparing for it and fighting it—was the primary vocation of the ali'i, and as was customary, Kameha had commenced his military training at about the age of ten, when a new influence entered his young life: his military tutor, Kekūhaupi'o.

Kekūhaupi'o was the chief of Ke'ei, a village down the coast from Kailua just south of Kealakekua Bay. He was renowned throughout the islands as the greatest warrior of his generation because of his skill and ferocity in the sham battles that the ali'i warriors staged for sport and to hone their fighting skills. He was not as physically imposing as so many ali'i were. Even at six feet, two inches in height, he did not tower over many of his opponents. But he boasted a powerful build, long arms, and a quickness of hands and feet that mystified his foes.

Kekūhaupi'o was persuaded to take Kameha under his tutelage by Kalani'ōpu'u, who on one of his visits to Alapa'i's court came upon Kameha hurling a hau-wood stick at a banana tree in the courtyard of Kalola's hale. Kameha had been throwing the hau stick across the small courtyard repeatedly, with a single-minded determination that Kalani'ōpu'u found exceptional in a boy so young. His aim was straight and true. "It is my destiny to be a great warrior, Uncle," Kameha proudly told him.

"It is indeed your destiny to be a warrior," Kalani'ōpu'u replied. "That is the destiny of all ali'i men. And you are right; you must be a great one."

Soon after this, Kalani'ōpu'u went to visit Kekūhaupi'o at Ke'ei. "My nephew Kamehameha will be a warrior one day," he said. "He has great need of your skills. Will you train him?"

Kekūhaupi'o was a distant kinsman of Kamehameha's first kahu, Nae'ole. Moreover, from his uncle Holo'ae—one of Alapa'i's kāhuna—he had heard of the mō'ī's plot against the life of the infant Kamehameha and he had disapproved. For all these reasons, he readily agreed. "It will be my great pleasure to train your nephew," he said.

Kekūhaupi'o was supremely skillful in throwing spears, and, perhaps more importantly for warfare in which shields were unknown, dodging and catching them. He was expert with the *'īkoi*, the tripping weapon;

the Pahoa dagger; the *lei o manō* shark-tooth weapon; the short *newa* war club; the long *lā'au palau* club; the *pohaku* stone hand club; the *ma'a* sling; and the *ka'ane* strangulation cord—there was no weapon that Kekūhaupi'o had not mastered. Above all, he was a master of *lua*, the art of breaking bones with bare hands. A combination of wrestling, punching, kicking, and paralyzing hand strikes, lua was the essential weapon in the arsenal of a well-trained warrior. As Kekūhaupi'o explained to Kameha one day, "You must know lua, because in close combat, even when you do not have a dagger, spear, or club, you will still have your feet and your hands."

Kamehameha began his military training with the spear, first with the ihe and later as he grew bigger, the longer pololu. His first target was a coconut tree. Kameha began by hurling an ihe spear from a distance of several times his height—about fifteen or sixteen feet at that time. As Kameha gained in accuracy and size, Kekūhaupi'o made him stand ever farther away from the tree. "You must be able to strike your enemy before he can carry the fight to you," he said, "no matter how far away he is." As his training progressed, Kameha could hit the tree unerringly from greater and greater distances, his spears striking the center of the trunk, penetrating deep into the rough bark, and quivering for many seconds afterward.

One day, Kekūhaupi'o said to him, "Kameha, your enemy will not stand before you like a coconut tree. Throw your spear at me."

Kameha's eyes widened. "Kekū, I cannot do that," he protested. "I do not want to harm you."

"You must throw your spear at a real man someday, boy," Kekūhaupi'o replied. "Throw it at me now." Kameha still hesitated. "Now!" Kekūhaupi'o commanded.

Kameha tossed his ihe spear in Kekūhaupi'o's general direction. It was a weak throw and the spear rattled flat on the ground at his kahu's feet.

"What?" Kekūhaupi'o snorted derisively. "You would go into battle throwing your spear like some woman? No, not like a woman—not even like a little girl." Kameha's tutor cocked his head. "Your little sister over there can throw better than that."

Kameha glanced in the direction of Kekūhaupiʻo's gesture. He saw that Kekuʻiapoiwa Liliha had been watching them. Now she was laughing at Kamehameha from behind an upraised, inverted palm. He reddened.

Kekūhaupiʻo retrieved the spear and tossed it back upright to Kameha, who caught it with his throwing hand. "Throw it!" Kekūhaupiʻo commanded again.

This time, Kameha hurled the short spear at his teacher with all the angry force he could muster. The missile flew straight across the space between them, its sharp point aimed at the very center of Kekūhaupiʻo's heavily muscled chest. But then, as if by magic, Kekūhaupiʻo was no longer in its path. In a movement almost too quick for Kameha's eyes to follow, Kekūhaupiʻo darted to the right while reaching out with his left hand to catch the spear's shaft as it sailed by him. Then, rapidly shifting the spear from his left hand to his right hand, Kekūhaupiʻo threw it straight back at Kamehameha. Kameha flung himself belly first to the ground and the ihe spear sailed harmlessly over his head, burying its point in the soft earth behind him. But before Kameha could get up, Kekūhaupiʻo was astride his back. He grabbed Kamehameha's long black hair and jerked his head up. Kameha felt the sharp point of a dagger against his throat. He gagged.

"You avoided my throw well," Kekūhaupiʻo said, withdrawing the blade and releasing his grip on his young pupil's hair. "But if this had been a real fight, you would surely be dead. You must always keep your feet under you. Your enemy will not let you rise once you are down. And he will show you no mercy."

This was the way of fighting among our people, who neither expected any quarter nor offered any. In the months that followed, Kameha not only learned to keep his feet when dodging spears, but to catch them and hurl them back.

One afternoon, after a furious exchange, Kameha found himself holding two spears to Kekūhaupiʻo's one. Instead of throwing again, Kameha waited to see if Kekūhaupiʻo would hurl his spear. His instructor nodded approvingly. "You have not only learned how to defend yourself," he said, "you have learned the virtue of patience. Now you have two spears and I have only one. What would you have me do with my spear?"

"You should not throw it," Kameha replied. "You would be defenseless."

"That is correct," Kekūhaupiʻo said. "I would keep this spear. So now, what will you do?"

"I will call for my brother over there to distract you with an attack on your flank so I can finish you off with one of my two spears." My father had been watching this exchange between Kameha and his instructor from the shade of a nearby breadfruit tree.

Kekūhaupiʻo laughed. "Very good. You do not have to finish every fight by yourself. You have also learned the virtue of discretion."

While Kekūhaupiʻo supervised Kamehameha's military training, Naeʻole continued to instruct him in the laws and lore of his people. One of the legends Naeʻole imparted to his pupil was the story of the *Pōhaku Naha*, the Naha Stone. The Naha Stone was in Hilo. People said a Kauaʻi chieftain had brought it there a score of generations ago. How the chief managed this feat, no one could say. The stone was rectangular in shape, and no one knew whose hands had shaped it or how. It was half again as long as the largest of the aliʻi was tall and it weighed a thousand pounds or more in the haole measure. It was said that if a newborn aliʻi baby did not cry when it was laid on this stone, then the blood of the chiefly naha line surely ran in its veins. It was also said that a man who could move this stone would become a great chief, destined to rule over all the Hawaiian Islands.

"Has any man ever moved the Naha Stone?" Kameha asked.

"No," Naeʻole replied, "it has never been done, and to my knowledge, it has never even been attempted."

"Why not?"

"Because the Naha Stone is kapu," Naeʻole said. "It is sacred. If a man were to attempt to move the stone and succeed, great things would be foretold for him. But if he were to try and fail, his reward would almost certainly be death—especially if he was not naha himself." Nae'ole paused. "And you are not naha."

Kameha had learned the virtue of discretion in battle, but he had not learned its value with respect to his own sexual exploits. Stories of Kameha's liaison with Kalola soon reached the ears of his cousin Kiwala'ō, who was furious that Kameha had lain with his mother. He would make Kameha pay for this affront. But mindful of Kamehameha's growing physical prowess, Kiwala'ō sought to exact his revenge at a distance.

"Eh, there goes Kamehameha, the terrible wohi warrior," he called out to Kameha one morning as the two approached each other on a footpath near Alapa'i's great hale. "I hear you are a great spearman, cousin." As he spoke, Kiwala'ō stood astride the path, blocking Kameha's way.

Kameha stopped a few feet short of Kiwala'ō and folded his arms. "I am still learning," he said.

"Perhaps you would like to test your skill in a spear-throwing contest with me," Kiwala'ō replied.

Kiwala'ō was supremely confident of his own skills with the spear, and he intended to teach Kameha a painful lesson in humility. Of his cousin's abilities, he knew little, since Kameha trained in private with Kekūhaupi'o.

"Perhaps you would like to test your skills in a wrestling contest with me," Kameha rejoined.

"Of course, you would prefer wrestling to spears, cousin," Kiwala'ō answered. "See how much bigger you are than I." Kamehameha was by this time an inch or two taller than Kiwala'ō and broader across the chest. "Are you afraid to face me with a spear?"

Kameha's face darkened. "I am not afraid to face you, Kiwala'ō," he said, "with or without spears."

"Then meet me at this time tomorrow on the games field," Kiwala'ō replied, stepping aside at last.

That night, Kameha told Nae'ole and Kekūhaupi'o of Kiwala'ō's challenge.

"If you show the same skill against Kiwala'ō that you have shown with me, Kameha, you will beat him handily," Kekūhaupi'o said. "Just remember to be patient."

"And remember that Kiwala'ō's father is your uncle Kalani'ōpu'u," Nae'ole said. "You will beat Kiwala'ō, of course. But you must take care not to inflict serious injury on him. It would not do well to anger your uncle."

The games field was an uneven grassy clearing inland of Kawaihae. Kamehameha and Kiwala'ō met there the next morning as the sun cleared the ridgeline to the east. Kiwala'ō was accompanied by a friend, a boy about his own age. For his part, Kameha brought along my father, Keli'imaika'i. Kekūhaupi'o also came, to act as referee.

Kekūhaupi'o laid three ihe spears on the ground in front of each boy. Then he stepped well out of their way and raised one arm. In his hand, he held a dagger. "I will drop the pahoa," Kekūhaupi'o said. "When it hits the ground, you may begin—but not before. You may not touch each other directly. This contest is with spears only. There are no other rules."

Kekūhaupi'o released the dagger. When it struck the earth, Kameha and Kiwala'ō each crouched and reached for a spear. Kiwala'ō came out of his crouch almost immediately and rocked back to throw. Then he hesitated. Kameha was still in a crouch, gripping his spear in both hands and extending it in front of him. He presented a difficult target. As Kiwala'ō hesitated, Kameha stood, drawing his right hand back as if preparing to hurl his spear. Now Kiwala'ō let fly his spear. But because of his hesitation, his motion was not fluid and his aim was not true. Kameha easily sidestepped Kiwala'ō's spear, picking up a second spear at the same time. Now he held two. Kiwala'ō was empty-handed. Kameha cocked his right arm again, but still he did not throw. Again, Kiwala'ō hesitated. He looked from Kameha to Kekūhaupi'o and back again. Kekūhaupi'o's face was impassive and unreadable.

Then, without taking his eyes off his opponent, Kiwala'ō stooped to gather up another spear. In a single, fluid motion that put the full force of his broad back into his throw, Kamehameha whipped his right arm forward and sent his first spear flying at Kiwala'ō. But instead of throwing directly at his cousin, Kameha aimed at the earth between him and his remaining spears. Kiwala'ō jumped aside to avoid the throw. Low to the ground and off balance, he sprawled on his back. Kiwala'ō scrambled to his feet and lunged for his remaining spear. But Kameha had gathered up his third spear and was racing across the field. Before Kiwala'ō could retrieve his last spear, Kameha leaped in front of him and planted a foot on the weapon, freezing it to the earth. Kiwala'ō scrambled backward as Kameha leveled the point of the spear in his right hand at his cousin's chest. Then, without warning, Kameha swung the spear in his left hand at Kiwala'ō, striking him in the side of the head with the shaft. Kiwala'ō reeled and fell to his knees. Kamehameha lightly jabbed Kiwala'ō's chest with the point of his other spear, drawing a trickle of blood. Kiwala'ō froze.

"Now, cousin," Kameha said, as he stood over his opponent, "if we were fighting in a real battle, you would surely die." Then he said with a smile, "Of course, we would never fight each other in a *real* battle."

Unnoticed by both Kameha and his cousin, Kiwala'ō's friend had crept close during this exchange. Still smarting from a beating Kameha had administered to him during a recent wrestling match, the other boy reached for a spear, intent on striking Kameha across the back. But before he could strike, Kekūhaupi'o slapped him aside.

"Enough!" Kekūhaupi'o said. "This contest is finished."

Tossing his spear aside, Kameha bent over his cousin and extended an open hand. The unhappy Kiwala'ō raised one arm to swat it away, whereupon Kameha grasped his hand and pulled him, against his will, to his feet. "*Now* this *wohi* warrior is satisfied," Kameha said.

"You are not even wohi," Kiwala'ō spat at him. "Everyone knows who your real father is, and it's not my uncle Keoua."

"What are you talking about?" Kameha demanded.

"Your father is Kahekili of Maui," Kiwala'ō jeered, "and you are no more than his kuhaulua cast-off."

Kameha tensed, ready to spring at Kiwala'ō, but Kekūhaupi'o swiftly stepped between them. "Your uncle Keoua is Kamehameha's acknowledged and true father, Kiwala'ō," Kekūhaupi'o said, "and you are foolish to say otherwise. I would advise you to hold your tongue on this subject, lest you convince Kameha here that he is not your cousin and therefore need not look to your continued health.

"And you, boy," said Kekū, turning to Kiwala'ō's friend, who was still rubbing his stinging cheek, "you should take more care about making enemies. You will have enough in your life without manufacturing them."

Gathering up the spears on the ground, Kekūhaupi'o said to Kameha, "Come, we are done here." They turned away and started down the footpath to the coast with my father trailing behind them. As my father told me later, Kekūhaupi'o was less than pleased with his student's performance.

"Kekū, would you agree that I fought well against Kiwala'ō?" Kameha asked as they made their way down the slope.

"Yes, you fought well," Kekūhaupi'o said, "but you neglected to watch your back."

Hilo and Kawaihae, 1761-1762

Raindrops as big as ʻōhelo berries pelted Kamehameha and Naeʻole as they descended the winding footpath to Hilo. It was the wettest time of the year on the Big Island's wet side, and it was the time of Makahiki, the four-month-long celebration dedicated to the god Lono. This was traditionally a time of peace. Warfare was suspended, as was human sacrifice. The temples of the sterner gods—Kāne, Kū and Kanaloa—were closed. Eating pig was kapu. Even without roast pig, there was much feasting and ʻawa drinking. It was an easygoing time.

Perhaps that is why this was also the time when the kāhuna collected taxes. During the Makahiki time, the priests circled the entire island on foot, carrying a pole bearing the likeness of Lono carved in wood. Along the way, they stopped at the border of each ahupuaʻa to collect tribute—feathers, kapa cloth, taro, pigs, and chickens. The Makahiki time ended when the kāhuna returned to their starting point, bearing their accumulated treasure to the king for propitiation of the gods and for distribution to the priests and the mōʻī's chieftains. At this time, the temples of Kāne, Kū, and Kanaloa were sanctified anew and reopened, the kapu on roast pig was lifted, and human sacrifice, and warfare, when required, were resumed.

"It would be best for you to attempt this feat during the Makahiki time," Naeʻole had advised when Kamehameha first voiced his intention to move the Naha Stone. "It is the god Lono's time of year and the kāhuna are most apt to be in a forgiving mood if you fail—though I would not wager on the extent of their mercy."

"You are right, as usual," Kameha replied, with a broad smile. "I do not intend to fail, but why tempt fate and the priests unnecessarily?"

Nae'ole had tried to talk Kameha out of this brash attempt to move the massive Naha Stone. "It has never been done," he reminded his pupil. "To try and fail can mean death—especially for a wohi such as you."

But Kamehameha would not be dissuaded. From the day Kiwala'ō had called him Kahekili's kuhaulua discard, Kameha had been eager almost to the point of desperation to prove his merit, once and for all. "You once told me that no ali'i can change the circumstances of his birth, but any ali'i can change his destiny," Kameha reminded his tutor. "I will go to Hilo, move the Naha Stone, and change mine."

"You will go to Hilo, without question," Nae'ole had said, shaking his head. He frowned at Kamehameha, but inwardly—he later told my father—he was smiling. "Your brother's will was so strong that I believed he just might be the one to move it."

Kameha and Nae'ole left Kawaihae early one morning while the village still slept. The day's first light was just touching the sky east of Mt. Kohala. They had told no one other than Kekūhaupi'o of their plan. "No others here must know where you have gone or why," Nae'ole told Kamehameha. "There are some who might try to stop you." When Kameha asked who at court would try to bar him from going to Hilo to move the stone, Nae'ole had replied, "Ka'akau, for one." Alapa'i's decision to welcome Kamehameha to court some eight years earlier had displeased the kahuna nui, who had foretold that the infant Kameha would someday become a threat to the mō'ī if he were allowed to live. "Ka'akau still bears you ill will," said Nae'ole, "and he does not want you to distinguish yourself in any way."

To further cloak their purpose in secrecy, Nae'ole insisted that they travel to Hilo by foot rather than canoe. Kamehameha assented to this, but he objected when his kahu said they must take the longer, more taxing route over the mountains. "Why must we go that way, rather than by the coast?" he asked. "It will be faster and more pleasant."

"Too many eyes will be upon us if we go that way," Nae'ole countered.

"Remember, Kameha, the strength to move the stone is in your legs," Kekūhaupiʻo said. "Going across the mountains will surely strengthen them for the challenge ahead."

Kiwalaʻō's contemptuous epithet on the games field still echoed in Kameha's mind as he and Naeʻole set off for Hilo. The spears Kiwalaʻō had thrown might have flown wide of their mark, but "kuhaulua cast-off" had struck home. In the days following the spear-throwing contest, the story of Kameha's victory over Kiwalaʻō circulated widely among the young aliʻi at Alapaʻi's court, and the many retellings always ended with a recounting of Kiwalaʻō's verbal slap. Among Kameha's young friends at court—and there were many—Kiwalaʻō's gracelessness in defeat was seen as foolish, even stupid. But Kameha's enemies—and there were more than a few—saw Kiwalaʻō's parting shot as a well-deserved rebuke. These boys regarded Kameha as somewhat of an interloper at court and resented King Alapaʻi's solicitousness toward him. They laughed about Kiwalaʻō's insult—though not to Kameha's face, of course. Nevertheless, Kameha was well aware of their ridicule and he was determined to make certain that no one on the Big Island, at least, should ever think to question his parentage and status again. Moving the Naha Stone would settle the issue.

When Kameha first spoke of his intention to move the great stone, Kekūhaupiʻo had told him that he was not yet ready for the challenge. "You are strong, Kamehameha," Kekūhaupiʻo had said, "but to move the Naha Stone, you must become stronger still."

Thus, Kameha had postponed his quest for more than a year while he worked to further strengthen himself for the task ahead. Whenever he went surf riding at Kawaihae, he selected the longest, heaviest board he could find, hoisting it high above his head as he carried it to and from the beach. After canoe races, Kameha would stay behind, alone, to lift one of the heavy dugout canoes. Squatting, he would grip the canoe's prow in his large hands and then, holding his arms tightly to his body, would thrust upward with both legs. Kameha repeated this exercise many times until he could lift the canoe almost to his full height in one swift, practiced movement.

By age fourteen he already stood nearly six feet, six inches tall and towered over the other ali'i, who as a group stood much taller than the common folk. He was broad across the shoulders and chest. His pectoral muscles and biceps swelled with the slightest tension. His thighs were huge, his powerful calf muscles explosive. Finally, in Kekūhaupi'o's judgment, Kameha was ready for the stone.

"If any man can move the Naha Stone, you are the one who can do it, Kameha," Kekūhaupi'o said. "You are strong, but physical strength alone will not be enough. Your mana must be strong as well." Kekūhaupi'o opened a small kapa cloth bag that he wore around his neck and extracted a shark tooth, which had been polished to a high sheen. "Take this to Hilo with you," he said. "It is from a tiger shark. Wear it when you lift the stone. Your mana will draw strength from it."

"*Mahalo,* Kekū. Is this from the shark that you killed with your own hands?"

"Yes it is, Kameha."

Kamehameha well knew the story of how as a young man, Kekūhaupi'o had jumped into the sea and slain a tiger shark, the most feared predator of the waters surrounding our islands. "Then your spirit is in this tooth, Kekū. I will wear it and add your mana to mine when I move the stone." Kameha said. "Together, we cannot fail."

The route Nae'ole and Kameha followed overland to Hilo had taken them over the Big Island's central massif along a footpath nestled in the saddle between Hawai'i's two towering volcanoes: Mauna Loa, the "long mountain;" and Mauna a Wakea, nowadays more commonly called Mauna Kea.

At this time of year, Mauna a Wakea slept under a white blanket that gleamed in the sunlight. "It is the home of the Wakea, the father of the islands," Nae'ole had told Kamehameha when he was younger. "It is holy and thus only the highest-born chiefs may go there." Nae'ole had explained to Kameha that Hawai'i was the oldest child of Wakea and his partner, Papa, and that, as the highest point on the island of Hawai'i, the summit of Mauna a Wakea was the island-child's navel. Mauna Loa was not sacred and therefore not forbidden to people, said Nae'ole, but it was a hazardous place because Pele, the fire goddess who lived in Ka'ū at Kīlauea, sometimes came there.

Kamehameha devoutly believed in Pele, as he did in all of his people's myriad gods. "If I am wrong to try to lift the stone," he had told Nae'ole at the beginning of their trek to Hilo, "Pele will not permit me to cross the mountain." Pele had not troubled them during their journey, and now Kameha was brimming with confidence.

"They are expecting you," Nae'ole told Kameha as the two made their way through the rain down the serpentine trail to Hilo. The evening before, while Kameha had made camp in the shelter of a hillside cave, Nae'ole had gone ahead to the village to announce his protégé's presence and purpose to the high chief of Hilo, the kāhuna at the heiau, and to the people in general. "The kāhuna will allow you to attempt to lift the stone, but they will be very harsh with you if you fail."

Indeed, his failure would signal the priests that Kamehameha's brash attempt to lift the stone was kapu from the start, and they would be in their rights to exact a swift and severe penalty: strangling in the heiau and sacrifice to the god.

"I am not concerned about the kāhuna because I will not fail, Nae'ole."

The rain had cleared and the sun was shining through parting clouds by the time Kameha and Nae'ole entered the village of Hilo. Word of Kamehameha's impending attempt had preceded him. Villagers thronged both sides of the path. They threw themselves to the ground as Kameha and Nae'ole approached, as the kapu required, but scrambled to their feet again and followed at a respectful distance after the two had passed. Kameha and Nae'ole were nearing the Naha Stone when a burly kahuna, a priest from the adjacent temple of Lono, stepped in front of them, blocking their way.

"Who is this who comes here and what is his purpose?" the kahuna said, addressing his question to Nae'ole. The priest knew Kamehameha's identity and intention, but he required a public declaration before he would allow Kameha to pass.

"This is Kamehameha, son of Keoua, grandson of Kalanike'eaumoku and great-grandson of the mighty Keawe," Nae'ole replied. "He has come to move the Naha Stone."

"He is not naha," the kahuna said. "It is kapu for him to challenge the stone."

"No, he is not naha by luck of birth," Kameha's kahu confirmed, "but he would prove that his mana is naha by moving the great stone."

Now the priest looked directly at Nae'ole's protégé. "Boy," he said, even as he tilted his head back to address Kameha, who towered over him, "do you understand that if you fail to move the Naha Stone, the consequences will be most severe?"

"Yes," said Kameha, "but I do not intend fail."

"Then see to it that you don't, *boy*," the priest said, and he stepped aside.

For all his outward confidence, Kamehameha was inwardly shaken as he regarded the Naha Stone for the first time. The great block of stone hulked in front of him, forbidding and ominous. Its pitted surface regarded him with a thousand malevolent eyes. *Do you truly believe you can move me, wohi?* the stone whispered. *Try if you dare, and prepare to die when you fail.*

The Naha Stone was tapered at one end, like the prow of a canoe. Kameha decided that he would mount his assault on the great stone from its narrower end, where it would be easier to grip and easier to move.

As Kamehameha advanced on the stone, the swelling crowd took his measure. The priest of Lono had called Kameha a "boy," but the spectators saw an imposing young man with legs thick as koa trunks who stood taller than all the other men present. He wore a simple malo and nothing else, save for the gleaming shark tooth that hung around his neck on a slender cord. Taking care to stay well out of his sight, the people of Hilo formed a wide semi-circle behind Kamehameha as he stood before the Naha Stone, studying it in silence. Muscles rippled across his broad back as he clenched his fists and tensed his shoulders in preparation for the great effort to come. His mouth was set in a deep frown and his eyes seemed to blaze. To the onlookers, it appeared as if Kameha meant to move the stone by staring at it.

Now Kamehameha squatted in front of the Naha Stone, encircling its tapered end with his arms and tightly gripping his elbows. In his mind he heard Kekūhaupi'o's admonition to rely on his legs. He took several deep breaths. Then he pushed upward with both legs. The stone did not move. A murmur arose from the crowd. The priest edged closer.

Kameha relaxed his legs and wrapped his arms still more tightly around the stone. Again, he breathed deeply. The crowd of onlookers buzzed with anticipation. Then, with a loud grunt, Kamehameha thrust upward once more. The Naha Stone did not move. Out of the corner of his eye, Kameha saw Nae'ole, a few steps away. "Whatever you do," Nae'ole whispered, "do not release your hold on the Naha Stone. The kahuna will interpret that as an admission of failure." Kamehameha frowned in acknowledgement.

As he braced himself for a third attempt, the crowd behind him stirred. A second priest was approaching through the villagers, who flung themselves to the earth again. The priest strode to the end of the stone opposite Kamehameha and glared at him. He was slender and tall, and carried a standard bearing the fearsome, carved likeness of Kūkā'ilimoku, the war god. This priest was the kahuna nui of Keawemauhili, the high chief of Hilo. The villagers were astonished to see the war god, for this was Lono's time of year, when the heiaus of Kūkā'ilimoku were closed. Normally, the kāhuna would sequester the god's fierce idol in his temple during the Makahiki time. But Kamehameha's challenge to the Naha Stone's kapu was extraordinary, and the second priest had decided that the god Kūkā'ilimoku should manifest himself, as further warning of the dire consequences of failure. Now the priest fixed Kamehameha with a hard stare and vigorously shook the god's standard.

Kameha met the kahuna's stare over the top of the Naha Stone. Without taking his eyes off the priest, he changed his grip, grasping the end of the stone in both hands, drawing his arms to his side and locking his elbows. Kamehameha tensed his legs, drew a deep breath, and then, with a sudden exhalation of air, drove upward with all his might. The Naha Stone began to move. Filling his lungs again, Kamehameha battled the stone's dead weight, thrusting forward and pushing upward. The big muscles of his calves and thighs swelled with exertion. At last, he released the stone and it thumped to the ground.

The kahuna nui ceased brandishing the god. The common folk behind Kameha prostrated themselves anew. Kamehameha stood over the Naha Stone like a warrior standing over a fallen foe in battle. He was breathing hard and his heart was racing.

This much of the story seems credible to me. I cannot vouch for what is said to have come next. In this telling, Kamehameha had conquered the stone, but he was not finished with it—not yet.

Kameha stared at the stone. To those among the onlookers who dared look at his face, Kamehameha's stare seemed as hard as the Naha Stone itself. He breathed deeply and slowly, willing his heart to slacken its pace. His hands hung loosely at his sides. Kameha stood this way for several minutes—inhaling, exhaling, and never taking his eyes off the massive rock.

Now Kameha stepped to the Naha Stone once more. He flexed his hands and fingers. Then he stroked the shark's tooth that hung at his neck. "Your mana and my mana will conquer all, Kekū," he whispered.

Squatting again in front of the Naha Stone, so the story goes, Kameha gripped it tightly, drawing his elbows close to his chest and pressing his chin tightly against the stone itself. He filled his lungs to capacity and then emptied them with a loud burst of air. He breathed in and out again. Then Kameha slowly drew one more deep breath and held it. His chest swelled and his face contorted. The crowd held its breath with him.

Kamehameha locked eyes with the high priest of Hilo over the stone's length. The kahuna now regarded Kameha with wary respect, and was gripping the standard of Kūkā'ilimoku so tightly that the blood had drained from his knuckles.

"Kū!" Kameha shouted, simultaneously driving his legs upward and thrusting his body forward under the stone as it rose with him. Wedging himself hard against the stone to counter its terrible weight with his whole body, Kameha drew another deep breath. "Kāʻili!" he cried, pressing forward with his all his might and extending his arms with a sharp up-thrust. The Naha Stone rose again. Kamehameha filled his lungs once more. "Moku!" he shouted, digging his toes into the soil, powering his legs forward and driving his left shoulder into the stone. People say that under the force of Kameha's final assault, the Naha Stone rose until it was upright, and then toppled over, slamming into the ground and spraying dirt in all directions. They say that the kahuna nui of Hilo leaped out of its way with a surprising nimbleness that denied his many years.

The two priests now stood shoulder to shoulder, gaping at Kamehameha, whose chest still heaved from his exertions. Then those among the crowd who still dared to look witnessed something remarkable. The two priests dropped to their knees before the young man. This was unheard of; kāhuna never paid obeisance to low-ranking aliʻi such as Kamehameha.

Kamehameha gestured toward the priests and was about to speak when Naeʻole stepped to his side. "Do not let mere words spoil the mystery of this moment, Kameha," he whispered. "Let us go now and leave the talking to the storytellers."

Word of Kamehameha's victory over the Naha Stone preceded him across the mountain to Kawaihae. As Naeʻole had predicted, the storytellers embellished Kameha's exploits with their own fabulist inventions. They spoke of a mysterious young man who had appeared out of a mist to challenge the great stone's dire kapu. They described Kameha as a silent giant—seven feet tall with a massive chest and biceps as thick as a koa trunk. His hands were as broad as canoe paddles and so powerful that Kameha could crack open a coconut by clenching it in one fist. They said that Kameha's body had glowed as he approached the stone, his bronze skin enveloped in a nimbus of golden light, and his long, black hair sparking in the sun. His eyes gleamed like polished black coral. According to one account, Kameha had flipped the stone end over end in one fluid movement. In another version, he had not only upended the stone, but sent it flying through the air like an ihe spear. In the most fabulous telling, the god Kūkā'ilimoku himself had invested Kamehameha, lending him his supernatural strength. How else to explain how a mere man could have moved the Naha Stone? In any event, no one any longer referred to Kameha as a "boy."

Of course, these stories soon reached the ears of old King Alapa'i'nui, who summoned Kamehameha shortly after his return from Hilo. News of Kameha's arrival and Alapa'i's summons spread quickly through the royal compound at Kawaihae, and by the time Kameha was ushered into the mō'ī's presence, the king's courtyard was packed with ali'i. Alapa'i was resting on a mat in his hale. He peered at Kamehameha through bleary eyes as Kameha and Kalani'ōpu'u approached and squatted before him. Though it was only mid-morning, Alapa'i was already muzzy from 'awa and his speech was slurred. "Ah, Kamehameha," he said, "is it true that you picked up the Naha Stone and hurled it into Hilo Bay like an ihe spear?"

"No, Lord," Kameha replied, "that is just a kaao story for little children. I did not throw the Naha Stone into the bay, but I did move it."

"Ah," said Alapa'i, "but is it not true that in your moment of greatest exertion, Kūkā'ilimoku himself entered your body to give you the strength you required?"

"Lord, I do not know if Kūkā'ilimoku gave me his own strength. But it is true that I called upon him."

"Well then, he must have heard you," said Alapa'i, "and the god would not have listened unless your spirit was pure. Your mana must be great indeed. No doubt, your father Keoua will be very proud of you." Alapa'i's declaration before his courtiers served to quiet the gossip about Kameha's real parentage.

"Thank you, Lord," Kameha said.

"And I am proud to have a strong warrior such as you in my ranks," said Alapa'i, returning his attention to his 'awa cup.

As Nae'ole had warned, Ka'akau was not pleased to see Kamehameha when he returned from Hilo. The kahuna nui confronted Kamehameha at the doorway of Alapa'i's hale as he and Kalani'ōpu'u were departing. "So, Kamehameha, you have moved the Naha Stone. Are you a great chief now? Are you now even greater than our mō'ī, and will you rule Hawai'i in his place?"

Unsure how to respond, Kamehameha hesitated. Interposing himself between his nephew and the kahuna, Kalani'ōpu'u answered for Kameha. "Mover of the Naha Stone or not, you can be sure that Kamehameha will become a great chief someday, *priest*," growled. "But no one would presume to say that he is greater than Alapa'i, or who will rule the island after him. Now step aside and let us pass."

Ka'akau gave way, but persisted. "The succession has already been settled by your mō'ī, Kalani'ōpu'u, as you and your nephew well know," he said.

"Thank you, Uncle," Kamehameha murmured as they walked away from the glowering priest. "I feared to offend the kahuna nui."

"Pay Ka'akau no mind," Kalani'ōpu'u replied. "It is Alapa'i's regard that matters, for now at least." Then Kalani'ōpu'u said, "Kamehameha, I know that there has been some ill feeling between you and Kiwala'ō. But the two of you must make amends. The time is fast approaching when I shall need both of you at my side."

"I want no quarrel with Kiwala'ō," Kameha replied. "You have treated me like a son, and therefore he is my brother as well as my cousin."

"Good," Kalani'ōpu'u said. "Then come with me now and make peace with your 'brother.'"

Kameha and Kiwala'ō met at the men's eating house—the *mua*—at Alapa'i's compound. There, sitting cross-legged opposite each other under Kalani'ōpu'u's benevolent gaze, they made a peace of sorts.

Kameha made the first gesture. "Cousin, for the sake of your father—who has been like a father to me—I wish to put aside any ill words of mine that have come between us," he said.

"Yes, for my father's sake, I would have no quarrel with you, Kamehameha," Kiwala'ō replied. Though they had spoken words of peace, the chill between them was still palpable.

Kalani'ōpu'u had been squatting between the cousins. Now he jumped to his feet. "Rise and embrace," he commanded. Kameha and Kiwala'ō rose slowly to their feet. Gingerly, they wrapped their arms around each other. Now Kamehameha, who stood two inches taller than Kiwala'ō, tightened his hold. "I am devoted to your father," he whispered in Kiwala'ō's ear, "and as long as he shall live, I will always make common cause with you."

Kiwala'ō broke Kameha's embrace, stepping away and regarding him with wary understanding.

"Good, good," Kalani'ōpu'u exclaimed, clapping his hands. "It is settled between you, then."

As the chill between Kamehameha and Kiwala'ō abated, Keawe'ōpala turned cool toward my uncle. Keawe'ōpala was disturbed by Kameha's newfound celebrity as the mover of the Naha Stone. Moreover he was reminded by the kahuna nui Ka'akau of an ancient prediction that the person who moved the stone would one day rule over all the Hawaiian Islands. "You may be Alapa'i's chosen successor, but beware of Kamehameha," the priest warned him. "One day, that one will become a slayer of chiefs. Even you will not be safe when that day comes."

Thus warned, Keawe'ōpala came to see Kameha as a potential threat to his future rule. Anticipating Alapa'i's death, he began making his own plans for Kameha. Careful to mask his true feelings, he always spoke kindly to Kameha as if nothing had changed between them. Nae'ole learned of

Keawe'ōpala's real intentions and cautioned Kameha to be on guard against his intrigues.

"No matter how much he may smile at you now, Keawe'ōpala does not wish you well," he warned. "He will move against you when the old king dies."

"Don't worry," Kameha replied, "I will be more than ready for him when that day arrives."

If Kamehameha gave short shrift to Keawe'ōpala's unfriendly intentions toward him, it may have been because he was preoccupied at the time with the tender attentions of Kalani'ōpu'u's youngest wife, Kaneikapolei. She was about eleven years older than Kamehameha. She had accompanied Kalani'ōpu'u to Alapa'i's court on one of his periodic visits there and then begged to remain behind when he returned to Ka'ū, saying that she preferred Kawaihae's greenery and sandy beaches to the barren landscape of the Ka'ū District.

Kaneikapolei had already borne Kalani'ōpu'u two sons, Keōua Kū'ahu'ula and Keōuape'e'ale. She had heard of Kalola's liaison with Kameha, and after his triumphant return from Hilo, she wanted him as well. She contrived "chance" encounters with him on the footpaths near the royal compound at Kawaihae, but in these brief meetings, Kameha had been merely pleasant—and always respectful to his aunt by marriage. Finally, Kaneikapolei set out one evening to seduce Kameha while dancing the hula with the other young women of Alapa'i's court. Her husband, Kalani'ōpu'u, was not at court at the time, but it would have mattered little to Kaneikapolei if he had been. Such were our ways in those days.

Kaneikapolei was wide in the hips from the birth of her two sons. Still, at twenty-five, her waist had not yet caught up with her hips in girth, and her breasts were still firm. Waggling her hips and shaking her shoulders, she danced provocatively close to Kameha. The seductive movements of her pelvis and bare bosom under her swaying ti-leaf skirt and flower lei aroused him.

When the dancing had concluded, the old king repaired to his hale with his cronies to while away the night drinking ʻawa. The younger people remained in the courtyard. Amid the young men's boisterous laughter and the women's demure giggles, they seated themselves in a circle on the ground. It was time to play *ʻume.*

ʻUme was a game of sexual pairing, usually played by commoners or lower-ranking chiefs and chiefesses. The game was conducted by a *mau*—a man who walked around the circle of seated men and women with a special wand of kauila wood trimmed with red and black feathers. As the mau circled the players, he would touch a man with his feathered wand. If the man desired a particular woman, he would give the mau something of value and the mau, in turn, would touch the woman indicated by the man. The man would then leave the ʻume enclosure or hale with the woman of his choice. Away from the other players, they would spend the rest of the night together, provided the woman consented. In the game of ʻume, the men were always careful to choose women who they knew would consent, for to return to the game rejected was profoundly embarrassing.

A more elaborate and refined version of this game, called *kilu,* was played by high-ranking aliʻi. But this version of ʻume took much longer and the only prize was a chaste nose-rub kiss. So this night, hot-blooded after the sensuous revelry of the hula, the young aliʻi opted for the simpler game, which was more directly suited to their immediate purposes.

As the mau circled the gathering, Kaneikapolei met Kamehameha's gaze across the circle and smiled at him, her eyes spoke of passionate desire. The mau neared. Kameha grasped the shark's tooth that Kekūhaupiʻo had given him and lifted the cord over his head. He caught the mau's eye and nodded at him. The mau stopped in front of Kamehameha and tapped his shoulder with the feathered wand. Silently, Kameha handed the shark tooth to the mau and gestured at Kaneikapolei. The mau smiled. He knew that Kameha had worn the tooth at Hilo. It was something of value indeed.

Now the mau circled around to the other side of the ring of seated ali'i and touched Kaneikapolei with his wand. Simultaneously and without a word, Kamehameha and Kaneikapolei rose and left the brightness of the 'ume circle for the darkness of the night. As they departed, murmurs and soft laughter trailed after them. The ali'i remaining in the circle knew that they would not see Kameha and Kaneikapolei again before morning.

Kamehameha led Kaneikapolei up the footpath to the games field where he had bested Kiwala'ō in spear throwing. The night was clear and a full moon bathed the deserted field in silver light. Tearing hungrily at each other's garments, Kameha and Kaneikapolei sank to the soft grass at the field's edge. They were both naked by the time their knees touched the earth.

"Come, Kamehameha," said Kaneikapolei, "move me the way you did the Naha Stone." Kameha, who had enjoyed other sexual liaisons since his first intimate encounter with Kalola, did not disappoint her.

"Foolish kāne!" snapped Kekūhaupi'o. "You were thinking with your worm instead of your head."

Kamehameha hung his head. "I am sorry Kekū. You are right; it was very foolish of me."

Kekūhaupi'o was aghast when he learned Kameha had surrendered his shark tooth to the mau. "That tooth was strong with mana, Kameha. No wahine's favors could match its worth," he scolded. "You have weakened your own mana by this rash act."

Kameha could not meet his kahu's eyes. He stared at the ground and said nothing.

"You must restore your mana," Kekūhaupi'o said.

"How shall I do that, Kekū?" Kameha asked.

"There is only one way," Kekūhaupi'o said. "You must kill a shark."

Thus it was that as dawn broke off the Ka'ū coast several weeks later, Kamehameha found himself in a double-hulled canoe preparing to do battle. Kameha and Kekūhaupi'o had put to sea from Kawaihae two days earlier. Thanks to favorable winds and currents, their canoe made good time down the leeward coast and was now rolling in gentle swells in the lee of Ka Lae, at the Big Island's southernmost extremity. It was here, according to the two fishermen who had accompanied Kameha, Kekūhaupi'o, and a half-dozen paddlers on this voyage, that the fierce *niuhi* were most plentiful at this time of year.

The canoe stank with the rancid smell of rotting pig's flesh. Before departing Kawaihae, Kekūhaupi'o had directed a kanaka to kill an old sow, butcher the carcass, wrap the raw meat in ti-leaf bundles, and load them onto the canoe. The meat had ripened rapidly under the hot sun as the canoe made its way south. "By the time we get to Ka'ū, the sharks will be jumping out of the water to eat this pig meat," Kekūhaupi'o had joked.

"By the time we get to Ka'ū, I will be jumping into the water to get away from it," Kameha had responded.

In fact, the ripened pig flesh preceded Kamehameha into the sea. The fishermen tied the bundles of meat to a long piece of wood and lowered them into the water between the canoe's double hulls. Then they pierced the ti-leaf wrappings with sharp sticks. Soon, the canoe was surrounded by a slick of smelly grease.

"Are you in a hurry to jump into the water now?" Kekūhaupi'o asked Kameha.

"I can wait for the shark, Kekū."

A shark was not long in coming. They saw its dorsal fin first, slicing through the water as the big predator arrowed toward them. Then its broad gray back broke the surface. It was a tiger shark. As it approached the slow-moving canoe from the stern, the fishermen and the two paddlers raised the long piece of wood again so that the bundled meat was now several feet above the water's surface.

"*E Kameha!*" exclaimed Kekūhaupiʻo. "Here is a big *manō paʻele*, come to test your mana."

"*E Kekū!*" Kamehameha replied. "Here is a big sea slug come to die by my spear." Kameha was kneeling at the rear of the platform between the canoe's twin hulls. Now he leaned over the edge to get a better look at the shark, which was swimming just behind the double hulls and lunging at the bundles of pig meat, just out of its reach. The shark was twice Kameha's height in length. Its mouth was several feet across, wide enough to swallow a man whole—even a man as large as Kameha. As the shark lunged at the bundle, its razor-sharp teeth glinted in the morning sun.

"I looked directly into that manō paʻele's eyes," Kamehameha later told my father. "They were as dark as night. The shark was very angry because it couldn't reach the pig meat, and as our eyes met, I was sure that it blamed me."

Kamehameha's bravado was shaken. Speaking softly to the shark so that no one else on the canoe would hear, he said, "My apologies. I was wrong to call you a 'slug.' Kanaloa has sent you and your mana is strong."

The fishermen continued to poke at the bundles with their sticks, spilling more grease and bits of meat into the water. A light breeze filled the canoe's sail and kept the vessel slightly ahead of the shark. Kameha slowly untied his malo, letting it fall to the deck. Now he stood naked and ready for battle with the man-eater. He was breathing quickly and his hands and legs were shaking. He hoped that none of the others would notice.

"Remember, Kameha, do not rush into this fight," Kekūhaupiʻo said. "Let the manō paʻele fill its belly with greasy water first."

"You can be sure that I am in no hurry," Kameha replied.

In its furious efforts to reach the pig meat and its ravenous hunger for the small morsels of flesh that had fallen into the sea, the tiger shark was steadily gulping greasy salt water. Eventually, the big animal would become sluggish from all its inadvertent drinking. Kamehameha would wait for his moment.

At last, the shark's thrusts at the suspended meat slowed. Kekūhaupiʻo signaled to the paddlers, who lowered the sail, allowing the shark to overtake the canoe. Now the big tiger shark was swimming directly between the double hulls, still snapping lethargically at the ti-leaf bundles just above its snout. Careful to keep one of the canoe's hulls between himself and the shark, Kameha slipped into the water with a short spear tied to his wrist. Before the animal became aware of his presence, he filled his lungs, doubled over, and slid beneath the water's surface. When he was several feet below the underside of the shallow hull, Kameha kicked hard and angled upward toward the shark, which was now a dark, blurry shadow against the water's bright surface.

Suddenly, the great predator sensed Kameha's approach and turned toward him. Ignoring the painful knot in his stomach, Kamehameha kicked hard again, driving himself against the animal's flank and grasping it across its back, just behind its head, before the shark could turn on him. Now the shark dove, trying to shake Kameha off. But bloated and enfeebled, the beast could not break his iron grip. Pain stabbed at Kamehameha's ears as he sank deeper with the descending animal. His lungs burned. Still maintaining his grip on the shark with his left arm, Kameha jammed his spear deep into the shark's gill, as Kekūhaupiʻo had taught him. "Drive your spear through its gill and into its liver," his kahu advised. "That is the surest killing blow."

The big shark shuddered with pain, shock, and fury. It jerked back and forth in frenzy as it tried to shake its tormentor. Kamehameha clung to the shark and the spear shaft and pressed the weapon home with all his might. A dark red cloud now surrounded him, and Kameha could see nothing in the murk.

Kekūhaupiʻo and the others on the canoe could not see what was happening. Kamehameha and the shark had disappeared from sight. But now they saw the water around the vessel turn red. Moments later, Kameha's head and shoulders broke the surface several yards behind the canoe. Greasy, bloodstained water streamed from his hair and into his face. He shook his head, blinked his eyes, and gasped for air.

"Where is the shark, Kameha?" Kekūhaupiʻo cried.

"Here it is, Kekū," Kameha answered. He pulled on the spear, still stuck deep in the tiger shark's gills, and the big fish's snout and gaping maw rose with it. The monster's eyes were empty. Kameha let go of the spear and the tiger shark rolled onto its back.

Regaining the canoe's deck, Kamehameha helped the fishermen and paddlers lash the predator's carcass between the vessel's double hulls. "*E Kameha!*" Kekūhaupiʻo exclaimed when this task was completed, "it is a good thing you waited for that manō paʻele to fill its belly with greasy sea water, because otherwise it would have had plenty of room in there for you."

Indeed, the tiger shark was massive. It was easily two-thirds the length of the thirty-foot deck. Kekūhaupiʻo handed Kameha a sharp pahoa dagger. "Cut the belly open and give the shark's entrails to Kanaloa in thanks," he said.

Reaching down, Kameha thrust the blade deep into the shark's throat and sliced the beast open with one long sweep of his arm. The animal's heart, liver, pancreas, and guts were exposed, along with something else. "Kekū," Kameha shouted, "I don't think this shark would have had any room for me in its belly after all."

Kekūhaupiʻo and the others gaped in wonderment. For amid the mess of guts and other organs were some twenty small forms—unborn shark pups. "Kameha," Kekūhaupiʻo said softly, "the mana of this she-shark is powerful indeed. Now you must make it your own by offering the shark and her pups to Lono at the heiau at Kalalea."

"But first, Kekū, let's not forget Kanaloa," Kameha said, and he gathered up the tiger shark's organs and entrails and held them out over the side of the canoe. "Oh Kanaloa, god of the deep waters," Kameha chanted, "accept this offering and watch over this canoe and all who journey in it this day and keep them from coming to harm at sea." He tossed the shark's innards into the water. Then, at Kekūhaupiʻo's order, the paddlers made for Kalalea.

The sun was approaching its zenith when the paddlers beached the double-hulled canoe on the narrow strand of sand just below the heiau at Kalalea. As Kameha and Kekūhaupiʻo disembarked, a kahuna from the heiau came forward to meet them. "Who comes here?" the priest demanded. He was an old man, stooped over a walking stick. His hair had long ago turned white.

"This is Kamehameha, the mover of the Naha Stone," Kekūhaupi'o replied. "He has slain a great she-shark—a manō pa'ele—with his own hand, and he would offer it and its pups to Lono this very night."

The aging priest's eyes widened. "Truly?" he said. "This is he who picked up the stone and hurled it over the head of the high-priest of Kū?"

"Yes, he is the one," answered Kekūhaupi'o.

"The god Lono will be pleased to accept his offering," the kahuna said to Kekūhaupi'o. Then, looking up at Kameha, who towered over him, he added, "You do this humble heiau a great honor."

The temple of Lono at Kalalea was indeed humble. It was much smaller than the heiaus at Hilo and Kawaihae. The strong winds that prevailed at Ka Lae, which the haoles now call South Point, buffeted the heiau daily, and its thatching was frayed and badly in need of repair. Sited as it was in the most remote corner of the arid Ka'ū district, the temple received few visitors and was mostly overlooked when the tributes collected during the Makahiki time were distributed. In later years, stories about Kamehameha's offering there this day would significantly raise its status.

The fishermen hauled the tiger shark's gutted body from the shore to the temple's small courtyard. There they laid it out, together with the big shark's dead pups. Then Kekūhaupi'o sent the fishermen and the canoe paddlers into the uplands to forage for firewood. Other than short grass and some stunted shrubs, there was little vegetation at the coast, where rainfall was sparse, and the men were gone for several hours before they returned with enough dry wood for a cooking fire. Kekūhaupi'o sent them off to the nearby village for the night.

After the other men had left, Kameha and Kekūhaupi'o sat down to rest in the shade of the heiau. Before them, the Kona Coast stretched away to the north, hooking northwest, and bracketing the deep blue of the ocean with the soft greens and tans of the rising landmass, which faded from sight amid the clouds and haze that gathered on the flanks of the great volcano, Mauna Loa.

"Kekū," Kameha asked, after they had sat in silence for some time, "why do we offer the shark and her pups to Lono? Why not the war god Kūkā'ilimoku? Is he not more terrible and therefore more powerful than Lono?"

"Kūkā'ilimoku is more terrible, but not necessarily more powerful," Kekūhaupi'o replied. "You must never confuse harshness with superior power, Kameha."

"But Kūkā'ilimoku brings victory in battle," Kameha persisted. "What is Lono's power?"

"Kūkā'ilimoku's power is the power of blood and conquest, and therefore, destruction," Kekūhaupi'o replied. "Lono's power is the power of clouds and rain and, therefore, creation. And creation is always more powerful than destruction."

Kamehameha pondered this for a moment. Then he said, "But we are warriors, Kekū. We should not offend Kūkā'ilimoku."

"He will not be offended by this offering to Lono," Kekūhaupi'o said. "Kūkā'ilimoku requires his tributes in times of war. This is a time of peace. In any case, he would not be pleased by an offering of dead fish."

Kameha nodded. The appropriate offering for the war god was the body of a warrior. Kamehameha was ever mindful of the many gods' demands. He believed, as did all our people, that the gods were everywhere and invested in everything. Throughout his life, Kameha tried to keep faith with all of them.

In the temple courtyard, there was a small imu lined with loose *a'a* lava stones, covered by a thick layer of ash. Kameha and Kekūhaupi'o brushed the ashes aside and set about laying a fire in the pit. They started their fire as our people had done for generations, setting the sharpened point of a stick of hard koa wood into a groove cut in a flat piece of softer *hau* wood and spinning this stick at high speed until the small wood particles and coconut fibers laid around it ignited. Today we have sulfur matches and everyone has forgotten this.

Kekūhaupi'o unsheathed his dagger and cut a large slab of meat from the shark's side. "We will save some of this fish for ourselves," he said. "Lono will not be offended, because we offer him the pups as well as the she-shark." Kekūhaupi'o sliced the shark meat into several pieces, which he wrapped in ti leaves that he had brought from Kawaihae. He bundled several yams with taro leaves and wrapped them in ti leaves as well.

The sun lowered in the west, a fat ball of flame that painted the sky orange and red, tinted the clouds congregating on Mauna Loa pink, and turned the sea purple. As dusk settled on the courtyard, the old kahuna hobbled forward with a bit of kapa cloth wrapped around a stick and ignited it in the flames. This he carried into the heiau to light the oil lamps.

When the fire had burned down to coals, Kekūhaupiʻo placed the ti-leaf-covered shark meat and yams atop the embers and used a stick to push more coals on top of them. "Our dinner will cook while you make your offering to Lono," he said. Then, with some effort, he and Kamehameha carried the shark's carcass into the heiau, where they laid it on the floor in front of the altar, along with the bodies of the aborted pups. By this time, Kamehameha's face, chest, hands, and thighs were covered with ashes and earth. His kahu sent him to the beach to clean himself. "Lono would surely reject an offering from such filthy hands," he said.

"Cut out the shark's eyeballs," Kekūhaupiʻo said when Kamehameha returned. It was time for the *ʻailolo* ceremony. Kameha had been anticipating this moment with some distaste. For while the animal's left eye would be offered to Lono, Kameha was required to eat the shark's raw right eyeball.

As Kameha sliced the eyeballs from the shark's massive head, the old kahuna stood at his side and chanted:

Lono of the heavens,
Lono of the thunder,
Lono of the wind,
Lono of the rainbow,
Lono of the clouds,
Lono of the rain,
Lono, who makes the earth fertile,
Lono, who quickens the womb,
Lono, who makes all things grow,

Accept this young warrior's humble offering,
Hear his prayer,
Watch over him,
Bless him,
Lono!

Kamehameha gave the shark's left eyeball to the priest, who laid it on the altar. Then, as he had been instructed by Kekūhaupiʻo, he raised the other eyeball above his head in both hands. "Lono of the heavens," he chanted, "Lono of the thunder, wind, rainbow, clouds, and rain. Lono, accept my humble offering. Lono, see how I consume the eyeball of the great niuhi shark. Lono, see how I make the great she-shark's mana my own and dedicate my strengthened spirit to you. Lono!" With that, Kameha lowered the gelatinous orb to his mouth and swallowed it whole.

When they returned to the temple courtyard, Kekūhaupiʻo handed Kameha a drinking gourd. Kameha tilted his head back, inverted the gourd, and let a stream of sweet water cascade into his open mouth, washing away the aftertaste of the shark's eyeball.

"If the mana of that she-shark is as strong as the taste of its eyeball, it is powerful indeed, Kekū," Kameha said, passing the gourd back to his kahu.

"It is powerful enough to make up for the mana you foolishly squandered on the favors of a wahine," Kekūhaupiʻo replied. "Do not surrender this shark's teeth so easily."

"I will not be so foolish again, Kekū," Kameha said, "but you must take one tooth now, for I would share this shark's strong mana with you." Grunting appreciatively, Kekūhaupiʻo accepted the shark tooth, one of several Kameha had knocked out earlier.

The old priest joined them. "Lono will be pleased by your offering," he said. As he spoke, he eyed the fire pit, and his nostrils widened visibly as he savored the aroma of the roasting shark meat.

"And we will be pleased if Lono's kahuna offers to share this shark flesh with us," said Kameha.

Later, as they reclined on sleeping mats in the heiau, where the priest had invited them to spend the night, Kekūhaupiʻo said, "You did well to invite the kahuna to eat with us."

"We are guests here—guests of Lono and his priest. It only seemed right. And besides, Kekū, even though it was no more than a simple meal for us, the old kahuna will make it a feast for the entire district."

"Ah, Kameha," Kekūhaupiʻo said, "You are thinking like a chief."

Kameha was still thinking like a lusty youth when he returned to Kawaihae, where he and Kaneikapolei resumed their lovemaking. The pair's carefree love sport produced the usual result. Kameha was no more than three or four months beyond his fifteenth birthday.

Kalaniʻōpuʻu was in Kawaihae on one of his periodic visits to pay his respects to Alapaʻi and take the measure of his own standing at the royal court. His visits to the court were becoming increasingly rare as Alapaʻi aged and Keaweʻōpala prepared to succeed him. Kalaniʻōpuʻu sensed that the time of open conflict was nearing and could well erupt even while Alapaʻi still lived, despite his uncle's repeated avowals of affection for him.

Even removed from court in Kaʻū, Kalaniʻōpuʻu had heard how Kameha had given his shark tooth for the chance to sport with Kaneikapolei. He had chuckled when he heard the story. In Kalaniʻōpuʻu's eyes, the value Kameha placed on Kaneikapolei's favors reflected well on him. After all, she was his own wife. Now he was proud that the baby in Kaneikapolei's belly was the child of Kamehameha, the mover of the Naha Stone. He hugged Kaneikapolei, patted her stomach, and exclaimed, "*E Kameha!* This child's mana will be very strong!"

Kalaniʻōpuʻu signaled Kaneikapolei to leave them. She smiled coyly at her husband and his nephew. Her smile was demure, but her manner was bold. She swayed her hips provocatively as she turned away. Kalaniʻōpuʻu and Kameha watched her departing figure with equal appreciation.

In the mua, Kameha and Kalani'ōpu'u shared a wooden bowl of sweet-potato poi that Kalani'ōpu'u had himself prepared. When he and Kameha had eaten their fill, Kalani'ōpu'u said, "Kamehameha, you are still too young to concern yourself with raising a child. Perhaps I should take this child in hanai and raise it as my own."

"You are right, Uncle," Kameha replied. "I am not ready for this responsibility. I would be pleased if you would raise this child."

"Then it is settled," Kalani'ōpu'u said.

At about this time, Alapa'i decided to move his court to Hilo. In his old age, the mō'ī of Hawai'i found the heat of Kawaihae oppressive and longed for the soothing daily rains of the island's wet side. Kamehameha traveled to Hilo with the king. It was there, after years of separation, that he was reunited with his father, who was then living at Pauka'a, a few miles north of the village of Hilo, with several of his many wives.

Keoua greeted Kameha in the courtyard in front of his hale, where he was reclining on a mat in the shade of a soapbey tree. Kamehameha's father had always been trim, but now he was thin and appeared frail. He did not get up.

"Come, my son, sit here beside me," Keoua said, "and tell me, is it true that you killed a manō pa'ele with your bare hands and hurled the Naha Stone into Hilo Bay?"

"I used a short spear to kill the tiger shark, father," Kameha replied. "And I moved the stone; although not nearly as far as many people now believe."

Keoua smiled. "What people believe is often more important than what really happens," he said. "Did you know, Kameha, that many people believe the mover of the Naha Stone is destined to rule over all of our islands?"

Kameha nodded. "I know some have said as much."

"And did you know that because of your exploits, Alapa'i believes your mana is exceptionally powerful?"

"He has always treated me kindly and with respect," Kameha replied.

"Ah, but did you know that Alapa'i and his son Keawe'ōpala fear you?" Keoua asked.

Kamehameha looked at his father and frowned. "Nae'ole has warned me that Keawe'ōpala may wish me ill, father," he said, "but I had not heard that he and Alapa'i fear me."

"You may be aware that there is no love lost between Alapa'i and his son and your uncle, Kalani'ōpu'u," Keoua continued. "I have never desired any land or authority beyond the Kohala District, but my brother Kalani's ambition acknowledges no boundaries, and certainly will not be confined to Ka'ū. Alapa'i and Keawe'ōpala understand this. You are like a son to Kalani, and they worry that if the other chiefs see you with him, it will strengthen his hand against them, because the other chiefs believe that as the mover of the Naha Stone, your mana is strong. That is why Alapa'i and Keawe'ōpala fear you. And that is why they will try to keep you close to them, to deny your mana to your uncle."

"What should I do?" Kameha asked.

Keoua was silent for a moment. Then he said, "Remember that you are a true descendant of the great Keawe, and be ready when the time comes."

The time was not long in coming.

Pauka'a, 1763

"Kameha! Come away quickly. Your father is very sick."

Startled, Kamehameha looked up at the big warrior who had burst into the hale of Keawema'uhili, the high chief of Hilo, whom Kameha had been visiting. The man was Puna, Kalani'ōpu'u's kahu and war counselor. Kameha scrambled to his feet.

"I fear he is dying," Puna said. "Your uncle is already at his side. You must come to Pauka'a at once."

"You must hurry to your father before his spirit leaves his body," said Keawema'uhili. He was fond of Keoua, and had invited him to live at Pauka'a after Kamehameha moved the Naha Stone. Rising from his sedge mat, he embraced Kameha, who stood taller by at least six inches. As soon as Kamehameha and Puna had departed, Keawema'uhili dispatched a messenger to the nearby hale of his mō'ī, old Alapa'i, to inform him of the news.

The sun was sinking behind Mauna Kea by the time Kamehameha and Puna reached Pauka'a. As they hurried north along the footpath, Puna told Kameha about the growing rift between Kalani'ōpu'u and Alapa'i.

"Old Alapa'i invited Kalani'ōpu'u to live at his court in Hilo, but your uncle would not go." Puna said. "Now the mō'ī is angry with him."

"Why does my uncle refuse?" Kameha asked.

"He fears a plot against his life. He believes that if he comes to court, Alapa'i will try to kill him to make the throne safe for Keawe'ōpala. So your uncle keeps to Ka'ū."

"Is he not then at risk by coming to Pauka'a?"

"Kalani'ōpu'u brought warriors with him to Pauka'a," Puna replied. "His canoes are close by. If needs be, he could be well out to sea before Alapa'i could spring a trap. But that is not the old mō'ī's way. He does not want Kalani'ōpu'u's blood on his hands for all the other chiefs to see. He would prefer to arrange a bloodless end for your uncle, by poisoning, perhaps. So Kalani'ōpu'u will not go to Alapa'i's court."

Though Kamehameha and Puna made all haste to reach Pauka'a, Keoua's spirit was swifter still in departing. Loud lamentations reached their ears as they neared Keoua's hale.

Kamehameha and Puna rushed inside. Kameha found his uncle swaying unsteadily on his knees next to Keoua's body. Kalani'ōpu'u's face was buried in his cupped hands. His shoulders convulsed in anguish. Keoua's head was thrown back, his lips still parted from his final struggle for breath. His empty eyes stared at the feeble light that filtered through small gaps in the hale's thatched roof. Keoua had not been a big man in life, but he was vigorous, and his vitality lent him stature. Now, in death, he looked like a diminished parody of himself. This was Keoua's body, but it was not his father. Truly, his spirit had fled.

Kalani'ōpu'u struggled to his feet. He and Kameha fell into each other's arms and wailed—Kalani'ōpu'u for the brother who had fought at his side in so many bygone battles, and Kameha for the father he had hardly known.

All this was described to me many years later by my father, Keli'imaika'i, who was there. By chance, my father had been visiting with Keoua when he fell deathly ill. "I had come to live with Kameha at old King Alapa'i's court in Hilo," he said. "Kameha and I did not see our father very often, and I decided to spend some time with him. I had been staying with him at Pauka'a for just a few days when he became very sick.

"Our uncle Kalani'ōpu'u and his kahu Puna had also come to visit Keoua at this time. They knew that open conflict with Alapa'i and Keawe'ōpala was drawing near, and they wanted to consult with our father. Keoua could barely hold his head up to speak to them. When our uncle realized that Keoua's time was very short, he sent Puna to fetch Kameha.

"At the end, your grandfather's face turned the color of fire ash and he could scarcely breathe," my father recalled. "His last thoughts were for your uncle Kameha. He said to Kalaniʻōpuʻu, 'Keep Kamehameha away from Alapaʻi,' and then he died. Your uncle Kameha arrived not long afterward. He did not see me at first."

Indeed, it was only after falling into his uncle's embrace that Kameha saw his younger brother huddled in a dim corner, his knees drawn up to his chin and his arms wrapped tightly around his legs. Their eyes met across their father's lifeless form. Kameha disengaged from his uncle and rushed to his brother. Reaching down, he grasped Keliʻimaikaʻi by the elbows and gently raised him to his feet.

"Little brother," Kameha said, "I am grieved that I could not reach Paukaʻa sooner. It is good that you were here at the end."

Keliʻimaikaʻi looked up into Kamehameha's broad face. He was on the verge of tears and his mouth quivered. Then he saw that his older brother was fighting to maintain his own composure and he resolved to be strong for him. "You could not know when father's spirit would leave this world," he said. "It was just my fortune to be here. Keoua loved you and his last words were for you." At this, the two brothers surrendered to their grief and wailed loudly.

Now Kalaniʻōpuʻu came to them. Kneeling and wrapping his arms around the young men's shoulders, he said, "Kamehameha, now that Keoua is gone, you should come away with me to Kaʻū—and your brother, too. It was your father's dying wish."

Puna agreed. "Yes," he said. "Listen to your uncle. It is best that you return with us to Kaʻū. Hilo is not a good place for you."

Remembering his father's warning about Alapaʻi and Keaweʻōpala, Kamehameha was inclined to agree with his uncle and his kahu. Before he could respond, however, there was a commotion outside the hale, where the last light of day was fast waning. Torchlight flared in the darkness beyond the hale's doorway.

Puna rushed to the door, filling it with his immense bulk. "Who comes here?" he demanded.

Three men stood immediately outside—Alapa'i's son, Keawe'ōpala, and two ali'i chieftains, Kame'iamoku and his half-brother, Ke'eaumoku, who were nephews of King Alapa'i'nui. Keawe'ōpala stepped forward. He was not as tall as his ali'i contemporaries, but much broader in girth, and soft in body to the point of appearing womanish. In the gathering darkness, the flickering torchlight cast unflattering shadows across his soft chest and flaccid belly. "We have come to join you in grieving for the noble Keoua," he said. "My father, the great Alapa'i'nui, is too grief-stricken to travel. Even now, he wails for Keoua at his hale in Hilo, and he bids Keoua's eldest son, Kamehameha, to return with us to Hilo to ease his sorrow."

Kalani'ōpu'u pushed past Puna to confront Keawe'ōpala. Kamehameha and Keli'imaika'i followed him. "Kamehameha is returning to Ka'ū with us," he said. As he spoke, Kalani'ōpu'u gestured toward the edge of the courtyard. Some two score warriors armed with war clubs and spears emerged from the shadows there.

"Why deny Alapa'i this small comfort in his old age, cousin?" Keawe'ōpala demanded. As he put this question to Kalani'ōpu'u, a larger group of armed warriors, as menacing as the first group, stepped out of the darkness. The two bands glowered at each other across the courtyard.

Now the massive Puna advanced on Keawe'ōpala, his big fists clenched. "What kind of 'comfort' does Alapa'i seek from the grandson of Kalanike'eaumoku, whom he killed to usurp the throne of Hawai'i?" he snarled. "Kamehameha goes to Ka'ū with us."

Taking a war club from one of Alapa'i's warriors, Ke'eaumoku stepped between Puna and Keawe'ōpala. "Would you openly defy the will of your mō'ī, Puna?" he rejoined, brandishing the weapon. "You talk treason." Puna, though unarmed, tensed as if to spring at him.

It was Ke'eaumoku's cooler-headed half-brother Kame'iamoku who spoke next and broke the mounting tension. "I can vouch that no harm will come to Kamehameha from Alapa'i, Puna, and I will lay my head under your war club if it does," he said. "In any case," he continued, addressing Keawe'ōpala and Kalani'ōpu'u, "Kamehameha is no mere boy to be led here or there. He is the mover of the Naha Stone, after all. Perhaps it is for him to decide where he will go."

Kalaniʻōpuʻu nodded assent. Keaweʻōpala frowned and then grunted, "Let Kamehameha decide."

Now all eyes turned to Kamehameha, who hesitated. He worried that if he chose to leave with his uncle now, he would almost certainly precipitate a bloody fight. On the other hand, if he agreed to travel to Hilo with Keaweʻōpala and his men, it might be at the peril of his own life, mover of the Naha Stone or no.

"For now, my place is with Keoua," he finally said. "I will stay here to await the arrival of the kāhuna and give my father's bones a proper burial. Later, I will come to Hilo to grieve for Keoua with King Alapaʻi. If you like, Keaweʻōpala, Kameʻiamoku can accompany me there."

Keaweʻōpala furrowed his brow as he considered Kamehameha's proposal. He was unhappy at being thwarted in his mission. Nevertheless, he could not reasonably refuse Kameha's desire to pay proper respects to his late father. "Well enough," he said. "I will return to Hilo and tell my father that you will come soon. Kameʻiamoku here can conduct you to court." Keaweʻōpala gestured to his warriors to withdraw from the courtyard.

"I have every confidence in my good cousin, Kameʻiamoku," Kalaniʻōpuʻu said. Then, forcing a smile at Keaweʻōpala, he added, "and I know that your father, King Alapaʻi, will treat Kamehameha well, as he has always done—*brother*." Kalaniʻōpuʻu nodded to his warriors, and they withdrew as well.

"Then it is settled," said Kameʻiamoku. "Come now, let us go in and grieve together for the noble Keoua."

Early the next morning, before first light, Kalaniʻōpuʻu and his small party stole away to the canoe landing at Paukaʻa and put to sea. Later that morning Keaweʻōpala demanded to know why Kalaniʻōpuʻu had left so suddenly. Kamehameha shrugged and said truthfully, "I do not know."

A procession of priests from Hilo had arrived at Pauka'a. Dispatched by Alapa'i, they were led by the kahuna nui Ka'akau and the priest of Kūkā'ilimoku who had silently challenged Kamehameha at the Naha Stone just a year or two earlier. Ka'akau acknowledged Kamehameha with a tight-lipped smile, but the priest of Kūkā'ilimoku greeted him warmly.

"*E Kamehameha!*" the priest said. "When you moved the Naha Stone, you brought your father, Keoua Kalanikupuapa'ikalaninui, much honor. Only a noble warrior and chief could have sired a son such as you. We have come to help you, his first-born, safeguard his spirit."

"*Mahalo*," Kameha replied. "Show me all the things that I must do to honor my father."

The priests commenced Keoua's funeral rites with a lengthy chant over his body. They sang of Keoua's long and illustrious royal lineage, dating back to 'Umi, who had ruled the Big Island wisely some two hundred years earlier. They chanted of his ferocity in battle and his gentleness in peace. Kamehameha and my father stood with the priests, their heads bowed and their bodies swaying with the repetitive rhythms of the kāhuna's dirge.

Several *kauwa-maoli*—defiled ones—were called to wrap Keoua's body in banana leaves from head to toe and to carry it to the imu they had dug in his courtyard. Since early morning, a fire had been burning in the imu, where a bed of glowing coals now overlaid white-hot stones. As Kamehameha, my father, Keoua's wives, and his other children watched, the defiled ones laid Keoua's corpse atop the stones and covered it with more wood, which soon ignited. For the next ten days, Kameha, Keli'imaika'i, and Keoua's other sons shared memories of their father as they waited for the imu's heat to sear the flesh from Keoua's bones.

When the imu had done its work, a kauwa-maoli retrieved Keoua's charred internal organs and intestines—the body's "unclean" parts—and wrapped them tightly in ti leaves. This bundle the priest of Kūkā'ilimoku gave to Kamehameha and Keli'imaika'i. "Take this flesh of Keoua *makai*, the priest instructed them, "and give it to Kanaloa."

Thus it was that the night's deepest hour found Kamehameha and my father in a small outrigger canoe in the middle of the bay, where

Kamehameha cast Keoua's remains into the water. The sky was clear and the moon was full. The sea glinted with silver light. As Keoua's scorched remains struck the water, Kameha implored Kanaloa to send a niuhi shark to consume them. "Let the flesh of our father become one with the flesh of a powerful shark, and not food for lowly carrion eaters," he prayed. Kameha and my father returned to the beach, where they kept a silent vigil for the rest of the night.

When they returned to Pauka'a at dawn, the priests presented Kamehameha with a kapa cloth bundle. In it were Keoua's skull, hands, and the long bones of his arms and legs. "Hide your father's bones well and tell no one where you have hidden them," the war god's priest instructed Kamehameha, "lest some foe vandalize his grave, steal his bones, and desecrate his mana."

The haoles who later came to our islands were horrified by these funeral rituals, scorning them as barbaric and worse. But among our people, they were regarded as a mark of great respect for the dead.

Alapa'i came to Pauka'a after all. Journeying up the coast by canoe to join his son Keawe'ōpala at Keoua's hale, he brought more warriors with him. Kamehameha's kahus, Kekūhaupi'o and Nae'ole, also accompanied the aging mō'ī to Pauka'a. Kameha greeted the mō'ī in the courtyard where Keawe'ōpala and Kalani'ōpu'u had confronted each other eleven days earlier. Observing the *kapu a noho*, Kamehameha sat on the ground with all the other people in the courtyard as the king approached.

"*E Kameha!*" Alapa'i cried when he saw Keoua's oldest son seated before him. "Keoua was a noble warrior who served me well and loyally. I am sorely grieved by his death. Stand so that I may embrace you."

Kamehameha rose to his full height and then, according to custom, he and Alapa'i hugged and wailed for the deceased. The old king, bent and diminished by his many years, was almost lost from sight in Kamehameha's embrace. As they mourned together, Keoua's women raised their voices anew in lamentation, augmenting their cries of grief.

"My father was ever devoted to you, my lord," Kameha said, bending over Alapa'i and speaking loudly so that all within earshot could hear. "He bid me to serve you as faithfully as he did—and this I pledged to him."

Alapa'i stepped back and cocked his head at the towering youth. The courtyard fell silent as the assemblage awaited the mōʻī's response. "Keoua was like a son to me, Kamehameha," Alapa'i said, "and as Keoua's son you will always have a place of affection in my heart and honor at my court." Alapa'i glanced pointedly at Keawe'ōpala as he said this. At his advanced age, he plainly had no appetite for whatever intrigues his son and his allies were plotting. Now he looked around the courtyard and pursed his thin lips. "But where is Keoua's brother, my own son Kalani'ōpu'u?" he asked.

"I believe he returned to his own domains to attend to some important matters, Lord," Kameha replied.

"These matters could not wait until he greeted his mōʻī?"

"Alas, Lord, he did not expect you to come this soon," Kameha replied.

"Ah, well," Alapa'i sighed, "the responsibilities of administering even a poor district such as Ka'ū can often be demanding. I expect that Kalani'ōpu'u will come again soon enough. And of course, you will come to stay with me in Hilo again after you are done grieving for your father, isn't that so?"

"I shall indeed, my lord," Kamehameha replied.

Two days later, amid a drenching rain, Kamehameha began a lonely trek up one of the many footpaths that climbed the gentle slopes above Hilo. He was making for an area along the Wailuku River, where the mountainside was riddled with caves formed by lava which had flowed since time immemorial from the now-slumbering summit of Mauna Kea. In one of these caves, which would remain known only to him, Kameha hid the mortal remains of his father, Keoua Kalanikupuapa'ikalaninui.

He had left Kame'iamoku standing with Nae'ole, Kekūhaupi'o, and my father, Keli'imaika'i, at the foot of the trail. "The remainder of this journey is yours alone, Kameha," Nae'ole had said. "Hide Keoua's long bones well. We will wait here for your return."

"And when you return, I will accompany you to Hilo," Kame'iamoku had said, as if Kamehameha required reminding. Then he added pointedly, "Your mō'ī, Alapa'i, will be happy to see you."

Now Kamehameha wondered anew what awaited him at Alapa'i's court. "*Alapa'i and Keawe'ōpala fear you...that is why they will try to keep you close to them,*" Keoua had said. Would Alapa'i indeed be happy to see him? And to what end? As hostage against Kalani'ōpu'u's presumed ambition to rule the whole of the Big Island? And even if the old king had no such thoughts and genuinely meant him no harm, what of his son, Keawe'ōpala? If his uncle moved against Alapa'i, how safe would his own life be at the king's court, despite Alapa'i's assurances? In his waning days, the king's good will might not be sufficient to prevent an enemy from poisoning his food or drink or arranging for a convenient "accident" to befall him.

Be ready when the time comes. Keoua's words echoed in Kameha's mind as he followed the river into the uplands.

Keli'imaika'i rushed to Kameha upon his return. They fell into each other's arms and wailed for Keoua one last time. He did not ask where Keoua's bones were hidden, either then or later. The secret belonged to Kameha alone.

Kame'iamoku stepped forward and gently clasped Kameha by the arm. "We should return to Hilo now," he said. "King Alapa'i is expecting you."

"I will come with you to Hilo, Kameha," said Kekūhaupi'o, stepping to Kamehameha's side. He had no intention of leaving Kameha to fend for himself amid the intrigues that undoubtedly awaited him at Alapa'i's court.

"And what of your brother?" Kame'iamoku asked, gesturing at Keli'imaika'i. "Will he also come to Hilo?"

"No," Kamehameha replied, without hesitation. "He should go to our uncle in Ka'ū." At this, Kame'iamoku frowned. Kameha continued, "My brother is still undergoing his military training and his kahu is with Kalani'ōpu'u. He must return to Ka'ū to continue his instruction. Nae'ole will accompany him there."

"Alapa'i will no doubt be disappointed," said Kame'iamoku. "But he will understand that your brother must improve his skills as a warrior. It is sufficient that you are coming to Hilo with me."

The small traveling party separated, with Kamehameha, Kekūhaupi'o, and Kame'iamoku heading almost due east for Hilo and Nae'ole and my father making their way south toward the Puna District by a different trail. When they reached the coast at Kapoho, Nae'ole told my father, they would continue to Ka'ū by canoe. In this way, he explained, they would avoid the hazards of walking in the lava shadow of the great caldera at Kilauea. "The goddess Pele can be fickle," Nae'ole said. "We will not tempt her anger by traveling overland to Ka'ū."

As they set off on their trek to the Puna Coast, Nae'ole told my father that Kamehameha had done well to send him away. "Your brother may have to break with Alapa'i or Keawe'ōpala one day," he said. "And when that day comes, it will be best that Kameha need only look after himself." Then Nae'ole chuckled. "Kameha has ever been a good *kōnane* player. He has always thought several moves ahead. He played well today." Nae'ole grew somber again. "But of course," he reminded my father, "the game your brother plays now is much more serious than checkers."

My father's name was not always Keli'imaika'i. The people of Maui gave him that name when he was well into adulthood. At his birth, my father's parents named him Kalanimālokulokuikapo'okalani. Until he took the Maui people's name for him as his own, everyone called my father Kalanimālokuloku, or just Kalani.

Throughout his life, my father lived in the big shadow of my Uncle Kamehameha, who eclipsed him both physically and by force of personality. Where my uncle was forceful, my father was mild. Where my uncle was unyielding, my father was accommodating. When my uncle and my father were together, even when they stood side by side, my father often receded into the background. Other men were drawn to Kameha like iron filings to a haole magnet. My father rarely attracted attention.

Though he was skilled in the arts of war, as were most ali'i, my father was nowhere near as adept as Kameha. He was well-coordinated, but he was not an exceptional performer in sporting contests. My uncle, on the other hand, excelled in every contest he entered. In wrestling and spear throwing he was nearly always the best. He was perhaps the most formidable surf rider of his time. His all-around athletic prowess was legendary among our people. And of course, Kamehameha was famous throughout our islands as the mover of the Naha Stone.

My father never bridled at Kamehameha's primacy. As Kameha's younger brother, my father was his lifelong subordinate, and happy to serve him. My uncle never had a lieutenant more faithful than he. Once I asked my father if my uncle's preeminence upset him. "He is my own brother," he said, with a look of puzzlement. And when my expression revealed that I had failed to comprehend, my father said, "Why should I resent your uncle's many triumphs? How could I? Kameha's achievements have always reflected well on me because I am his brother, and everyone knows it."

Kamehameha loved my father. He loved him for his even disposition, easygoing ways, good humor, and most of all, for his gentle candor. Though my father stood in Kameha's shadow, he did not stand in awe of him. If he believed that Kameha was wrong, he would not hesitate to tell him, even with regard to personal matters. Once, when Kamehameha lusted for a particularly beautiful woman he had spied in a small fishing village on the Kohala Coast, my father warned him to avoid the liaison. "Brother," he said, "that wahine is truly beautiful, but she is not ali'i. You will abase yourself if you lie with her."

"You are right, of course, Kalanimālokuloku," he said. Then he laughed and said, "Nevertheless, I see how you look at her, little brother. I trust that you have no intention of abasing your own self with her when I am not looking."

Kalaniʻōpuʻu greeted my father warmly when he and Naeʻole reached Kaʻū.

"Welcome, Kalanimālokuloku," he cried, embracing him. "Welcome to my hale, nephew. How goes it with Kamehameha?"

"He is well, Uncle," my father replied. "He is at Alapaʻi's court in Hilo. Kekūhaupiʻo is with him."

"It is good that Kameha keeps his kahu close to him. He has many enemies at Alapaʻi's court. No matter how much Alapaʻi proclaims his love for Kameha, the old man cannot protect him from them. They will try to do him harm if they can."

Alapaʻi had also professed great love for Kalaniʻōpuʻu. But Kalaniʻōpuʻu's heart was not warmed by the mōʻī's affectionate words. "It is the ʻawa speaking," he scoffed. "And Keaweʻōpala and his allies are only waiting for the old man to die before they move against me. They may not even wait until then."

To his kahu, Puna, he said, "We must make ready to strike our enemies before they can attack us. I will not stand still, waiting to dodge the first spear."

While Kalaniʻōpuʻu readied for war, my father resumed his military training with his own kahu, Mulihele. My father had already been under Mulihele's tutelage for several years, studying spear-throwing, dodging, and catching, dagger thrusting and club wielding, the pīkoi, or tripping weapon, and the sling. He taught my father well enough so that when the time came, as it inevitably did for all aliʻi, my father could hold his own in battle. And, like all the kahus of old Hawaii, Mulihele fought always at his student's side, saving my father's life on more than one occasion—a favor which my father repaid more than once.

As Kalaniʻōpuʻu had promised Puna, he did not wait for his enemies to throw the first spear, and thus began a time of war. Kalaniʻōpuʻu first attacked Hilo from the sea, but he was repulsed, so he then mounted an overland assault from the Puna district, only to be pushed back again. Hundreds of men died on both sides in these battles, which altered nothing.

Keaweʻōpala vociferously advocated reprisal raids against the Puna and Kaʻū districts after Kalaniʻōpuʻu's second failed campaign, but his father showed no interest in pursuing Kalaniʻōpuʻu or punishing his people. Nor would he countenance any act of revenge against Kamehameha.

"Kalaniʻōpuʻu has behaved brashly, and he has paid for his foolishness," Alapaʻi said. "As long as he keeps to Kaʻū, we will let him be. As for Kameha, he has committed no offense against me and he remains my honored guest." When Keaweʻōpala began to protest, Alapaʻi cut him off with an abrupt wave of his hand. "I'm old and I'm weary of fighting," he said. "Be patient, Keaweʻōpala. You will have your own war with Kalaniʻōpuʻu soon enough after I am gone."

Kawaihae, 1764

In the year following Kalaniʻōpuʻu's failed rebellion, Alapaʻi relocated his court several times: first to the lush, intimate confines of Waipiʻo; then to the drier, open highlands of Waimea; and finally to Kawaihae and its humid coastal heat. To some extent, Alapaʻi's own restless nature induced these moves. He had been in constant motion around the Big Island, and for that matter among all our islands, throughout his life. But at this time they were compelled by the mōʻī's declining health.

When his health first began to fail him in Hilo, Alapaʻi's priests, Holo'ae and Kaʻakau, had consulted with his healers and advised him, "Waipiʻo's waters will revive you, Lord." When Alapaʻi's condition failed to improve after several months in the valley, they said, "Waimea's sweet air will prove restorative." And when that remedy also brought no relief, they told him, "Kawaihae's heat will purge your illness."

Kamehameha and his kahu Kekūhaupiʻo accompanied Alapaʻi in his travels around the Big Island—at the mōʻī's insistence. Throughout this time, they were treated as honored guests at the old king's court, despite Kalaniʻōpuʻu's revolt. They were not comforted by this, for they knew it was only by Alapaʻi's command. There were others, Keaweʻōpala foremost among them, who did not wish them well. Holoʻae, who was Kekūhaupiʻo's uncle, kept them abreast of their adversaries' intentions.

"Alapa'i's son does not share his father's kind feelings toward you, Kameha," Holo'ae reminded him one night. The priest had come to see Kamehameha and Kekūhaupi'o at the hale they shared in the newly relocated royal compound at Waimea. Kameha and the two older men sat cross-legged on sedge mats around a kukui- oil lamp. The lamp's trembling flame illuminated their faces but little else in the hale. "Keawe'ōpala will move against you. He only waits for his father to die."

"And yet Kameha and I cannot leave court while Alapa'i still lives," Kekūhaupi'o said. "We must stand here waiting to catch Keawe'ōpala's spear."

"Trust me," replied Holo'ae. "I will let you know when he is about to throw it."

That year Kamehameha became a father for the first of many times. His lover, Kaneikapolei, gave birth to a son at Ka'ū. She named the baby Pauli Ka'ōleiokū, though throughout his life he would be known by his nickname, Pauli. As he had promised, Kalani'ōpu'u adopted the child.

"Here is your new brother," Kalani'ōpu'u said, holding up the squalling newborn for his own sons Kiwala'ō, Keōua Kū'ahu'ula, and Keōuape'e'ale to see.

"He is no brother to me, Father," objected Kiwala'ō.

"He is the son of your cousin Kamehameha, the mover of the Naha Stone, and the grandson of your late uncle, my beloved brother, Keoua," Kalani'ōpu'u replied. "He will be a son to me and therefore a brother to you, Kiwala'ō."

The younger boys, who shared the same mother with Pauli, needed no such explanation from their father. Keōua Kū'ahu'ula and Keōuape'e'ale eyed the baby with mild curiosity before returning to their play. Their new brother would hold little interest for them until he learned to walk. Even then, because of the difference in their ages, he would be relegated to trailing after the older boys, more tolerated than accepted. Thus did Pauli, the first son of the man who would unite all of our islands, become a born follower.

Kiwala'ō may have wanted little or nothing to do with Pauli, but he was friendly to my father. During their time together at Ka'ū, my father and Kiwala'ō engaged in spirited but amiable competitions in spear throwing and wrestling. They rode the surf together at Kāwā Bay. "Kiwala'ō always treated me well," my father told me. "Of course," he added, "it helped that he never saw me as a potential rival for power."

It also no doubt helped that Kiwala'ō never saw my father as a potential rival for the affections of his own mother, Kalola. Kalola was very kind to my father, but only in the manner of a loving aunt. She showed no interest in initiating him into the rites of manhood, as she had Kamehameha.

Keku'iapoiwa Liliha, who was Kalola's daughter by Keoua, was taken with Kiwala'ō, and followed her half-brother everywhere. Lili, as she was affectionately called, was about ten or eleven years old at this time. She was a lithe girl on the cusp of womanhood with flashing eyes and an infectious giggle. Kiwala'ō hardly seemed to notice her, though she contrived to be in close proximity to him whenever she could. "That little wahine is always getting underfoot," he told my father with some irritation. "One day, I will fall on her." Indeed, one day he would, but not in the manner he then imagined.

Pauli's birth turned Kalani'ōpu'u's thoughts anew to the infant's father, Kamehameha. "I am worried about Kameha," he told his nephew's old kahu, Nae'ole, one day. "Alapa'i himself may mean the boy no harm, but I fear that some of his people wish Kameha ill. We must extricate him from my uncle's court."

Nae'ole, who shared Kalani'ōpu'u's concern, volunteered to undertake a mission to Alapa'i. "I will go see the mō'ī," he said. "I will tell him that you desire peace with him, and that you wish to see your nephew again. Perhaps Alapa'i will give Kameha leave to go."

"Or perhaps you can devise a means for Kameha to slip away, whether Alapa'i agrees to his leaving or no," said Kalani'ōpu'u.

Nae'ole set out for Waimea, where Alapa'i was by this time, traveling first by canoe to Kailua and then ascending on foot to the cool highlands below the summit of Mauna Kea. He found the old king reclining on a sedge mat in the courtyard of his hale.

In observance of the kapu, Nae'ole squatted before the mō'ī. "I bring greetings from Kalani'ōpu'u, my lord," he said. "He wishes you well and desires nothing more than peace between you and him."

"So my nephew now regrets his past impertinence?" Alapa'i replied. Nae'ole said nothing, merely lowering his head as if to suggest agreement. "Then why does he not come to see me himself with this news?"

"He is much occupied with matters of governance at Ka'ū and he regrets that he could not come in person, my lord," Nae'ole said. "But he begs that his beloved nephew Kamehameha join him in Ka'ū."

"It is sad that a man as young as Kalani'ōpu'u should already have so many regrets, Nae'ole," Alapa'i responded, part in jest and part in irritation. "Ah well, I welcome Kalani'ōpu'u's offer of peace. You may return to Ka'ū and tell him so. As for young Kamehameha, his company pleases me. My time grows short and I would keep him by my side. He may leave after I am gone, if he wishes. Tell Kalani'ōpu'u that also."

"Thank you, my lord," Nae'ole replied. "I will tell him all you have said."

Later, Nae'ole visited Kamehameha and Kekūhaupi'o.

"Kameha, you have a child, a healthy boy," Nae'ole said, after the three men had wailed and hugged each other in greeting. "The baby's name is Pauli Ka'ōleiokū and Kalani'ōpu'u has adopted him as his own son."

Kamehameha smiled. In truth, he had all but forgotten Kaneikapolei's pregnancy. But he well remembered her pliant body and her gentle favors. "And how is Kaneikapolei?" he asked.

"She is well," Nae'ole said.

"I hope I will see her again soon," Kameha said.

"You won't," said Nae'ole. "The old man will not hear of you leaving his side while he lives."

"And if we do not take care, Nae'ole, others will ensure that Kameha never again sees Kaneikapolei, or Kalani'ōpu'u, or his own new child," said Kekūhaupi'o, emphasizing the last three words. "You still think too much with your worm," he reprimanded Kameha.

"Then it is true that Kameha is in danger here, Kekū?"

"He is in grave danger, Nae'ole," Kekūhaupi'o replied. "Already, Keawe'ōpala plots against him. In truth, Kameha's life depends upon Alapa'i's breath. And Alapa'i is not well." Kamehameha remained silent as the two men spoke, glancing from one to the other.

"And what will you and Kameha do when Alapa'i breathes no more?"

"Holo'ae will help us," Kameha said at last.

"Alapa'i's own kahuna?" Nae'ole was surprised. "How can he help?"

"He has promised to warn us when Keawe'ōpala decides to move against us. At least, Keawe'ōpala will not be able to surprise us."

"Kameha," Nae'ole replied, "it is one thing to know when your enemy will strike and another to be prepared for it." He turned to Kekūhaupi'o. "Kekū, what will you do when Alapa'i dies?"

"You can be sure we will not stay long to mourn him," Kekūhaupi'o said. "But in truth, I do not yet know how we will contrive to leave."

"Perhaps you should leave before the old man dies," Nae'ole said.

"It is kapu for Kameha to leave the court while Alapa'i still lives, Nae'ole. And Keawe'ōpala's people watch us very closely. If Kameha were caught trying to leave without Alapa'i's permission, it would almost certainly mean death for him."

"Then he must find a way to quit the court without being perceived as leaving," Nae'ole replied.

Quitting Alapa'i's court—in any manner—was not possible for Kamehameha while the old king remained in Waimea. Still alert and in good spirits despite his failing health, Alapa'i would summon Kameha to his side almost daily to regale him with stories of his old battles and to demand of the young man: "Kameha, tell me again how you moved the Naha Stone." Alapa'i never tired of hearing this story. Kamehameha would always relate it in the same laconic fashion, concluding on the same self-effacing yet immodest note: "It was not I who moved the stone, my lord. It was the god Kūkā'ilimoku who moved it from within me." And Alapa'i's response was inevitably the same: "*E Kameha!* Kūkā'ilimoku truly moves within you? He favors you then?"

"No, Lord," Kameha would always reply. "He does not move in me or favor me. He merely took pity on me that one time."

Alapa'i would smile. "And how many can say even that, eh Kameha? How many, indeed?"

"Old Alapa'i truly believed that the god was in me," Kameha told my father later. "I think he was convinced that by keeping me close to him, his mana would be strengthened by mine."

Even if the old mō'ī had not taken such an interest in Kameha, it would have been very difficult for him to get away from the king's court at Waimea. The surrounding countryside was open grassland that afforded little cover, and all the trails were closely watched, by day and by night. And had he tried to leave, he would not have gotten far, for Waimea was a long way mauka from the sea, which offered the only truly feasible avenue of escape. Ironically, it was Alapa'i himself who opened that avenue for Kameha.

Alapa'i set Kameha's escape plan in motion by relocating his court from the highlands of Waimea to the Kohala Coast. "Kekū," Kamehameha exclaimed to his kahu soon after their arrival in Kawaihae, "I know how it can be done."

"How, Kameha?"

"I can take my leave on a surf-riding board. Keawe'ōpala will not be looking for that."

Kekūhaupi'o was skeptical at first. "And how far do you think you can paddle on a surf-riding board, Kameha?" he asked.

Kamehameha pursed his lips and furrowed his brow in thought for a moment. Then he said, "I will paddle as far as I must to meet a canoe that you will arrange, Kekū."

At about this time, Alapa'i lapsed into his final illness. What was wrong with Alapa'i, no one could say for certain. His breathing became labored. He walked with great difficulty. His appetite was failing. He even lost the taste for his beloved 'awa. The healers generally agreed that Alapa'i was afflicted by a loss of mana. But they differed on the cause.

"Evil spirits have entered the king's body," one said.

"His ancestral god is displeased with him," another said.

"The source of Alapa'i's illness is surely sorcery," a third argued. "Kalani'ōpu'u is praying him to death." This last diagnosis was taken very seriously.

These healers of Alapa'i's court, kāhuna whose vocation was the treatment of illness, administered a variety of cures to the ailing monarch. They restricted his diet, barring him from eating squid, sea snails, and moss. They plied him with a potion made from 'ōlena root—turmeric—and bark of the koa and mountain apple trees, to cleanse his blood. They fed him a tonic made of baked laukahi leaves to restore his strength. None of these remedies succeeded.

Now, in a *hale hau*—a small sick house—at Kawaihae, the healers called upon higher powers. First they gave the ailing Alapa'i a steam bath, followed by such nourishment as he was still able to take. They sacrificed a hog to Alapa'i's family god; they seized an unfortunate commoner on the pretext of violating some petty kapu and dragged him to the heiau of Alapa'i's war god, Kūkā'ilimoku, where they strangled him and left his body to rot on the god's altar. Finally, in the gathering dusk, they prayed to Kanaloa to drive the sickness from the king and restore his mana.

O Kanaloa, god of the squid!
Here is your patient, Alapa'i
O squid of the deep blue sea,
Squid that inhabits the coral reef,
Squid that burrows in the sand,
Squid that squirts water from its sack!
Here is a sick man for you to heal, Alapa'i
A patient put to bed for treatment
By the squid that lies flat.

Then they waited through the night for a sign from the god. If no rain fell, Alapa'i would surely live. In that case, in the morning a fisherman would be dispatched to catch a "squid that lies flat"—an octopus—to cook and feed to the king. But if rain fell during the night, Alapa'i would almost certainly die. Kawaihae was just north of the Kohala Coast's lava desert, so the odds of a night without precipitation were in the king's favor. But there was no need for the kāhuna to send out a fisherman the next morning. Rain did fall that night.

Alapa'i summoned Keawe'ōpala to his side. Holo'ae and Ka'akau were hovering over the king as he lay on his sleeping mat. The once mighty war chief struggled to raise himself on one elbow. "Keawe'ōpala," he said, "my time is almost at an end. When I die, you shall succeed me as mō'ī of all Hawai'i. All the chiefs know that this is my will."

"Father, the chiefs will respect your wishes, or I will—" Keawe'ōpala began, but Alapa'i weakly waved him to be silent. Then, with much effort, he spoke in a tremulous voice that underscored his dire condition.

"Keawe'ōpala, my desire in this matter of succession is only as good as your own judgment," he said. "Always remember: Intelligence without strength is surely impotent, but firmness without astuteness is foolhardy. You must rule with a strong hand but also with wisdom. If you fail in this, those who should be your allies will challenge you. Do you understand me?"

"Yes, Father, I understand," Keaweʻōpala replied.

Alapaʻi died the next day.

In those days, our people believed that when a chief of Alapaʻi's stature died, his passing defiled the entire surrounding district. To avoid being defiled himself, his heir was required to immediately remove himself to another district until such time as the dead flesh had been burned away from the late mōʻī's bones and the bones were ready for consecration and burial. Hence, on the morning of Alapaʻi's passing, Keaweʻōpala journeyed south by canoe to the coastal village of Kailua. Before he left, he instructed two of his personal guards to remain behind and keep a close watch on Kamehameha at all times. "He is beside himself with grief for my beloved father," he told them. "I fear he may do himself serious harm."

While Keaweʻōpala professed concern for Kameha's well-being to his guards, he disclosed the darkest of intents to Kaʻakau, his high priest, and foolishly, within Holoʻae's hearing. "Kaʻakau," he said, "Isn't it true that when Kamehameha was born you prophesied that he would become a slayer of chiefs, and my father ordered him slain at birth?"

"Yes," replied Kaʻakau, "but old Naeʻole took him away to Waipiʻo before it could be done."

"Just so," said Keaweʻōpala. "Now I believe that the prophecy was meant for me. Kamehameha must die."

"Lord," said Kaʻakau, "there is an old one, a *kahuna hoʻonuana* well-practiced in the arts of sorcery, who can assure that Kamehameha will never live to fulfill this prophecy. This old one can cast a spell that will make Kamehameha suddenly take sick and die. People will believe that his death was out of grief for old Alapaʻi."

"Good," Keawe'ōpala said. "See to it then."

"It shall be done, Lord," replied Ka'akau. Holo'ae said nothing. Why Keawe'ōpala issued this order with Kekūhaupi'o's own uncle, Holo'ae, close by, I do not know. "Keawe'ōpala was an arrogant fool," was my father's only explanation.

Soon thereafter, Keawe'ōpala departed by canoe for Kailua, and Holo'ae stole away to see Kekūhaupi'o and Kamehameha. "Keawe'ōpala has thrown his spear," he said.

"When and how will it strike?" asked Kameha.

"I do not yet know when, Kameha. As for how, I know only that Keawe'ōpala has set his high priest, Ka'akau, to have you slain. Even now, Ka'akau goes to seek out an old kahuna ho'onuana."

"A kahuna ho'onuana? Ka'akau would slay me by sorcery then?"

"It will be by poison, more likely," Kekūhaupi'o said. "As long as you remain in Kawaihae, do not eat any food unless it is prepared by your own hand or mine. And do not drink any water that you have not fetched for yourself. In the meantime, we will be watchful."

Alapa'i had enabled Kameha's escape by moving his court to Kawaihae. Now, Keawe'ōpala's followers gave him the opportunity by mourning the dead mō'ī according to the traditions of old Hawai'i. In those days, when a king died, people were free to behave in ways that would never be countenanced at other times. Women were allowed to enter the heiaus, which were otherwise closed to them on pain of death. They were permitted to eat all manner of foods otherwise forbidden to them, such as roast pork, coconut, and bananas. Women could even eat with men. Men drank more than usual. Men and women engaged in love sport more freely than usual. An atmosphere of general debauchery—including widespread thievery and other low crimes—prevailed, all in the midst of great wailing and lamentations for the departed mō'ī.

The kāhuna and the chiefs, who at other times would severely punish such behavior, would look away. If asked why, they would explain that the people were so undone by their grief that they had taken all leave of their senses and forgotten the strict kapus, even those punishable by death. I think they believed otherwise, however. As my father once told me, "Our laws are so strict and so numerous that our people must of occasion have some relief from them, lest the kapus become too much to bear and provoke revolt." The death of a revered high chief like Alapa'i provided just such an occasion. Thus, as the news of his death spread through Kawaihae, disorder and confusion spread swiftly in its wake. The disorder was further compounded by Keawe'ōpala's withdrawal to the Kona District.

The guards promised Keawe'ōpala that they would never let Kamehameha out of their sight, not even for an instant. But in their chief's absence and amid the prevailing atmosphere of dissipation, their attention to duty would prove less than constant.

Ka'akau sent for an old kahuna ho'onuana named Lilihae. Lilihae, it was said, was a sorcerer well-practiced in the art of praying people to death. In truth, he was a skilled herbalist who put his expansive knowledge of plants to perverse use. He was intimately familiar with all the trees, shrubs, and seaweed of our islands, and especially those that produced deadly toxins. He knew how to extract these poisons and mix them with food and drink so that his intended victims would consume them undetected, and he offered his dark skills for hire. When someone truly wished another man or woman dead, but dared not lift their own hand against them, they would seek out Lilihae. After accepting pigs, bananas, taro, kapa cloth, or whatever other goods his prospective client might offer in payment, he would make a great show of performing malevolent chants and invoking the wrath of evil spirits. Some days later, the object of his client's enmity would die. It was said that he could slay from afar with a mere look, and none risked offending him.

Ka'akau and some other priests who knew the truth about the old kahuna's art kept it to themselves and maintained the fiction of his sorcery. Ka'akau met with Lilihae in secret. "Old one," he said, "there is a young ali'i who has profaned the memory of our late king, Alapa'i'nui, because he lacks respect for our new mō'ī, Keawe'ōpala. He must die."

"Who is this ali'i?" Lilihae asked.

"His name is Kamehameha," Ka'akau replied.

"Kamehameha?" Lilihae asked, surprised. "The son of the noble Keoua, the blood-nephew of Kalani'ōpu'u, and the mover of the Naha Stone?"

"The same one," Ka'akau said.

"His mana is very powerful. It is no small matter to slay one such as he."

"I am confident your magic is more powerful."

"Oh, it almost certainly is," Lilihae said, "but one cannot put too high a value on such a life," he said.

"And how much value would you place on this life?" Ka'akau asked.

"I will require a portion of the new mō'ī's share of the next Makahiki tribute—equivalent to the tribute collected from one ahupua'a, shall we say?"

"That is very steep," Ka'akau said, thinking of the large quantities of pigs, kapa cloth, taro, rare feathers, and various implements.

"It is what is required," Lilihae said, implacable now. "Shall we say, the Waipi'o ahupua'a?"

"No," said Ka'akau, "that is too much, even for a life as valuable as this one. Perhaps the Lapakahi ahupua'a will provide sufficient compensation." Though not as rich as Waipi'o, Lapakahi was a prosperous fishing village on the northern Kohala Coast. The ahupua'a's uplands were well watered and bountiful, producing taro, bananas, coconut, yams, and other produce in abundance. Koa trees, prized for canoes, also flourished on its slopes.

"It will do," Lilihae said.

Ka'akau went to find Holo'ae, who was supervising the slow baking of Alapa'i's corpse. "Holo'ae," he said, "I cannot stay here until the imu has finished its work. Keawe'ōpala has summoned me to Kailua. I will return with him when Alapa'i's bones are ready for burial."

Holoʻae nodded his assent. "And did you find the old one whom you sought?" he asked.

"Yes, I did," Kaʻakau replied.

"Keaweʻōpala will be pleased," Holoʻae said. "This old one, when will he work his sorcery?"

"Soon," said Kaʻakau, biting off the word. Holoʻae did not press him further.

Unlike Keaweʻōpala, Kaʻakau was wary of Holoʻae, convinced that he was not to be trusted where matters involving Kameha were concerned. Before departing for Kailua, Kaʻakau ordered a young novitiate priest named Maile to spy on Holoʻae. This youth, who was about my father's age, was already assisting Holoʻae with the purification of Alapaʻi's long bones, so it was not difficult for him to follow the kahuna here and there without arousing his suspicion.

"Maile," Holoʻae said to Maile, "I need more wood for the imu. Go fetch some."

Maile, who was squatting near the fire, looked up at the kahuna questioningly. There was already sufficient wood at hand to fuel the fire for another day. Moreover, Holoʻae could order any kanaka in the vicinity to go for wood. This menial task would necessitate a sweaty ascent of the slopes above Kawaihae in search of downed branches and dry brush.

"Why do you hesitate, boy?" Holoʻae demanded. "Go at once."

Maile shrugged sullenly and rose to his feet. Just as he was turning to go, he noticed Kekūhaupiʻo approaching the courtyard, and he hesitated. "Go now," Holoʻae ordered. Maile trudged off, but he did not go far.

Holoʻae did not yet suspect that Maile was spying for Kaʻakau, but he believed that the less others at Kawaihae knew about his dealings with Kekūhaupiʻo, the better. Thus, he'd sent Maile away.

"Greetings, nephew," Holoʻae said, as Kekūhaupiʻo drew near. As he spoke, he stepped away from his other assistants. Keeping his voice low, he asked, "How is Kamehameha?"

"He is well, Uncle," Kekūhaupiʻo replied.

"And does he eat well?"

"He eats well, and carefully," Kekūhaupi'o said. Then, looking about to see if anyone was watching or listening, he said, "Uncle, we need your help. Kameha has need of a canoe and two or three men who can be trusted. Can you arrange it?"

"What will be required of these men?" Holo'ae asked. Kekūhaupi'o explained Kamehameha's plan.

Hiding within a copse of soapberry trees whose broad leaves afforded him sufficient concealment, Maile watched the two men as they conferred. They spoke in low voices and he could not hear what they said. But the fact that they took such care to mask their words convinced Maile that Holo'ae and Kekūhaupi'o were plotting something. Unable to overhear their conversation and unwilling to risk edging closer, Maile broke off his surveillance to search for some commoners to help him gather firewood.

The sun was merging with the sea's horizon when Maile returned to King Alapa'i's courtyard followed by several maka'āinana men sweating heavily under their loads of brush and dead branches. "Here is the firewood," he announced.

"Good. Put it there," Holo'ae said, gesturing at the already-large pile of wood near the fire pit. "I must attend to some matters," he then told Maile. "Stay here and supervise the others until I return." Holo'ae turned away and amid gathering shadows, he set off down a footpath leading to the beach. Maile waited until Holo'ae was out of sight and then, after ensuring that no one was watching him, he followed the kahuna.

At the beach, the priest spoke to two fishermen who were readying their gear for the next morning. As earlier, when he had spied on Holo'ae and Kekūhaupi'o, Maile did not dare approach close enough to hear the kahuna's actual words to the men. He could only observe Holo'ae gestures. The sun had slipped below the horizon, and the three men's forms were silhouetted against the sky's dying embers. Maile could see the fishermen nodding as Holo'ae talked. He turned and hurried to Alapa'i's courtyard.

Lilihae was ready. Years ago, he had collected bark from the *nioi* tree, which was only found on the island of Moloka'i. The bark of this tree, no longer extant in our islands, was deadly poisonous. Lilihae ground the bark into a fine powder and mixed it with sweet potato poi in a gourd bowl. The bark powder would only slightly darken and thicken the orange paste, which he sweetened further with coconut milk to mask the powder's faint bitter taste. The old kahuna ho'onuana judged that one handful of the poisoned poi would be sufficient to fatally sicken Kamehameha. Now he required a means to deliver it. He could not set the bowl before Kameha himself. It would have to be introduced into Kameha's hale without drawing notice somehow. To this end, Lilihae approached an ali'i boy who could cross the threshold of Kamehameha's dwelling without fear of violating the kapu that proscribed commoners from entering the hales of the nobility.

"Do you know me, boy?" Lilihae asked. The boy shook his head. Lilihae shrugged, indicating that this was of no particular concern. "Do you know where Kamehameha's hale is?" Lilihae asked. The boy nodded. "Then take this there for me," he said. Lilihae handed the bowl to the boy. "It is a special poi to strengthen Kamehameha's mana in his time of mourning for the great Alapa'i. If no one is there, you may leave this bowl in the hale, but if Kamehameha or his kahu should see you and ask about it, say it is from the old kahuna Holo'ae."

As it happened, Kameha did see the boy as he approached the hale. "What do you have there?" he asked as the boy entered the courtyard.

"It is a special poi from Holo'ae," the boy replied, handing the bowl to Kameha. "He said it will strengthen your mana. He told me to bring it to you."

After speaking to the fishermen, Holo'ae went to see Kamehameha. "It is all arranged, Kameha," he said as he entered the hale. Kamehameha and Kekūhaupi'o looked up at him. They were both sitting cross-legged on sedge mats. Darkness had fallen and the hale was illuminated by several kukui-oil lamps. Bowls and platters with sweet potatoes, yams, breadfruit, and baked chicken were spread out before them. "Two fishermen will be waiting for you tomorrow between Kawaihae and Kukui Point," Holo'ae said. "They will take you down the coast as far as Hāpuna. Don't worry; they can be trusted."

"Thank you, Holo'ae," Kamehameha said. "We were just about to eat. Will you join us?" Kameha raised the gourd bowl that the boy had brought earlier. "I have been looking forward to tasting this special poi that you sent me," he said. "Will you have some?" As he spoke, Kameha dipped three fingers into the bowl and scooped out some of the sticky orange paste before extending the bowl to Holo'ae.

The kahuna looked puzzled. "I sent you no poi," he said. Kamehameha's fingers, dripping with poi, froze just inches from his lips. "Where did *this* poi come from?" Holo'ae demanded.

"A boy brought it to me late this afternoon," Kameha replied as he set the bowl down and carefully wiped his fingers clean on the mat. "He said it was from you."

"Do you know this boy?"

"No, I never saw him before."

"Would you know him if you saw him again?"

"Yes," Kamehameha replied.

"Keawe'ōpala! Kamehameha is gone!"

Keawe'ōpala, the new mō'ī, gawked at the high priest Ka'akau, who had stammered out this news after falling to his knees in front of his king.

"Gone, Ka'akau? How can this be?"

"He went to ride the surf at Kawaihae two days ago and he never returned, my lord. A messenger has only just now arrived with the news."

"Is he drowned then?"

"I cannot say for certain, Lord. They say the waves were big and he disappeared."

"I must know for certain, Ka'akau," Keawe'ōpala barked. "Search for his body, and find anyone who knows anything about this and bring them to me."

The waves were indeed big the day of Kamehameha's disappearance, driven against the Big Island's northwest coast by the same unseasonable weather that had brought rain to Kawaihae two nights before Alapa'i's death. Kamehameha joined a number of other young ali'i, men and women, who trooped down the footpath to the beach to ride the surf. A throng of children and adults followed them, eager to watch them challenge the big waves. Kekūhaupi'o walked at Kameha's side. At the beach, Kameha selected the longest board from an array laid out on the sand above the high-tide line. They were kapu boards; only ali'i could use them. And this day, the bay and its surf were kapu for common folk.

Kamehameha was about to heft the big board onto his shoulder when a young boy broke from the crowd of spectators and ran up to him. "Kamehameha," he cried, "let me help you!"

Kameha laughed as he easily swung the board over his shoulder. "Thank you, boy, but do you think the mover of the Naha Stone really needs your help lifting this trifling weight?"

The boy, who was about ten or twelve years old, dropped his eyes and looked at the ground in embarrassment. "No, of course not," he said. Then he brightened. "Was the special poi good? Did it strengthen your mana for riding those big waves?"

"Oh, no doubt it did," Kameha replied, still smiling broadly. He cocked an eye at Kekūhaupi'o, who was standing nearby, overhearing everything. "Here, boy," Kamehameha said, "hold this for me while I ride the waves." At this, he loosened his malo with a practiced flick of his wrist and handed the garment to the youth. In those days, it was the custom of our people—men and women equally—to sport in the water naked.

The boy regarded the kapa cloth in his hands as something akin to a sacred object. "Mover of the Naha Stone, I promise I will take good care of this. Not a grain of sand will soil it," he said.

Kameha laughed. "Wait here with Kekūhaupiʻo until I return," he said. "He is my honored kahu."

Kameha turned and waded into the bay. He slapped his board down on the water, threw himself flat on it, and stroked hard for the surf line. Soon, he was slipping in and out of sight amid the breakers.

"So," Kekūhaupiʻo asked the boy as they watched Kamehameha, "you know old Holoʻae?"

"Yes, I know him. He asked me to bring the special poi to Kamehameha." The boy drew himself up proudly as he said this.

"I have been looking for him this morning, but I have not seen him," Kekūhaupiʻo said. "Do you know where he is?"

"But surely you have seen him, for he is over there." The boy pointed to an old man hovering on the periphery of the spectators. It was Lilihae, who had also followed Kamehameha to the beach, expecting to see him stricken at any moment. Now he watched in consternation as Kameha stroked up and over the oncoming waves, which were growing higher every minute.

"Indeed he is," Kekūhaupiʻo said as he marked the man. "Thank you."

Lilihae had turned away and started back toward the village. Kekūhaupiʻo observed that the old man was moving with surprising speed and agility. He thought that he recognized him. "I must go now," he told the boy. "When Kamehameha returns from riding the waves, tell him to look for me at our hale. And take care to guard that malo well." Then Kekūhaupiʻo set off in pursuit of Lilihae. The boy watched him go and then returned his attention to the bay, where Kamehameha was already racing a rising swell to catch his first wave.

Lilihae's hale was mauka of Kawaihae proper, in the uplands overlooking the bay. He preferred this separation. It added to the air of mystery he sought to cultivate among the people. As he marched up the hill to his dwelling he could not understand why the poison-laced poi hadn't produced any ill effects yet. The young man was strong, surely, but not indestructible. If the deadly bark of the nioi tree was not lethal enough to kill Kamehameha, what other poison would work? How would he manage to administer it? Preoccupied with these thoughts, Lilihae did not notice that he had been followed nearly to the threshold of his hale.

Kekūhaupiʻo returned to the beach the way he had come, walking slowly and deep in thought. The old man was Lilihae, the much-feared kahuna hoʻonuana, of this he had no doubt. Sorcerer or not, Lilihae must die for his attempt on Kameha's life.

But Holoʻae counseled patience. "Lilihae does not yet know for certain that his scheme has failed, nephew," the kahuna said, when Kekūhaupiʻo came to see him in the courtyard of Alapaʻi's hale. "And Kaʻakau still believes it proceeds. But if something were to happen to Lilihae, Kaʻakau might have cause for doubt. Therefore, stay your hand against that old one for the time being, for if we can assuage his uncertainty, he may prove useful to us."

As the two men spoke, they were careful to keep their voices low and their faces turned away from Maile, who was hovering nearby, making a great show of tending to the imu. Once again, he could not hear what passed between them, but he was sure it was more than idle talk.

"That one has been keeping an overly close eye on me," Holoʻae whispered to Kekūhaupiʻo. "Be careful what you say around him. I think he may be spying for Kaʻakau."

Sometime after mid-morning, the boy whom Kameha had entrusted to hold his malo rushed into the courtyard of the hale shared by Kekūhaupiʻo and Kamehameha. Kekūhaupiʻo was resting on a mat in the shade of the thatched house. "Kamehameha is missing," the boy shouted. "He was riding a huge wave when he disappeared. He is gone!"

Kekūhaupiʻo jumped to his feet. "I am going to the beach to help search for Kameha," he said. "Someone must tell old Holoʻae. Do you know where to find him?" The boy shook his head. "Come, I will show you," Kekūhaupiʻo said. He led the boy to a path that climbed the hill beyond the village. "He is up there," he said, pointing to a lone dwelling. The boy ran off, still carrying Kameha's malo. Kekūhaupiʻo smiled as he watched him go.

Kamehameha attacked the sea with abandon that morning, as the waves continued to build, higher and higher. He was already well known among the people of the Big Island for his surf-riding prowess. While many of his contemporaries rode the waves lying flat on their boards or kneeling on them, Kameha would most often stand on his—even when riding the crests of the highest waves. This day, he rose to his feet time after time, to great cheers from the spectators on shore. Always, he would stay with the waves until just before they collapsed. Sometimes he would dive into them at the last moment and recover his board wherever it washed up on the beach, and sometimes he would turn his board seaward and slip down the backside of the waves. Kamehameha was one of the few surf riders of his time to have perfected this maneuver. Most would simply dive from their boards while the water was still deep enough for them to avoid being slammed against the sand or dashed against jagged rocks at the shore.

While he delighted the onlookers on the beach with his surf-riding display, Kamehameha was in fact playing for time, and waiting for the fishermen to get into position. Holoʻae had told him that the men would head for their usual fishing grounds that morning, so as not to arouse any notice. At first, they would be well seaward of Kameha. But when Kāne's sun had climbed halfway to its midday position in the sky, the fishermen would turn shoreward again, angling toward the bay at Kawaihae. It was then, Holoʻae advised, that Kamehameha should make his escape. Now it was time.

Though Kamehameha had thought to escape on his surf-riding board, too many eyes were on him now. People would see him trying to paddle away. He would have to abandon his board and swim. The waves were now towering as high as ten feet in the haole measure as they rushed toward shore. Holding his position in the rolling swells beyond the surf line, Kameha saw an oncoming upwelling of water that promised to eclipse the already powerful waves ahead of it. Suffused with sunlight, its steadily rising mound glowed blue-green. Kameha could see the shadowy forms of small fish swimming about in its interior. As the last intervening swell slipped away beneath his board, Kameha commenced paddling furiously toward the beach. The powerful wave soon overtook him and lifted him on its broad shoulders. The watchers on the beach gasped as Kamehameha gained the crest of the biggest wave of the morning, now nearly fifteen feet high. Kameha could see them gaping up at him. It was time. He had been standing, evenly balanced, in the middle of his board as he rode atop the wall of rushing water. Now he moved toward the front of the board and forced its nose into the wave crest. "I meant to flip the board and fling myself into the wave," he told my father much later. "But this is not what happened."

Instead of upending tail over nose and throwing him into the clutches of Kanaloa, as he had intended, Kamehameha's surf-riding board dipped below the wave's crest and into its massive, rolling face. Reacting instinctively to maintain his balance, Kameha moved back to the middle of the board. Now he was traversing the front of the wave without losing any height as the wave's onrushing underbelly surged under his board and its towering crest boiled above his head. The wave's roar filled his ears; a light spray teased his face. The people on the beach seemed to vanish. Time seemed to vanish as well. "I felt that I could stay in that place forever," Kameha told my father later. "I wanted to stay there." The moment passed. He took a deep breath and let the wave overtake him.

To the people on the beach, it appeared as if Kameha had been swallowed by the huge wave. They waited anxiously for him to reappear after the wave had spent itself against the shore. His surf-riding board washed up on the beach, but there was no sign of Kamehameha. Among the spectators were the two men whom Keaweʻōpala had ordered to keep close watch on Kameha. "Do not allow him to leave Kawaihae—under any circumstances," he had told them before he left for Kailua. But instead of taking to the waves with Kamehameha that morning, they had come late to the beach, having caroused to excess the night before. By the time they arrived, there were no more surf-riding boards to be had. They could only watch from the shore with the others.

Many minutes passed without any sign of Kameha. The spectators began murmuring among themselves. "He has not surfaced," said one. "I can't see him," said another. "Kanaloa has taken him," a third exclaimed. "No!" said another. "He is the mover of the Naha Stone. Kanaloa would not take him." "Perhaps he was injured," still another cried, as the murmurs rose to shouts. The people began gesturing wildly and calling to the surf riders still in the water. "Kamehameha has disappeared. A huge wave took him. Find him! Find him!" Some of the riders turned their boards around and started paddling toward the horizon. Others paddled parallel to the shore in opposite directions. As they searched, they called out Kamehameha's name. There was no method or coordination in their efforts.

Keaweʻōpala's men watched the frenetic search until they were convinced that Kamehameha was unlikely to be found. Then they left the beach. One immediately headed south, to bring the news of Kameha's disappearance to Keaweʻōpala. The other man would remain in Kawaihae, to await the recovery of Kameha's body, if he had indeed drowned. There was a small outrigger canoe pulled up on the beach near the canoe shed, but the spies saw no point in joining the search.

At about the same time that Keaweʻōpala's spy set off for Kailua, the boy bearing Kameha's malo reached Lilihae's hale. "Holoʻae! Holoʻae!" he shouted as he neared the threshold. "Kamehameha has gone missing in the bay. The other surf riders are looking for him even now, but they fear he has drowned!"

Emerging from the dark interior of his dwelling into bright sunlight, Lilihae squinted at the boy. "Kameha? Drowned? But he is a powerful swimmer. How could this happen?" the old man demanded.

"He was riding a huge wave when he suddenly fell from his board. No one has seen him since."

"This is terrible! I must go to Kailua to bring Keaweʻōpala this awful news. He will be sorely grieved."

There was one in Kawaihae who suspected that Kamehameha was not truly missing. Maile could now begin to make sense of what he had observed—Holoʻae's hushed consultations with Kekūhaupiʻo and his late-afternoon visit to the fishermen. Perhaps Kameha did not drown, he thought. What if he had been trying to leave Kawaihae undetected? He could have used the big waves to mask his escape. He might have sent Kekūhaupiʻo to Holoʻae for help. That would explain Holoʻae's business with the fishermen. Maile was pleased with himself. Now he would have some important intelligence to share with Kaʻakau when he returned from Kailua. He was sure that he would be well rewarded for his efforts.

Upon reaching the beach, Kekūhaupiʻo made a great show of agitation and grief. "Kamehameha!" he wailed. "What has become of him?" Kekūhaupiʻo saw the beached outrigger canoe, ran to it, and pushed it into the water. "I will help you look for him," Kekūhaupiʻo called to the other surf riders, who were still frantically paddling here and there. Jumping into the canoe, he set out to confuse the search.

Holding his breath for as long as he could, Kamehameha stroked and kicked hard under the water to distance himself from the other surf riders. When he could no longer bear the burning in his lungs, he rose to the surface for air. Too close by, he could hear the other surfers' first notes of alarm. "Where is Kamehameha? Have you seen him?" called one. "His surf-riding board washed up on the beach," cried another. "I never saw him come up," called a third man. "Surely, he is about somewhere," said a fourth. "He must be!" Kameha took a deep breath and dove again.

He kept on in this fashion for a long time, always making for the horizon. Each time he broke the surface to breathe, the searchers' calls were weaker. At last, when he was beyond the bay's southern point, he surfaced for good and began swimming down the coast. "Head toward the beach at Ōhai'ula," Holo'ae had said. "The fishermen will look for you in the waters there." But they would be watching for someone on a surf-riding board, not a swimmer. Kamehameha hoped that he would be able to find them and attract their attention, for surely they would not see him first.

Kameha had never attempted a swim of this duration before. He did not know how long or how far he would have to swim to find the fishermen. He could not swim to shore this close to Kawaihae, lest he be discovered by any searchers who might be ranging along the coastline looking for him. All he could do was to continue swimming south, parallel to the shoreline, until he spotted the canoe. To conserve his strength, he kicked and stroked slowly, keeping his arms always in the water. He kept on this way for a long time. Kāne's sun was more than halfway through its daily course across the sky when he finally saw a lone canoe.

At first, he was not sure that it was the one he sought. But then he heard voices calling his name. "Kamehameha! Is that you? Answer us!" The two fishermen had been about to abandon their search when they saw something in the water. They were not sure if it was a person, a dolphin, or a bit of flotsam, but they had called out just the same. "Yes, yes! Over here!" Kameha called. He kicked hard to elevate himself in the water and waved his arms at them. The canoe's prow turned toward him.

The fishermen put Kamehameha ashore at the sandy beach at Hāpuna. He stank of fish. His rescuers had spent the hours before the time appointed for their rendezvous productively, filling their small craft with an abundant catch. When he hauled himself up and over the side of the canoe, Kameha had landed in a slick bed of scales and fins. Now he hurriedly rinsed himself in the surf and tied on a plain kapa cloth malo that one of the fishermen had given him. There was no one else about. "You must not stay near the coast," Kekūhaupi'o had told him. "There is a stream that empties into the bay at Hāpuna. Follow it into the uplands. Find a secure place of concealment and wait for me there. I will come to you." His muscles aching from hours of swimming and treading water, Kamehameha set out.

Once he had cleared the surf line, Kekūhaupi'o pointed the prow of the small canoe north, opposite the way he knew Kameha must be heading. After paddling hard in this direction for several minutes, he pointed and cried out, "There! I see something there!" All the surf riders began paddling toward him. Before they got too close, Kekūhaupi'o pointed seaward and cried, "No, over there! I think I see Kamehameha over there!" And stroking furiously, he set off in a new direction. Again, the surf riders followed. Kekūhaupi'o continued this for some time. Each time he changed direction, the surf riders followed, but they could not catch up with him. At last, when he was sure that Kamehameha had put too much distance between himself and the searchers to be spotted, Kekūhaupi'o stopped paddling and slumped over in his seat as the now-exhausted surf riders collected around his canoe. "Forgive me," he wailed. "My eyes have been playing tricks on me. He is truly lost!" He began paddling desultorily toward the beach, the picture of complete dejection.

Late that night, under cover of darkness, Kekūhaupi'o stole away from Kawaihae. No one saw him go, save one. All that afternoon and evening, Maile had kept watch on the hale that Kekūhaupi'o and Kamehameha shared. He had seen Kekūhaupi'o return from the beach. Now he saw a shadowy form emerge from the dwelling's doorway and pause momentarily before disappearing among the gray shapes of the surrounding palm and breadfruit trees. Maile thought for a moment to follow, but immediately checked himself. Kekūhaupi'o, the renowned warrior, would surely detect his presence in a moment, and under the circumstances, that could well spell his own end. It was enough that he had seen him abruptly quit the village in the dead of night. Clearly, he was up to something. Precisely what it might be was for others to discover.

Kamehameha was hungry. The fishermen had given him some roasted sweet potato and breadfruit to eat, and he had eagerly consumed it. As he ascended into the uplands, he had gathered as many ripe bananas as he could carry from the trees that grew wild along the narrow gulch. These too he had voraciously devoured. Now, crouched in a thicket of grass and shrubs where he was confident he could not be seen, he felt new pangs of hunger. The light was fading as the sun set; a light drizzle was falling from the low clouds that had blown in from the sea late in the day and fetched up against the mountainside, and he was chilled. Kameha drew his knees up against his chest and hugged them close against the cooling air. Trying to ignore the growling in his stomach, he shivered and waited. Kekūhaupiʻo had promised he would come.

After slipping out of Kawaihae, Kekūhaupiʻo had climbed the hillside above the bay and then turned south. He made sure that he was well clear of any outlying dwellings before he descended again to the rocky beach. The need for stealth slowed his progress and he did not reach the bay at Hāpuna until late that night. Turning his face mauka, he followed the stream into the uplands. Kekūhaupiʻo expected that Kamehameha would be well hidden. He knew he would not be able to find him easily in the darkness. But he expected Kameha to see or hear him.

The dark of night was giving way to the gray of the last hour before dawn when the sounds of rustling foliage and splashing water awakened Kamehameha from a fitful doze. "Kekū," he called softly, "is that you?"

"Yes, it is me!" Kekūhaupiʻo, who could steal through any terrain without making a sound or leaving a trace if he chose, had made a steady commotion as he ascended the stream bed. He was counting on Kameha to be the sole audience for his performance.

Kamehameha surged from his hiding place and embraced his tutor. "Kekū," he exclaimed, "have you brought anything to eat?"

Much later, after Kameha had taken the edge off of his appetite with some dried fish his kahu had brought, the pair set off for Ke'ei, Kekūhaupi'o's own village just below the bay at Kealakekua. Kamehameha would be safe there—for a time, at least.

Traveling on foot and by canoe, Lilihae reached Kailua soon after the news of Kamehameha's apparent drowning. By this time, Kameha and Kekūhaupi'o had ascended well into the south Kohala highlands. Lilihae found Ka'akau in the courtyard of Keawe'ōpala's hale.

"Kamehameha is no more," Lilihae announced with a grim smile.

"You are certain he is dead then?" Ka'akau demanded.

"I worked a powerful magic on him the night before he disappeared in the sea," Lilihae said. "The spell did not take effect at once because he was too strong. But as you know, Kamehameha was also a very strong wave rider. No mere wave could have broken him. Only a mighty spell such as mine could do that. Surely, he is in the depths with Kanaloa now."

Ka'akau said nothing.

"You will arrange for the Makahiki tribute of the Lapakahi ahupua'a to be delivered to me as promised, of course?" Lilihae ventured.

"When Kanaloa returns Kamehameha's body to us, then you shall have your tribute—as promised," Ka'akau replied.

"And if his body is never found?" Lilihae asked.

"In that case, we may have to wait until the next Makahiki time, when I can be sure that he is truly gone," Ka'akau said. He turned on his heel and disappeared into the mō'ī's hale.

"Do you have news of Kamehameha?" Keawe'ōpala asked.

"No one yet knows what has become of him, Lord," Ka'akau said.

ensure that Holoʻae would not escape his trap, Kaʻakau ordered the two men to keep watch on the kahuna's hale throughout the night.

Holoʻae was suspicious of Keaweʻōpala's intentions toward Kalaniʻōpuʻu. How genuine could Keaweʻōpala's desire for peace be so soon after he had sought the death of Kalaniʻōpuʻu's beloved nephew, Kamehameha? Holoʻae suspected that his mission to Kaʻū was merely a ruse meant to lull Kalaniʻōpuʻu into dropping his guard. He would not lend himself to such a deception. Nevertheless, he welcomed Keaweʻōpala's charade as an opportunity to escape from Kawaihae.

His two escorts arrived at his hale just after dark and bedded down on mats outside his doorway.

"Why have you come here now?" Holoʻae demanded of the two men.

"The journey to Kaʻū is long and we must depart early," one of the men explained. "We will sleep here so that we will be ready to leave with you at first light."

"It is not necessary for you to sleep at my door," Holoʻae said. "Come back in the morning to fetch me when you are ready to leave."

"No," the second man said. "We will stay here."

"Well then, stay here if you must," replied Holoʻae, smiling despite his suspicion. "Perhaps you are hungry?" he asked. "I have some poi. I would be pleased to share it with you, if you would like."

The two men nodded. Holoʻae fetched a calabash full of poi from his hale. After he and his two "guests" licked the last of the sticky poi from their fingers, Holoʻae asked the men, "Do you wish for anything else?"

"Thank you for the poi, *Lord,*" one of the men replied, "but we have imposed on your hospitality enough for one evening. We have a long journey tomorrow and we must rest now."

"Indeed," said Holoʻae. Pausing at his doorway, he turned back to them and said, "When you see Kaʻakau and Keaweʻōpala tomorrow night, please tell them how grateful I was for your assistance."

"*Mahalo*, Lord," the second man said. "We will tell them."

Inside, Holoʻae extinguished the oil lamp and lay very still in the dark. After some time, he heard one of the men on his threshold mutter to the other, "You fool. What were you thinking?" The other man did not respond. But Holo'ae had heard enough.

Holo'ae said nothing as he walked with the two men to the beach the next morning, even as they tried to engage him in conversation.

"It is a fine day for a sea journey, is it not, old man?" asked one.

In response, Holo'ae merely grunted and pursed his lips.

"See how calm the water is this morning," exclaimed the other as they neared the beach. "We will make good time today and reach Ka'ū before you know it."

Holo'ae held his silence and kept his eyes fixed on the shore, where a light surf was breaking.

The kahuna knew that physically, he was no match for either of the two younger men, and certainly not both in combination. And yet in the close quarters of a small voyaging canoe, he might achieve a momentary advantage. Toward that end he had donned a kapa cloth robe to hide the bulge in the belt of his malo, where he had concealed a newly sharpened wooden dagger. "To protect my old bones against the damp sea air," Holo'ae had explained to one of the men when the latter remarked about his robe.

Preoccupied as they were with their own scheme, neither of Holo'ae's two would-be assassins noticed that the kahuna's right hand never wavered from his midsection, even as he stepped into the canoe.

Their plan was simple. When they reached Pauoa Bay, about five miles south of Kawaihae, the warrior at the stern of the boat would strike Holo'ae sharply from behind with his paddle. They would throw the stunned kahuna overboard and watch him to make sure he drowned. If need be, one of them would jump into the water to hold Holo'ae under until he died. When they were certain that the kahuna was dead, they would abandon the canoe and swim ashore. Pauoa Bay was close enough to Kawaihae that they could easily regain the village—with their tale of the day's "tragic" events—before nightfall.

The warriors did not anticipate any problems. They were confident that it would not be difficult to slay Holo'ae. In their eyes, he was an old man, while they were young and strong. But Holo'ae, who was at this time about forty years old, was in fact exceptionally fit; he was trim and still blessed with quick reflexes.

The warriors chatted idly as they paddled southward. They told bawdy jokes that drew no laughter from Holo'ae. The kahuna smiled as if amused, but his smile was tight and his grip on the dagger hidden under his robe was tighter still. Neither of the two men seemed aware of his alert posture. The warrior in the stern who was to strike the first blow never noticed the tension in the kahuna's neck and shoulders.

At length, the warrior in the bow turned around to speak directly to him for the first time since they had set out from Kawaihae. "Are you enjoying the voyage, old man?" he asked with a broad smile. Holo'ae ignored the man's too-wide grin and fixed instead on his eyes, which now were not on him.

Sweeping his robe aside, the kahuna dropped to the bottom of the canoe, rolled onto his back and braced the dagger point-upward against himself just as the warrior in the stern raised his paddle to strike him. The paddle blade cut through empty air, and the warrior stumbled and fell upon Holo'ae and his waiting blade. The man's weight and the momentum of his fall drove the dagger deep into his stomach. He screamed.

The man in the bow froze, uncomprehending. Holo'ae rolled the writhing wounded warrior aside, simultaneously wrenching the bloody dagger from the man's stomach, and flew at the other man, driving the blade into his throat before he could raise his arms to ward off the blow. Choking on his own blood, the warrior could not even scream as he tumbled into the sea. Struggling to keep his grip on the dagger, Holo'ae was only just able to arrest his own momentum before it carried him over the side with his second victim.

Breathing heavily from his exertions, the kahuna turned back to the first man, who was now feebly trying to raise himself on one elbow. "Let me help you, my son," Holo'ae said. He grabbed a handful of the warrior's long black hair, jerked his head up, and slit his throat. The younger man gurgled and lay still. Holo'ae was very tired now. He rested for some time before he was able to summon the strength to heft the warrior's considerable dead weight over the side of the canoe. Then at last, he seated himself at the stern, picked up a paddle and began stroking. "It is indeed a fine day for a sea journey," he said aloud, as the canoe resumed its progress toward Ka'ū. Several shark fins broke the bloodied waters' surface as he paddled away. The two warriors' bodies were never found.

Holo'ae made slow progress in his voyage south. He did not come ashore for the rest of the first day. He was still too close to Kawaihae and he dared not risk being seen. Even if he was not recognized, talk of an "old one" alone in a canoe would soon reach Ka'akau and Keawe'ōpala. Keeping well to sea, Holo'ae paddled slowly but steadily, pausing only occasionally to eat or drink. At last, as the day's last light was fading, he beached the canoe in a secluded cove, where he dozed fitfully next to the vessel, ready to put to sea should anyone venture near. Holo'ae kept on for several days, slipping ashore only at night, until he reached his ancestral home at Ke'ei, where his nephew Kekūhaupi'o still reigned as village chief. The kahuna hoped to find Kekūhaupi'o and Kamehameha already there, but no one had seen them, nor had they heard any word of them. Taking advantage of his status as a priest and Kekūhaupi'o's uncle, he requisitioned a sail canoe and two young warriors to man it and reached Kalani'ōpu'u's village at Ka Lae the next day.

Kalani'ōpu'u already knew of Alapa'i's death and Keawe'ōpala's succession, but Holo'ae was the first to tell him of the attempt on Kamehameha's life and of his beloved nephew's narrow escape. This news enraged Kalani'ōpu'u. "I will sacrifice that pig Keawe'ōpala on the altar of Kū before the next full moon!" he exclaimed. Kalaniʻōpuʻu turned to his military kahu, who was seated on an adjacent mat in the courtyard of the chieftain's hale. "Puna! We must gather our warriors at once to march on Kawaihae!"

The big warrior grunted and said, "Keaweʻōpala must be destroyed, but we will surely need many allies in such a fight, and at present we have few."

"In that case Puna, I will leave it to you to amass an army of sufficient strength to defeat Keaweʻōpala," Kalaniʻōpuʻu replied. "But move quickly, for my patience is nearing an end."

Puna did not have to search long for allies. They came to him, and it was mostly Keaweʻōpala's doing. Among our people in those days, no one held permanent title to the land. All land belonged to the reigning mōʻī, who divided it among his followers. Upon his death, their claims lapsed and his successor was free to redistribute the land among his own followers as he chose. Land was distributed in whole districts to high chiefs, who then subdivided it among lesser chiefs in smaller parcels, ranging from *okanas* down to *ahupuaʻas* and the smallest plots—*ilis*. Sometimes, these last would even be granted to commoners.

Inevitably, some chiefs would be dissatisfied with the new land dispositions, and conflict would often ensue. When Keaweʻōpala parceled out landholdings after old Alapaʻi's death, he greatly offended his cousin, Keʻeaumoku. Keʻeaumoku believed that as a nephew of the late King Alapaʻi, he was entitled to more land than Keaweʻōpala had granted him. Always quick to anger and nearly always as quick to act on it, Keʻeaumoku resolved to settle his claim by force.

"Brother, you do not have sufficient strength to defeat Keaweʻōpala in battle, if it comes to that," his half-brother, Kameʻiamoku, counseled. But Keʻeaumoku would not be dissuaded.

"I will take what should be mine by right of birth," he rejoined. "Let Keaweʻōpala try to stop me." Thereafter, he moved swiftly to expand his land holdings beyond his fiefdom in Kekaha. He ordered his people to tear down the pile of lava stones that marked the boundary between his own okana and a smaller, adjacent ahupuaʻa. "It is all Kekaha now," he declared.

When Keaweʻōpala learned of Keʻeaumoku's defiance, he was furious. "I am the mōʻī," he thundered. "My will in this matter is final. Keʻeaumoku should have been satisfied with Kekaha. Now my cousin shall have only the sea for his okana!"

Mustering a force of more than a thousand warriors at Kawaihae and collecting hundreds more in the course of a swift, forced march south, the new mōʻī descended upon Keʻeaumoku and his people with such suddenness and ferocity that they were thrown back upon the beach at Kiholo village in disarray. Keʻeaumoku's fighters rallied at the water's edge just long enough to allow their chief and most of his men to escape in canoes.

Keʻeaumoku had avoided annihilation, but he and his people could not come ashore for provisions because Keaweʻōpala's forces ranged along the coastline opposite them, making landing perilous. They had come away with few provisions, and hunger gnawed at their bellies. They were forced to eat raw fish, when they could catch them. Their only source of drinking water was the occasional rain that fell from passing squalls and collected in the bottom of their canoes.

At last, Keʻeaumoku dispatched four of his youngest and strongest warriors in a light canoe to race farther south to Kaʻū while he feinted a landing on the Kona Coast. The ruse worked. Their attention drawn to the oncoming war canoes, Keaweʻōpala's soldiers' did not see the lone craft stealing away amid the concealing swells. When the young men reached Kaʻū with the news of Keʻeaumoku's rebellion, Kalaniʻōpuʻu was elated.

"Now we have the allies we need!" he shouted to his kahu. "Now we go to finish the dog."

Since his lord first swore to destroy Keaweʻōpala, Puna had been diligently assembling warriors and canoes from throughout the Kaʻū and Puna districts at Ka Lae. The giant warrior had also enlisted the support of Keawemaʻuhili, high chief of Hilo. Though Keawemaʻuhili had always been grateful to the late Alapaʻi for placing him over the eastern half of the Big Island, he distrusted Keaweʻōpala. He came to his half-brother Kalaniʻōpuʻu's side, bringing hundreds of warriors with him. Thus, Kalaniʻōpuʻu was able to set forth with a war fleet manned by some several thousand warriors. He made straight for Hōnaunau.

Hōnaunau, 1764

Hōnaunau was a royal retreat, a sacred place of refuge, and a place of great beauty. The kings of the Big Island were drawn there by the soft breezes that whispered in the crowns of its many shade-providing palm trees, by the sweet, fresh-water springs that flowed down the slopes of Mauna Loa, and by its abundant marine life, which included all manner of colorful fish and many *honu*—green sea turtles—that bobbed in the swells as they fed on the algae and the sea grasses that flourished among the submerged rocks there. Great pods of dolphins often played in the outer waters of the bay. A small inlet opening onto a sandy beach afforded a protected canoe landing, where a fierce wooden likeness of the war god Kū warned all that it was kapu for any but ali'i to set foot there.

The royal compound at Hōnaunau was composed of a dozen or so hales with steep thatched roofs. A high wall of lava stones separated the compound from the *pu'uhonua*, the place of refuge, where the bones of the great king Keawe, grandfather of Kalani'ōpu'u and Kamehameha's father Keoua, reposed in the Hale ō Keawe Heiau. Kameha's own grandfather, Kalanike'eaumoku, had erected the heiau. In those days, our people believed that Keawe's powerful mana protected the ground there. There was no kapu on that side of the wall. Any person, regardless of status, could enter. And anyone who reached it—such as a kapu violator or a defeated warrior—could find sanctuary, expunction of their transgression or shame, and forgiveness when they returned home. That the pu'uhonua at Hōnaunau was hallowed ground and inviolate was understood and respected by all on the Big Island. Perhaps that is why Kalani'ōpu'u was eager to muster his forces in its precincts. "He knew he would not be attacked there," my father explained.

It was at Hōnaunau that the forces of Kalani'ōpu'u and Ke'eaumoku converged. And it was at Hōnaunau that Kalani'ōpu'u and his beloved nephew Kamehameha were reunited at last.

Kamehameha and Kekūhaupi'o had kept to footpaths mauka of the coast as they fled south from the Kohala District, avoiding the coastal villages and their many curious eyes. They foraged for food as they traveled, raiding patches of sweet potatoes and yams and picking bananas from the trees that grew on Mauna Loa's lush flanks. Though they did not go hungry during their journey, neither did they once know the satisfaction of a full belly.

"*E Kekū!*" Kameha grumbled one evening, as he and Kekūhaupi'o finished a meager meal of bananas and yams. "My belly is not happy with this poor food. If it is not satisfied soon, it may go makai to find something better."

"*E Kameha!*" Kekūhaupi'o rejoined. "When we reach Ke'ei, your belly can have its fill. But until then, it will not be safe for us to go down to the coast, so tell your belly to be patient and stay mauka with us."

"I am trying, Kekū," Kamehameha sighed, "I am trying." Even as he spoke, his stomach groaned in protest. Unfortunately for his belly, Kamehameha and Kekūhaupi'o had precious little time to eat when at last they reached Ke'ei.

They had just sat down to a meal of roast pig, poi, and baked yams when a young warrior rushed into the courtyard of Kekūhaupi'o's hale. Nearly breathless from running, he could barely speak. "Keawe'ōpala comes!" he cried. "Keawe'ōpala comes!"

"Keawe'ōpala comes himself? Where is he now?" Kekūhaupi'o demanded.

"He is at Ka'awaloa with thousands of men," the warrior panted.

"Then he is not yet too close," said Kameha, who desperately wanted to slake his hunger. "We can stay here a little while longer."

Ka'awaloa was nearly opposite Ke'ei on the north side of Kealakekua Bay. It was not far from Ke'ei as a dolphin swims, but a strenuous climb to the high cliffs at the base of the bay's great horseshoe made for a longer journey on foot.

"An advance guard precedes him," the young man said. "They are already nearing the village."

Kekūhaupi'o was incredulous. "Keawe'ōpala comes here with thousands of men? He comes all this distance from Kawaihae with an army to catch Kamehameha?"

"Oh no," the warrior replied. "He comes with an army to catch Ke'eaumoku."

This was the first Kamehameha and Kekūhaupi'o had heard of Ke'eaumoku's rebellion. "Ke'eaumoku was driven into the sea," the young warrior explained. "Keawe'ōpala and his people have been chasing him down the coast ever since. Keawe'ōpala means to destroy him when he comes ashore."

"Where is Ke'eaumoku now?" Kekūhaupi'o asked.

"He has reached the bay at Kealakekua," the warrior said. "He is making for Hōnaunau."

"He is seeking sanctuary, no doubt," said Kekūhaupi'o. "And, Kameha, we must as well."

Still regarding the repast laid out before them, Kamehameha hesitated.

"Now!" Kekūhaupi'o commanded.

Kamehameha and Kekūhaupi'o set off for Hōnaunau at a swift trot. Keawe'ōpala's vanguard entered Ke'ei soon afterward. The soldiers did not notice the two fleeing figures. Their attention was fixed on the sea, where Ke'eaumoku's flotilla was just then drawing abreast of the village. They lined up along the shore, leaping about, screaming and waving their spears, daring Ke'eaumoku and his people to land. Hearing the commotion, Kameha and Kekūhaupi'o—still only a few hundred yards distant—stopped to watch.

At about this time, Keawe'ōpala himself reached Ke'ei, accompanied by his personal guard and his kahuna nui, Ka'akau. As he pushed through the village with his men, the mō'ī's eyes were on the hubbub at the shore, but his kahuna's eyes were elsewhere.

"Look over there," Ka'akau exclaimed, pointing at the two distant onlookers, "that big one there; it is almost certainly Kamehameha!"

Keawe'ōpala turned and squinted his eyes. "I think you are right, Ka'akau," he said. Then he shouted to a score of warriors nearby, "See those two men there! Go after them at once and bring them to me!" The soldiers rushed off, the flaps of their malos whipping around them.

Kekūhaupi'o saw them coming. "Run!" he cried. A desperate foot race now commenced.

The village of Ke'ei is about four miles distant from Hōnaunau. A lava shelf overgrown with grasses and shrubs lies between them. The ground is uneven, and because of the thick ground cover, treacherous. Walking at a leisurely pace is not easy. Forced marching is difficult. Running can be hazardous. In those days, shoes and sandals were unknown among our people. As Kameha and Kekūhaupi'o ran, jagged lava stones concealed by the grasses gashed their feet. They repeatedly stumbled in hidden depressions. Their pursuers suffered in like manner. But they were many and even though some might stumble and fall, there were always more to continue the chase. Kamehameha and Kekūhaupi'o, on the other hand, could not afford a misstep.

It was Kameha who fell, landing hard on one knee as he fought to keep his balance. A sharp lava stone gashed his kneecap. As he struggled to his feet, one of his nearest pursuers rushed at him, waving a war club. This man was off balance and his swing lacked force. Kamehameha fended off the blow with his forearm, but he was knocked to his knees again. Standing over Kameha, the other man raised his arm for a second blow that was almost sure to incapacitate him. The blow never came. Kekūhaupi'o charged him at full force, bowling him over. The club flew from the man's hand and Kekūhaupi'o was astride him before he could recover. Kekūhaupi'o grasped the warrior's head about the ears and twisted it sharply. Bones cracked. The man's body went limp. "Get up! Get up!" Kekūhaupi'o shouted. "They are coming!"

Slowly, Kamehameha rose to his feet. His arm ached where the war club had struck him and both his knees were bleeding. There was nowhere left for him and Kekūhaupi'o to run. Their other pursuers had caught up with them and their only remaining escape route was the sea. Their opponents, all armed, formed a wide semicircle around them. Kekūhaupi'o and Kamehameha had only one weapon between them, the war club that Kekūhaupi'o had taken from the fallen warrior. Yet the others held back. "That is Kamehameha, the mover of the Naha Stone," one murmured. "He did not drown after all," said another. "Why do you run from us?" a third man asked. "The mō'ī merely wants to see you."

"The mō'ī wants more than that. He tried to kill Kamehameha," snapped Kekūhaupi'o. "Let us go!"

"You're coming with us, now!" the third man said, brandishing his war club. Still, he and his comrades hesitated.

It was not the reputation or spectacle of Kamehameha, who easily towered over every other man there, which kept them momentarily in check. Though Kameha was large and powerful, he had yet to be tested in battle. No, my father told me, it was their fear of Kekūhaupi'o, the Big Island's most celebrated warrior, that held them back. The body lying at his feet served as further warning. Slowly, warily, the warriors tightened their circle.

Standing shoulder-to-shoulder, Kamehameha and Kekūhaupi'o faced their assailants. "You take this," Kekūhaupi'o said, handing the club to Kameha. "I do not need it." The weapon nearly disappeared in Kamehameha's big hand. Kekūhaupi'o growled at the advancing warriors. "Who wishes to die next?" he asked.

The first of Ke'eaumoku's canoes had now drawn even with the spot where Kameha, Kekūhaupi'o, and their pursuers stood. Ke'eaumoku was in the lead canoe. Seeing the commotion on the shore, he had ordered his paddlers to steer closer to land. His boat and several others were now just a hundred yards or so from the rocky beach. "We must swim for it, Kekū!" Kamehameha shouted. He hurled the club at the nearest warrior, striking him square in the chest. The man toppled over, gasping for breath. Kameha turned, ran the few remaining yards to the water's edge, and splashed into the surf. Kekūhaupiʻo followed close behind him. They discarded their malos as they ran. This happened so quickly that Keaweʻōpala's warriors scarcely had time to react before Kamehameha and his kahu had reached waist-deep water and dived into the waves. Like Kameha, Kekūhaupiʻo was a strong swimmer. Stripped to their bare skin, they soon outdistanced several warriors who had followed them into the water, but had failed to likewise remove their malos in their hurry.

Keʻeaumoku could see Kameha and Kekūhaupiʻo swimming toward him, but he could not make out who they were. Nevertheless, he reasoned that anyone fleeing from Keaweʻōpala's people was bound to be an ally. "See those two in the water there!" he shouted. "We must help them!" His canoe veered sharply toward Kamehameha and Kekūhaupiʻo. Realizing that they were now in peril, Keaweʻōpala's warriors gave up the chase and swam back to shore.

As his canoe drew closer to the two figures bobbing in the swells, Keʻeaumoku recognized them. "It is Kamehameha and Kekūhaupiʻo," he exulted. Assisted by the canoe paddlers, Kameha and Kekūhaupiʻo clambered over the side of the nearest hull and joined Keʻeaumoku on the war canoe's central deck. They greeted him with hugs and loud wails.

"We go now to Puʻuhonua o Hōnaunau," Keʻeaumoku said at last. "Keaweʻōpala cannot follow us there." As it turned out, they would have no need of refuge.

Keaweʻōpala, who lived much of his life on the edge of anger, was furious. Keʻeaumoku had escaped. Kamehameha had eluded his grasp. And now they were with Kalaniʻōpuʻu, who, his scouts told him, was encamped at Hōnaunau with many hundreds of warriors. He knew that the combined forces of Kalaniʻōpuʻu and Keʻeaumoku most probably numbered several thousand or more. They would be a formidable match for his own army, which was now massing in and around the village of Ke'ei. If only Ke'eaumoku had not slipped away at Kiholo, he could be more confident of crushing Kalani'ōpu'u. If only his people had captured Kamehameha near Ke'ei, he would now hold a valuable hostage. Kalani'ōpu'u would not dare attack him if he understood that his beloved nephew's life would be forfeit. Keawe'ōpala could then withdraw without dishonor and meet Kalani'ōpu'u in battle—as he knew he eventually must—at a time and place of his own choosing. Instead, his hand was forced. He must confront Kalani'ōpu'u now. Failure to do so would risk humiliation in the eyes of his subordinates. In that direction lay only further rebellion. No, he was the mō'ī of the Big Island, and if he wanted to remain so, he had no choice. Keawe'ōpala blamed his own people for this.

"They all failed me!" he railed at Ka'akau. "They failed to catch Ke'eaumoku! They let Kamehameha escape! Well, now they must fight, even if it costs them dearly!"

"Perhaps there is still an alternative to giving battle at this time, Lord," soothed Ka'akau, who understood that his mō'ī's bluster concealed his own dread of fighting on near-equal terms with his now-united foes.

"And what is that?" Keawe'ōpala demanded.

"The *kanapī* has many limbs," the kahuna replied, speaking of the poisonous Hawaiian centipede. "But if the head of the kanapī is cut off, then body and limbs die. We will cut off the head."

Keawe'ōpala looked at Ka'akau in puzzlement.

"We will slay Kalani'ōpu'u," the priest explained, "and his army will melt away."

Lilihae had followed Keawe'ōpala and Ka'akau to Ke'ei. Still believing that a poison-weakened Kamehameha had drowned in the big waves off Kawaihae, he was determined to collect his payment for eliminating him. When Ka'akau finally received news that the youth's body had washed ashore, Lilihae could press the high priest to hand over the Makahiki tribute from the Lapakahi ahupua'a at once. He was old, and did not want to wait for another turn of the seasons to claim his just due. When Ka'akau finally sent for him at Ke'ei, Lilihae was sure that he was being summoned to receive his reward. Instead, he was surprised to find the priest scowling at him.

"You failed, old one," Ka'akau said. "Kamehameha lives. He was seen here at Ke'ei just today. He escaped from our people and he has fled to Hōnaunau with Ke'eaumoku."

"How is that possible?" Lilihae protested. "My sorcery was very powerful. No one, not even one as strong as Kamehameha, could have withstood it."

"There was another whose own magic was evidently mightier still," Ka'akau replied. "Holo'ae interfered with your 'spell.'"

"Holo'ae!" Lilihae sputtered indignantly. "What powers does that one have?"

"None, any longer," Ka'akau said with a grimace that encompassed both loathing and satisfaction. "He is dead. He will not trouble you anymore. Now I give you another chance to work your sorcery, and if you succeed this time, you shall have your reward."

"It will be more difficult now, with Kamehameha at Hōnaunau," Lilihae said, "but he will not elude me this time."

"I do not care about Kamehameha," Ka'akau replied. "It is Kalani'ōpu'u whom I want you to slay."

Lilihae's rheumy eyes widened and he gasped. "That will require very powerful magic, more costly magic," he said. "And I must get very close; it will be dangerous."

"Do it, old one, and you will have the Lapakahi tribute for two Makahiki times."

"I will do it," he said, "but I will need assistance."

Ka'akau clapped his hands. "Maile, come here," he called.

"Kalani! Come quickly!" Puna exclaimed. "Ke'eaumoku has come with many warriors, and Kamehameha is with him!"

Kalani'ōpu'u rose from the mat where he had been resting in the heat of the late afternoon. Laughing, he reached up and clapped Puna on the shoulder. "Kamehameha too? Well, it is about time my nephew decided to come join me!"

Joined by Holo'ae, who had journeyed with them from Ka'ū, Kalani'ōpu'u and Puna made their way across the royal compound, past the ponds stocked with fish for easy capture by the ali'i, and through a gap in the lava-stone wall that separated the compound from the place of refuge. A multitude of Kalani'ōpu'u's fighters were gathered on the broad bench of smooth pahoehoe lava that fronted the sea, cheering and shouting greetings to Ke'eaumoku and his people as their canoes neared the beach.

My father was one of the many people who had rushed to the pu'uhonua when the first canoes had arrived and Ke'eaumoku, his brother, Kame'iamoku, Kamehameha, and Kekūhaupi'o stepped ashore. Breaking from the crowd, my father ran to Kameha, who threw his arms around him. "Little brother," he wailed, enveloping my father in a fierce hug, "it is so good to see you again."

Now Kalani'ōpu'u, Puna, and Holo'ae made their way through the throng as Kalani'ōpu'u's men opened a path for them. Holo'ae and his nephew, Kekūhaupi'o, clasped arms, hugged, and laughed. Kalani'ōpu'u warmly embraced Kamehameha and then Ke'eaumoku and Kame'iamoku. Turning to his kahu, he asked, "What do you say now Puna? Do we have warriors enough for a fight?"

"Yes, Lord," Puna replied.

"Good," Kalani'ōpu'u said. "Then there is no cause for further delay. Let us go find Keawe'ōpala and finish with him."

"You will not have to go far to find him," Ke'eaumoku replied. "Keawe'ōpala is already at Ke'ei."

Having shed their malos at Ke'ei, Kamehameha and Kekūhaupi'o were still naked when they came ashore at Hōnaunau. In the exhilaration of their escape, it hadn't occurred to them to cover themselves again before they reached the place of refuge. As I have said, it was customary for our people—even women—to swim nude in those days. Thus, no one had remarked on their nakedness aboard the canoe or as they stood amid the crowd of cheering, laughing men on the lava shelf. So now, forgetful of their unclothed state, Kameha and his kahu strode through the opening in the lava wall to the adjacent royal compound. Abruptly, Kamehameha, who had been jesting and laughing with my father, stepped behind him. His eyes had met Kaneikapolei's, and she was most certainly mindful of his nakedness.

"Kaneikapolei was smiling at him," my father recalled. "Kameha gripped my shoulder very hard and ordered me to keep in front of him. Kalani'ōpu'u saw this and made fun of him."

"Why are you so shy about your manhood, nephew?" Kalani'ōpu'u laughed. "You have nothing that wahine hasn't seen before."

Though this was true, Kalani'ōpu'u's jest in front of so many others made Kamehameha, already flushed with embarrassment, turn redder still. He averted his eyes from Kaneikapolei, as if he could lessen his own mortification by not acknowledging her. As for Kaneikapolei, my father said, "Her eyes never left my brother." And when Kameha at last dared to meet her steady, unabashed gaze again, he saw his infant son, Pauli, suckling at her engorged breast.

Kamehameha's feelings toward Pauli were ambivalent. He was proud to have fathered a child, but he had never regarded the infant as his own. When Kaneikapolei offered the baby to Kameha later that day, he drew back. "Don't you want to hold your son?" she asked.

"He is Kalani'ōpu'u's son now," Kamehameha replied. Then, seeing that Kaneikapolei was dismayed, he relented and gingerly took the baby from her. Sensing perhaps that this big stranger was reluctant to hold him, Pauli began to bawl. Kameha thrust him back into his mother's arms. "See, the boy does not like me," he protested.

"He does not yet know you, Kameha," Kaneikapolei said. "When he comes to know you, he will like you well enough." Her words would prove true, but it would be many years before he came to know his true father.

Kamehameha and Kaneikapolei wasted no time renewing their knowledge of each other. Kiwalaʻō's mother Kalola had also accompanied Kalaniʻōpuʻu to Hōnaunau, and she looked after Pauli in Kaneikapolei's absence. Kalaniʻōpuʻu, who spent that night with Kalola, greeted Kamehameha with a broad smile the next day. "I trust you slept well last night, nephew," he said. Kameha had slept very well that night and would sleep equally well on several more nights to follow. Kalaniʻōpuʻu paid it no mind.

For Kamehameha and my father, those days at Hōnaunau, just before Kalaniʻōpuʻu's battle with Keaweʻōpala, were carefree. As happy as they were, though, Kiwalaʻō was dour. He was not enthusiastic about seeing his cousin Kameha. "Kiwalaʻō was always very quiet around Kameha then—almost sullen," my father recalled. "It may be that he was jealous of all the attention Kameha received from Kalaniʻōpuʻu." Kamehameha also received much attention from Kalola. Although she was no longer amorous for Kameha, she felt a fondness for him that would last the balance of her life. It was a fondness that was much different from that of a mother toward a son, one that her own son Kiwalaʻō would never experience. And perhaps this, too, embittered him toward Kamehameha. He sulked and kept his distance.

Kaneikapolei's young sons, Keōua Kūʻahuʻula and Keōuapeʻeʻale, on the other hand, followed Kameha everywhere. He towered over all of his contemporaries, including their own father, a great chieftain. In their eyes, Kameha was a giant and they were awestruck. Their attention amused Kamehameha and he would occasionally pick up one or the other brother and toss him into the air, to great shrieks of delight.

This time at Hōnaunau was largely given over to martial sports and feasting. There were wrestling and spear catching contests every day. These games enabled the warriors to sharpen their skills and provided an outlet for the tension that was building steadily in anticipation of the big fight to come. At Kekūhaupiʻo's instruction, Kamehameha was always careful to ensure that he never drew Kiwala'ō as his opponent. "It would not do well to embarrass him," Kekūhaupi'o said.

The nightly luaus were lavish. Kalani'ōpu'u and Ke'eaumoku dispatched their warriors to nearby villages to gather provisions from the commoners: fresh fish, pigs, taro for poi, coconuts, sweet potatoes, and yams. Keawe'ōpala's people were doing likewise at Ke'ei, demanding tribute from villages as far away as Keauhou, well back up the coast. With thousands of warriors to feed in both camps, there was little left over for ordinary folk. All around, the common people only wished for the day when the two opposing armies would have their battle and the warriors would go away and leave them alone. The outcome of the impending conflict was immaterial to them.

Food preparation for so many warriors consumed the efforts of several scores of men for much of the day. It was into this group that the old sorcerer Lilihae and the young novice kahuna Maile inserted themselves. Lilihae and Maile had stolen into the outskirts of Kalani'ōpu'u's encampment in the depths of night. Bedding down among a group of men who were sound asleep on mats in the open air, they arose in the morning as if they belonged there. Some warriors were still trickling in from Ka'ū at this time and thus their arrival aroused no suspicions. Lilihae had been counting on this. "If we are asked, we can say that we only lately learned of Kalani'ōpu'u's intention to give battle," he had told Maile as they set out from Ke'ei. "And that we have just come from the Puna district. No one will challenge us, because no one at Hōnaunau has seen us before."

Despite his confidence that he was unknown to Kalani'ōpu'u's people, Lilihae did not want to be seen in close proximity to the high chief of Ka'ū. His fearsome reputation as a sorcerer depended on people believing that he could cast his deadly spells from a distance. It would not do for anyone to know that he required direct access to his victims for his spells to work. Nor could he allow anyone to suspect that poison, rather than magic, was the agent of his sorcery. He needed Maile's help to poison Kalani'ōpu'u, yet he could not reveal the truth of his dark art to his helper. So he dissembled.

"Kalani'ōpu'u is a powerful high chief," he explained, as they made their way toward Hōnaunau. "Only an extraordinarily powerful spell can overcome him—an eating spell." Lilihae told Maile that he would cast this spell over a bowl of poi that he himself would prepare. "You will carry this bowl to Kalani'ōpu'u's luau and place it where he is sure to eat from it," he said. "You must watch to make sure that he eats this poi."

"What if someone else eats it?" Maile asked.

"It is not important," Lilihae lied. "The spell will only affect Kalani'ōpu'u."

After sending Maile off to mingle with the food preparers, with instructions to "learn where Kalani'ōpu'u will feast tonight," Lilihae made his preparations. He ascended into the hills above Hōnaunau and gathered some small apples from a *noho-malie*—yellow oleander—tree that he found growing there. The fruit of this tree, as well as any part of it, is deadly poisonous. With a rounded stone, Lilihae mashed the oleander fruit into a paste, mixing in bits of shaved coconut meat to cover its sour taste. Before returning to Hōnaunau, he wrapped this mixture in ti leaves he had earlier gathered for this purpose.

Upon his return, Lilihae found Maile among the food preparers, pounding steamed taro stems into poi for the evening's feast. Squatting next to his young assistant, the old kahuna ho'onuana reached across him to scoop up a handful of cut, peeled stems, intentionally knocking over a hollowed-out calabash full of water with the back of his arm. "Go fetch some more water," Lilihae ordered. Maile hurried away with the bowl. Lilihae watched the other men, who were vigorously pounding taro into thick paste and regaling each other with lewd jokes. They were paying no attention to him. He reached under his malo for the ti leaf bundle, unwrapped it, and mixed the oleander paste into his pile of taro stems. He commenced pounding the stems just as Maile returned with the bowl of water.

"Here, take this," he said to Maile, handing him the blunt pounding stone. "You are younger and stronger and it will go faster if you do it. When you have finished, bring the poi to me. I will be resting in the shade there." Lilihae gestured at a grove of palm trees some forty or fifty yards distant. He rose slowly to his feet and walked away.

"This work is too much for that old one," one of the other men said as he watched Lilihae go.

"But he will surely come back when it is time to eat," said another. The men laughed and resumed their work. Maile said nothing.

His chest heaving, Maile stumbled through the moonless night. Kalaniʻōpuʻu's people were steadily closing on him, their shouts growing louder by the minute. Maile's pursuers had spread out in a ragged line marked by the streaming light of their torches and the wavering shadows preceding them among the low shrubs growing here and there amid the broken lava stones. There was nowhere to hide. He had to keep going. Short of reaching Keʻei and Keaweʻōpala's people before he was overtaken, there would be no sanctuary for Maile.

Nothing had gone as expected after Maile carried Lilihae's bowl of bewitched poi into the courtyard of Kalaniʻōpuʻu's hale at Hōnaunau. While Lilihae hid himself in the shadows on the outskirts of the royal compound, Maile entered with the other young aliʻi food bearers and set the bowl of poi before the high chief of Kaʻū.

Holoʻae was engrossed in conversation with his nephew Kekūhaupiʻo and thus had not noticed Maile when he knelt to place the bowl of poi before Kalaniʻōpuʻu. Nor, intent as he was on setting the bowl down just where Kalaniʻōpuʻu was sure to reach for it, had Maile noticed the kahuna. But now, as he watched from the edge of the courtyard, his eyes met the priest's. For an instant, Maile froze in disbelief. He had believed Holoʻae to be dead. Now he saw the kahuna staring at him across the courtyard. The priest's eyes were deep shadows and unreadable in the uneven light of the kukui-oil lamps. Maile lowered his eyes and turned away, but it was too late.

"You! Maile!" Holoʻae called out sharply. "Come here!"

Kalaniʻōpuʻu, who was about to dip his fingers in the bowl of poi, looked up. His hand paused in midair and then fell to his side again. "Who is that, Holoʻae?" he asked.

"That is Maile, Kaʻakau's spy," he spat. "He can be up to no good here." As Holoʻae spoke, Maile edged into the shadows beyond the reach of the oil lamps' illumination. "See, he is already trying to flee!" the kahuna exclaimed.

Kalaniʻōpuʻu gestured to several young warriors nearby. "See that one there," he said, pointing at Maile's receding, now-shadowy form. "Bring him to me at once." The young men jumped to their feet and ran after Maile, picking up and lighting kukui-oil torches as they went.

Kamehameha, who was sitting nearby, leaped to his feet. "I will catch him myself!" he declared. He ran after the warriors into the darkness. My father and Kiwalaʻō raced after him.

Old Naeʻole was baffled by the sudden commotion. He turned to Kekūhaupiʻo. "What is this foot race in the middle of a feast?" he asked.

"They are chasing Kaʻakau's spy," Kekūhaupiʻo said.

"Kalaniʻōpuʻu is here. He has come to fight," said Naeʻole. "What does Kaʻakau expect to learn from his spy that he does not already know?"

"We will have the answer to that question when they catch him," said Kekūhaupiʻo. "I do not think we will have to wait long."

"No doubt you are right," Naeʻole said. "In the meantime, would you please pass that bowl of poi to me?"

It was Kamehameha who caught Maile. Overtaking the other pursuers, and bursting through their ranks, he hurled himself at Maile's back and brought him down with such breath-expelling force that Maile could not even cry out.

Kamehameha sat on the prostrate fugitive to restrain him until the others caught up. Then he grabbed Maile under one armpit and hauled him roughly to his feet. "What are you doing here?" he demanded. Still gasping for breath, Maile looked up at him and said nothing. But his eyes, wide with fear, spoke volumes. "Never mind," Kameha said. "You can come with us and explain yourself."

"Who sent you and why?" Kalaniʻōpuʻu roared at Maile, who lay prone and quivering in the sandy soil where Kamehameha had thrown him. The high chief of Kaʻū, who had risen from his place at the feasting mat, now stood over Maile, brandishing a heavy war club. "Answer me or you'll answer to this club and your body will be sacrificed this same night to Kūkāʻilimoku!"

Maile raised his head to look up at Kalaniʻōpuʻu. His face was covered with dirty smudges and streaked by his copious tears. "Kaʻakau sent me," he blubbered.

"To what end?" thundered Kalaniʻōpuʻu. He shoved the butt end of his club under Maile's jaw and jerked his head up. "Speak!"

"To…slay…you," Maile gasped.

"You? You are nothing!" Kalaniʻōpuʻu sneered. "Kaʻakau sent you to slay me? Tell me the whole truth and perhaps you shall yet survive this night."

"I came with another," Maile said. "A powerful kahuna hoʻonuana. He cast a spell to cause you to sicken and die."

"But what kind of spell was this? I am not in the least sick, and I am certainly not dying," Kalaniʻōpuʻu rejoined.

"It was a food spell. The kahuna cast a spell over a bowl of poi. I carried it to the feast for him."

"Poi?" Kalaniʻōpuʻu was incredulous. "Where is this bowl of poi?"

Before Maile could answer, there came a loud groan from behind the high chief. Naeʻole was slumped over and shaking violently. Thick spittle had formed on his lips. He was clutching his stomach with sticky hands. The sweetened poi had been tasty, and while the chase after Maile was on, Naeʻole had consumed it with gusto.

Kamehameha had been standing next to Kalaniʻōpuʻu. Upon seeing his first kahu in agony, he rushed to the old man's side, gathered him into his lap, and cried, "Naeʻole! Naeʻole! What is wrong?"

Nae'ole did not reply; he only looked up at Kamehameha through glazed eyes. His breathing was fast and shallow; his face was gray. His whole body continued to quiver. Kamehameha enfolded his beloved kahu more tightly in his arms and pulled him closer. My father watched in horror as the old man—whom he loved no less than Kamehameha himself—died in his older brother's arms.

For a short time, Kamehameha and my father sat there in stunned silence. Then they began to wail. Others soon joined them in loud lamentations and a cacophony of grief enveloped the once-joyous luau.

Kalani'ōpu'u was not to be diverted. Yanking Maile to his feet and digging his fingers into the young man's throat, he hissed, "Do you know where this kahuna ho'onuana is now?"

"Yes, my lord," Maile croaked.

"Then take us to him," snarled Kalani'ōpu'u.

Resting on a kapa mat in the darkness well away from the feast, Lilihae heard the great commotion and clenched his fist, confident that his "sorcery" had achieved its end. Thus, as Maile approached, he was certain that his young assistant was coming to confirm what his ears had already surmised. Then he made out the shadowy forms of the other men following Maile, and his mood turned to dismay. Lilihae struggled to his feet and tried to flee, but a powerful blow knocked him to the ground. A heavy foot landed in the middle of his back. Yet even now, the old kahuna ho'onuana clung to his arrogance.

"How dare you strike me?" he shouted at his unknown assailant. "Don't you know who I am? I am Lilihae, the sorcerer. It is certain death to threaten me."

"And I am Kalani'ōpu'u, the high chief of Ka'ū," came the cold reply from the darkness above him. "And for certain, dead sorcerers are no threat!"

A sudden chill coursed through Lilihae's thin frame. The last sound he heard was the rush of air that preceded the skull-smashing blow of Kalani'ōpu'u's war club.

"Kamehameha and Kekūhaupi'o wanted to slay Maile on the spot," my father recounted, "but Kalani'ōpu'u would not allow it."

"No," Kalani'ōpu'u said. "We will send him back to Keawe'ōpala and his dog, Ka'akau." He turned to Maile, who quavered on his knees before him. "Go and tell the son of the usurper to meet me in open battle, if he dares."

Though both were now old enough to fight, neither Kamehameha nor Kiwala'ō took part in the great battle that ended in Kalani'ōpu'u's accession to the throne of the Big Island. Kalani'ōpu'u would not permit it. "Neither of you have experienced war," he told them, "and this is not the place to begin. I could not bear it if either of you should fall today. You will have many opportunities to prove yourselves as warriors, but I must defeat Keawe'ōpala first." Kameha and Kiwala'ō were thus kept well away from the fray, as was my father. They remained in the rear with Kalani'ōpu'u, only later learning of the battle's bloody events.

"It was a terrible fight that went on for several days," my father told me many years later. "The ground was rough and uneven, with many hidden holes, and thus the warriors could not fight and support each other in orderly lines," he said. Instead, my father explained, they fought *makawalu*—in roving bands—and so it was very difficult for one side to gain a clear advantage over the other. "At first, much blood was spilled with no gain," he said.

Kalani'ōpu'u finally turned the awful tide in his favor by violating a sacred custom. In those days, when a clash of great significance occurred, such as a contest for the kingship of the entire island, it was customary for the high priests of each side to lead their people into battle. These kāhuna nui were the *mihaus*, chaplains of their respective armies, and by tradition, their persons were kapu—inviolate by any combatant—even in the midst of the fiercest fighting. They would carry a tall branch stripped from a *hau* tree and topped with white feathers so that their own people could see them and no opposing soldiers would mistake them for warriors. Wherever they stood, the mihaus would often plant this branch in the ground or among the lava rocks. Most fighters believed that their own side would prevail as long as they could still see their mihau's hau branch.

It was Holo'ae, newly installed as Kalani'ōpu'u's high priest, who urged him to disregard the kapu, sending the message through Kekūhaupi'o. "If that is what must be done," Kalani'ōpu'u responded, "then do it, and quickly!"

At this time, Kalani'ōpu'u was still keeping well removed from the fighting, standing with Kameha, Kiwala'ō, and my father in the middle of a large group of young, relatively untried warriors armed with long pololu spears. This was the way of things for the high chiefs when the order of battle was the helter-skelter fighting of makawalu. Keawe'ōpala was doing likewise at the opposite end of the sprawling battleground.

Kekūhaupi'o set off with some of Kalani'ōpu'u's personal guards. He had no trouble finding Ka'akau, standing as he was where fighters on both sides could easily see him. He was holding his hau branch high and waving it back and forth. Maile was with him. Maile was alarmed when he saw Kekūhaupi'o and the enemy warriors running toward them, but Ka'akau did not flinch. "They will not harm me," he said. "I am mihau." Squaring his shoulders, Ka'akau watched with amusement as Kekūhaupi'o and his men approached.

"What brings you here to me, Kekū?" he asked, when Kekūhaupi'o stood before him at last. "Has Kalani'ōpu'u sent you to sue for peace?" It was not uncommon when two sides were evenly matched for one or the other to suggest a truce to avoid further bloodshed, and this battle had already been raging without resolution for several days.

Kekūhaupi'o smiled at Ka'akau, but said nothing. He moved toward the priest as if to hug him. Ka'akau stepped forward as well. Maile, who saw in Kekūhaupi'o's broadening smile only the cold whiteness of his teeth below the hard glitter of his eyes, took a step backward.

Now Ka'akau planted his hau branch in the ground and opened his arms. Kekūhaupi'o gripped the priest tightly by his shoulders and murmured into his ear, "Don't be so familiar with me, old man. I was never

'Kekū' to you." At this, Ka'akau stiffened and tried to pull away, but it was too late. Kekūhaupi'o grasped his head, twisted it sharply, and snapped his neck. Ka'akau's spirit fled at once. With a sigh of disgust, Kekūhaupi'o flung the priest's body aside and kicked over the kahuna's hau branch.

Horrified, Maile turned and fled. "Let him go!" Kekūhaupi'o ordered, as several warriors made to run after him. "He is of no consequence now. I will settle with him later." Then, pointing at Ka'akau's body, Kekūhaupi'o said, "Pick that up and take it to Kalani'ōpu'u."

Maile proved to be of some consequence after all. For as he fled from the awful scene of Ka'akau's murder, he spread panic among Keawe'ōpala's people. "Ka'akau is dead! Ka'akau is dead! His hau branch has fallen," he wailed. "We are lost!" His fear was contagious, and soon many of Keawe'ōpala's warriors had joined Maile in his headlong flight from the field of battle.

While Kalani'ōpu'u remained in the rear, Ke'eaumoku and his half-brother Kame'iamoku had led the fight against Keawe'ōpala's forces. When they saw their enemies begin to break and run back towards Ke'ei, they shouted for their own men to pursue them. A disjointed chase commenced as their orders were relayed from fighting group to fighting group. In some places, small bands of Keawe'ōpala's people turned and fought, inflicting serious casualties among their pursuers before they were overwhelmed. In other places, larger groups fled like flocks of *nene*—mountain geese—flushed from cover. Some were cut down as they ran, but many others escaped. As the rout of Keawe'ōpala's warriors began, Kekūhaupi'o sent a young warrior back to Kalani'ōpu'u to tell him to join the pursuit. Then, with a jubilant shout, he joined the chase himself.

Well to the battle's rear, Keawe'ōpala did not understand what was happening at first. When he saw his own people running toward him, he thought they were coming with news of victory. But then he made out the cries of distress. He could not fathom what had changed. Both sides were still more or less equally matched. If anything, he held a slight numerical advantage. His warriors had matched the enemy in ferocity, but now many of them were in flight. Why?

As if in answer to his puzzlement, a ragged form burst through the phalanx of warriors in front of Keaweʻōpala and collapsed at his feet. It was Maile.

"My lord, we are lost!" he gasped. "Kaʻakau is dead and his hau branch has fallen."

"Kaʻakau, dead? The branch fallen? How can this be?"

"Kekūhaupiʻo slew him," Maile wailed. "He kicked over the hau branch."

Keaweʻōpala exploded. "And for this reason, our people are running away?" he shouted. "Kaʻakau is mihau. It is kapu to harm him! It is kapu for any man to touch the hau branch. Kekūhaupiʻo has offended the god Kūkāʻilimoku, and Kalaniʻōpuʻu will surely pay for it!" Without a further word to his retinue, Keaweʻōpala rushed forward to rally his scattered warriors.

A more cautious leader might not have acted so hastily amid all the confusion. But Keaweʻōpala had never been one for circumspection. For that, he had depended first on Alapaʻi, and then on his high priest, Kaʻakau. But Kaʻakau was gone, and so now, certain of his own cause and with no one to restrain him, Keaweʻōpala dashed onto the battlefield well ahead of his personal guard. It was a foolhardy move, for it was not his own people he found first, but Kalaniʻōpuʻu's.

Keaweʻōpala saw a group of men running in his direction, and thinking they were warriors loyal to him, shouted at them to turn back. "This battle is not yet decided!" he cried. "Stand and fight! I order you to stand and fight!"

"We are fighting," one of the warriors shouted back as the group closed on Keaweʻōpala. "And who are you to order us?" he demanded. This particular band of warriors was composed of younger men from the Puna District who did not know Keaweʻōpala on sight.

The warrior's challenge brought Keaweʻōpala up short. He froze in his tracks, dumbfounded by the question. "Who am I to order you?" he roared at the men, who had likewise stopped running and were now arrayed in a semicircle some ten or fifteen paces from him. "I am your mōʻī, Keaweʻōpala!"

"Then we do not answer to you," replied the warrior, who was the group's leader. "Our 'mōʻī' is Kalaniʻōpuʻu."

Realizing his mistake, Keaweʻōpala glanced back to see the warriors of his personal guard racing toward him. "To me! To me!" he shouted to them over his shoulder. "Come kill these dogs of Kalaniʻōpuʻu!"

Kalaniʻōpuʻu's warriors exchanged apprehensive looks. They were isolated on the battlefield and suddenly outnumbered, with little chance of outrunning their foes. But their young leader understood what must be done. Without hesitation, he hurled his long pololu spear at the mōʻī of the Big Island.

When he was younger, Keaweʻōpala had taken part in mock battles, like all aliʻi warriors, but he was clumsy and had never excelled at throwing, catching, or dodging spears. As he grew older and more fearful of injury, he avoided these competitions. Now he was out of practice. He tried to sidestep the oncoming spear, but he stumbled and the weapon caught him almost squarely in the middle of his chest. Keaweʻōpala screamed in agony and sagged to his knees, clutching the spear's shaft. At this moment, his guards arrived.

"Kill them! Kill them, now!" Keaweʻōpala moaned. He was still on his knees, and as he spoke, blood poured from his mouth.

For a brief moment, no one on either side moved. Keaweʻōpala's guards gaped in disbelief at their gravely wounded king. Kalaniʻōpuʻu's warriors stood by as if they were no more than shocked bystanders at a terrible event.

"Kill them," Keaweʻōpala moaned again. "Kill them." He fought desperately to remain on his knees. He could no longer hold his head up and he was mumbling into his own chest.

The leader of Kalaniʻōpuʻu's small warrior band locked eyes with his counterpart among Keaweʻōpala's guards over their chieftain's bowed head. Then, before any of Keaweʻōpala's people could react, he grabbed a war club from one of his comrades and swung it at Keawe'ōpala's skull. It was a mortal blow. Keawe'ōpala sighed once and toppled over.

The opposing warrior bands faced each other in silence. No one moved. Then, almost in unison, Keawe'ōpala's guards dropped their weapons, fell to their knees, and commenced wailing. With their mō'ī dead, their cause was lost. For Keawe'ōpala himself was their cause, and now they had no one and nothing left to fight for. Kalani'ōpu'u's young warriors made no move to harm them. They did not cheer or gloat. Instead, they stood by quietly.

It was upon this tableau of death, sorrow, and subdued satisfaction that Kalani'ōpu'u's party and the forces led by Ke'eaumoku converged some time later, drawn from various quarters of the battlefield by the loud keening of Keawe'ōpala's people. Kekūhaupi'o, who arrived soon afterwards, set off almost immediately in search of Maile.

All the fighting ceased with Keawe'ōpala's death. Kalani'ōpu'u took Keawe'ōpala's body back to Hōnaunau and ordered his corpse baked with Ka'akau's in a special imu. He sacrificed their charred flesh on the altar of Kūkā'ilimoku. Holo'ae presided at this ceremony, and father said that he "took great pleasure in it." Afterward, Kalani'ōpu'u ordered Ka'akau's remains thrown into the sea. He ordered Keawe'ōpala's flesh stripped from his long bones and likewise discarded. He kept the bones for himself. "He had them carved into fish hooks and other trinkets which he distributed to the chiefs, and to Kiwala'o, Kamehameha, and me," my father said.

Kalani'ōpu'u claimed that by acquiring Keawe'ōpala's relics, one would also appropriate the slain man's mana. Kamehameha was dubious as to its value, however. "Keawe'ōpala was so easily defeated that his mana cannot be very strong," he said.

Kekūhaupi'o did not return to Hōnaunau until well after dusk that day. When Kamehameha and my father asked him where he had gone, he replied simply, “I went to settle a debt for Nae‘ole’s spirit.” Maile was never seen again.

That night, there was a great feast. There was much dancing and chanting. In the midst of this celebration, Ke‘eaumoku turned to Kalani‘ōpu‘u and asked, “What shall be done with Keawe‘ōpala’s people?”

The new mō‘ī of the Big Island looked at him with some puzzlement and then replied, “Why, nothing, of course. They are all *my* people now.”

Pauoa, O'ahu 1858

In the night I have a disturbing dream. In my dream, I am alone in a traditional hale of pili-grass construction. It is nighttime and a single kukui-oil lamp lights the hale. A gust of wind blows open the hale's door, extinguishes the lamp's flame, and plunges me into total darkness. I cannot see my own hand in front of my face, nor can I hear anything, not even when I snap my fingers. I feel panicky. Wakefulness rescues me from this nightmare, and I sit up in bed and take quick stock of my surroundings. I am cocooned in the vague shadows of a moonless night. Esther slumbers peacefully next to me. Her soft breathing calms me and I lie back once more. I fall asleep wondering if my dream is a presentiment of my own death or of something more.

I have been unwell and I have not touched my manuscript for several weeks. As always when I am indisposed, Esther is especially attentive to me. She has canceled her social engagements in town without complaint to stay home and care for me.

At times like this, when I feel poorly and am reluctant to rise from our bed in the morning, Esther brings me my breakfast. She plies me with hot tea and with juice which our servants have squeezed from the guavas and passion fruit they collect each morning from our trees. She brings me a tray with cut-up bananas—again from our own trees—soft-boiled eggs, from our own hens of course, and store-bought biscuits if I can bear them, or some porridge or broth if I cannot. I could not ask for a more loving partner in my old age.

Esther Kapi'olani and I have been married for six years. She was just eighteen when we wed, and I was already an old man of sixty-one. Among our people, so many of whom have died prematurely of haole diseases, I am very fortunate to have lived as long as I have. In 1848 and 1849, successive epidemics of measles, mumps, whooping cough, and influenza—illnesses generally not fatal among haoles—took the lives of ten thousand people, and perhaps more. Thousands more died of smallpox in 1852 and 1853.

The haoles estimate that when Captain Cook first came upon our islands in 1778, the entire archipelago's population numbered some four hundred thousand souls. Though I cannot prove it, I believe there were more than that. Today, according to the government's last census, we number fewer than one hundred thousand.

Esther and I still entertain hopes of retarding this decline, at least in our own household. To date, unfortunately, we have tried without success, although certainly not without pleasure. My young wife is most pleasant to look upon. Her face is open, her eyes bright, her lips beckoning, and her shoulders elegant. And when Esther comes to me in her shift, as she has this morning, her bosom on glorious display, I yearn to reach out to her. But this day I do not. I hope Esther is not disappointed with me. It would not surprise me if she has taken a lover in town, but she never fails to return to me by evening and I am grateful to her.

This morning, Esther radiates warmth as she sits beside me in bed and shares breakfast with me. I cannot imagine now how I once took it on faith that women must neither prepare food for men nor eat with us. In some things, haole ways are preferable.

Are you feeling better today, husband? Esther asks me as she softly strokes my arm.

Yes, I say.

Esther tells me she has been reading my manuscript. *It is wonderful,* she says. *Promise me you will finish it.*

I promise, I say. Eventually I rouse myself from our bed, throw on a robe, and return to my desk on the lanai to commence writing once more.

Kalani'ōpu'u

E hume i ka malo, e ho'okala i ka ihe

Gird the loincloth, sharpen the spear

Kawaihae and Hana, Maui 1766-1768

After the defeat of Keawe'ōpala, Kalani'ōpu'u moved his court north to Kawaihae and consolidated his hold over the Big Island. Keawe'ōpala's own people had mostly sworn obeisance and Kalani'ōpu'u rewarded their submission by dividing the island equitably among his own followers and the former adherents of the fallen mō'ī alike. Keawe'ōpala's lieutenants were grateful to Kalani'ōpu'u for this generous treatment. To those of his people who voiced dissatisfaction with this arrangement, Kalani'ōpu'u said, "We are all kinsmen here, and we must share our island as kinsmen." Given the tangle of interrelationships among Hawai'i's noble families, this was the truth. The dissidents still grumbled among themselves, but they assented nevertheless. And thus, the island's peace was secured for the time being.

Kamehameha and my father remained with Kalani'ōpu'u at his court at Kawaihae for some months. Life was pleasant there. They continued their rigorous military training with Kekūhaupi'o and Mulihele, but they also had ample time for surf riding, swimming, and other sports. There were feasts nearly every night, followed by dancing, singing, and storytelling. And of course, there were wāhine—many wāhine. Kamehameha continued his amorous liaisons with Kaneikapolei. But he also found time to sport with other women.

During this period at Kawaihae, Kiwala'ō and Kamehameha often faced each other as opposing "generals" in mock battles. Though these were sham fights, they were rough and tumble. Opponents hurled blunted spears at each other with real force. Serious injury was always a risk for warriors who failed to dodge or catch these weapons, and sometimes they died of their wounds. The battles were not open-ended. They would conclude at fixed times, such as the moment when the orange rim of Kāne's setting sun first touched the ocean's horizon. Each side commenced these frays with an equal number of men. The side with the most able-bodied combatants at a fight's end was declared the winner. In addition to providing a means for warriors to sharpen their fighting skills during intervals between actual warfare, the mock battles helped identify the most skilled fighters. These men would advance to positions of leadership within a chief's forces when real fighting commenced.

Kamehameha and Kiwala'ō took care not to confront each other directly during these martial contests. Both understood that Kalani'ōpu'u would be most unhappy if either of them harmed the other. The two cousins were fiercely competitive nonetheless. They would both range the mock battlefield, exhorting their warriors to ever-greater efforts, intervening in the fighting here and there to turn the advantage to their respective sides. And though they avoided throwing spears at each other, they often hurled taunts.

"Your people are fighting like old men," Kiwala'ō shouted across the field at Kameha one afternoon.

"The way my people are fighting, they will more likely live to be old men than yours," Kamehameha shouted back.

"Your people will live to be old men because they run away," Kiwala'ō answered, throwing a spear at the nearest opposing warrior, who dodged it handily.

"My people will live to be old men because they do not stand in front of your spears like breadfruit trees," Kameha replied.

With both sides evenly matched at the outset, Kamehameha's and Kiwala'ō's respective teams lost as often as they won. And it was through these mock clashes that Kamehameha came to a grudging respect for his cousin. "Kiwala'ō is courageous," he told my father. "I would not worry about fighting at his side."

While Kamehameha and Kiwala'ō waged sham battles, Kalani'ōpu'u prepared for real warfare. Undisputed rule of the Big Island was not enough for him. Almost as soon as he had dispatched Keawe'ōpala, he set his sights on Maui. He ordered his lieutenant, Puna, to muster thousands of warriors in northern Kohala and assemble a fleet of war canoes to carry them across the ʻAlenuihāhā Channel. "We will descend upon Maui like a powerful storm, Puna," Kalaniʻōpuʻu exulted. "And no one will be able to stop us!"

There was one who tried to stop Kalaniʻōpuʻu: his senior wife, Kalola, the full sister of Maui's reigning king, Kamehamehaʻnui, and his younger brother, Kahekili. "Why do you go to make war on my own brothers, your own son's uncles?" she demanded. Kalaniʻōpuʻu, who was taking his ease in his hale, where he was sheltering from the muggy, mid-afternoon heat of the Kohala Coast, frowned at his wife, who knelt before him. "Why can't rule of Hawaiʻi be sufficient for you, Kalani?" Kalola pleaded, crying now. Her tears were to no avail.

Glowering at Kalola now, Kalaniʻōpuʻu retorted, "It is my decision, and it is not your place to question it!"

Kalola rose from the floor, sobbing. "I will not go with you to Maui to make war on my own brothers," she cried. "And you will not take Kiwalaʻō there to make war on his own uncles."

"Come with me or not, it is your choice," Kalaniʻōpuʻu replied with an indifferent shrug. "As for Kiwalaʻō, he is not ready for serious battle. He will stay here, with you."

So Kiwalaʻō remained behind, as did Kamehameha and my father. "Kalaniʻōpuʻu could not very well take Kameha to war with him if he was not taking his own son," my father explained. "And of course, if my older brother could not go, then neither could I."

Kalaniʻōpuʻu resolved matters by elevating Kamehameha and Kiwalaʻō to chiefly status, bedecking them with magnificent feather robes—*'ahu'ula*—and imposing feathered helmets. He presented them with these treasured items during a ceremony at Kawaihae, and invested Kiwalaʻō and Kamehameha as the high chiefs of the Kaʻū and Kohala districts, respectively. These land dispositions reaffirmed the paternal legacies of both young men, since Kaʻū had long been Kalaniʻōpuʻu's fiefdom, while Kameha's father, Keoua, had been the high chief of Kohala. Kalaniʻōpuʻu dispatched

Kamehameha and Kiwala'ō to administer their own districts during his absence at Maui.

Kalani'ōpu'u's first foray against Maui yielded an easy conquest. Landing at Hana in eastern Maui, he met little opposition. He occupied Hana and the neighboring Kipahulu District and took possession of a fort on Kauwiki Hill, a supremely strong defensive position overlooking the harbor. Kalani'ōpu'u installed Puna as governor of the two districts, and once he was satisfied that everything was in order administratively, returned to Hawai'i.

Kalani'ōpu'u had caught Kamehameha'nui napping, but the king of Maui did not slumber for long. Gathering warriors from throughout his own island and the nearby islands of Moloka'i and Lanai, he launched a furious assault on the Hawai'ians. After several battles in which Kamehameha'nui's forces triumphed, Puna withdrew his surviving warriors to the fort at Kauwiki, where they resisted all further attempts to dislodge them. Weary of bloodshed and tired of the prolonged siege, Kamehameha'nui finally broke it off, leaving the Hawai'ians to their own devices in Hana. "Let Kalani'ōpu'u have this little bite," he is said to have told his lieutenants. "No matter how hard he tries, he cannot swallow the rest of our island."

While Puna fought with Kamehameha'nui for control of Hana and East Maui, Kalani'ōpu'u faced a struggle of his own at home. Ke'eaumoku, evidently dissatisfied with his own lot once again, revolted. Many years later, no one could really explain why the mercurial Ke'eaumoku had gone to war against his mō'ī. "Kalani'ōpu'u had treated him fairly when he redistributed the Big Island's land after Keawe'ōpala's death," my father said. "He gave Ke'eaumoku and his brothers all they had wanted, and more." Indeed, Kalani'ōpu'u had extended their holdings well northward along the Kona Coast toward Kohala, an enlargement that encompassed several valuable fishponds. Ke'eaumoku's half-brothers, Kame'iamoku and Kamanawa, were content enough with this arrangement. "Perhaps Ke'eaumoku did not want to share with them," my father speculated.

Crossing over Mt. Kohala, Ke'eaumoku and his people occupied some land overlooking the sea between Pololū and Honokāne. Throwing up a makeshift fort of tree branches at the top of a cliff, Ke'eaumoku claimed this place and the surrounding countryside on the island's rainy side for himself.

If an easy life on Hawai'i's northeastern coast, where almost anything will grow, was Ke'eaumoku's hope, he was destined to be disappointed. Knowing that his continued hold on the Big Island depended on his subjects' conviction that he would brook no opposition, Kalani'ōpu'u moved swiftly against the rebellious chief. Collecting a force of several thousand warriors, he followed Ke'eaumoku over the mountains, put his foe's hastily built fort to the torch, and defeated the rebels after a fierce fight. Kalani'ōpu'u surely would have killed Ke'eaumoku then if he could have, but his quarry escaped.

Leaving nothing to chance, Ke'eaumoku had directed his people to make a rope long enough and strong enough to lower him from the top of the cliff to the sea below. When it was clear that the battle was irretrievably lost, Ke'eaumoku tied one end of the rope around his waist and ordered several men to lower him to the small, sandy cove at the base of the pali. One of his men had earlier beached a small sail canoe there.

Well concealed by the pall of smoke that now covered the hill, Ke'eaumoku's escape went undetected by Kalani'ōpu'u's warriors. His own eyes stinging from the smoke, Kalani'ōpu'u reached the edge of the cliff just in time to see his enemy putting to sea.

Ke'eaumoku fled to Maui, where he was given refuge by Kamehameha'nui, who welcomed him as a fellow enemy of Kalani'ōpu'u. Soon after his arrival, Ke'eaumoku was strongly attracted to one of the Maui king's wives, Nāmāhana. The attraction was mutual, and after Kamehameha'nui became ill and died later that same year, she and Ke'eaumoku "married." Their union sorely displeased Kamehameha'nui's younger brother and successor Kahekili, who wanted his own half-sister Nāmāhana as an accessory to the throne he had just inherited.

Oblivious to Kahekili's displeasure, Ke'eaumoku and his new bride established their own court at Waihee, amid Nāmāhana's landholdings on Maui's northeast coast. The country there was well watered, the soil was rich and productive, and the fishponds well-stocked. Ke'eaumoku and Nāmāhana lived lavishly at Waihee and shared their bounty with many visitors. Kahekili, who meanwhile had set up his own court at nearby Wailuku, tolerated them.

Ke'eaumoku and Kahekili eventually had a bloody falling out. After several days of brutal fighting, Kahekili's warriors expelled Ke'eaumoku and his people, who fled to Ka'anapali on Maui's west coast, and then to the smaller neighboring island of Moloka'i. Once more, Kahekili pursued them. Ke'eaumoku escaped again, and this time he and Nāmāhana fled to Hana, where they were welcomed and given refuge by the new governor, Mahihelelima, who had recently replaced Puna in that post.

"Mahihelelima did not bother to consult with Kalani'ōpu'u about this," my father told me. "If he had, Kalani'ōpu'u surely would have ordered him to send Ke'eaumoku away." But by the time Kalani'ōpu'u learned that Ke'eaumoku and Nāmāhana were sheltering at the fort on Kauwiki Hill, his anger at his sometime ally and sometime adversary had cooled and he decided to let the matter go.

It was at Kauwiki, in the year of 1768 by haole reckoning, that Nāmāhana bore Ke'eaumoku a daughter. They named the baby Ka'ahumanu.

Kaupō, Maui 1775

Ambitious to expand his holdings on Maui, still angered by the defeat that Kamehameha'nui had inflicted on Puna some nine years earlier, and thwarted from moving northward from Hana by Kahekili's forces, Kalani'ōpu'u attacked Kaupō, southwest of Hana. Having first demanded that the Kaupō's chiefs swear loyalty to him—a demand they rejected—he landed at Kalaeokilio Point and led his forces in a bloody rampage through the defenseless district. Pillaging as they went, Kalani'ōpu'u's warriors razed whole villages, destroyed taro patches, clubbed simple farmers and fishermen to death, and ravished their women.

Kahekili had continued his late brother's policy of tolerating the presence of Kalani'ōpu'u's people at Hana. As long as they kept to themselves, the new king of Maui was content to leave them unmolested. He had not even bothered to pursue Ke'eaumoku when he finally took refuge there. But news of Kalani'ōpu'u's depredations in Kaupō roused him. Mustering thousands of warriors along the length of the Maui coast from Wailuku to Wailua, he sent them south under his leading general, Kāne'olaelae, with orders to expel the intruders from Kaupō, and, if possible, drive them from his island once and for all. As they entered Kaupō, even the most hardened of Kahekili's men were shocked at the devastation wreaked by Kalani'ōpu'u's people, and they fell upon the marauders lusting for their blood. Kamehameha and Kekūhaupi'o nearly paid for Kalani'ōpu'u's wanton pillaging with their own lives.

Kalaniʻōpuʻu had summoned Kameha and his kahu Kekūhaupiʻo from Hawaiʻi to join him in Hana for the assault. My father came as well. Kalaniʻōpuʻu's own son Kiwalaʻō had remained behind, still forbidden by Kalola from taking part in any assault on the people of her beloved home island of Maui.

Kamehameha did not approve of his uncle's plans to invade Kaupō. "Uncle, the people of Kaupō have done nothing to offend you. Why do you make war on them?" Kameha asked Kalaniʻōpuʻu one night, soon after he had arrived in Hana.

Kamehameha and Kekūhaupiʻo were sitting with the mōʻī of the Big Island in the courtyard of his hale on Kauwiki Hill. Kalaniʻōpuʻu was angered by his nephew's challenge.

"They have refused me allegiance," Kalaniʻōpuʻu replied sharply, "and that is offense enough!"

Kameha ignored his uncle's irritation and pressed on. "But Uncle, they have not provoked you. The god Kūkāʻilimoku may not help you in this fight. He may see it as unworthy."

At this, Kalaniʻōpuʻu jumped to his feet and loomed over Kamehameha, who remained motionless, cross-legged, and concentrating intently now on his own lap. "Do not question my judgment," he shouted. "I am your mōʻī. I will go where I will. And you shall go with me if I so command it, and command it I do!"

"Kameha was deeply embarrassed," my father recounted. "He had thought that our uncle's affection for him was such that he could freely share his doubts with him. But now he understood that he had presumed too much. He never challenged Kalaniʻōpuʻu to his face again. And of course, he went on that raid to Kaupō."

My father did not accompany him, however. "You will stay here at Kauwiki," Kameha told him. "Our uncle will not miss you. The god Kūkāʻilimoku will not bless this raid, and there is no point in bringing his terrible wrath down upon both of us."

The god's wrath nearly fell upon Kekūhaupi'o amid a tangle of sweet potato vines in a sloping field above Kalaeokilio, where Kalani'ōpu'u's war fleet was drawn up on a wide, black-sand beach in the lee of the point.

Like Kalani'ōpu'u, Kāne'olaelae came by sea. He landed his forces unseen at Kamanawa Bay, just to the east of Kalaeokilio Point. Deploying his warriors from Waipu cliff on the west to Pahonu on the east, Kāne'olaelae led them uphill through the sweet potato vines towards Kalani'ōpu'u's forces. They affixed sweet potato leaves in their hair and moved slowly and stealthily, advancing in a low crouch, using the potato plants for cover. They held their war clubs low to the ground and trailed their spears behind them. Their bobbing, leaf-cloaked heads barely topped the vines. To observers mauka, the line of oncoming warriors seemed nothing more than a wave among the leaves, rolling slowly uphill toward them before the prevailing onshore wind. "We didn't see them until they were upon us," Kamehameha told my father afterwards.

The soft rippling among the leaves was replaced by a howling surge of human flesh as Kāne'olaelae's people suddenly rose out of the sweet potato field, screaming and brandishing their weapons. Thinking they were under attack by the field's guardian spirits, Kalani'ōpu'u's warriors turned and fled uphill. Kāne'olaelae's men gave chase and cut the Hawai'ians down as they ran, impaling them with spears and felling them with their war clubs. The battle soon devolved into a chaotic melee as attackers closed and intermingled with defenders in hand-to-hand combat. No match for the furious warriors of Maui, Kalani'ōpu'u's men died in great numbers. Those who were not killed outright were dragged wounded and bleeding from the battlefield by their assailants, for later sacrifice to Kahekili's war god.

Amid the carnage, the confusion of battle became Kalani'ōpu'u's ally. Dodging spears and eluding several oncoming foes, he ran down the slope into the sweet potato field, whirled about, and called out to his surviving warriors, "On me, men of Hawai'i!" Fall back to the canoes!" The Hawai'ians need no encouragement. Abruptly breaking off contact with Kāne'olaelae's men, they ran pell-mell down the hill with their would-be assailants in hot pursuit. Kekūhaupi'o and Kamehameha had become separated in the fierce fighting and were among the last to withdraw. Keeping their faces to their foes, they backed slowly downhill through the sweet potato vines.

Though this was Kamehameha's first taste of real battle, it felt familiar to him. Attackers hurled spears at him from all sides, just as his opponents had in so many mock fights before. And as he had so many other times, he dodged their missiles, or knocked them down and picked them up and hurled them back with brutal force. Whenever they found their targets, they struck with lethal effect.

Realizing that they were doing little more than re-arming Kamehameha at their own painful expense, the warriors of Maui ceased throwing spears at him. Now, brandishing their weapons while being careful to keep out of his range, they began to encircle him. Still facing his assailants, and menacing them with his one remaining spear, he retreated deeper into the sweet-potato field, but more swiftly now, high-stepping to clear the vines. The Maui warriors rushed forward, trying to stay out of spear range yet still moving fast enough to get behind him. But as the men on the flanks rushed to close the circle, they tripped and stumbled in the vines. Kamehameha continued to outdistance them.

Now, out of the corner of his eye, Kameha saw a commotion to his left. Kekūhaupiʻo, who had been retreating before another band of Maui men, had himself become entangled in the vines and was down on one knee, struggling to regain his footing. Several enemy warriors were closing on him. Abruptly, Kamehameha changed direction and raced across the hillside toward his kahu. His sudden move caught the nearest of his foes off guard and he easily eluded them. One of Kekūhaupiʻo's assailants saw Kameha approaching, and turning toward him, he raised his war club. Kamehameha leaped into the air, and with all the compounded force of his momentum and his own strength, hurled his spear at the man. The spear struck the Maui warrior in his chest, piercing him through and propelling him backwards into the potato plants. Kameha never broke stride. The mortally wounded man had barely struck the ground when Kamehameha ripped the war club from his still-outstretched hand and rushed at the other enemy warriors, laying about in all directions as he hurtled forward. The air was rent with the terrible sound of cracking skulls and the shrill cries of dying men as Kameha's blows struck home. Kekūhaupiʻo, meanwhile, had regained his feet. Now, as his erstwhile attackers backed away before Kamehameha's furious assault, Kekūhaupiʻo struck them from the rear, spearing one man, gutting a second with his dagger, and breaking the neck of a third with his hands. In short order, moaning men writhing in their own blood surrounded Kamehameha and his kahu.

The other warriors who had been pursuing Kameha pulled up short, frozen by this grisly spectacle. They gaped at the gore-splattered forms of Kamehameha and Kekūhaupiʻo. Kameha was in a crouch, his war club still buried in the skull of a fallen foe.

"Aieee!" one of the Maui men cried, gesturing at Kamehameha. "Look out for that one. He is as tough as a *paiʻea*!" It was the first time anyone had called him "paiʻea"—a hard-shelled crab—since his earliest years in Waipiʻo.

In response, Kameha rose to his full height, waved the bloody club over his head, and howled at the enemy warriors. His shout carried down the hillside to the rear-most ranks of Kalaniʻōpuʻu's retreating fighters. A dozen Hawaiʻi men turned and ran toward Kamehameha. At once, the men of Maui spun away and fled. Kamehameha reached down to retrieve a discarded spear and threw it at one of the fleeing warriors. But he was spent now; there was little force in his throw and the missile fell harmlessly to earth. He clenched his fist in frustration.

Kekūhaupiʻo clasped Kameha's arm. "It is enough," he said. "You have proven yourself to be a true warrior today, and you have saved my life, Kameha." Kamehameha nodded to Kekūhaupiʻo but said nothing. Then, stepping over the dead and the dying warriors who lay all about them, he and Kekūhaupiʻo walked slowly down the hill toward their comrades and the waiting canoes. As he walked, Kamehameha's thoughts turned to the men he had just killed and his stomach began to churn; bile rose into his throat and he battled a sudden urge to vomit. Kekūhaupiʻo sensed his distress. Lightly brushing Kamehameha's hand, he said, "It is the way of all of us to be troubled the first time, Kameha. Do not worry, it *will* get easier."

Later, after Kamehameha had returned to the fort at Kauwiki, my father asked him what it was like to kill a man. "It was much better than being killed myself, brother," Kameha replied. My father pressed him for more details of the fight, but Kamehameha only shook his head, scowled at my father, and turned away.

It was mid-afternoon when Kalaniʻōpuʻu and his surviving warriors put to sea from Kalaeokilio Point. The sun had set by the time they reached Hana Bay, some twelve miles distant. Propelled by fear for their own lives, they paddled without let-up against unfavorable winds through the gathering dusk.

Upon reaching Hana Bay, Kamehameha picked his way in the dark up the steep, uneven path that wound through thick foliage from the beach to the fort atop Kauwiki Hill. There he collapsed onto a mat in Kalaniʻōpuʻu's hale and fell into a deep sleep. When he awoke early the next morning, he realized that his body was still caked with dried blood from the killing of the day before. Taking a flat lava stone, Kameha descended the narrow path to the beach, where the village fishermen were already preparing their nets in the pale, pre-dawn light. Ignoring these commoners, Kamehameha untied his malo, let it fall to the sand, and waded into the surf. As he scrubbed the blood from his chest, arms, and legs with the rough stone, it etched small scratches in his skin that stung in the salt water.

Keeping his face to the sea as he bathed, Kamehameha watched the progress of Kāne's sun as it breached Kanaloa's waters and ascended into Lono's sky. He thought about the warriors he had slain the previous day, men who would never see another sunrise. Then, as quickly as this thought had come to him, he banished it from his mind. He was young. Kalaniʻōpuʻu was bent on war. Kameha had no doubt that he would deprive many more foes of future sunrises in the service of his mōʻī. And as he alluded to my father later the same day, he could ill afford sentimentality about such things. Kamehameha sighed and turned back to shore.

As Kameha emerged from the water, he saw a young girl, no more than eight or nine years old, sitting cross-legged on the sand. She was staring brazenly at his dripping loins. As natural as public nudity was for our people in those days, this child's gaze suggested knowledge beyond her years and bordered on impudence. Kameha halted abruptly and stared back at her. "You!" he shouted, reflexively shielding his manhood with both hands. "What are you looking at?"

At this, the girl giggled, and grabbing Kamehameha's discarded malo, leaped to her feet and fled. "You! Girl! Bring that back!" Kameha shouted at her. She paid him no mind and despite his anger, and as she disappeared into the heavy undergrowth at the base of Kauwiki Hill, Kamehameha could not help admiring her lissome form, already presaging the young woman she would become. Irritated and bemused, he trudged after her, not caring now who might see him.

When he reached Kalaniʻōpuʻu's hale, Kamehameha was greeted by raucous laughter. He found his uncle seated in the courtyard with Puna, Kekūhaupiʻo, Keʻeaumoku, and Mahihelelima. Kalaniʻōpuʻu pointed at Kameha and hooted. "That one, she will have that one!" He continued to point and guffaw until Kamehameha realized that his uncle, the mōʻī all Hawaiʻi, was gesturing at his own exposed penis. Again, without thinking, he covered himself. This led to a further explosion of hilarity by Kalaniʻōpuʻu and his companions.

"Kameha, you were wrong to tempt my *keiki ponoʻi* so," said Keʻeaumoku, who tried to maintain a stern countenance as he spoke. But he could not suppress his amusement and began to cackle even as the last syllable escaped his lips. This prompted still more boisterous laughter from the entire group.

Kalaniʻōpuʻu picked up something from his mat and tossed it at his nephew. It was Kameha's stolen malo. "You should not expose yourself thus to impressionable young women," he snapped. More laughter erupted.

"It transpired that the keiki pono'i who had run off with my brother's malo was Ke'eaumoku's own daughter, Ka'ahumanu," my father told me. "She ran straight to her parents with it, told them what she had seen and declared, 'I will have that big *kāne* one day.' Kameha was mortified when he learned this."

Kalani'ōpu'u sought to soothe him. "'That one, that one,'" he sighed. "Well, I suppose it could not be helped. She is an impertinent child. You really must do something about her, Ke'eaumoku." Now the mō'ī of the Big Island smiled benevolently at Kamehameha. "Come sit, nephew," he said, "and join us for breakfast."

Ke'eaumoku patted an empty place on his mat, and Kamehameha sat beside him. The older man gave him a mock-serious look and jabbed him lightly in the ribs and laughed again, as did the others. This time, Kameha laughed with them.

In hopes of reinstating himself in Kalani'ōpu'u's good graces, Ke'eaumoku had volunteered to join the ill-fated expedition to Kaupō. Kalani'ōpu'u had accepted his offer. But perhaps because he still did not trust Ke'eaumoku sufficiently to risk having him by his side in battle, Kalani'ōpu'u had ordered him to remain at Kalaeokilio Point to guard the fleet. Now in the afterglow of their shared laughter, Kalani'ōpu'u turned to him and said, "Brother, let us put aside the unpleasantness of Pololū and be forever reconciled."

"Brother," Ke'eaumoku replied tearfully, "there is nothing I want more."

With this, the two men jumped to their feet and fell into each other's arms, wailing with joy.

Some days after that, Kalani'ōpu'u returned to Hawai'i, and my father, Kekūhaupi'o, and Kamehameha returned with him. Ke'eaumoku, his wife, Nāmāhana, and their daughter, Ka'ahumanu, also made the journey back across the 'Alenuihāhā Channel to the Big Island, settling in Honokua, below Hōnaunau in South Kona, where Kalaniʻōpuʻu installed Keʻeaumoku as chief.

Within days after Kalaniʻōpuʻu's return, the story of Kamehameha's bravery at Kaupō spread rapidly throughout the Big Island, as did the terrified Maui warrior's comparison of the embattled Kameha to a paiʻea. This time, among Kamehameha's aliʻi peers, and especially among his intimates, the name adhered.

Ka'awaloa, 1775

"Nephew," Kalani'ōpu'u said, "it is past time for you to take a wife." Kamehameha and his uncle were seated on mats in the courtyard of Kalani'ōpu'u's hale at Ka'awaloa, on the north side of Kealakekua Bay. The mō'ī of Hawai'i had relocated his court there after returning from Maui.

Despite his setbacks on Maui, Kalani'ōpu'u had not abandoned his territorial ambitions. His people still held the fort at Kauwiki Hill, and he was determined to expand his holdings beyond Hana. He would invade Maui again, with more canoes and more warriors than before. But this time, he would attack Kahekili directly. He was done with half measures. When he returned to Maui, he would go to conquer. While he made ready for renewed warfare, Kalani'ōpu'u also sought to resolve some family matters. Chief among his domestic concerns were marriage arrangements for his son, Kiwala'ō, and his nephew, Kamehameha.

"You would do well to marry Pele'uli," Kalani'ōpu'u advised Kameha. "She is a good match for you; her consanguinity with you is very strong." Pele'uli's great-grandmother on her father's side was also Kamehameha's great-grandmother twice over, being the grandmother of each of his parents. "Royal blood will run pure in your children," Kalani'ōpu'u continued enthusiastically. Kamehameha accepted his uncle's logic and readily assented to the match. But of course, physical attraction had played no small part in his own decision.

Pele'uli was then eighteen, about nine years younger than Kamehameha. She had burst into full womanhood several years earlier. Her belly, as yet untouched by motherhood, was a tight, eye-pleasing fulcrum between her inviting hips and her swelling breasts. Kameha and my father had both noticed her for the first time as she danced a hula with other women after one of Kalani'ōpu'u's nightly feasts. "She was a great beauty back then," my father recalled. "I would have liked to have had her for myself." But in this, as in so many other matters in his life, my father's elder brother Kameha came first.

As solicitous as he was of the lineage of Kamehameha's future children, Kalani'ōpu'u was even more attentive to the dynastic interests of his own son, Kiwala'ō. "You should take Keku'iapoiwa Liliha as your wife," he counseled. "Lili," as she was called, was the half-sister of both Kiwala'ō and Kamehameha—the child of a union between Kiwala'ō's mother, Kalola, and Kamehameha's father, Keoua.

While Kamehameha and his new bride Pele'uli could trace their common ancestry back to one of Keawe the Great's wives, Kiwala'ō and Lili could trace theirs back to Keawe himself, through Kalani'ōpu'u's and Keoua's fathers. Because of this, and because they themselves were siblings, royal blood would run even purer in the veins of their children than in Kameha's and Pele'uli's. As Kalani'ōpu'u summed up for his son, "Any male child that Lili bears for you would have the most sacred of kapus, and the strongest claim to the throne of our island."

The superior pedigrees of his and Lili's future children were not foremost on Kiwala'ō's mind when he agreed to partner with her. He was thinking of Lili's nubile body. The pesky child who had so annoyed him at Ka'ū had matured into a willowy young woman. She was about the same age as Pele'uli, with flashing eyes, a radiant smile, and swaying hips under a flaring *pa'u*—woman's skirt—that dared exploration.

"That little wahine's passion fruit will be sweet," Kiwala'ō told my father.

Kamehameha was equally unconcerned about issues of lineage. "Pele'uli will be a good wife," he said to my father. "But I will also have other wāhine, and by them, other children. Who knows what their kapus will be?"

Unions of royal consequence were often occasions for elaborate public ceremonies and even more elaborate feasts. The double unions of Kamehameha and his cousin Kiwala'ō were marked by a feast so sumptuous that it would be fondly remembered many years later.

"Kalaniʻōpuʻu ordered villages throughout the Kaʻū, Kona, and Kohala districts to send pigs for the feast," my father recalled. "They were baked in two score or more imus. There were heaps of roasted yams and bananas, fish of all kinds, and, of course, endless servings of poi. Aliʻi came from all over the Big Island."

Kalaniʻōpuʻu summoned all the chiefs to his hale and proclaimed the unions, garlanding the young couples with flower leis as they knelt before him. Amid much cheering and laughter, the men and women then departed to their respective feasts. The men's feast lasted deep into the night. Kalaniʻōpuʻu sat between his son and his nephew. "You, Kiwalaʻō and Kamehameha, are now brothers," he said, throwing his arms over the two young men's shoulders. "For your own sister, Kameha, is now Kiwalaʻō's wahine. But he is also your own sister's brother. You are both *kaikunāne ponoʻī* to Kekuʻiapoiwa Liliha." Blood brothers. "And therefore…therefore…" Kalaniʻōpuʻu's voice trailed off as his train of thought, muzzy with ʻawa, momentarily lost its way in the tangled web of blood ties. Kameha and Kiwalaʻō waited respectfully for him to finish. "Therefore," Kalaniʻōpuʻu finally concluded, "because you are both Lili's true brothers, you must love each other as brothers."

Kamehameha and Kiwalaʻō both smiled indulgently at Kalaniʻōpuʻu, but neither said anything in response. "You must love each other," Kalaniʻōpuʻu said again, with a note of pleading in his voice. "Come now," he urged. "Rise and embrace as true brothers."

Kameha and Kiwalaʻō clambered to their feet and embraced awkwardly over their mōʻī's head. Swiveling from side to side, Kalaniʻōpuʻu beamed broadly at them as they sat down again. "Good, good," he said. "It is good." Soon after this, his eyes fluttered shut, his head tilted forward and his chin fell against his chest. He dozed where he sat. No one disturbed him.

Keōua Kūʻahuʻula and Keōuapeʻeʻale, Kalaniʻōpuʻu's sons by Kaneikapolei, were among the revelers this night. At fourteen and thirteen years old, they were on the cusp of manhood. Pauli, who was then about ten, was there, too, seated near his half-brothers.

Keōua Kūʻahuʻula, whose name meant Keōua Red Cloak, looked upon his cousin Kamehameha with considerable awe. He had heard the stories of Kameha's bravery and prowess at Kaupō, and on this night, Keōua Kū'ahu'ula sought to impress him. But lacking true experience in battle and still a neophyte in mock combat, he had little to offer besides bravado.

"Pai'ea," he loudly declared, "I will go to Maui with my father when he next returns there, and like you, I will slay many Maui warriors."

There was a lull in the many overlapping conversations as the revelers' attention was drawn by this outburst from an untested youth. All eyes turned toward Kamehameha to see how he would respond. Kameha's own eyes narrowed and his countenance, which moments before had been lively with uncharacteristic merriment, became stern. Since Kaupō, no one except warriors blooded in the same battle, his closest friends, and the chiefs of the Big Island had called him Pai'ea, and he was offended by Keōua Kū'ahu'ula's presumption.

"Well, little cousin," Kamehameha replied, his voice full of disdain, "I look forward to hearing the stories of your own bravery when your war club is finally the same color as your red cloak."

At this, the gathering exploded in raucous laughter. "Yes, Red Cloak, come back and tell us when your own name matches your true deeds," someone cried.

"Meanwhile, go find a wahine and show her your other club," another man jibed. "Maybe she will be impressed."

Mortified and blushing, Keōua Kū'ahu'ula scrambled to his feet and fled the feast, with Keōuape'e'ale and Pauli trailing in his wake.

Kamehameha returned to Kohala with his new wife and new resolve. Among his contemporaries, Kamehameha had always been known as the solemn one. He was invariably the last in a group to laugh at a joke, the slowest to smile. Now he laughed even more rarely and his broad features seemed set in a state of permanent gravity. Formerly, he had devoted his days to recreational pursuits such as surf riding and holua sledding; now he tended diligently to the most mundane matters of local governance. He oversaw the construction of fishponds, supervised the building of canoes, looked after taro cultivation, and encouraged production of kapa cloth. He consulted regularly with his astrologer to determine what days would be best for planting, fishing, and other activities. He held court almost daily to settle disputes among the people of his district.

Kameha also attended conscientiously to his young wife, Pele'uli. She would eventually give him four children, one of whom died in infancy. The surviving children, two boys and a girl, would make no impression on the momentous events of the years ahead.

As busy as he was with his domestic responsibilities, Kamehameha never failed to join Kekūhaupi'o, my father, and Mulihele for daily combat training. They practiced with spears, daggers, and slings. They honed their lua wrestling skills. They ran foot races on coastal benches of uneven pahoehoe lava to improve their agility. Recalling that time years later, my father said, "In those days, your uncle and I were ever preparing for war, which was as certain to come as the daily rains in Hilo."

WAILUA, NORTHEAST MAUI; NOVEMBER, 1778

When the two great canoes with masts like tall trees and sails like billowing white clouds appeared off the northeast coast of Maui, where Kalaniʻōpuʻu was once again laying waste to the countryside, he was not in the least surprised. He had already heard stories of a "moving island" inhabited by strange creatures, which had visited Kauaʻi the previous Makahiki season. Now Kalaniʻōpuʻu stood with a number of his people, including Puna, Kiwalaʻō, Holoʻae, Kamehameha, and my father at the edge of a cliff at Wailua Bay, pondering this strange sight. "So, Puna," he said, turning to his trusted lieutenant, "it seems that the god 'Lono' has come to see me now."

The arrival of a god, if a god this truly was, came at an opportune moment for the mōʻī of the Big Island. Two years previously, Kalaniʻōpuʻu had invaded Maui anew with disastrous results. Over two days of fighting, he had lost thousands of men, including eight hundred warriors in two elite divisions known as the Ālapa and Piʻipiʻi. These men had set off early in the morning from Māʻalaea Bay on Maui's south shore, boasting that they would "drink the waters of Wailuku" by nightfall, only to be slaughtered to a man by late afternoon. When next day found him hemmed in by Kahekili's people at Māʻalaea and cut off from his own fleet down the coast, Kalaniʻōpuʻu was forced to send Kiwalaʻō to sue his uncle, Kahekili, the ruler of Maui, for peace. Kahekili had assented, in return for Kalaniʻōpuʻu's promise to keep to his own island in the future.

Kalaniʻōpuʻu brooded for nearly a year over this latest defeat at the hands of Kahekili and then, despite his pledge, prepared to invade Maui again. Kalaniʻōpuʻu's decision to attack Kahekili once more had infuriated his favorite wife, Kalola. "You are breaking your promise to my own brother," she stormed at Kalaniʻōpuʻu, when she learned of his intentions. Kalola had reluctantly accompanied Kalaniʻōpuʻu on his previous expedition to Maui, but she refused to go with him now. "Do not expect me to come with you this time. I will have nothing to do with this," she cried, "or with you either if you persist!"

"Fine!" Kalaniʻōpuʻu had snapped. "Remain here in Hawaiʻi. But our son Kiwalaʻō comes with me again! Kaneikapolei will be happy to accompany me to Maui and comfort me at night and I will surely have no need of you." This exchange marked the beginning of a permanent estrangement between Kalola and Kalaniʻōpuʻu.

Leaving his embittered senior wife behind, Kalaniʻōpuʻu had crossed the channel to Maui again. Once more unable to defeat Kahekili, he was reduced to raiding coastal villages and visiting a yearlong reign of terror upon the people of Maui and neighboring Lanai.

Kamehameha saw no point to any of it. "Our uncle has no plan," he complained to my father one night. "He strikes here; he strikes there, but what does he have to show for it? He has inflicted much pain and suffering on old men, women, and children, and squandered the lives of our own men, but after all this time, he has not added even one more ahupuaʻa to his holdings on this island."

Now, after another season of disappointment, Kalaniʻōpuʻu welcomed the appearance of "Lono." "Kalaniʻōpuʻu was already looking for a reason to break off the fighting without acknowledging defeat," said my father, "and what better justification could he have had than the coming of a 'god?'"

Kalaniʻōpuʻu had first learned of the "god's" previous appearance in our islands shortly after his latest landing at Hana, where he was gathering his forces for yet another assault on Kaupō. A Hawaiʻian named Moho had come to Hana from Oʻahu with news of strange happenings on Kauaʻi the previous year.

Moho, who swore he had spoken with people who had witnessed these things, told a story of a floating island with tall trees hung with billowing white clouds, of strange beings with wrinkled white skin, cornered heads, and flashing eyes who spoke in a strange, twittering tongue. They blew smoke from their mouths and had holes in their sides from which they would extract various objects. They carried long, black sticks that roared and belched streams of dirty, gray smoke that looked like Lono's rain clouds. Moho said the Kauaʻi people called these sticks "water squirters." These strange beings also had many shiny objects, including long, sharp daggers made of the very same pahoa that Kanaloa sometimes surrendered from the sea. They were happy to trade their pahoa for produce and hogs, but they became angry when one Kauaʻi man tried to take one of these things from their floating island; Moho said that one of the beings pointed a water squirter at this man and killed him.

The Kauaʻi people thought that these beings must be gods. They learned that what they thought was an island was in fact a *waʻa nui*, a great canoe. Many of their women swam to the waʻa nui to have congress with these gods. One of the gods was particularly unhappy about this and sent the women away. He was much taller than the others, who all paid obeisance to him, and because he had come on his great canoe, which looked like a floating island, at the Makahiki time, the people of Kauaʻi believed that the tall one must be the god Lono, returned to them as prophesied of old.

Now, in the new Makahiki season, "Lono" was back. Surveying the two ships from his vantage point on the cliff above the bay, Kalaniʻōpuʻu turned to his people and said, "Come, let us go out to these great canoes and see if Moho spoke the truth."

Moho told the truth as best he knew it at the time. Our people would learn soon enough that these unusual beings were not gods but men—haoles from a faraway island—and that "Lono's" true name was Captain James Cook. Cook and his people kept their own accounts of Cook's visits to our islands, reports that have recently reached our shores. In truth, their own telling of their encounters with the people of Kaua'i is at some variance with Moho's as my father remembered it. Similarly, their accounts of Cook's visit to the Big Island—his own account and others'—are in disagreement here and there with our own stories. While I will from time to time refer to these haoles' reports, I will not muddle this narrative overmuch with theirs, for this, after all, is our people's mo'olelo.

The "floating heiau" was much bigger up close than it had seemed from the top of the cliff. Kalani'ōpu'u had ridden out to the nearest vessel in his grand double-hulled war canoe, with a full complement of warrior-paddlers and more than a dozen ali'i attendants who stood with their mō'ī on the long deck between the hulls, among them Kamehameha and my father.

Remembering Moho's account of the vigorous bartering between the strange beings and the Kaua'i people, Kalani'ōpu'u had brought several small pigs with him and ordered a second canoe to follow, loaded with taro, sweet potatoes, bananas, breadfruit, and more pigs.

"Kalani'ōpu'u was garbed in his best chiefly finery, to alert the strange beings of his high status," my father said. "He wore his full-length cloak of bright red and yellow feathers, his high, feathered helmet, and a feathered malo that covered his loins and draped over his left shoulder. And he carried two pieces of pahoa." These were elongated bits of iron, long ago extracted from flotsam. They were among Kalani'ōpu'u's most prized possessions and rarely displayed by the mō'ī. The members of Kalani'ōpu'u's retinue were all appropriately attired for the occasion. "All of his companions had donned colorful feather cloaks and helmets. Even the warriors paddling his canoe were arrayed in fresh loin cloths of the best quality," my father said.

Kalaniʻōpuʻu's canoe flew across the placid bay as the warriors dug their paddles deep into the water in rhythmic unison. Manned by fewer paddlers and weighed down with goods, the second canoe soon fell behind.

My father said that as they drew nearer to Lono's great canoe, they could see that it was oddly shaped. Whereas our people's canoes were pointed at both ends, he said, Lono's was pointed at one end and broad and flat at the other. The canoe's broad end was intercut with many square openings that glistened in Kāne's light. "We remarked among ourselves that the canoe's pointed end must be its front, since no canoe with a flat nose could make much progress through the water," he said. "But we wondered why this canoe of 'Lono' would have eyes in the back of its head." The great canoe of "Lono" loomed ever larger as they drew closer. "When we reached 'Lono's' canoe, it was as if we had come alongside a wall rising out of the water," my father said. "We had to stretch our necks to see to the top of it."

At close quarters, Kameha, my father, and the others could see that the "floating heiau" was fashioned of many long, flat pieces of wood. The paddlers seated in the hull closest to the great canoe reached out and stroked its side in wonder. Its construction was strange and yet familiar. Our people of course knew nothing of milled lumber or wooden planking in those days, but they had seen similar odd-looking pieces of wood that the sea god Kanaloa had sometimes delivered to our shores—wood pieces embedded with the much-prized pahoa. No doubt, they had come from great canoes like this one.

The great canoe's masts transfixed my father. "There were three of them," he said. "They were taller than many of our trees. They were strung with many stout cords, much thicker than any of the ropes we used to lash the outriggers and decks of our canoes. Each of these tall masts had two or three cross pieces from which sails—much larger than any of ours—were hung, at this time partially furled. And as I looked up, I could see a number of the strangers climbing the masts and sitting on these cross pieces."

Kamehameha was not looking up at the masts. He was looking at several openings in the side of the great canoe, through which he could see round objects with deep, dark holes at their centers. "See those things there, brother," he said to my father, drawing his attention away from the masts' towering spectacle. "I think they are made of pahoa. I wonder what their purpose is."

"Look there," exclaimed Kiwala'ō, pointing at a large banner that fluttered gently from a much shorter mast at what they surmised was the great canoe's rear. "That must be 'Lono's' standard." The banner was bright red, except where it was inset with a strange symbol in red, dark blue, and white. Our people had heretofore only seen such a vivid red in the feathers of birds, and nowhere had they seen such a bright blue except in Lono's sky, but this banner was not crafted of feathers, nor was it a piece of the sky.

Now, Kalani'ōpu'u and his people saw that Moho's "strange beings" were regarding them from the great canoe's heights. At the canoe's broad rear, where the banner of "Lono" waved, they could see beings with "cornered heads" and "wrinkled white skin" looking at them. They could see others whose "skins" were white below the waist and improbably pink from the waist up leaning over the canoe's side, waving at them and shouting unintelligibly. It was mostly the "strange twittering speech" Moho had spoken of. But then, through the gabble, they heard distinctly, "Welcome. Come up, come up. See you there, the steps; come up."

The one who had thus spoken pointed to the side of the great canoe. They now noticed the wooden steps that were affixed to the canoe's side. These were shaped so that a man's hand could fit in and around them and his feet could still gain purchase on them. Without hesitation, Kamehameha jumped from the central platform of Kalani'ōpu'u's war canoe to the hull closest to the side of the strangers' great canoe, grasped the first of these steps and began to climb.

Kiwala'ō was furious with Kamehameha for preceding Kalani'ōpu'u on board. "You should have waited for your mō'ī, Pai'ea," he chastised his cousin, upon gaining the deck. But Kiwala'ō had not waited upon Kalani'ōpu'u either. Slowed by his own infirmities, his father was not quick enough for him and he too was impatient to board.

Kalani'ōpu'u scaled the steps on the great canoe's side with some difficulty, steadied from above by my father and supported from below by his trusted lieutenant Puna. Holo'ae followed them, handing up Kalani'ōpu'u's treasured pieces of pahoa before himself ascending. Last were the paddlers, who were charged with bringing the pigs up the steps, a task that proved impossible. After some shouting and gesturing, the strange beings above lowered a large basket to the paddlers, who deposited the pigs in it and then followed the others up the steps.

The mō'ī of all Hawai'i was in some disarray by the time he reached the deck. He was breathing hard, shaking, and leaning heavily against Puna. His cloak had shed some of its bright feathers and his feathered helmet was askew. In the eyes of his own people, he was still a potent figure, imbued with the power of the prostrating kapu. The great canoe's strange beings saw him quite differently, however. One of them later recorded that the mō'ī's eyes were red, his skin "encrusted with scabs," and that he was shaking all over "as if from palsy." In fact, it was not palsy, but excessive 'awa consumption that troubled Kalani'ōpu'u.

Clustered behind their mō'ī, the Hawai'ians now stood facing "Lono," who was surrounded by others of his kind. The contrast between the shambling figure of their king and "Lono" as he stepped forward to welcome the Hawai'ians could not have been more striking, even to the Hawai'ians themselves. Six feet tall in the haole measure and ramrod straight in bearing, "Lono" seemed to tower over Kalani'ōpu'u, who now slowly backed away, along with his entire entourage, wide-eyed at the sight of the "god."

"Imagine," my father told me, "there before us were the very beings of whom Moho had spoken. We could now see for ourselves their cornered heads and their wrinkled white 'skin.' And some of them were indeed breathing smoke from their mouths." The Hawai'ians were not surprised by the smoke-breathing, which they had been led to expect. But their eyes were now drawn to a startling aspect of these beings that Moho had not mentioned. "First, we saw that what the Kaua'i people and Moho had taken for these strange beings' 'skin' was in places dark blue like Lono's sky in the early morning or evening, as well as white. Then we saw that their blue 'skin' was edged in bright yellow. And finally, we saw that from their necks to their waists, these beings' white 'skin' was punctuated by flat, round things that gleamed in the sunlight and could only be pahoa."

Some of Kalani'ōpu'u's company took these objects for the beings' own navels and sank to their knees. Kalani'ōpu'u himself trembled with fear. It was Kamehameha who broke the spell. Gesturing at the gleaming round objects and speaking loudly enough for all to hear, he proclaimed, "I do not know what those things are, Uncle, but they are not 'skin.'"

Now Kameha did something so bold that it took his comrades' breath away. He stepped forward and lightly brushed his hand across "Lono's" arm. "See," he said, "it is their own kapa cloth. They wear it. That is their skin." At this, Kamehameha pointed at "Lono's" face, with its strangely thin lips, sharp nose, and pink hue. "And," he said, with a sweeping gesture at "Lono's" company, "those cornered things are not the beings' heads; they are helmets, like ours—but not of feathers." With this, Kameha fell silent, though to my father he whispered, "Do not fear these beings, brother, for I think they are men, not gods."

"Lono" had remained impassive throughout this display. Ignoring Kamehameha, he addressed Kalani'ōpu'u. "What your name?" he asked.

Heartened by his nephew's boldness, the mō'ī of Hawai'i drew himself up to his full height, looked directly at "Lono," and replied. "I am Kalani'ōpu'u."

"Lono" looked at Kalani'ōpu'u quizzically and pursed his thin lips. "*Teereeeohbooo*," he repeated, speaking the syllables slowly as if experimenting with them. "Welcome, Terrioboo."

If Kalani'ōpu'u was puzzled by this response, he gave no indication of it. Turning to Puna, he said, "Tell our people to bring the pigs here." Puna gestured at the paddlers, who had retrieved the squealing creatures from the net basket, to come forward with them. They gave one to Puna, who passed it on to Kalaniʻōpuʻu, who took two unsteady steps toward "Lono" and held the animal out to him in trembling hands. "Welcome to our beloved land," he said. "Please accept this gift of pigs from my people, who have longed for your foretold return, divine Lono."

"Lono" again regarded Kalaniʻōpuʻu with puzzlement. "'*Orono*?' *Orono*?'" he said, looking now at the pig the mōʻī of Hawaiʻi had extended to him. A younger man hurried to his side. He was attired much like "Lono," although not so finely, and wore a cornered helmet. This was the man who had called to them from the deck of the great canoe, beckoning them to come aboard. "Lono" bent toward him and the man whispered into his ear. "Ah, yes," he said, straightening. Smiling now, he thanked Kalaniʻōpuʻu in Hawaiian. "I, Orono, accept pig from you, Terrioboo. *Maururu*."

Now it was the Hawaiʻians who were puzzled. "'*Maururu, maururu*?'" they murmured among themselves. What could this mean?

"Lono" signaled to his people and several stepped forward. They laid a number of gifts on the deck at Kalaniʻōpuʻu's feet: a roll of their unusual kapa cloth, bright red; a tool resembling our people's stone adzes, but fashioned instead with a blade of shining pahoa; a dagger similarly made; and a pouch containing more pieces of pahoa, these being thin, round, and pointed at one end and flattened at the other, like the pahoa our people had sometimes retrieved from the odd-looking pieces of wood that washed up on our beaches. As the kapu mōʻī of all Hawaiʻi, Kalaniʻōpuʻu declined to bend low to examine these offerings. Instead, he gestured to Puna to retrieve the pouch for him. Kalaniʻōpuʻu fingered the pouch curiously, its texture unfamiliar to him. This was very strange kapa cloth, indeed. The Hawaiʻians had never seen leather before.

Now Kalaniʻōpuʻu addressed "Lono." "Mahalo for these gifts," he said.

"'*Mahalo*? *Mahalo*?'" "Lono" queried. "Ah," he said, glancing at the younger man who had lately whispered to him, "Understand." Then, smiling as broadly as his thin lips would allow and baring his yellowed teeth, he said, "Mahalo, maururu—same thing. Mahalo, Terrioboo!" At this, "Lono" laughed, and his company joined in.

Now Kalani'ōpu'u smiled. "Yes," he said, "Maururu, mahalo, maururu. Maururu to you as well, Lono." And then he too began to laugh, and all of his people with him. They did not know then that this strange word for thank you, maururu, had come from their own faraway ancestral islands.

After the laughter subsided, "Lono" spoke once more to the younger man, who then addressed Kalani'ōpu'u. "*Orono* wishes to trade for more pigs, fruit, and other foods. He invites you to bring whatever you can spare. For this he will pay generously in cloth and iron."

"*Ailon'e*? What is ailon'e?" Kalani'ōpu'u asked.

"That, in there, is iron," the younger man said, pointing at the pouch in Kalani'ōpu'u's hands. "And that is iron," he said, pointing at the strange adze that still lay on the deck. "And that is iron," he said, pointing at the dagger.

Addressing this man as "One-Who-Speaks-for-Lono," Kalani'ōpu'u replied, "We have more pigs as well as taro, sweet potatoes, bananas, and breadfruit. We will trade them for more of your ailon'e." One-Who-Speaks, as he became known to our people, arranged for the big basket to be lowered again. The paddlers in the Hawai'ians' second canoe, now arrived, loaded all their goods into it and then climbed to the great canoe's deck as the basket was raised. A brisk trade, ultimately satisfying to both sides, now commenced.

While the trading proceeded under Puna's supervision, "Lono" and One-Who-Speaks conducted Kalani'ōpu'u, Kiwala'ō, Kamehameha, Kekūhaupi'o, and Holo'ae on a tour of the great canoe's deck. My father trailed after them. "Kalani'ōpu'u marched around the deck as if it belonged to him," my father said. "I think he was trying to show his people that he was not intimidated by 'Lono,' that his mana was still powerful even in the presence of a god."

As the tour progressed, Kalani'ōpu'u pointed at various objects and asked One-Who-Speaks what they were. Few of his answers were intelligible to the Hawai'ians, as our people's own language had no equivalents for them. But despite this, Kalani'ōpu'u made a great show of understanding, pursing his lips and nodding at each answer. "Lono" walked alongside the pair throughout this interrogation, listening intently, but interjecting nothing himself.

When the group reached the front of the vessel, ascending some steps to a raised platform, Kamehameha spoke up. "And what is that?" he asked, pointing at a dark cylindrical object. Clearly made of "ailon'e," it resembled the larger objects he had seen in the square openings in the great canoe's side.

"That is a small cannon," One-Who-Speaks replied.

"*Kano'ono*," Kameha said, repeating the unfamiliar sounds. "What is it for?"

One-Who-Speaks turned to "Lono" and spoke rapidly to him in his strange, twittering tongue. "Lono" called out to his men, who moved to the cannon. One carried a container that looked to be made of iron and the other a wooden rod that was round and blunt on one end. These men had no helmets and were bare to the waist. Their chests, arms, and backs were reddened, and they wore nothing on their heads. One man's hair was yellow, and the other's was bright red. "Look there!" Kiwala'ō cried. "Flames shoot from that one's head, and the other has hair like Kāne's sun."

The Hawai'ians watched as the men loaded the cannon and primed the fuse, gaping at their unfamiliar tools and procedures, unsure of their purpose. Particularly shocking was the ease with which they produced a spark, using a flint, to ignite a piece of oiled rope. "We had never before seen a fire started in this manner, or so easily," my father said.

The two men now stood erect, looking expectantly at "Lono," who said a single word in his unintelligible tongue. Now, one of the men touched the rope's smoldering end to a small hole at the rear of the cannon. None of the Hawai'ians was prepared for what happened next.

"We heard a sudden boom," my father said. "It was loud and sharp, like the sound of Pele's fury. The weapon my brother called a 'kano'ono' spit smoke and fire."

Nearly all the Hawai'ians recoiled in terror from this spectacle. Kalani'ōpu'u stumbled backward and collided with Kiwala'ō. The two of them hugged each other and wailed. Kekūhaupi'o fell to his knees. Holo'ae reflexively raised his arms in supplication. Many of the paddlers jumped into the bay. My father bolted toward the deck railing and would have followed them if his own brother had not restrained him.

"Kamehameha was no less unnerved by the gun's firing than the rest of us," my father recalled, "but he was determined not to show it. He held me tightly by one arm and said, 'Do not flee brother; no harm has come to us from this kano'ono. It is all noise and smoke. Noise and smoke has never hurt anyone.'"

The Hawai'ians' reaction to this demonstration seemed to amuse "Lono," who smiled and tipped his bi-cornered helmet toward them. The rest of his company erupted in boisterous laughter.

"See, brother," Kamehameha said, "how terrible can this kano'ono be if these strange people laugh at it? Perhaps it is for driving away evil spirits. It may be that we have nothing to fear from it."

"In that moment," my father recalled many years later, "I think Kameha was merely trying to reassure me. He was mindful of Moho's story of the death-dealing 'water-squirters' at Kaua'i. I think he suspected the danger they presented, and was determined to find out for himself."

The firing of the cannon brought an abrupt end to Kalani'ōpu'u's visit to "Lono's" great canoe. Untangling himself from Kiwala'ō and straining to maintain his dignity, Kalani'ōpu'u motioned One-Who-Speaks to his side. "I must go ashore now, on matters of urgent business," he said.

Disembarking from the great canoe proved to be more awkward for Kalani'ōpu'u than boarding it, for the demonstration of the cannon had left the mō'ī of Hawai'i too unsteady to descend the ladder. He quavered at the edge of the deck and then almost lost his grip on the railing as he tried to set foot on the first step. It was clear that even with the powerful Puna positioned below to steady him, Kalani'ōpu'u was in danger of falling to the deck of his own canoe. At last, "Lono's" people lowered him, along with the Hawai'ians' newly obtained iron, in the same large net basket that had earlier brought the trade goods and pigs on board. His people followed, some descending the steps while others clambered over the great canoe's side railings and dropped or dove into the water and swam to their canoes.

The iron Kalaniʻōpuʻu's people had acquired in trade was not the only prize the Hawaiʻians came away with that day. "Whenever our people saw something of interest, and provided none of the strange beings were looking their way," my father said, "they took it."

Not all of the Hawaiʻians came away with Kalaniʻōpuʻu from "Lono's" great canoe. Kamehameha and Kekūhaupiʻo remained on board, as did my father.

Before Kalaniʻōpuʻu departed, Kamehameha asked him for permission to remain for some time with "Lono." Kalaniʻōpuʻu was reluctant at first to give his assent. "'Lono' and these strange beings may be gods," he said. "And what if we have somehow offended them? Who knows how they will treat you if you stay."

"Uncle, they are exceedingly strange, but they are only men," Kamehameha replied. "If you allow Kekū, my brother, and me to stay with them for a while, we may be able to learn more about them. I do not believe any harm will come to us."

Kalaniʻōpuʻu then turned to his kahuna nui, Holoʻae. "What is your opinion of these beings?" he asked.

Holoʻae frowned and furrowed his brow. "Lord, I am still undecided about this," he replied. Then, glancing at Kameha, he said, "But I do not believe 'Lono' would allow any harm to befall Kamehameha or his companions. His intentions so far have seemed entirely benevolent. Let 'Lono's' great canoe take one of our canoes in tow and leave some paddlers here with Kameha so that he can easily return to us when he is ready."

Kalaniʻōpuʻu summoned One-Who-Speaks to his side and explained matters to him. One-Who-Speaks in turn spoke in his twittering tongue to "Lono," who readily assented to this plan.

And so it was settled.

Sailing on "Lono's" great canoe proved a wondrous adventure for the Hawaiians. Kamehameha, my father and Kekūhaupi'o moved to the high deck at the rear of the great canoe, where they could see nearly everything.

"As soon as Kalani'ōpu'u's canoe was away and our remaining double-hulled canoe was secured to the back of 'Lono's' vessel with a stout line, a great commotion began," said my father. There was much loud calling back and forth among 'Lono's' people, commencing with 'Lono' himself. The men with the cornered helmets called out in succession to each other and finally to the other men with the bare chests and pink skin, and they in turn rushed this way and that. Two men ran to a large vertically mounted cylinder at the front of the great canoe and commenced pulling on long bars to turn it. The Hawai'ians, who had never before seen such a device, nor a wheel of any kind, watched in fascination as the haoles labored to weigh the ship's anchors. "Look!" exclaimed Kamehameha, pointing to the heavy chain of iron links wrapping around the cylinder, "They bring up a rope made of *ailon'e*!"

"We heard much creaking and groaning as the haoles turned this thing," my father said. "We knew that there must be something very heavy at the end of that big ailon'e rope."

Responding to the barked commands, other bare-chested people leaped to the masts and climbed into their branches on wide rope ladders that could hold a half-dozen or more men at once. They wrapped their legs around the branches and unfurled the great canoe's square sails. Dirty white like the true Lono's scudding rain clouds, the sails soon filled with the god's own breeze. Then, at first barely discernibly to the Hawai'ians, the ship began to move.

"First, we heard the water slapping against the sides of the great canoe," my father said. "Then we noticed the rolling of the deck. Next, we looked to its front and saw that its long nose was now rising and falling. And then we looked behind us. We could barely credit our own eyes. We saw a broad wake spreading behind the great canoe. The island of Maui was receding from us at great speed. Our paddlers were huddled together on the lower deck at the middle of the great canoe. They began to wail and hug each other in fright."

Through all this, Kamehameha, Kekūhaupiʻo, and my father kept their places. Kameha never ceased looking about this way and that, observing everything. "This is all most interesting," he said to my father and his kahu.

Kamehameha, Kekū, and my father made the most of their brief stay aboard the great canoe. With One-Who-Speaks acting as their guide, they explored every part of the vessel, visiting the hold, where the bare-chested ones slept in hammocks amid the canoe's stores; the galley, where food was prepared; and the gun deck, where the cannons peered out at the sea through openings in the great canoe's side.

The gun deck was a cave-like place divided into several compartments. Its confined spaces were sparingly illuminated by daylight admitted through the open gun ports. The Hawaiʻians were forced to stoop to avoid striking their heads against the cross beams of the deck's low ceiling. "What are those for?" Kamehameha asked One-Who-Speaks, pointing at the black iron balls nestled in a groove along the bottom of one of the gun deck's walls.

One-Who-Speaks paused before answering, pondering how best to explain a cannonball's purpose. "Those are food for the cannons," he said. "We feed them to the cannons and they spit them out at our enemies."

Kameha continued his interrogation. "The kanoʻono spit out these things when your people touch them with their fire ropes?" he asked.

"Yes," replied One-Who-Speaks.

From that moment, Kameha and Kekūhaupiʻo were most interested in learning about these unusual weapons. They put many more questions to One-Who-Speaks. They asked him about the nature of the black "sand" that was poured into the mouths of the cannons; about how the people who fired the weapons could ignite their "fire ropes" so easily; about the smoke that streamed from the cannons' mouths; about the nature and power of the iron balls that the cannons spat. One-Who-Speaks answered their questions as best he could.

"The black 'sand' is a powder that burns and becomes very angry when it is ignited," he said.

"We strike iron against a special stone to make a spark," he said.

"The smoke is from the fire which burns very hot inside the cannon when the black sand is lit," he said.

"The cannon spits out the 'food' when the fire burns hot inside it," he said, "and the cannon 'food' flies swift and far."

"With this kanoʻono food, you can slay your enemies from afar, just as we do with our sling stones, is that so?" Kamehameha asked. It was more of a statement than a question.

"Yes," replied One-Who-Speaks. "But it is much more powerful and travels much farther than the stones from your slings. It is so heavy, flies so fast, and strikes so hard that not even the side of a great canoe can stand up to it, let alone a man," he said, with some pride.

Kamehameha nodded at this. He pondered the cannon and its "food" for a moment, saying nothing. Then, baring his teeth, which glinted white against his dark face in the gun deck's dim light, he grinned at One-Who-Speaks. "Mahalo," was all that he said.

One-Who-Speaks smiled back at Kameha, somewhat uneasily now.

Later, Kamehameha, Kekū, and my father saw some people on the great canoe's top deck who were dressed very differently from the others. They wore red cloaks that shone brightly in the sun and some carried long iron sticks.

"Who are those people?" Kekūhaupiʻo asked.

"They are marines," replied One-Who-Speaks, "soldiers-of-the-sea."

"What is it that they carry, those sea soldiers, those *mālīnʻe*?" Kamehameha asked, wrestling with the unfamiliar consonants.

"They are called muskets," said One-Who-Speaks.

"*Mūkʻe*?" Kameha repeated, struggling anew with the strange sounds. "What are mūkʻe?"

"They are little cannons," answered One-Who-Speaks.

And so it went.

When Kamehameha and his kahu were not questioning One-Who-Speaks about weaponry, my father questioned him about "Lono" and the people on the great canoe. "I was most interested in discovering what I could about their customs aboard that vessel, their true names, and whence they had come," he told me.

"One-Who-Speaks, what is that twittering sound you make with the others on this canoe?" my father asked.

"It is our own way of talking. It is called English."

"*Ī'ïklī?*" My father repeated, tentatively.

"Yes," said One-Who-Speaks, smiling, "that is close enough." Then he asked, "Tell me, why do you call me 'One-Who-Speaks'?"

"Because we know you as the one who speaks to us for Lono."

"Ah yes, for *Orono*. I see," said One-Who-Speaks. "But my true name is Jem Burney. What is your name?"

"*Pu'unē... Pu'unē,*" my father said, trying again to negotiate the unfamiliar sounds of this strange talk called Ī'īklī. He could not manage Jem. "Pu'unē," he said, "my name is Kalanimālokuloku."

Now it was Jem Burney's turn to stumble over strange sounds. "*Tala... Talani... Talani-ma...*" Finally, he said, "It is too much for my simple tongue. May I call you Talani?"

"That is close enough, Pu'unē," my father replied, and then he and Burney began to laugh.

From Pu'unē, my father learned that "Lono" was the captain of both great canoes, and that his true name was Cook; *Kāpena Kuke*, my father and my uncle called him. Those in the cornered helmets were Kuke's sub-chiefs, among them John Gore and James King. *Ko'o'e* and *Ki'ine*, my father called them. In my father's understanding, Gore and King ruled the lesser chiefs and the bare-chested, helmetless ones—the commoners—in Cook's absence. Charles Clerke—*Kale'eke* was the best my father could manage—was chief of the other great canoe, answering to Cook. "Pu'unē" was one of Clerke's lesser chieftains. Clerke had seconded him to Cook to serve as his interpreter because of his exceptional facility with our people's tongue. There was no priest on either of the two great canoes as far as my father knew.

"So this 'Lono,' or 'Kuke' as you call him, is the great canoes' mōʻī and the ones with the cornered helmets are their aliʻi," Kamehameha said, when my father explained this to him. "And the rest are kānaka. Why do they not prostrate themselves before their chiefs? Do they have no kapus?"

"They do not prostrate themselves, nor do they sit or kneel before their chiefs," my father said, "but they must obey them."

Indeed, my father had learned, the penalties for disrespect, or, worse still, for outright disobedience aboard the great canoe, were quite harsh. "We do have *tapus*," Burney had assured him. "If a man insults or disobeys one of our aliʻi, he can be whipped, provided our chief, Cook, orders it." And in cases of severe disobedience, a man could be "keel hauled." Those were the words Burney used, because he could not express them in our own language.

"What is *keʻelʻe haʻolo*?" my father asked.

"The keel is under the bottom of the great canoe. It runs from the front to the back," Burney replied. "When a man is keel hauled, his hands are tied to the end of one rope and his feet to the end of another and he is pulled under the keel for its entire length."

My father looked up and down the length of the great canoe's deck. "That is a long way to be dragged under water, especially if a man is not pulled quickly," he said. "Can your people hold their breath that long?"

"Some cannot," Burney said.

"What?" Kameha had asked, upon hearing of these punishments. "They do not immediately slay those kānaka who violate their kapus? What kind of justice is that?"

"Oh, they do slay them if they deem the violation sufficiently serious," my father said, "but not while they are still on the great canoe."

"We take those men back to England," Burney had explained when my father questioned him on this point.

"*Ī'īklī'ana?* What is *Ī'īklī'ana*?" asked my father.

"It is our own island," Burney said. "It is far away. There, our highest chiefs consider those men's offenses. And if they so decree, those men are slain."

"How are they slain?" my father asked.

"We tie ropes around their necks and drop them from a yardarm."

"*Hi'ah'ama?*" My father looked uncomprehendingly at Burney.

"There," said Burney, pointing at one of the highest crosspieces on the nearest mast. "That is a yardarm." My father understood him now.

"That is a novel way to slay an offender," Kamehameha said when he heard of this.

"On your island, Ī'īklī'ana, do all the people talk Ī'īklī?" my father asked Burney.

"Oh yes," Burney answered, "for that is the talk we learn as infants."

"Then how is it that you can speak our talk?"

"I learned it from the people of *Otahiete*," said Burney, referring to Tahiti. "They look much like you and they speak much the same."

"'*Okahiki*?' Where is this Okahiki?" my father asked.

"It is that way," Burney said, pointing southwest, where Maui now lay. "Otahiete is on the other side of your island, but it is far, far away. You cannot see it from here."

"But that is not our island," my father exclaimed. He pointed southeast. "Our island is that way," he said.

This news greatly excited Burney. "Wait here!" he exclaimed. He hurried to where Cook was conferring with two of his ali'i sub chiefs. He raised his right hand briskly to his forehead, and then spoke rapidly. Cook turned and regarded the Hawai'ians, whom he had mostly ignored until now. He spoke to Burney, who hastened back to my father and the others. "Come," he said, with an enveloping gesture. "Captain Cook wishes to speak with you."

"Pu'unē conducted us to the higher deck, where Kāpena Kuke was standing before a piece of flat wood on two pedestals," my father told me. "He had spread out a large piece of very thin kapa cloth before him. It was held in place against the wind by several small pieces of ailonʻe. We did not know what to make of it." The Hawaiʻians had never before seen a map, let alone paper.

Now it was Cook who asked the questions. Stabbing the paper with one finger and then turning to point at the island behind them, he asked, "What island that? What name that island?"

"That is Maui," Kamehameha replied.

"*Mow'ēē*," Cook slowly repeated. Then he asked, "What name your island?"

"Hawaiʻi," Kameha said.

"*O'why'hee*," Cook said, savoring the syllables. "Where this *O'why'hee*?"

Kamehameha pointed in the general direction of the Alenuihāhā Channel. "There is Hawaiʻi," he said.

Now Cook stabbed at the paper and spoke rapidly in English to his sub chiefs, who immediately scurried away, issuing urgent commands to the great canoe's commoners. Then Cook turned to Kameha once again. "Good," he said. "We go this *O'why'hee*."

The winds abated with the setting sun, so it was not until morning that the Big Island came into view. The Hawaiʻians had passed a pleasant night. Kamehameha, Kekūhaupiʻo, and my father spent the evening on the vessel's elevated rear deck with Burney, while the canoe paddlers gathered with the great canoe's commoners on the main deck.

Cook's people offered to share their evening meal with their guests. Earlier in the day, the great canoe's deck had reverberated with terrified squeals as the pigs brought aboard by the Hawaiʻians were slaughtered. Now the vessel's cook served up a watery stew of pork and local yams. This meal was apportioned amongst the crew in large wooden vessels of a sort that the Hawaiʻians had never seen before. One such vessel was set before Kamehameha, Kekūhaupiʻo, and my father. "We call them 'meal buckets,'" explained Burney.

"*Me'ele pu'uke*?" my father hazarded.

"Close enough," Burney said, laughing.

Distributed with the meal buckets were smaller vessels shaped like our people's eating and drinking gourds, but also fashioned of wood—as well as pewter ladles and spoons, implements new to the Hawai'ians.

"*Lāke'el'e*; *po'ole*; *pū'ūn'e*," my father repeated, twisting his tongue around the unfamiliar sounds of this new language. "What kind of ailon'e is that?" he asked, pointing at the implements.

"It is called pewter," Burney replied.

"*P'uke?*" my father tried.

"Close enough," said Burney, laughing again.

Now Burney commenced to demonstrate the purpose of the ladle and spoons. The Hawai'ians watched in rapt attention as he plunged the ladle into the bucket, filled it with stew, and poured the stew into the bowl, whereupon he dipped the spoon into this same bowl and raised it to his own mouth. Then, with much show, Burney sucked the food from the spoon and chewed vigorously on a bit of pork while some of the juice dribbled down his chin. Wiping his chin clean with the back of his hand, Burney dipped the ladle into the meal bucket, filled three more bowls, and set them, with spoons, before my father, Kameha, and his kahu. "Now you try," he said.

Accustomed to dining on savory meat and vegetables wrapped in ti leaves and baked in their imus, the Hawai'ians were repulsed by this fare. "We beheld these bits of pig meat and shreds of yam floating in a malodorous, oily broth," my father told me, "and it turned our stomachs." But out of politeness, they tried it anyway. Then, with murmurs of "Mahalo, mahalo," they begged off eating any more of this concoction and commenced instead to dine on the provisions they had brought on board—bananas, baked yams, and dried fish.

"Our food is not to your liking?" Burney asked.

In answer, Kekūhaupi'o screwed up his face and grunted. Kamehameha looked embarrassed.

"It is too new to us," my father replied diplomatically. "Perhaps we will come to like it in time."

"Tell us about this Okahiki and its people," Kamehameha said, changing the subject. My father had told him of Burney's revelation concerning this faraway land.

Burney went on to describe the far-off archipelago, its people and language, and some of the crew's experiences there. Then he began to tell a story of how Cook had been forced to retaliate against the people of one of these islands, "Eimeo," when they stole some goats, but Kamehameha interrupted him almost at once.

"What is a *kōʻoko*?" he asked.

"A goat is a four-footed animal with horns."

The Hawaiʻians stared at Burney without comprehension. "We have them on board. I will show you later," he said. Then he recommenced his tale.

These people of Eimeo, he said, had taken two of several goats that Cook had temporarily put ashore to feed. The previous day, Cook had refused a request by the island's chief to give these animals to him. "They already had two goats," Burney explained. "Captain Cook could not obtain any more such animals and he was husbanding the rest for settlement on other islands. So he was determined to recover these thieved creatures."

Cook succeeded in persuading the Eimeo people to return one of the goats, Burney continued, but the other they still withheld. "It was a female goat, heavy with a baby, and Captain Cook would not put to sea without it."

The next day, Cook led a shore party on a fatiguing and ultimately fruitless overland march to find and recover the goat. Not finding the animal in any of the villages along the way, Cook became angry and ordered his men to burn the houses and canoes at the last village they visited. On his orders, his shore party burned more canoes on their march back to their own boats.

The following morning, Burney said, "Captain Cook sent a message to the chief of Eimeo with a warning that he would destroy every canoe on the island if the goat was not returned to him." He first demonstrated his resolve by destroying every canoe in the bay where his own ship was anchored and moving on to a neighboring bay where his people destroyed more canoes. “By the time he regained the ship,” Burney concluded with a smile, “the goat had been returned—from one of the villages the captain had visited the previous day. Captain Cook was much irritated by the inconvenience this incident had caused, for he had meant to put to sea again much sooner, but he was well satisfied that he had taught these people a lesson they would not soon forget.”

Thinking of Kalani’ōpu‘u‘s recent depredations on Maui, Kamehameha said to my father, “This Kāpena Kuke is not so different from our own uncle.” Then he turned to Burney and said, “I would like to see these kō‘oko now.”

Burney conducted Kamehameha, Kekūhaupi‘o, and my father to the ship’s lower deck, where they had earlier seen the cannons, galley, ship’s stores, and the crew’s quarters. But now he led them to a different compartment—illuminated by a single oil lantern hanging from a beam—where the livestock was kept. The goats, tethered with ropes, were lying amid dried grass that had been laid upon the deck. The air was close and reeked of the sickly sweet smell of dried excrement. Wrinkling their noses, the Hawai‘ians inspected these goats and their formidable horns with great interest, but did not touch them.

“They are good to eat?” Kamehameha asked.

“Yes,” replied Burney, “especially when we can cook them over an open fire, instead of boiling their meat, as we must do on board the ship. They also give milk, which we can drink.”

“Milk such as that from the breast of a wahine? You drink it?” Kameha queried. This was new, the thought of people other than infants drinking milk—and animals’ milk at that. Infants and little children suckled, but only at their mothers’ or some other wahine’s breasts. The Hawai‘ians had never heard of people, adult or otherwise, consuming animals' milk—and certainly not that of dogs or pigs, which were the only domesticated animals they knew.

Kamehameha screwed up his face in disgust. "What kind of lamp is that?" he said now, pointing at the compartment's sole source of light. Like many of the articles on the ship, it was fashioned of some sort of iron. Its essential workings were familiar to the Hawai'ians, but they had never seen glass before.

"It is a lantern," said Burney. "It is enclosed in glass to prevent the flame from escaping and starting a fire."

"*La'an'ak'en'e, ka'ala,*" my father tried to repeat the strange new words.

While this conversation continued, Kekūhaupi'o noticed a doorway leading to another compartment near the front of the ship. It was darker than the first, for its only light came from the adjacent compartment where the animals were kept. Peering in, he could make out the shadowy forms of two men reclining against the compartment's sloping wall. They were shackled at their ankles by thick bracelets of iron which were in turn affixed to heavy chains which were themselves firmly connected to the compartment wall.

"Pu'unē, why are these two confined here?" he asked.

"Ah, those men," Burney said. "They are down here by the will of Captain Cook. He ordered them bound in irons after they deserted from our ships at Ulietea and were caught. They did not want to return to England with us. Now they will—poor wretches."

"What will happen to them in Ī'īklī'ana?" my father asked.

"They will both hang by their necks from a yardarm, no doubt."

"For violating the kapu of your chief, Kāpena Kuke?" Kamehameha asked.

"Yes," answered Burney.

"It is only fitting," said Kameha.

When Burney, Kamehameha, and his companions regained the great canoe's main deck at last, they encountered a scene of rollicking merriment among the ship's commoners and their own canoe paddlers, who were in the midst of demonstrating their peoples' dance customs to one another. They had gathered near a mast, to which several oil lamps had been hung to afford them some light.

"First, some of the Ī'īklī people would jump up and down upon the deck on their toes, twirling around with their hands in the air while one of their number played a strange wooden instrument that made whining sounds when he pulled a stick across some thin ropes pulled tight upon it," my father told me. Then, he said, the Hawai'ians, six in number, would commence to dance. "They danced like the true men they were," my father said. "They thumped the deck with their feet and moved in unison while one of them drummed on the bottom of one of the Ī'īklī people's empty me'ele pu'uke." Throughout, my father said, the Hawai'ians would shout their fearsome war chants, much to the amusement of the Englishmen, who would roar with laughter. Then it was the Englishmen's turn to resume their dance, to their guests' equal amusement.

Finally, they turned to mimicking each other. The Englishman with the strange rope-strung instrument and stick gestured to his Hawai'ian counterpart that he wished to exchange his own instrument for the meal bucket. The trade was accomplished and a scene of even greater hilarity ensued.

"Now the Ī'īklī man began to beat on the me'ele pu'uke while his fellows jumped here and there loudly chanting nonsense," my father said. "Then the Hawai'ian with the Ī'īklī instrument commenced drawing the stick across it, eliciting from it horrible sounds while all the while his comrades spun around feverishly. Soon both sides began dancing in mockery of each other all at once, mixing in together amid great laughter."

But the laughter came to an abrupt end with the arrival of short, stout haole who kicked the meal bucket away from his own man and began shouting at his people. They dispersed at once. Next he sought to recover the crewman's instrument from the Hawai'ian, who would not release it. The Hawai'ian was taller than the haole, strong and wiry in build, but not nearly as heavy. The two men struggled mightily for the instrument, the haole leveraging his superior bulk against the Hawai'ian's longer reach and greater agility.

"They might have come to blows," my father said, "had not Pu'unē and Kamehameha intervened." These two stepped forward simultaneously. At a word from Burney, the stout haole let go of the instrument and stepped away. Meanwhile, Kameha spoke sharply to his own man who immediately dropped to knees before his ali'i lord, still holding the foreign instrument in his now-shaking hands. Kamehameha said nothing, but merely gestured at the Hawai'ian, who handed him the instrument while keeping his head down and his eyes on the ship's deck. Ignoring the stout haole, Kamehameha returned the instrument to Burney. Burney spoke softly in his twittering tongue to the stout haole, who shot Kameha a withering look and stalked away.

Kamehameha asked, "Is that man one of your lesser chiefs—a lesser chief than you?"

"Yes," Burney replied. "He is the ship's master. He helps us find our way on the seas. His name is Bligh…William Bligh."

"This *Ūli'iama P'ulī*, why did he order those people away? Were they violating a kapu?"

"Yes," said Burney, an unmistakable note of disapproval in his voice. "They were violating his kapu."

Bligh stood at the deck railing, glowering down at the Hawai'ians as they departed in their canoe the next morning. Burney, standing nearby, waved to them. Several of the canoe paddlers waved back. The morning sunlight reflected dully off the pewter spoons in their hands.

"Uncle, this 'Lono' and his people are not gods," Kamehameha declared to Kalani'ōpu'u upon returning to Maui. "They are only men."

Kalani'ōpu'u, reclining on a sedge mat in the hale he had appropriated at Wailua, regarded his nephew quizzically and said nothing.

"I have observed them closely," Kameha continued. "They eat and drink like men; they urinate and defecate like men—and they smell bad, like men who have not bathed for a long time. They are not divine."

"Nephew, do they bleed like men?" Kalaniʻōpuʻu asked at last.

"This I do not yet know, Uncle," Kamehameha said.

"Perhaps you are right, Kameha," said Kalaniʻōpuʻu. "But until we know the answer to that question, we must reserve judgment."

Kealakekua Bay, January, 1779

While Kalaniʻōpuʻu withheld judgment at Maui, Cook unwittingly assumed the mantle of a god upon reaching the Big Island. Coincidence combined with the Hawaiʻians' own legends to confer divinity upon him.

As he had at Kauaʻi, Cook arrived in the middle of the Makahiki season—Lono's time. Upon his first close approach to the coast at Kukuipahu in Northern Kohala, Cook was greeted by the villagers there, much as the people of Waimea had greeted him at Kauaʻi. "When the Kohala people saw Kuke's ship with its great square sails, they likened it to a floating island with its own clouds—Lono's clouds, just as the Kauaʻi people had," my father told me. "And they said to each other, 'Surely, this is Lono returned to us from Kahiki, as the prophecy foretold that he would in the Makahiki time.'"

The Hawaiʻians gathered along the Kohala cliffs and waved white kapa cloth banners at "Lono's" vessel. Others ran to their canoes and raced out to the ship, flying similar ensigns. In answer, Cook ordered his people to break out his red flag, with its red, white, and blue cross. The Hawaiʻians took this as a sign of Cook's godhead, too, for the prophecy also foretold that "Lono" would respond by displaying a banner of his own. "When the people in the canoes drew closer to Kuke's ship," my father recounted, "they saw that some of the men watching them from the deck railings were blowing smoke from their mouths and they said, 'Surely there is no question that these people who breathe fire are gods.'"

Gods or no, the people of Kohala struck up a brisk commerce with these strangers, trading pigs, fruit, roots, and sugar cane for pieces of iron that they transformed into weapons and fishhooks. "Even some haole axes changed hands," my father told me.

Intent on charting the Big Island and defining the extent of his latest "discovery," and in search of a safe harbor for his ships, which were in need of repairs, Cook sailed on: down the Hāmākua Coast; past Hilo; around Cape Kumukahi, the island's easternmost point; past the forbidding lava desert of the Ka'ū district where gouts of fiery lava flowing down from Kilauea met the cold sea, sending up white clouds of steam; and around the island's southernmost extent at Ka Lae and up the Kona Coast. Although he found no welcoming anchorages for much of the way, he repeatedly closed with the shore—"stood in"—for trade. Everywhere Cook's ship appeared, events unfolded much as they had at Kohala. The Hawai'ians waved their white banners; Cook in turn broke out his colorful ensign. The people of the coastal villages paddled out to his ship in their canoes and clambered aboard to exchange hogs, vegetables, and fruit for iron.

Some came aboard for other reasons, including women eager to mate with these unusual and perhaps godly beings, as at Kaua'i the previous year, and also men seeking relief from heretofore unknown ailments in their nether parts—bloody urine and painful urination, yellow discharges, and swelling in their groins. The Hawai'ians had no idea that the one was related to the other. Unbeknownst to them, they were suffering from the gift Cook's sailors had uncaringly proffered on the women of Kaua'i the year before, and which by now had spread throughout the archipelago.

Throughout his circumnavigation of the Big Island, Cook took the Hawai'ians' white banners for, as he wrote in his journals, "a signal of peace and friendship." But for our people, of course, they meant much more than that. For by circling the island as he had, Cook had fulfilled the other part of the prophecy: that Lono would not only return during the Makahiki season, but that he would circle the entirety of the Big Island, commencing in Kohala and traveling from the island's wet side to Kealakekua Bay on its dry side—just as Cook in fact did. Kealakekua was revered as the ancestral home of the god, Lono, to which he would one day return. There was little question that Cook was Lono, indeed.

It was at Kealakekua that Koa, the priest of Lono, officially proclaimed the British sea captain's divinity.

Cook first sighted Kealakekua Bay at daybreak on January 16, 1779, as the haoles marked the date. At this time, Cook's ship, the Resolution, and its sister ship, the Discovery, were by his reckoning still some three leagues, or nine miles, distant from the bay itself. Cook dispatched a party commanded by Bligh in two small boats to reconnoiter it. While Bligh and his men were away, the two ships continued to sail in the bay's direction, making slow progress as they tacked northward against the prevailing winds. Upon seeing these large vessels with their majestic sails, villagers the length of the South Kona Coast rushed to the beaches, leaped into their canoes and paddled out to the ships in great numbers, intent on trading pigs and whatever else they had for iron.

Bligh spent the night at Kealakekua. Upon his return to the Resolution late the next day, he reported that the bay afforded an excellent anchorage with an ample supply of fresh water. At eleven in the morning, the Resolution and the Discovery dropped their anchors at Kealakekua. The bay's pali, which rises abruptly from a narrow, pebbled beach, towered above them. It is this cliff, in fact, that gives the bay its name. Kealakekua means "path of the gods." If any of our ancient gods had been looking down upon the bay this day, they would have comprehended that after generations, everything was about to change for our people.

According to Cook's own account, the greeting he received at Kealakekua was unlike any he had heretofore witnessed. "I have no where in this

Sea seen such a number of people assembled at one place," he wrote in his journal. "Besides those in the Canoes all the Shore of the bay was covered with people and hundreds were swimming about the Ships like shoals of fish. We should have found it difficult to have kept them in order had not a Chief or Servant of Terrioboo's named Parea now and then exerted his authority by turning or rather driving them all out of the Ships." For a time, at least, order had been restored.

Palea, for that was his name, was followed to the ships by Koa. Koa arrived at Cook's ship in his own canoe, paddled by acolytes, after Palea and another chief had expelled the common people from the decks of the Resolution and the Discovery. Koa and Palea were conducted into Cook's cabin on the Resolution. Speaking to Cook through Burney, Palea explained that his mōʻī was still at Maui but would soon return. He then introduced Koa to Cook. A scene ensued that would propel much of the subsequent events. As neither my father nor Kamehameha were there to vouch for it, perhaps it is best to describe it as the haoles witnessed it. Wrote Cook: "Among our numerous Visitors was a man named Tou-ah-ah, who we soon found belonged to the Church, he introduced himself with much ceremony, in the Course of which he presented me with a small pig, two Cocoanuts and a piece of red cloth which he wrapped around me." "Tou-ah-ah,"—Koa—presented Cook with other gifts as well: "He brought with him a large hog and a quant'y of fruits and roots all of which he included in the present."

Koa was the keeper of the Hikiau Heiau, Lono's temple at Nāpoʻopoʻo on the south side of the bay, opposite Kaʻawaloa. Little remains of the heiau today, save for its enduring platform of layered lava stones, meticulously selected many generations ago by craftsmen who knew nothing of mortar. The temple's ruins are but a few steps from the edge of the bay. The lava-stone foundation stands more than twice the height of a full-grown man at its highest. Its top is level and commodious. When Koa presided, the heiau platform was the site of a number of structures, including fencing, scaffolding, and two small hales, constructed with wooden poles, woven grass walls, and thatched roofs held together with coconut-fiber cordage. These have long since vanished, as have so many of our people's old ways.

No sooner had Cook come ashore at Kealakekua for the first time than Koa conducted him to the heiau, where he officiated a lengthy and elaborate ceremony, no doubt incomprehensible to Cook, in which he paid obeisance to the Englishman as a deity. Some Hawai'ians and haoles looking back upon these distant events have lately debated whether Cook understood that our people regarded him as an actual god, and if so, whether he actively encouraged and exploited this perception. I suspect that Cook might well have deduced the import of this event from the sight of people prostrating themselves before him on his way to the heiau. Moreover, whenever Cook came ashore thereafter, he was greeted with gifts of hogs, coconuts, breadfruit, and vegetables, and was at all times accompanied by a wand-waving kahuna who commanded all to prostrate themselves as he went by. How Cook might have taken these demonstrations for anything other than idolatry, I do not know. Certainly, Cook came to understand that he and his people could gain advantage from our own people's rituals and beliefs, and was happy to do so.

Cook was not happy, however, about our people's propensity to filch anything made of iron from his ships. While most people who came aboard his ships that first day at Kealakekua had come to trade Hawaiian goods and produce for the precious haole metal, those with nothing to trade did not hesitate to take whatever items struck their fancies.

Some came away with lids from the ships' copper kettles; others dove into the water to pry nails out of the vessels' copper hull sheathing. One man took a rudder from one of the Resolution's small boats. This passed unnoticed by Cook and the ship's crew until the man was well away in his own canoe, whereupon, determined to put an end to such activities, Cook ordered his people to demonstrate to the Hawai'ians the fearsome power of their weaponry. He ordered a volley of warning shots from the ship's smaller cannons and the marines' muskets. The spectacle failed to elicit the desired response, however, and islanders of what Cook called "thievish disposition" continued to steal from the haoles.

"I do not truly know if this Kāpena Kuke is Lono come back to us," Kalani'ōpu'u acknowledged to Holo'ae, upon their return to Hawai'i some days later. "But Koa has thus proclaimed it and many of our people seem to believe it, so let us leave it at that for now."

Kalani'ōpu'u's first act upon his return to Kealakekua some seven days after Cook's arrival there was to impose a kapu on the bay. The kapu discomfited the haoles. Accustomed to daily consignments of fresh fruits and vegetables, the men of the Resolution and Discovery were dismayed when no victual-ladened canoes ventured out into the bay all the next day after Kalani'ōpu'u's return. The following morning, some of our people—as hungry for the haoles' iron as the haoles were for their produce—endeavored to reach the ships despite the kapu, and one of the minor chieftains, I know not who, tried to drive them off. Cook's people would not have it. They fired their muskets over the chief's head and drove him away instead. Trading resumed, albeit limited.

Kalani'ōpu'u could not permit this to stand. Yet, he could not undo it. He resolved to make a show of meeting with "Lono" that same afternoon. "The people defy the kapu, so great is their desire for ailon'e, and Lono's people aid them in this," he told Holo'ae. "I must myself go to the great canoe at once, to demonstrate that the kapu is only lifted by my will."

Kalani'ōpu'u's first visit to the Resolution at Kealakekua Bay was without fanfare. After dispatching his subordinates to clear the bay of all other vessels and assert the kapu once again on pain of death, the mō'ī of the Big Island ventured forth in his double-hulled canoe, accompanied by Kaneikapolei, Keōua Red Cloak, and Keōuape'e'ale. Kalola, now refusing to reside on the same island as Kalani'ōpu'u, had fled to Maui and Kiwala'ō had remained there with her. Kalani'ōpu'u and his small party stayed on board Cook's ship well into the evening.

That same night, Keōua Red Cloak and his brother related the events aboard the great canoe to Kamehameha and my father. "Lono," Red Cloak said, had greeted them on the main deck. After presenting Kaneikapolei with a mirror, and her sons with iron daggers, he had invited Kalani'ōpu'u into his own "hale"—his large private cabin at the rear of the ship. At this point in his story, Keōua paused and noted with some self-importance that Kalani'ōpu'u had insisted that his sons accompany him to Lono's cabin. Burney was also there to interpret. Keōua said that his father had beseeched "Lono" to respect the customs of his own people, and especially their kapus.

"Oh hear me please, Lono," Kalani'ōpu'u had said, "I know that these kapus are beneath you and your people, who have come here from Kahiki, but they are laws of my own people and I beg you, please do not encourage them to transgress these laws. Without our kapus, we have no order." When all this had been translated by Burney, Cook nodded gravely and said, simply, "I understand. We not want weaken your tapus. We not do so from now on."

After their parley in Cook's cabin, Cook and Burney conducted Kalani'ōpu'u, Kaneikapolei, and his sons on a tour of the ship, which took some time, as the boys paused frequently to ask questions regarding the nature of the various objects they observed. Like Kamehameha, they were especially interested in the ship's cannons. Cook indulged them in a detailed explanation, but Burney, perhaps remembering Kameha's keen and somewhat unsettling interest in the workings of these armaments, offered a much-abridged translation. "Lono spoke at great length about these kano'ono," Keōua reported, "but One-Who-Speaks explained them to us very quickly. He said that the kano'ono eat fire and defecate ailon'e on their enemies. I cannot imagine why Lono would take so long to say such a simple thing. In any case, I see no advantage in it. Any Hawai'ian warrior could easily dodge such a weapon. It seems like a waste of ailon'e."

Kamehameha listened and said nothing in response.

"Look at the fine ailon'e daggers that Lono gave us," Keōua Red Cloak exulted, brandishing his weapon inches in front of Kamehameha's face. The blade gleamed in the light of the kukui-oil lamps. "Do you yet have a dagger as fine as this?"

"No," Kameha replied, "but I will."

"Do you have any food?" asked Red Cloak's brother, Keōuape'e'ale. "Lono's people shared theirs with us, but we ate no more than courtesy required. It was terrible."

Kalani'ōpu'u returned to the bay the next day, this time with all the trappings of his high station, saying to Holo'ae, "This day, Lono shall come to me."

The mō'ī of the Big Island and his retinue embarked in three double-hulled canoes. Kalani'ōpu'u and his most important chieftains rode in one; Holo'ae and his fellow kāhuna traveled in another, bedecked with idols. A third canoe heavily ladened with hogs and vegetables followed them. Save for the two ships and Kalani'ōpu'u's three canoes, the bay was empty.

Kalani'ōpu'u did not board Cook's ship. Instead, his small flotilla circled once around the Resolution and the Discovery and then made directly for the place onshore where King and his people had established an astronomical observatory. Holo'ae, who took the haoles' astronomical instruments to be holy objects, believed the haoles had established Cook's own heiau at this place.

Cook, realizing that Kalani'ōpu'u had no intention of calling on him on his own ship this day, followed Kalani'ōpu'u to shore in the Resolution's pinnace. He gained the beach at about the same time as the mō'ī.

Though Ki'ine—Lieutenant King—had earlier encountered Kalani'ōpu'u at Maui, he had not understood then that the latter was the Big Island's ruler. King recorded later in his own journal that he was "surprised to see, in the person of this king, the same infirm and emaciated old man that came on board the Resolution when we were off the north-east side of the island of Mowee." King also noted the presence of Kamehameha, whom he called "Maiha-Maiha," saying that at first he did not recognize him, "his hair being plastered over with a dirty brown paste and powder, which was no mean heightening to the most savage face I ever beheld." Kameha had merely adorned himself in a manner reflective of his status as Kalaniʻōpuʻu's nephew and a warrior chieftain of high station.

Of course, the haoles—with their pale skin, strange eyes, narrow noses and mouths, and oddly variant hair coloration—looked equally strange to our people. All the same, these differences did not induce mockery among us.

Kameha described the proceedings at the haoles' observatory to my father. "We were invited into a strange hale made entirely of some kind of heavy cloth that the haoles had thrown over wooden poles and lashed to the ground," he said. Burney later told Kameha that this material was called canvas, which Kamehameha called *kaʻanwa*. Burney said that his people called the structure itself a tent. Kamehameha called it a *hale o kaʻanwa*. "This hale o kaʻanwa provided surprisingly good shelter from both the sun and the rain," Kamehameha said.

At the makeshift hale that day, Kalaniʻōpuʻu presented Cook with many gifts. "He gave Kāpena Kuke pigs, yams, sweet potatoes, sugar cane, fruits, and vegetables," Kamehameha recounted. "He gave him his own feather cloak and helmet and several more feather cloaks besides. Kalaniʻōpuʻu gave the haole his finest red kapa cloth." This, the mōʻī had ceremoniously draped over the Englishman's shoulders. "Kuke seemed very pleased with these gifts," Kamehameha said.

Kalaniʻōpuʻu's attendants spread mats on the sand and the mōʻī invited Cook to join him in sitting on the ground. Holoʻae seated himself at Kalaniʻōpuʻu's other hand and then led Koa and the other priests in a lengthy chant. At the conclusion of this ritual, Cook invited Kalaniʻōpuʻu and his entire party to visit the Resolution. "He insisted that we travel with him in his own canoe," said Kameha. "It was a good-size canoe, but it could not accommodate everyone. Holoʻae and the other priests stayed behind."

Aboard the Resolution, in exchange for the brilliant feather cloaks Kalaniʻōpuʻu had given him, Cook presented the mōʻī with the two goats he had labored so mightily to recover from the people of Eimeo, a white haole shirt, and, most impressively to Kameha, his own exceptionally long, iron dagger with a gleaming handle. He unstrapped this weapon from his waist and girded Kalani'ōpu'u with it with a flourish. When Kamehameha asked what this weapon was, Burney told him that it was a "sword." Try as he might, Kameha could not pronounce this word. Instead, he called it a pahoa nui—a big dagger. "This pahoa nui would be very useful in battle at close quarters," Kamehameha told my father. "I will obtain one for myself." Meanwhile, Cook had obtained what he wanted from Kalani'ōpu'u: permission for the Hawai'ians to resume trade with his people.

The resumption of trade meant continued depletion of our peoples' food stores—of hogs, vegetables, and fruit. Fish, the haoles could obtain themselves. Iron continued to be the haoles' currency of exchange; most often nails, but occasionally tools or daggers. As the days passed, iron became more plentiful and food became scarcer, and Kalani'ōpu'u began to worry. "Makahiki time is nearly over," he said to Holo'ae one day. "When will Lono leave?"

"Who knows the mind of a god?" Holo'ae replied.

"His name is Kuke, not 'Lono,' and he is no god," Kamehameha declared anew to Holo'ae. "He and his people are men, as we are, but they are foreigners—*haoles*. We are being too generous with them." Kameha insisted that the people of the Big Island should demand more iron—and most especially iron daggers—in exchange for their hogs and produce.

While our people exchanged their goods for the haoles' iron, my father and Burney conducted a brisk trade in words. "I was determined to learn more of the strange haole talk and I spent as much time as I could with Pu'unē so that I could learn something of their language," my father said.

"*Me*," Burney said, touching his forefinger to his chest. "Me," he said, touching his chest again.

"Mi," said my father, tentatively pointing his own forefinger at Burney. "Mi?"

"No, *Talani*," Burney said, laughing. "A'u; *me*." He jabbed at his own chest once again.

Now my father understood. "Mi," he said, and he pointed to himself.

"Yes, yes, very good," said Burney. He pointed at my father. "*You*," he said.

My father was once again confused. He tapped his own chest again "Yu? Mi? Yu?"

Burney laughed again. "No," he said. "A'u; *Me*," he said, pointing to himself. "'Oe. *You*." Now he pointed at my father.

Now it was my father's turn to smile and laugh. He understood. "Mi!" he said, tapping his chest. "Yu!" he declared, pointing at Burney.

"Yes, yes, Talani," Burney cried. "Very good; very good."

My father now pointed at Burney. "Yu Pu'unē; 'Oe Pu'unē." he said.

Burney nodded vigorously. "Yes, yes," he said, and pointed to himself. "Me *Burney*. A'u *Burney*." He pointed at my father again. "*You* Talani," he said. "Yes!"

"*Ni'eh*!" said my father. *Yes*. "Mi Kalani; yu Pu'unē!"

They laughed together.

And so it went.

The haoles became quite comfortable in their visits to the shore, walking freely among our people and consorting with our women, who continued to welcome their attentions. Our people paid little mind to this, but more and more they grew anxious about their own rapidly depleting food stocks. Kameha and some others now took to greeting the haoles by rubbing their own stomachs and then patting the haoles' bellies—thereby signifying to them that our people's capacity to meet their needs was not without limits. Yet, despite the growing concern, the munificence continued.

When the haoles at the observatory expressed an interest in venturing mauka to explore the countryside inland of the coastal villages, Holo'ae instructed the villagers to supply them with every provision they desired, with no expectation of recompense. He sent runners ahead to instruct the people in the uplands to do likewise.

Now came an event that would have a marked impact on the Hawai'ians' perceptions of the haoles. One of them died. This man, whose name was Watman, was popular among Cook's people and well-liked by Cook himself. Knowing of Cook's affection for "*Wakma'ana*," Koa invited the haoles to inter the dead man's body at the Hikiau Heiau. "Koa still believed Kuke to be the god Lono," my father said. "No doubt, he thought that the burial of one of 'Lono's' people at the temple he administered would further enhance his own status."

Watman's bones—still encased in his decomposing flesh, much to the priests' dismay—were laid to rest at the Hikiau Heiau on February 1, 1779, as the haoles reckoned the day on their calendar. Cook conducted a burial ceremony in the haoles' queer, twittering speech. Immediately thereafter, Koa led his acolytes in a series of solemn and lengthy chants for the departed seaman. They deposited a dead hog, vegetables, and fruit in his grave to nourish his spirit. Cook's people erected a post at the gravesite and hung a piece of wood upon it to mark the final resting place of Watman's bones. On this board they had carved symbols that remained entirely mysterious even to those among our people who could interpret the most obscure of the symbols etched on lava stones throughout the Big Island:

Georgius tertius Rex 1779
Hic jacet Gulielmus Watman

Upon learning of Watman's death, some chieftains, Palea foremost among them, joined Kamehameha in questioning the haoles' divinity. "If these beings are gods and not men," Palea wondered, "how can they die? And if they are men and not gods, why do we still empty our food stores for them?" These questions began to gather over the haoles like the dusky clouds that obscured the upland slopes in the late afternoons.

Still, our people's generosity toward the haoles was not yet exhausted. For in the waning days of his visit to Kealakekua, Cook made an unusual request of Koa. "There was an old fence around the Hikiau Heiau," my father told me. "Kuke wanted the railings for firewood. He asked Koa if he could tear them down and take them away in trade for ailon'e." The kahuna of Lono granted Cook's request, but refused to accept any payment for the fence railings. Under King's direction, and with the help of some of our people, Cook's men demolished the fence, loaded the rotting wood into their boats, and took it back to their ships. They also removed the temple's carved images. King reported this theft to Koa, who was not concerned. Said my father, "Koa only asked for the return of an image of Lono that he and Kuke had earlier kissed during the ceremony at the heiau." Thus, Koa permitted the despoilment of the heiau by Cook's people. And why not? It was, after all, Lono's temple, and was not Cook Lono personified? He could hardly refuse him.

Not long after this event, Lieutenant King informed Koa that Cook and his people would shortly take their leave of the Big Island. The priest was distraught. "Koa begged Ki'ine, whom he believed to be Lono's son, to remain behind," said my father. King declined this invitation as politely as he could, but Koa persisted, telling King that he would hide him in the uplands and keep him safe there until his father, Lono, had departed for Kahiki, his paradise. Again, King gently refused. Koa then appealed directly to Cook, who told the priest that he would give his request serious consideration but that he would need more time to deliberate about it. "Kuke had no intention of granting the kahuna's request, of course," my father said.

Holo'ae, meanwhile, had concluded that Cook was not a god, but merely a high chief of his people like his own lord, Kalani'ōpu'u. The death of the haole Watman had greatly influenced his thinking in this regard. Holo'ae now believed that Cook and his people were refugees from some far-off land where food was in short supply. "That must be why they are so eager for our own provisions," he said. Regarding Koa's continued reverence toward Cook, Holo'ae said to Kamehameha and Kekūhaupi'o, "Old Koa is acting quite foolishly." Still, he would not openly refute his priestly colleague in

Kalaniʻōpuʻu's presence. "There is no need for that," he said. "Kuke will soon depart and all will be as it was."

Kalaniʻōpuʻu, for his part, remained ambivalent on the question of Cook's godhead. "You may be correct, nephew," he told Kameha, who persisted in voicing his objections. "But perhaps it is Koa who is right after all. And if he is right, then we should continue to propitiate 'Lono.' And if he is wrong, we will have lost nothing of importance." And so it was that on the day of Cook's departure, Kalaniʻōpuʻu and Koa presented Cook and his people with one last gift.

Upon learning that Cook would shortly leave, Kalaniʻōpuʻu ordered the inhabitants of all the nearby villages to deliver up their best produce and fattest hogs and invited Cook and his officers to his own hale at Kaʻawaloa. Cook and his men found a bounteous array of vegetables and fruit and many tethered pigs awaiting them when they reached Kalaniʻōpuʻu's courtyard. Kalaniʻōpuʻu greeted his guests reclining on a mat. His chiefs and kāhuna sat behind him. Cook, King, and Burney seated themselves opposite the mōʻī on mats that had been thoughtfully placed there for them.

Koa now commenced a lengthy speech. He heaped many praises upon "Lono" and begged him to grant the people of Hawaiʻi future harvests as fruitful as the offerings they had laid before him. Then he once more appealed to Cook to permit his "son," "Kiʻine," to remain behind on the Big Island to "assure our people of everlasting plenty." Burney translated all this over the loud squeals of the pigs, which were protesting their restraints. "When at last Pūʻune finished," my father said, "Kuke smiled at Koa and said that he indeed wished our people well, but that he could not spare his own 'son.'" Thus did Cook continue to uphold the old priest's belief that he was Lono incarnate. The high priest Holoʻae observed all this impassively and said nothing.

It was near midday when Cook's ships sailed away from Kealakekua Bay. The scene accompanying their departure was as tumultuous as the one that marked their arrival. The bay filled with canoes as thousands of people put out from shore to bid "Lono" a final farewell. Many thousands more lined the beaches waving white banners. All joined in loud lamentations over the "god's" departure. Their clamorous, grief-stricken cries echoed off the pali. Kamehameha, Kekūhaupiʻo, and my father were among the many who embarked in canoes to escort the Resolution and the Discovery as they put to sea. They joined Palea and several other chieftains on the deck of a double-hulled war canoe. Their canoe kept pace with the ships during a leisurely progress up the Kohala Coast under light winds. Drawing alongside the Discovery, they saw Burney waving to them from its quarterdeck. They waved back.

The ships kept close to the coast throughout the afternoon, their gently billowing sails presenting a majestic spectacle to those on shore. At every coastal village, the sight was the same: villagers lamented, chanted, and waved their white banners. "It seemed as if all the people of Hawaiʻi had come out to pay homage to 'Lono' that day," my father said.

As the Resolution and Discovery continued north, their escort flotilla steadily diminished in size. By the time the ships reached Keāhole Point in North Kona, only a few canoes remained. "We were among the last to turn back to Kealakekua," my father said. "I kept my face toward Kuke's ships and continued to watch them until I could see them no more." As the two haole ships shrank in the distance and were lost to sight in the hazy light of the late afternoon, my father tried to envision the journey ahead of them. "Pūʻune had told me that Kuke intended to sail first to Maui and then to visit the neighboring islands they still had not seen before returning to their own island of Īʻīklī," he said. "He had tried to describe the vastness of water they must cross to reach their home, but I, who had never journeyed farther than Maui, could scarcely comprehend it. Even though many others have come since Kuke, I still cannot grasp it to this day."

Cook's ships took their leave of Kealakekua Bay on February 4, 1779. Several days later, a fierce storm struck the Big Island and continued to lash its normally sheltered dry side for several days more. Koa said this unusual storm had come to carry Lono back to Kahiki. Lono's Makahiki season of peace had drawn to a close and the time of Kūkāʻilimoku, and war, had come round again.

Little did the priest, the people, or their mōʻī imagine that "Lono" would soon return.

Kealakekua Bay, February, 1779

"Father, father! Lono is back!" Keōua Red Cloak and Keōuape'e'ale burst in upon Kalani'ōpu'u in his hale while he was yet barely awake and still rubbing his eyes, which were bleary from the previous night's 'awa drinking. He blinked at them in the morning light streaming through the hale's open door.

"Lono? He has returned from Kahiki?" Kalani'ōpu'u exclaimed. "What more can he want of us?"

Indeed, just the night before, Kalani'ōpu'u had feasted with his favorite chieftains in celebration of both "Lono's" departure and the return of clement weather. The intense storm that followed the sailing of the Resolution and the Discovery had driven all of the bay's inhabitants inside and prevented the kindling and tending of fires to heat the stones of their imus. Without the hot stones, pigs and vegetables could not be baked and no feasts were possible. But the weather had turned at last and Kalani'ōpu'u had ordered the imu fires lit and a general feast prepared, despite the scarcity of provisions. "Though we have sacrificed much for 'Lono,' we have surely met all his desires and he has returned to Kahiki well satisfied with us," he had declared. "'Lono' will certainly shower his favors upon us, and with his blessings, we will prosper for many seasons to come. So let us celebrate."

"In truth, Kalani'ōpu'u did not much believe this," my father told me many years later, "but after several days of heavy rain and no cooking fires, he hungered for pig meat and roasted bananas and yearned for a big banquet."

And so new imu pits were dug, stones were laid, and fires were lit. Precious hogs were slaughtered; scarce vegetables were wrapped in ti leaves and placed with the pigs in the heated pits. An aromatic haze gathered above Ka'awaloa and the other villages around the bay, causing people to rub their bellies and lick their lips in anticipation. With the onset of dusk, the pigs were unearthed from the smoldering holes, their roasted flesh falling away from their bones. The steaming vegetables were unwrapped. The poi, pounded from taro roots earlier in the day, was portioned out. Men chewed pepper-plant roots, spat the juice into gourd cups, and mixed it with water to make 'awa. The feasting commenced and continued deep into the night in the light of kukui-oil lamps. And afterwards, men with full stomachs staggered back to their own hales and their sleeping mats, certain that even if their food stores were now scarce, they would soon be replenished many times over by the grace of Lono's bounty. The god had returned to his paradise, Kahiki, and from there all blessings would flow to them. But now, unaccountably, Lono was back.

Kalani'ōpu'u struggled to his feet and reeled out into brightening morning, supported by his sons. He called for runners to summon his high priest Holo'ae and those of his chieftains who still remained at court to his hale. Kamehameha came, as did Palea and several other chiefs. When those who could be found were assembled, the mō'ī of the Big Island slowly made his way to the beach with his retinue in tow. My father trailed after them, as did a growing throng of minor ali'i, including some women folk. The common people kept to their hales.

Cook's ships were at the same anchorages they had previously occupied, as if they had never left. The date was the twelfth of February.

The Resolution and Discovery entered the bay under the cover of early morning darkness. Red Cloak and his brother had taken their sleeping mats to the beach the night before. They awakened to the startling sight of the two "great canoes" sitting in the bay like floating islands once more. Now Kalani'ōpu'u surveyed the two vessels and scowled. "We are short of food," he said. "We cannot afford more trade with the haoles, not for any amount of ailon'e. The bay is kapu, on pain of death." It did not pass unnoticed that Kalani'ōpu'u had referred to Cook and his people as haoles, rather than gods.

Word of the kapu spread swiftly from one side of the bay to the other. No canoes came out from the beaches. For the rest of that day and into the next, the two ships remained majestically isolated. For much of the first day, there was a flurry of activity aboard the Resolution. From shore, people watched the haoles remove all the spars and rigging from the ship's foremast and slowly lower it to the deck. Early in the morning of the second day, some of the haoles were seen making for the former site of King's observatory, near the Hikiau Heiau, in two small boats. The Resolution's foremast was lashed to one of the boats. This, the haoles hauled up on the beach, where they set about working on it.

"We must go out to the great canoe and learn why the haoles have returned," Kalaniʻōpuʻu said at last. Arrayed once more in his finest chiefly regalia, Kalaniʻōpuʻu went out to the Resolution in his great double-hulled war canoe, accompanied by Keōuapeʻeʻale and Keōua Red Cloak, Holoʻae, Kamehameha, and my father. Cook, Lt. King, and Burney came forward to greet the mōʻī as he gained the deck with his sons' help.

"Why have you returned?" Kalaniʻōpuʻu asked. His sons, who flanked him, steadied him against the gentle roll of the Resolution's deck. There was no hint of hospitality in his voice.

Burney, interpreting, spoke softly to Cook, who answered immediately. His response was abrupt, delivered from the summit of his tall frame. "Mast break, and must fix before can go on," he said, gesturing at the far shore, where his people labored. "We find no good place for this work, except this one. So we come back."

Frowning now, Kalaniʻōpuʻu said, "Tell me, Kuke, how long you will stay this time, and what is it that you will require of us."

Cook, who seemed to understand, made to answer, but Burney stopped him, nervously pulling on his coat sleeve and speaking hurriedly to him.

"I could not understand what Puʻunē said to Kuke," my father told me, "for he was speaking too rapidly in his own tongue, but I did make out two words: 'Lono' and 'Kuke.'"

Now Cook regarded Kalaniʻōpuʻu again. His demeanor changed. Bowing his head ever so slightly toward Kalaniʻōpuʻu, he spoke rapidly to Burney, who now resumed his role as One-Who-Speaks.

"Kāpena Kuke begs the king to permit him to stay here only as long as necessary to repair our broken mast and make other repairs to our ships," Burney said. "He also asks for permission to resume trade for food and to collect fresh water for his people's long ocean journey."

Kalaniʻōpuʻu said nothing, only fixing Cook with a rheumy stare. An uneasy silence settled over the deck of the Resolution.

Finally Cook dipped his brow toward the mōʻī again and asked, somewhat uneasily, "You allow this?"

Placing one hand on each of his sons' shoulders, Kalaniʻōpuʻu shakily drew himself up to his full height, and looking directly into Cook's pale blue eyes, said, "I will allow it."

Kamehameha was quick to take advantage of Kalaniʻōpuʻu's lifting of the trading kapu. Stepping forward and removing his cloak of bright red and yellow feathers, he said, "I will trade this for ailonʻe." Burney motioned to one of the Resolution's crewmen to approach with the usual bag of nails. "No," Kamehameha said. "I will not trade this cloak for trifles. Only ailonʻe daggers will do—your longest daggers."

Bargaining commenced. It was brief. At Burney's direction, another seaman came forward with ten daggers, all of goodly length, and laid them on the deck at Kamehameha's feet. "Which one do you want?" Burney asked.

"All of them," Kamehameha said brusquely. "I want all of them." Burney seemed startled by his tone. He stiffened and, turning to Cook, spoke rapidly in their twittering tongue, all the while glancing nervously in Kamehameha's direction. Cook listened intently and then looked directly at Kamehameha. He smiled, without mirth, and nodded.

"It is agreed," Burney said. "They are yours." He extended his hands. Kamehameha gave him the cloak. The he scooped up the daggers from the deck, five in each of his big hands, and flourished them at Keōua Red Cloak, who reddened.

"Once again, Red Cloak felt willfully diminished by my brother," said my father, who also speculated that Cook had agreed to Kamehameha's terms because he did not want to offend anyone of importance.

But offenses—on both sides—were now unavoidable, and quick to come. My father suffered one of the first. He had stepped away from the group to explore the Resolution's deck. "I saw a haole ax that had been left on the deck near a railing and picked it up, but only to examine it," he said. "All at once, I was struck sharply from behind." The blow, to the side of his head, knocked my father to his knees. Scrambling to his feet and turning about he came face to face with his assailant. "It was Ūli'iam P'ulī," he said—William Bligh.

The Resolution's deck now became a scene of tumult. Kamehameha charged toward Bligh. He was still holding his newly acquired daggers. Bligh's blow and Kameha's reaction followed in such swift order that neither Cook, King, nor Burney had time to respond. They merely stood and gaped as Kamehameha hurtled across the deck toward the ship's stout master. As he ran, Kameha raised one arm, with the dagger hilts forward, to strike Bligh down. "Kameha was much bigger than P'ulī, and he would surely have knocked him over the ship's railing into the bay, and who knows what might have happened then," my father recalled years later. "But at the last moment, Ko'o'e stepped between them." John Gore, the Resolution's second in command, had been standing nearby and rushed to intervene. Kameha's hand, balled tightly around the dagger hilts and poised to strike, froze high over his head. Gore spoke sharply to Bligh, who saluted him desultorily and stalked away in obvious disgust.

Kamehameha's insistence on trading for daggers was a harbinger. The haoles soon found that the Hawai'ians would not trade their goods for anything else. And they found that many others were not interested in trading at all.

Bligh had thought my father meant to steal the ax, and well he might have suspected so, since during their previous visits aboard the Resolution and the Discovery, many of our people had taken to freely appropriating any easily portable haole articles that took their fancy. Others had refrained from this activity, out of respect for the god "Lono," even after the death of Watman seemed to confirm that Kuke's people were but mortals. But now that Cook had returned out of season, and from the wrong direction, many more of our people doubted that he was a god. Thus, those who might have been reluctant to steal from a "god" were now relieved of such reservations and felt free to pilfer from the ships whatever items of value they could, with no thought of honest exchange.

This change in the Hawai'ians' attitudes toward Cook and his men led to several unfortunate clashes of escalating severity throughout the day—February 13, 1779. Serious trouble began when one of our people took a liking to an unusual tool on Clerke's ship. This implement was a pair of iron tongs that the Discovery's blacksmith was using to manufacture the daggers that were in so much demand by the Hawai'ians. "This person—I do not know his name, but he was one of Palea's own people—took the tool and tried to jump into the water with it, but the haoles caught him," my father recounted. "Kale'eke was very angry." Captain Clerke ordered the man flogged and tied to one of the ship's shrouds.

Upon learning of this, my father said, "Palea went out at once to Kale'eke's ship. He told Kale'eke to free this man and warned him not to beat any of our people again. He said that Kalani'ōpu'u would be angry with him and that violence would surely follow if he did." Unfortunately, while Palea was upbraiding Captain Clerke, one of the men who had come aboard with him seized the tongs and a chisel, jumped overboard, and swam away. The deck of the Discovery erupted in an uproar as Clerke's people shouted and pointed at the man. The Discovery's marines had already been mustered on deck with their weapons. Clerke ordered them to fire at the fugitive. It was too late to stop him. Like all of our people then, he was a strong swimmer, even burdened as he was with the tools. "The man was already so far away that their mūk'e could not reach him," my father said. The marines' musket balls struck only water, sending up small sprays, much like pebbles thrown by little boys. In the meantime, Palea's canoe paddlers had pushed their vessel away from the Discovery's side and raced to aid the man, who threw his booty into the canoe clambered aboard after it.

Clerke now ordered four of his men—including the Discovery's master, Thomas Edgar, and a young junior officer named George Vancouver—to take one of the Discovery's small boats, a cutter, in pursuit of the Hawai'ians. But even with all four haoles pulling hard as they might on their own oars, they could not overtake the Hawai'ians' canoe.

The muskets' report rolled across the water from the deck of the Discovery and echoed off the high pali of Kealakekua Bay, startling Cook, who had gone ashore to inspect the progress of the repairs on the Resolution's broken mast. From his vantage point just south of the Hikiau Heiau, he watched Palea's people help the fleeing man into their canoe and elude his own people's pursuit. Vancouver was now standing in the bow of the haoles' boat and pointing in the direction of Nāpo'opo'o. Cook could see the Hawai'ians' canoe coming ashore there. Palea's men were greeted by a throng of laughing, cheering villagers who swarmed round to congratulate them on their courageous exploit. My father was there.

"After I had returned to Ka'awaloa and recovered from the pain of Ūli'iama P'ulī's blow to my head, I crossed to the other side of the bay to watch the haoles work on their mast," he said. "Kuke was already there with Ki'ine and his people. When I heard the sound of the guns and saw the haoles pursuing the men in the canoe, I ran at once toward Nāpo'opo'o. I got there just as the canoe reached the beach." Palea's man jumped from the canoe and waved his prizes for all to see. Cook and King also came running, but before they could gain Nāpo'opo'o, the crowd had enveloped the man. "One of the people told the man, 'Quick, run mauka while we distract the haoles,'" my father said. "The man ran off on one of the trails leading inland from the village, while several other people ran off in other directions, all pretending to carry something. By the time Kuke and Ki'ine reached the village, they did not know which way to turn."

Cook spoke sharply to the people who were still gathered on the beach, near the canoe. "Which way?" he demanded. "You tell me now which way him go!"

Cook's command was greeted with polite smiles. Several men pointed toward Ke'ei, down the coast. "*Him go* that way," they said.

"Kāpena Kuke could barely speak our language," my father said, "and now he spoke it even less well. The people were trying hard not to laugh at him." Indeed, Cook's rage at the theft of the tools had all but robbed him of his few Hawaiian words and limited grasp of syntax. His fury, registered in his countenance, was unmistakable to the Hawai'ians. "His white face had turned red and his lips were thinner and tighter than usual. He was waving his arms and he spoke very harshly," my father recalled. "I had not seen him like this before. I now remembered the story that Pu'unē had earlier told us about how angry Kuke became when the people of Eimeo took his kō'oko, and I wondered what he might do if he could not recover his tools."

Cook set off with long strides in the direction the Hawai'ians had indicated. King hastened to follow him. Neither man appeared to notice that the Hawai'ians no longer prostrated themselves as they passed.

While Cook was questioning the people on the beach at Nāpo'opo'o, Palea's men had returned to the Discovery to fetch him. Palea came ashore as Cook hurried toward Ke'ei with King following in his wake. "Palea asked the people where his man had taken the Discovery's tools," my father said, "and they told him where to find him." Palea went off and soon came back with the tongs and chisel. He told his men to go out to Vancouver and Edgar, who were still offshore in their boat, and return these tools to them. My father watched from the beach. "Palea's men drew their canoe alongside the haoles and gave them the tools. Then they turned around and began to paddle back to the beach. On shore, we all believed that the haoles would now be satisfied and would return to their great canoe," my father said. "But we were wrong."

Unfathomably to the onlookers and to Palea's men, Vancouver, Edgar and their people now gave chase. Edgar and Vancouver leaped ashore as their boat beached a short distance from Palea's canoe, followed in short order by their two comrades. The Discovery's master and the young officer ran to Palea's canoe and tried to push it back into the water.

"Palea had sent the tools back to them and now they were trying to take his own canoe," my father said. "We could not understand it." Palea would not countenance it. He ran toward the canoe, shouting at Edgar, who ignored him. Palea now seized Edgar, holding him by his own hair with one hand and twisting one of the master's arms behind his back with his other. "Palea was shouting at the haole all the while," my father said.

"I have returned your tools; why would you take my canoe?" Palea demanded, pulling ever harder on Edgar's hair and ever more tightly on his pinioned arm. Edgar screamed in pain. Vancouver stood by, frozen in shock. A score or more Hawaiʻians, including my father, gathered at a distance, transfixed by this heretofore unheard-of spectacle of a Hawaiʻian grappling with a haole.

Cook's own larger boat was pulled up on shore some paces away, his men idling around it as they awaited their captain's return. Upon hearing Edgar's cries, one of these men snatched an oar from Cook's boat and attacked Palea. "This haole beat Palea on his head and shoulders with his own big paddle until Palea stumbled under the repeated blows and released the other haole," my father said. "This assault on one of our chiefs angered people. Slings came out."

Now the air filled with stones as the Hawaiʻians unleashed a volley of missiles at the haoles. Several stones struck Edgar and Vancouver. Covering their heads with their hands, they backed away into the water. Meanwhile, Palea recovered his balance, wrested the oar from the man who had beaten him and snapped it in two as if it were nothing to him. He brandished the broken oar's jagged-edged handle at the haole, who retreated in fear.

More haoles now came running from Cook's boat, wielding their own oars. The Hawai'ians, who were many more in number, began closing in on Vancouver, Edgar, and these other men from all sides. My father, who had just joined this group, was swept along with them.

Fortunately, Palea himself had no thought for further fighting. "Enough!" he shouted to his own people. "Let these haoles be." Palea pointed at the haole who had first attacked him. "That one has beaten me," he said, "and in return, I have beaten him and therefore there is no further cause for conflict here. So let live."

Edgar, Vancouver, and their companions were now astounded as the Hawai'ians abruptly abandoned their hostility and with many friendly gestures urged them to regain their boat, which they then proceeded to help them launch. Cook's men watched this in relieved bafflement and returned to their own boat, shaking their heads and murmuring among themselves. There they waited, unmolested, for their captain's return. None of the haoles, save perhaps Burney, understood our people's language or idioms well enough to appreciate the full import of Palea's final words, "let live." For with those two words, he had commanded all of his people to disown their anger and they had cheerfully complied. Such were our ways in those days.

"Palea foresaw that if matters continued as they were," my father said, "someone on one side or the other, or both, would be killed, with serious and unpredictable consequences." While Palea wanted no bloodshed, he was still intent upon having satisfaction for the disrespect the haoles had shown him—with consequences that even he could not anticipate.

News of the fray spread rapidly around the bay. "Did any of the haoles have a mūk'e?" Kamehameha asked my father at Ka'awaloa that night. No, he answered, there was not a musket among them. "Then you were fortunate," Kameha said. "Those mūk'e are more dangerous than any canoe paddle. If a haole points one at you in the future, be sure to get out of his way—and quickly. *E wiki ʻoe, mai lohi,* Kalanimālokuloku," he said, tapping my father's chest. *Do not delay.*

"You can be sure of that, brother," my father replied.

When Vancouver and Edgar returned to the Discovery after the fight on the beach, they left the cutter in the water, tied to the ship's stern. In the night, while everyone on shore and nearly everyone aboard Cook's ships slept, Palea and one of his people paddled out to the Discovery in Palea's canoe, untied the cutter, and towed it away. "The haoles had tried to take Palea's own canoe," my father said. "Thus, he retaliated by taking the haoles' canoe." Palea and his man towed the cutter to the beach at Kaʻawaloa. With the help of some other men, they carried it mauka, where they broke it apart to extract its iron nails. The haoles on the Discovery did not miss the cutter until daybreak.

Cook was enraged when he learned of the theft, and as he had done when the people of Eimeo stole his goats, he resolved to recover his boat without regard to any pain he might cause the inhabitants of Kealakekua Bay. Cook had already set his plans in motion as the people around the bay were waking to the new day.

"When first we rose, Kamehameha and I knew nothing of Palea's actions during the night," my father said. "But we could already see much activity around the haoles' great canoes. It was unusual for so early in the morning and I wondered at the cause."

The first thing my father and Kameha saw was two boats, one from the Resolution and the other from the Discovery, making for opposite ends of the bay. "One boat went toward Palemanō Point and the other came toward us at Kaʻawaloa," he said. "They made no attempt to land and we could not divine their purpose." But others soon would, for at this time, a canoe put out from Kaʻawaloa, making toward the bay's northern point.

"Almost at once," my father said, "the haoles in the boat closest to us commenced pulling harder on their paddles. To those of us watching from the beach, it seemed that they were giving chase."

For the people in the canoe there was no doubt about this, because they could see the haoles shaking their fists at them and hear their shouts. Though the haoles' words were unintelligible to the Hawai'ians, their intent was clearly hostile. The Hawai'ians unfurled a sail, and their canoe began to pull away from the slower haole rowboat. There followed two events that shocked residents from one side of the bay to the other.

"Kuke's great canoe fired its cannon," my father said. A large spout of water suddenly erupted ahead of the fleeing canoe and the cannon's roar caromed off the bay's high cliff. People who had still been slumbering now came stumbling out of their hales, wide-eyed. "It was as if the goddess Pele had flown from her home at Kīlauea and descended suddenly upon Kealakekua," said my father. "People were all at once frightened and angered." The men in the sail canoe were now paddling frantically, trying to reach the presumed safety of the shore. But the wind shifted and the Hawai'ians lost the advantage of their sail. Now the haoles began closing on them in their own boat.

"I thought that perhaps the haoles meant to detain those men, though in that moment, I could not understand why," said my father. "But then one of the haoles shouted at the others and they pointed their guns at the three men in the canoe. We saw fire and smoke spout from the guns. One man fell into the bay; another collapsed in the canoe and the third man dove into the water and tried to swim away. The haoles shot at him, and we heard him scream." Above the screams of wounded and dying men, the crack of gunfire echoed off the pali. The haole who had ordered his people to fire on the Hawai'ians was William Bligh.

Once they learned that Palea had taken the boat, the people of Kealakekua Bay understood the haoles' anger. In those days, a vessel of any size was a valued possession among our people. Thus, they were not surprised that Kuke was unhappy. But they were shocked by the indiscriminate, sanguinary ferocity of his people's response. Palea had taken the cutter. Kuke's grievance was with him, not with the men his people had attacked. Only enemies punished each other in this way. Had "Lono" now become their enemy? Fearful of what was to come, the women fled mauka with their infants and small children. The men picked up their clubs and spears. Blowing on conch shells, they raised alarms from one side of the bay to the other.

"Kuke will not rest until he has retrieved his own canoe," Kamehameha said. "He will burn our canoes; he will burn our villages if he thinks he must; it will be for us as it was for the people of Eimeo."

Kameha spoke thus to my father while they were still standing on the rocky beach at Ka'awaloa, watching the tumult in the bay. Now they saw several boats pull away from the Resolution and head for the spot where they stood. A tall haole stood at the prow of one of the boats. His figure was unmistakable. "Look there, Kameha," my father said, "Kuke comes."

"No doubt he is coming to speak with Kalani'ōpu'u," Kamehameha said. "We must go to him at once." Kameha and my father turned back to the village. As they made their way through the palm trees to Kalani'ōpu'u's hale, they heard more musket fire and new cries coming from the direction of the bay.

Cook landed at Ka'awaloa with an escort of nine marines and one of their officers. The marines carried muskets; Cook and the officer each carried a sword and pistol. Another launch with more armed marines remained a short distance offshore. Once Cook and his people were away, the pinnace's crew likewise withdrew offshore.

Drawn by the commotion in the bay, a swelling crowd of Hawai'ians was on hand as Cook and his people stepped from his pinnace to the rocky shore. Out of respect either for Cook or for the "water-squirters" that his men carried, the people made way for them. But no one laid themselves on the ground at Cook's feet now.

Kalani'ōpu'u was still abed in his hale when Kamehameha and my father reached his courtyard. They sat down to wait for him to emerge. Keōua Red Cloak and Keōuape'e'ale, who had also gone down to the beach, now returned to their father's hale and seated themselves in the courtyard near my father and Kameha. "As was his custom then, Kalani'ōpu'u had indulged his love of 'awa well into the night," my father said. "The noise of the haoles' guns had failed to rouse him."

Cook and his marines now entered the village, trailed by scores of people who had followed them from the beach. Upon seeing Cook approaching, Keōuakuahu'ula and Keōuape'e'ale jumped up to fetch him. "Keōua Red Cloak and his brother were much enthralled with Kuke," my father told me. "They had visited his ship again as soon as they could after their father lifted the kapu on the bay." Taking Cook in hand, they led him to Kalani'ōpu'u's house. The marines followed their captain into the courtyard. The scores of Hawai'ians who had followed them halted at the courtyard's low fence. They were commoners and it was kapu for them to enter the mō'ī's courtyard.

Surveying the Hawai'ians gathered in and around the courtyard, Cook asked imperiously and of no one in particular, "Where Terrioboo is?" Keōua Red Cloak and his brother pointed at the hale. "Our father is in there," Red Cloak said. "He sleeps still." Though his grasp of our language was only rudimentary, Cook understood Red Cloak well enough. He turned to the officer of marines who had accompanied him, spoke rapidly and pointed at the hale. This man—his name was Phillips—darted through the hale's single doorway, disappearing into its darkened interior. Kalani'ōpu'u's people gasped. It was kapu to disturb the mō'ī during his time of rest, however long that might be. Moments later, Phillips emerged from the hale, leading Kalani'ōpu'u by one hand. The ruler of the Big Island blinked repeatedly against the bright light of morning into which he had been ushered so abruptly. He was bewildered.

"Kuke?" he said, looking first at Cook, then at the marines in their red uniforms, and then round at his own people, who were watching him.

"Why have you come here now?" Now his eyes fixed on the haoles' muskets. "Why do you come with so many water-squirters?"

"I come ask you come back to great canoe," Cook replied, touching Kalaniʻōpuʻu lightly on the shoulder. "I much wish see you more."

"Kuke was doing his best to issue a polite invitation," my father said. But as the haoles' own journals have since revealed, Cook's intention was anything but polite. His plan was to hold Kalaniʻōpuʻu hostage on the Resolution, against the return of the stolen cutter.

Kalaniʻōpuʻu nodded meekly to Cook. "I will come with you, Kuke," he said.

Cook signaled his people to turn back to the boats. Leading the way and parting the Hawaiʻians—hundreds of them now—before them like the prow of a canoe, the soldiers struck out for the shore. The boys followed them. Cook now took Kalaniʻōpuʻu lightly by the hand and led the mōʻī to the beach. Kamehameha and my father walked behind them. The crowd followed, swelling by the minute.

Cook's gesture of familiarity toward Kalaniʻōpuʻu drew muted protests from our people. "There was much muttering at this sight," said my father. "God or no, they thought it was improper for 'Lono' to take their mōʻī's hand."

The party had just emerged from the coconut grove mauka of the beach when four men in a canoe reached the shore. They were crying and wailing. "Kalimu is dead! Kalimu is dead! The haoles have killed him!"

Kalimu was a popular young chieftain who had been visiting with Kekūhaupiʻo in Keʻei. Shaken out of their sleep that morning by the boom and crack of cannon and musket fire reverberating off the pali at Kealakekua, he and Kekūhaupiʻo had run to Nāpoʻopoʻo and then set out by canoe for Kaʻawaloa. They had not gone more than a few hundred yards when sailors Cook had dispatched in the direction of Nāpoʻopoʻo confronted them. As part of his plan to recover the lost cutter, Cook had ordered his people to prevent all Hawai'ians from leaving the bay. Now the violence set in motion by his blockade order fell upon Kekūhaupi'o and Kalimu.

"As we neared their canoe, the haoles began to shout at us," Kekūhaupi'o told Kamehameha and my father that night, in the somber aftermath of the day's events. "We could not understand their words or what they wanted, but they seemed very angry." Kekūhaupi'o and Kalimu responded to the shouts by paddling harder as they tried to evade the irate haoles. "Our canoe was faster than theirs and we were easily outdistancing them. We were already near the middle of the bay," Kekūhaupi'o said. Then from behind them came a loud clap that made Kekūhaupi'o's ears ring. The small, two-man outrigger canoe rocked suddenly, and all at once Kekūhaupi'o felt as if he was paddling against a strong current. He turned and looked over his shoulder. Kalimu, at the canoe's opposite end, was now slumped over, blood gushing from his neck. Kekūhaupi'o looked back at the haoles, who were pulling hard on their oars and drawing ever closer. One of the haoles was pointing a musket at him. Now he understood. He raised his hands, palms open, to show he meant no offense. Then, turning around in order to propel the canoe as best he could with the dead weight of Kalimu's inert body now in front of him, Kekūhaupi'o had returned to the bay's southern shore. He landed at Nāpo'opo'o to the great cries and lamentations of the villagers, who had watched from the beach as this terrible event unfolded.

The men who carried the news to Ka'awaloa had departed at once by canoe, taking care to stay well inshore of the menacing haoles and their odd canoe. "Kalimu is dead! Kalimu is dead!" they wailed all the way across the bay. Their stricken cries echoed off the path of the gods.

The Hawai'ians trailing Cook and Kalani'ōpu'u to the beach were stunned as word of Kalimu's death at the haoles' hands spread among them. Kalani'ōpu'u seemed not to notice and was still walking hand-in-hand with Cook toward the waiting boats. Red Cloak and his brother ran ahead to the shore, plunged into the water, and swam to Cook's pinnace. Now there was a commotion at the front of the crowd. Kaneikapolei—the boys' mother—pushed her way through the throng and fell to her knees at Kalaniʻōpuʻu's feet. "Oh husband," she cried, seizing his free arm, "I beg you, do not go with Lono to his great canoe. It is death to go with him."

Unsteady in any case, and now pulled off balance by Kaneikapolei, the mōʻī of the Big Island staggered. His hand slipped from Cook's gentle grasp. Sensing what was happening, Cook tried to stay Kalaniʻōpuʻu's fall but it was too late. Kalaniʻōpuʻu fell, landing on his back in the sand. For a frozen instant, Cook's own hand remained raised above the fallen mōʻī. Anger now followed upon the crowd's shock.

"Kamehameha and I could see clearly what had happened," my father told me, "but the people behind us could not. They thought Kuke had struck Kalaniʻōpuʻu." Now, as their uncle struggled to regain his feet, Kameha and my father hurried to him, one to each side, and gently placed their hands on his shoulders to prevent him from rising. They knelt beside him. More frightened than before, Kaneikapolei retreated into the crowd. A single stone flew from the crowd's midst, narrowly missing one of the marines. Cook, who had done his best to maintain a pleasant manner until now, shouted angrily at the Hawaiʻians in his own tongue. "We could not understand his actual words," my father said, "but their meaning was clear." Phillips, a few paces ahead, turned round and called out to Cook, who nodded. Phillips then shouted to the marines, who hastened to the water's edge. The Hawaiʻians behind them parted to let them pass, thinking they meant to leave. But instead, the marines lined up abreast along the rocks and assumed a threatening posture. "All at once, the haole soldiers pointed their mūk'e at our people," my father recounted. More stones now sailed from the crowd, and one of them struck a haole soldier, driving him to his knees. "I heard angry shouts behind us," my father said, "and when I looked back I saw that many of our men were carrying daggers that they had gotten from the haoles in trade. They had been concealing them behind their backs."

Cook, his face to the crowd and his back to the sea, retreated slowly toward the line of marines.

Now one of the Hawai'ians stepped forward with a spear and thrust it at Cook. "This man did not intend to strike Kuke," my father said, "only to drive him farther away from Kalani'ōpu'u. Kuke did not even see him at first." Phillips said something to his captain. Cook was carrying a double-barreled pistol. He turned and pointed his weapon in the direction of his presumed assailant. "Many of the men there had brought along sleeping mats that they had soaked in water as protection against the haoles' guns," my father said. "When they saw Kuke point his small mūk'e at them, they raised their mats in front of them." Cook's pistol belched fire and smoke, but the barrel he had fired was loaded only with small shot. It had no effect on the Hawai'ians, and they laughed at Cook from behind their heavy mats. Enraged, he fired his second barrel. This one was loaded with a musket ball. One of the men toppled to the ground. Phillips again shouted something to Cook, who shouted back. Now Phillips pointed his musket at the man with the spear, fired, and killed him.

"Only then did the people begin to understand that their mats afforded them no true protection against the haoles' mūk'e," my father said.

Angrier still, but more wary now, the Hawai'ians facing Cook and his marines backed away slowly. Then for a time, no one moved. Kamehameha met my father's eyes with a concerned look and he understood at once. *"If a haole points a mūk'e at you, be sure to get out of his way."* They were in the way, as was their uncle, Kalani'ōpu'u. Without so much as a word passing between them, Kameha and my father now helped Kalani'ōpu'u to his feet. "We intended to guide him back to the village," my father said. "But we did not get far." They had only just managed to extract their uncle from the perilous ground between the opposing Hawai'ians and haoles when the Hawai'ians launched another volley of stones at the marines. Upon this provocation, the soldiers—their muskets already raised—fired as one into the Hawai'ians' ranks. Several more men fell and writhed or lay unmoving in the sand. "Our people were disheartened and might have fled in that moment," my father said, "had it not been for Kameha, who understood at once that the haoles were now vulnerable."

Kamehameha remembered Burney's earlier instruction in the workings of the cannon aboard the Resolution. The marines' muskets were little cannons. "They must stop to feed their mūk'e now!" he shouted to the crowd. "They cannot hurt you!" Spurred on by Pai'ea, the mover of the Naha Stone and the hero of Kaupō, the Hawai'ians now charged the marines. Cook shouted to his men: "Take to the boats!"

"All but two of the haoles dropped their guns and turned to flee," my father said. Of the remaining eight men, four managed to wade into the water and swim to Cook's pinnace, but the others stumbled and fell amid the rocks close to shore. Seeing what was befalling their comrades onshore, the marines in the launch fired their muskets. The rocking of the boat hindered their aim; their volleys thus found no targets and were to no effect, other than to frighten Keōuape'e'ale and Keōua Red Cloak. The latter, who had gained the pinnace, dove into the water and struck out toward the middle of the bay. His brother, still in the water nearby, disappeared beneath the surface and did not reappear until he had nearly reached the narrow rocky shelf below the bay's cliff face.

At this time, Cook backed a short distance into the water and gestured toward the launch, as if to signal the marines there to desist. The Hawai'ians had hesitated anew at the second round of musket fire, but now they resumed their assault. Neither my father nor Kamehameha, who were steadying Kalani'ōpu'u, joined in this attack. Instead, they watched from where they stood with their mō'ī.

Flowing around Cook, the Hawai'ians surged toward the four marines who were struggling amid the rocks in calf-deep water and overwhelmed them. "They cut one man to pieces with ailon'e axes," my father said. "They speared another in the face. He went down screaming and did not rise again. They surrounded a third man and broke his skull with sharp lava stones. A fourth they stabbed to death." The near-shore waters turned red with blood.

"The two haoles who did not flee had fed their mūk'e again. They were standing just in front of Kuke, among the rocks at the water's edge," my father said. One of these men was Phillips; the other was a haole named Thomas. Thomas was making ready to fire his weapon when one of the Hawai'ians lunged at him and plunged a long iron dagger deep into his stomach. He shrieked and collapsed, blood pouring from his wound. Phillips, meanwhile, tripped on a rock and fell as he was raising his musket. Another Hawai'ian stabbed him in the shoulder. Before the Hawai'ian could stab him again, Phillips raised his own weapon, fired, and killed the man at near point-blank range. Now he staggered to his feet, and despite his grave injury and a hail of stones thrown by the angry multitude, managed to reach deeper water and swim to the pinnace. Cook now stood alone amid the carnage at the shore.

"Throughout all, save for the one man who had threatened him with a spear, none of our people had yet dared attack Kuke," my father said. "Perhaps it was because they still thought of him as 'Lono.' But then, one man approached Kuke from behind and struck him in the head with a club, though not so hard as to kill him." Cook moaned and sank to his knees. His bi-cornered officer's hat had fallen among the rocks. He had lost his powdered wig as well. Trembling, Cook crawled toward the rocks, trying to regain his hat, wig, and his feet at the same time. Blood from a superficial wound seeped through his short-cropped brown hair. Upon seeing this, the people cried, "Look, he bleeds. He is not a god; he is only a man after all." The furious Hawai'ians swarmed the fallen haole explorer.

"From where we stood, Kamehameha and I could see nothing save the men's rising and falling arms and the long ailon'e daggers in their clenched fists." The daggers rose and plunged, rose and plunged, their blades dripping with Cook's blood. Offshore in their boats, Cook's people looked back over their shoulders in horror as they escaped to their ships. Exhausted by their own fury at last and fearing reprisal by the haoles on the Resolution and the Discovery, the Hawai'ians fled the beach, leaving Cook's sundered body to lie among the partially submerged lava rocks at the shore.

Supported on shaking legs by my father and Kamehameha, Kalaniʻōpuʻu had witnessed these events in a daze. Now as his nephews helped him from the beach, he looked up them and said sadly, "Our people have just slain a great chief."

Cook and the four slain marines lay in the shallows, where they had fallen. Taking care to stay out of sight of the ships, a number of Hawaiʻians returned to the palm grove to see if the haoles would come back to retrieve their people's bodies. Kamehameha and my father were among them. "Some of the people there wanted to go down to the shore and take the haoles' bodies immediately," my father said. "They said, 'The bones belong to us. Let us go now and take them.' But Kameha cautioned these men against hasty action."

"If the haoles return now with their mūkʻe, we would all be in peril," he said. "Let us wait here a while to see what they will do." When, after a time, Cook's people had not returned to the beach and showed no sign of doing so, the Hawaiʻians crept from the shelter of the trees and carried away the fallen haoles' bodies. They collected the foreigners' abandoned muskets as well.

"We took the bodies and guns to Kalaniʻōpuʻu," my father said. The mōʻī was sitting on a mat under a tree in the courtyard of his hale, still shaken by the morning's events. Kameha and the others laid the corpses on the ground just beyond the courtyard's low fence.

Kamehameha now entered the courtyard and knelt before Kalaniʻōpuʻu. "What shall we do with their bones, Uncle?" he asked.

Kalaniʻōpuʻu regarded the bodies for some time. Then, gesturing at the marines' remains, he said, "The bones of those others you may distribute among the chiefs. But 'Lono's' bones belong to me."

"And what of their mūkʻe?" Kamehameha asked.

"You may dispose of those as you see fit, nephew," Kalaniʻōpuʻu replied. Kamehameha decided to keep these weapons for himself, saying to my father, "Perhaps we will learn to use them someday."

Before setting out on his ill-considered and ill-fated attempt to take Kalaniʻōpuʻu hostage, Cook had dispatched King to Nāpoʻopoʻo to reassure the Hawaiʻians on that side of the bay that despite the previous day's incident, the haoles meant them no harm. The Resolution's carpenters were still laboring close by the Hikiau Heiau to repair the ship's broken mast and Cook wanted to ensure that the villagers would not disrupt their work, or worse still, attack his people outright. King had conveyed Cook's assurances and personal wishes for continued amity to Koa, the priest of Lono.

Promising King that his own people were equally desirous of harmony, Koa sent some of the villagers to assist the haoles in their work. But the musket fire that claimed the life of Kalimu shattered this interlude. The villagers helping the haoles fled the worksite even as King begged them to stay. At this time, no one on that side of the bay—neither the haole carpenters working to repair the Resolution's mast, nor King and the marines, nor the villagers of Nāpoʻopoʻo—had any hint of the bloody calamity unfolding on the beach at Kaʻawaloa.

Their first intimation that something had gone terribly wrong came in the form of a sudden bombardment of Nāpoʻopoʻo by the Discovery's cannons. The angry thunder of the ship's guns rolled across the bay to Kaʻawaloa. Kamehameha and my father watched as the barrage fell upon the defenseless village, demolishing hales and setting fires. Then they saw a haole boat set out from the far shore, its oarsmen pulling hard, making haste toward the Discovery. One man stood upright, waving frantically at the ship. It was King, pleading for the Discovery's gunners to cease fire. The cannon fire ceased, but for the people of Nāpoʻopoʻo, worse was yet to come.

John Gore, who had assumed command of the Resolution, had separately sent an armed party from that ship to reinforce the haoles still onshore. Unfortunately for the people of Nāpoʻopoʻo, the Resolution's sailing master, William Bligh, commanded this force. Though he had no orders to attack the village, Bligh assaulted it nevertheless.

Bligh's assault on Nāpoʻopoʻo continued until King returned to shore and ordered a halt. By then, a score or more of our people—women as well as men—lay dead. King now commanded all of his people to withdraw to the ships.

The pungent smell of burning human flesh hung in the air at Kaʻawaloa, and with it the question of what to do with the bones of Captain James Cook.

"The haoles will surely come for them in the morning," Kamehameha said to his uncle, Kalaniʻōpuʻu.

Kameha and Kekūhaupiʻo were sitting with Kalaniʻōpuʻu, Holoʻae, Palea, and my father in the mōʻī's hale, discussing the day's events. Hazy smoke from the kukui-oil lamps collected amid the rafters of the sharply slanted roof. The smoke's sweet smell could not mask the sharp odor drifting into the hale from the fire that Koa was tending in the darkness beyond Kalaniʻōpuʻu's courtyard. The old priest had arrived from Nāpoʻopoʻo at dusk, bringing news of the bloodletting there. Koa's anguish over the slayings at Nāpoʻopoʻo was soon overcome by his even sharper grief over the death of "Lono." Wailing and shaking, he begged to tend to the rendering of the "god's" earthly flesh and the recovery of his sacred long bones.

"In fact," my father said, "Kuke's body was already roasting in the pit by the time Koa arrived. Holoʻae had earlier seen to it." In his haste to begin this ritual, Holoʻae had not bothered to properly prepare the imu or Cook's corpse. Instead, he had directed two kauwa-maoli to toss Cook's naked body into the pit's open fire without waiting for the imu's stones to become hot. Now coals hissed continuously as the fire seared the flesh from Cook's bones. Holo'ae, who found Koa tiresome and wished to be rid of him, readily assented to the old priest's request to tend to Cook. The faint sound of the kahuna's mournful chanting drifted through the door of Kalani'ōpu'u's hale, while within, a debate about the fate of Cook's bones proceeded.

"We should not surrender Kuke's long bones to the haoles," declared Palea. "Our people slew him in battle and the bones rightfully belong to our mō'ī," he said, with a deferential nod toward Kalani'ōpu'u.

"You would provoke a new conflict with the haoles?" retorted Kekūhaupi'o. Palea tensed at this, taking it as a reprimand for his theft of the Discovery's cutter—which it was. Kekūhaupi'o could see that the young chieftain was growing angry. "That would make no more sense than Kuke having made such a big thing over the small canoe you took," he added. Palea relaxed.

"The haoles will come with their mūk'e. And more will come than before," Kamehameha said. "We cannot well stand against them in force, and if we attempt it, more of our people will surely die." Turning to Kalani'ōpu'u, he said, "We should give them Kuke's bones if they want them."

For a long moment, Kalani'ōpu'u said nothing, considering their arguments. "What need have I for 'Lono's' bones?" he said at last. "It is no matter to me if the haoles desire them. We shall give them over if that is what they want. Now where is my 'awa?"

Early the next morning, Burney and King set out in two boats for Ka'awaloa, intent on recovering the bodies of Cook and the slain marines. They were accompanied by a score of armed men. "Upon seeing the approaching haole canoes," my father said, our people made a great show of running to the shore and casting aside their spears and clubs." Holo'ae had ordered this display. Rather than wait for the haoles to come ashore, Koa plunged into the surf and swam to the boats, bearing a small, white banner that he waved above his head. Even though he was old and infirm on his feet, he was still a strong swimmer and managed this feat with no trouble. "Koa promised the haoles that he would deliver Kuke's remains to them the next day," my father said. It was a promise that the kahuna was unable to keep. Cook's body remained in the imu the following day, the heat of its stones having not yet parted all the flesh from his bones.

"I promised Ki'ine—Lono's son," Koa pleaded with Holo'ae. "I must bring him something of his father's."

Koa and Holo'ae were standing by the steaming imu beyond Kalani'ōpu'u's courtyard. The kahuna nui regarded Koa with barely disguised contempt. Picking up a long stick from a pile of firewood next to the pit, Holo'ae poked sharply at the body with end of the stick, separating piece of burnt flesh from its pelvic bone. "Here," Holo'ae said, spearing the it with the stick and brandishing it at Koa, "Take this to Ki'ine."

Thus it was that later that day, the haoles aboard the Resolution received from one of Koa's acolytes a partially charred piece of Cook's haunch. The priest's apologies for failing to deliver up more of their late captain's body notwithstanding, the haoles were horrified.

Their evident—and false—presumption of cannibalism on our people's part inflamed them with anger. And the actions of a few young warriors soon transformed their anger into deadly rage. "Holo'ae had instructed our people to make a great show of their desire for peaceful relations, but had neglected to forbid them from engaging in provocations," my father told me.

Thinking to amuse themselves, these young ali'i set out to mock the haoles. One young warrior, who had somehow acquired Cook's hat, paddled out to the Resolution from Ka'awaloa in a small canoe. "He stood up in his own canoe and waved Kuke's hat at the haoles on the great canoe," my father said. "And then he turned his back on them and exposed himself." Other young men taunted the haoles from the shore, waving the dead soldiers' red coats and likewise exposing themselves.

This was too much for the men on the Resolution, who responded by firing at the crowd on the shore with the ship's small cannons. "A number of our people were slain," said my father, who witnessed these events from a safe distance. "The others fled the shore, screaming as they ran."

The haoles wreaked even crueler vengeance upon the people of Nāpoʻopoʻo later that same day, but not without more serious provocation. "The haoles were collecting water from a stream there when the people in the village—enraged over the slaughter of the previous day—assaulted them with slings," my father said. The haoles responded by assaulting the village again. "They stormed through Nāpoʻopoʻo, slaying anyone they met and cutting off the heads of a number of their victims," said my father. "Then they put the entire village to the torch."

Kamehameha was sickened by these events. But his dismay was directed more at his own people than the haoles. "They acted foolishly," he told my father. "The haoles only wish to quit our islands. Where is the gain in provoking and attacking them since they are leaving? All that comes of it is pointless bloodshed."

At the urgent prompting of Kamehameha and Holoʻae, Kalaniʻōpuʻu once more imposed a kapu on Kealakekua Bay—on both its waters and shore. No one was permitted to approach the haoles' great canoes or show themselves to the haoles at the water's edge. Only one exception was allowed. "Koa was dispatched in a double-hulled canoe with Keōuapeʻeʻale and Keōua Red Cloak to reestablish peaceful relations with the haoles," my father said. "They traveled under the white banner of Lono, as a sign of their peaceful intent." Kalaniʻōpuʻu's sons and Koa stood on the canoe's deck. As they neared the Resolution, the three began to chant.

Oh Lono of the sky,
Oh Lono of the clouds,
Oh Lono of the wind,
Oh Lono of the thunder,

Oh Lono of the rain,
Oh Lono, hear us, your children,
Oh Lono, we come in peace,
Oh Lono, hear us and let live.

On the Resolution's deck, the marines had leveled their muskets at the approaching canoe. But upon recognizing Koa and the boys and hearing their chanting, Clerke signaled them to lower their weapons.

The kahuna and the boys clambered aboard the ship. Koa now delivered a grandiloquent appeal for peace, accompanied by many low bows in the direction of King, who was standing by Clerke's side, attempting to translate the old priest's words as best he could. "Koa still believed that Ki'ine was the son of Lono," my father said. When at last Koa fell silent, Clerke spoke to King, who turned to Koa and said sternly, "He say tell you no peace until you give to us bones of 'Orono' and the others."

Koa then explained to King and Clerke that it would be impossible to return the bones of the dead marines, as Kalani'ōpu'u had already divided them among his chieftains. But 'Lono's' bones, he assured them, would be delivered up the following day.

"You give us bones of 'Orono'," King replied, "and we have peace."

Holo'ae refused to let Koa return Cook's remains to the haoles the next day. "They are not yet sufficiently purified," the kahuna nui told the old priest of Lono. "Inform the haoles that they must wait another two days. On the morning of the third day, they will be ready."

"Uncle," Kamehameha urged Kalani'ōpu'u that evening, "since Kuke's bones will not be ready for two more days, let us appease the haoles by permitting them to trade with us as long as they remain here."

"Yes, yes," Kalani'ōpu'u replied. "Why not?"

Forced to return to the Resolution the next morning empty-handed, Koa threw himself upon the deck before Clerke and King and delivered an apology so abject that they could only shake their heads in weary resignation. They were, however, gratified to learn that Kalani'ōpu'u had rescinded the kapu on the bay. The Hawai'ians returned eagerly to the Resolution's and the Discovery's decks to exchange food for iron—always for iron in any form, whether nails, cooking pots, or daggers—and especially daggers. None of our people procured any items from the haoles except in trade. For while rescinding the kapu on commerce, Kalani'ōpu'u had imposed another on thievery.

For the next two days, relations between the haoles and the people of Kealakekua Bay remained peaceful, as if no blood had been shed between them. On the morning of the third day Kalani'ōpu'u led a procession of chieftains and priests to the canoe landing at Ka'awaloa village. Clerke, who had earlier been advised that the hour for the return of Cook's bones was at hand, was waiting for them a short distance offshore in the Resolution's pinnace. King was there too, in the ship's cutter.

"Kalani'ōpu'u carried Kuke's bones himself, as a mark of respect," my father told me. The priests had carefully wrapped the late captain's skull, scalp, lower jaw bone, thigh, and arm bones and his hands—bits of charred flesh still clinging to them—in white kapa cloth. This was covered with a cloak of black and white feathers, a symbol of mourning. "The haoles would not come ashore, such was their lingering distrust of our people," my father said. "So Kalani'ōpu'u, Holo'ae, Koa, Kamehameha, and some others boarded Kale'eke's canoe, which was sufficiently spacious to accommodate them."

With words and gestures of grief and remorse whose meaning was plain to the haoles, the mō'ī of Hawai'i presented Clerke with the sorrowful bundle. Clerke then bowed to Kalani'ōpu'u. "Mahalo," he said softly. This was one of the few words of our language that the Englishman knew. And then it was done, but not quite—for Koa suddenly grasped Clerke's hand and spoke to him urgently, wailing all the time. Clerke, who had not understood a word the priest had said, looked to King in the nearby cutter for an explanation. When the lieutenant responded with a rough translation of Koa's words, Clerke could only shake his head in utter surprise. "Koa asked Kale'eke when 'Lono' would return and if he would be angry with us," Kamehameha told my father. "What an old fool he is."

The Resolution and the Discovery remained at Kealakekua Bay for several days more. On the evening of February 22, the pali once again echoed with the booming of ships' cannons as the bones of Captain James Cook were consigned to the bay's deepest waters. On the following morning, people around the bay awoke to discover that the two ships were gone. In addition to Cook's remains, the departed haoles left behind them much iron, two goats, and intimations of external forces that would in time shake the very foundations of Hawaiian society.

Kamāʻoa, Kaʻū District, 1781

Kiwalaʻō was in the act of offering the pig to the god Kūkāʻilimoku when his cousin suddenly grasped the body of the slain rebel chieftain by an arm and a leg, lifted the still-bleeding corpse high over his own head, and cried, "Kūkāʻilimoku, see how I, Kamehameha, your highest servant, consecrate your new temple with the body of this fallen warrior!"

Kameha's action astonished the chieftains and kāhuna assembled at the new Pakini Heiau, for all assumed that it was Kiwalaʻō's right as Kalaniʻōpuʻu's chosen heir to present this fallen warrior's body to the god. None was more surprised than Kiwalaʻō, who had glimpsed Kamehameha's movement out of the corner of his eye. At first, he had assumed that his cousin was offering his own pig to the god, as planned. Now, upon hearing Kameha's declaration, Kiwalaʻō scowled at him.

Kamehameha ignored his royal cousin and advanced upon the heiau's altar in three long strides. As he stepped forward, the dead man's head lolled and his long dark hair brushed Kamehameha's own brow. Kameha dropped the body at the base of the altar and backed away, the entire time keeping his eyes fixed upon the fearsome grin of the god's idol, all teeth and mocking malevolence.

A disquieted murmur now arose from the onlookers. It might have escalated to a strident protest had not Holoʻae stepped forward. Without hesitation, the kahuna nui of the Big Island began to pray.

Lift up O Uli,
The prayer, torch of life
Strive onward,

Lift it toward Ke'ālohilani,
Seek the supernatural ones above,
Who is the ancestor?
Who is the daring one above?
'Io of the dark heavens,
'Io of the mist,
'Io without markings,
Kū of the long cloud,
Kū of the short cloud,
Kū of the red glowing cloud of the heavens
Long man of the mountain,
Kū of the forest underbrush,
The gods from the wet upland forest,
Kulipe'enuiahiahua, Kīkekalana, and Kauhinoelehua,
Kahuna of the raging fire.

As Holo'ae continued to chant, his sacred words hushed the gathering, and forced all the chiefs to turn their thoughts to the god. But Kiwala'ō's anger against his cousin continued to smolder in his heart after the kahuna's words faded. In due time, it would erupt.

Kalani'ōpu'u had unwittingly set Kamehameha's presumptuous act at the Pakini Heiau in motion the previous year. Knowing that his remaining time was short, Kalani'ōpu'u wished to ensure that his eldest son and his eldest nephew would not quarrel after his death. He had thus summoned Kiwala'ō from Maui to join him and Kameha in Waipi'o Valley, where he had moved his court, and where—in the presence of his chieftains—he had invested Kiwala'ō as his successor as mō'ī and Kamehameha as the keeper of the war god, Kūkā'ilimoku.

"All hear and bear witness," Kalani'ōpu'u had declared. "When I am gone, my beloved son Kiwala'ō shall rule over all the chiefs and the land. It shall be his sacred duty, and his alone, to divide the land among his subjects—all the land save for that of Kohala. Those lands I entrust to my beloved nephew Kamehameha, whose ancestral lands they are. And to him I also entrust the care of the god, Kūkā'ilimoku, and the god's sacred kapu. Only he shall have the right to consecrate the heiaus of the god."

"Kalani'ōpu'u hoped that by affirming Kameha's suzerainty over Kohala and by bestowing a high religious station upon him, he could slake his ambition, which he already knew to be great," my father said. "For what, after all, could bring greater honor to a warrior such as Kamehameha than the keeping of the war god?"

Kalani'ōpu'u was mistaken in this presumption. For Kamehameha's ambition would prove to encompass much more than a single district, or the god and his temples. Though Kameha understood it was only natural for Kalani'ōpu'u to name his own son Kiwala'ō to succeed him as ruler of all Hawai'i, he had accepted it only grudgingly.

Kameha gave voice to his discontent at the Pakini Heiau when he asserted his own primacy in the temple of "his" god—this, despite the fact that he was not yet the god's keeper while Kalani'ōpu'u still lived. And this, even though Kalani'ōpu'u had chosen Kiwala'ō to consecrate the heiau, and it was thus Kiwala'ō's right to offer the slain rebel warrior's body to Kūkā'ilimoku.

The dead man's name was 'Īmakakoloa. He was an important chieftain of the Puna District who had risen in revolt against Kalani'ōpu'u. According to my father, the mō'ī had brought this rebellion upon himself. After Cook's people departed for the final time, Kalani'ōpu'u gave himself over entirely to feasting and 'awa drinking. My father said that his revelry eventually became a great burden upon his own people—and too burdensome for 'Īmakakoloa.

"Kalani'ōpu'u remained for some time at Ka'awaloa after the haoles left. He was done with fighting and cared only for pleasure," said my father. Kalani'ōpu'u and the chieftains at his court feasted every night. They indulged themselves at the expense of the maka'āinana throughout the Kona District, who were called upon day after day to deliver up hogs, fish, taro, bananas, sweet potatoes, yams, and whatever other produce they had at hand, until finally they had nothing more to give, and were themselves on the verge of famine. Kalani'ōpu'u then moved his court to Kapa'au in Kohala and continued his dissipation there until the resources of the area's commoners were likewise exhausted.

"Our uncle should not behave in this fashion," Kamehameha said to my father one night at Kapa'au. Kalani'ōpu'u had feasted lavishly, and, intoxicated from much 'awa drinking, had joined his chiefs and chiefesses in a vigorous hula. Now he was reeling about his courtyard and colliding with other dancers, who pretended not to notice. "He will only incur the ill will of his own people," Kamehameha said.

"Kamehameha had become especially sensitive on this point once the court moved to Kohala," my father said, "since he was the district's high chief and the welfare of Kohala was his responsibility. But he dared not voice his objections to our uncle."

Far removed from Kalani'ōpu'u's court at the opposite end of the Big Island, 'Īmakakoloa had no reservations about confronting his king. When Kalani'ōpu'u sent emissaries from Kohala to Puna to demand tribute from 'Īmakakoloa's people, he refused. When Kalani'ōpu'u learned of this, he shook his head and declared, "Īmakakoloa will pay; his people will pay." Then he returned to his feasting and 'awa drinking.

The mō'ī was in no haste to move against 'Īmakakoloa, even after the recalcitrant chieftain rose in armed rebellion against him. He remained at Kapa'au, feasting nightly, drinking 'awa, and commanding all at his court—men, women and even children—to dance with him until at last the people of Kapa'au, like the people of Kona, had exhausted their food stores and had nothing left to give to their mō'ī. Kalani'ōpu'u next moved his court to Waipi'o. Kamehameha and my father moved on with him.

Having settled the issue of Kiwala'ō's succession at least to his own satisfaction at Waipi'o, Kalani'ōpu'u ordered a new heiau built there. He dedicated this heiau, Moa'ula, to the war god. "Look, nephew," he said to Kamehameha, to whom he had just entrusted the god's keeping, "see how I increase the number of your god's sacred houses." Kameha nodded his head but said nothing.

Next, Kalani'ōpu'u moved with his chiefs and warriors to Hilo, where he ordered the construction of yet another temple for the war god. From Hilo, he dispatched his army to the neighboring Puna District to subdue 'Īmakakoloa's rebellion. While his people fought in Puna, Kalani'ōpu'u dwelled at Waiākea, continuing to feast, drink, and dance the hula every night.

Though Kiwala'ō and Kamehameha wished to join the fighting, he kept them close to him. "It is not fitting that you should stoop to fight this renegade," he told them. My father thought that Kalani'ōpu'u had a different reason for keeping his son and nephew out of the fray. "Even though he hoped he had settled the succession at Waipi'o," my father said, "Kalani'ōpu'u feared that Kiwala'ō and Kamehameha would compete for glory in the fight against 'Īmakakoloa, and that a battlefield rivalry would only engender ill feelings between them." Kalani'ōpu'u did send his sons by Kaneikapolei to fight against 'Īmakakoloa. "Aside from joining their father in pillaging some defenseless villages on Maui, Keōuape'e'ale and Keōua Red Cloak had not as yet engaged in serious battle," said my father. "Kalani'ōpu'u decided that it was time for them to be tested as men. By all accounts, they acquitted themselves well."

'Īmakakoloa's men were defeated in a matter of months, but 'Īmakakoloa—sheltered by the people of Puna—eluded capture by Kalani'ōpu'u's forces for a full year. During this time, Kalani'ōpu'u moved his court from Hilo to Punalu'u in Ka'ū and then farther south and upcountry to Kamāʻoa. There he built another heiau for the war god and awaited word of ʻĪmakakoloa's capture.

At last Kalani'ōpu'u ordered one of his chiefs, Puhili, to lay waste to the entire Puna District until ʻĪmakakoloa's people gave him up. Starting at ʻĀpua, just across the Kaʻū-Puna border, Puhili burned whole villages, crops, and canoes. "Puhili went through Puna ahupuaʻa by ahupuaʻa, pillaging makai to mauka, until at last ʻĪmakakoloa's own kahu gave him up," my father told me. ʻĪmakakoloa was brought before Kalani'ōpu'u at the new Pakini Heiau. The mōʻī gave Puhili the honor of slaying the rebel chieftain. "ʻĪmakakoloa was forced to kneel at Kalani'ōpu'u's feet. His arms were tied behind his back," my father said. "Puhili set his foot on ʻĪmakakoloa's neck, gripped his long hair and pulled his head back. Then he reached down and slashed his throat with a lei o manō." The weapon's jagged shark teeth sliced through ʻĪmakakoloa's windpipe. He collapsed, still alive and struggling to breathe, even as his blood pooled beneath him on the heiau's lava-stone floor. Puhili then stove in ʻĪmakakoloa's skull with a war club. "He struck at ʻĪmakakoloa more than once," said my father. "It was not a merciful death."

"That was not wise, Paiʻea," Kekūhaupiʻo said quietly. Kamehameha and his kahu were sitting side by side at Kalani'ōpu'u's boisterous feast celebrating the capture, execution, and sacrifice of the rebel ʻĪmakakoloa. "You gained nothing by presuming to offer ʻĪmakakoloa's body to the god. You only angered your royal cousin, needlessly."

"I showed my royal cousin that I am not to be trifled with, Kekū," Kameha replied, making no attempt to mask his irritation.

"He will trifle with you all the same."

Though he would not then admit it, Kamehameha knew that Kekūhaupiʻo was right. "Kameha regretted his impetuous action," my father said. "He realized that he had angered not only Kiwalaʻō, for which he was not sorry, but also a number of chiefs whom he might one day need as allies, which he did regret."

The hostility toward Kamehameha among the chiefs at court soon reached a dangerous intensity. Keawema'uhili, high chief of Hilo, was heard to say that Kameha should be slain for his temerity. "It was kapu for anyone but Kiwala'ō to offer up 'Īmakakoloa's body to the god," he claimed.

Kalani'ōpu'u became so anxious for his nephew's safety that he urged him to leave the court. "It is time for you to return to your people in Kohala," he told Kamehameha one evening, a few days after the temple ceremony. "They require your presence more than I do." Kalani'ōpu'u needed to say no more. Kameha understood that it was dangerous for him to remain at Kamā'oa and he was grateful for his uncle's concern. He departed for Kohala the next morning and remained there until the following year, when Kalani'ōpu'u died.

Hōnaunau, 1782

My father insisted that it was Kiwala'ō, spurred on by his uncle Keawema'uhili, chief of Hilo, who provoked Kamehameha to battle. Others have claimed that it was Kekūhaupi'o and the other Kona chieftains who pushed Kameha into bloody conflict with his royal cousin. In any case, my uncle's rivalry with Kiwala'ō, if not yet bitter, was already pronounced, and I believe that after Kalani'ōpu'u's death, conflict between the two was inevitable. I can only recount the subsequent events as best I understand them.

The mō'ī of the Big Island died at Kā'iliki'i, a coastal village in southern Ka'ū. It was mid-1782 when Kalani'ōpu'u's mana fled his wasted body. Kamehameha was tending to his chiefly duties in Kohala when Kekūhaupi'o brought him the news.

As it happened, Kekūhaupi'o came upon Kamehameha while he and my father were engaged the sport of *lele kawa*—cliff jumping. In this sport, our people endeavored to jump from the highest palis into the sea and enter the water so cleanly as to barely make a splash. Kameha was just about to jump into the water when Kekūhaupi'o found him. Grasping his student by one elbow, he cried, "Kamehameha! Kalani'ōpu'u has died. You must come away with me at once." Kekūhaupi'o added reprovingly, "It is time to cease this sporting and devote yourself to serious matters."

"Kameha did not deserve this rebuke," my father told me. "For in truth, he was merely enjoying a brief respite from his obligations when Kekūhaupi'o chastised him."

Upon his return to Kohala the previous year, Kamehameha had devoted himself to improving the industry of his people, directing the maka'āinana in improvements in farming and fishing. He was not one to satisfy himself with simply ordering others about. As he led his warriors in battle, so he led his people in domestic labor. "Kameha worked alongside the people," my father said. "He suspended the kapus that required the common people to keep their distance from him so that he could share in the work of planting taro and building fish ponds. The people loved him for this."

Kameha also spent many hours training his warriors. "It was a peaceful time, but Kamehameha understood that the tranquility was no more than an interlude, and he wanted his people to be ready for the next fight, with whomever and wherever it might come," my father said.

"Why must we go at once?" Kameha demanded, visibly irritated at the reprimand. Kalani'ōpu'u was known to be ill and thus his passing was not unexpected. Mourning for any deceased mō'ī was a prolonged affair.

"You must come with me to Ka'ūpūlehu," Kekūhaupi'o said. Ka'ūpūlehu was a village in North Kona. "It is urgent. The Kona chiefs are gathering there even now. They are preparing for war."

"War? With whom, and why?" Kamehameha asked.

"Why with Kiwala'ō, of course," Kekūhaupi'o replied. "He is taking our lands from us."

Kalani'ōpu'u had commanded that his bones should be interred with the bones of other late rulers of the Big Island at the Hale o Keawe at Hōnaunau. After the old mō'ī's death, Kiwala'ō prepared to fulfill his father's last wish. The new king delegated his uncle and principal adviser, Keawema'uhili, to organize a flotilla that would convey Kalani'ōpu'u's bones and his funeral party from Ka'ū to the sacred place of refuge in South Kona. After ten days, when the heat of the funerary imu had melted the flesh from

Kalani'ōpu'u's bones, Kiwala'ō and his court embarked for Hōnaunau in four great double-hulled canoes.

Upon learning of Kalani'ōpu'u's death and seaborne funeral procession, Ke'eaumoku and several other Kona chiefs had hurried to the South Kona coastal village of Ho'ōpūloa, just above the Ka'ū border, to meet the mourners. "Ke'eaumoku and the other chiefs went aboard Keawema'uhili's canoe," Kekūhaupi'o told my father. "After they wailed together for Kalani'ōpu'u, Ke'eaumoku, knowing of Kalani'ōpu'u's desire to be interred at the Hale o Keawe, told Keawema'uhili that the Kona chiefs would accompany the funeral flotilla to Hōnaunau. But Keawema'uhili said they were taking Kalani'ōpu'u's bones to Kailua."

This news greatly disturbed the Kona chiefs. "Why else would Kiwala'ō bring his father's bones so far up the Kona Coast for burial, except to deprive us of our lands?" they asked. Kekūhaupi'o, Ke'eaumoku and the other Kona chiefs returned to their own canoes in a state of great agitation, breaking off from the funeral fleet and making for Ka'ūpūlehu to muster their forces for a fight with Kiwala'ō's people. As it happened, a storm descended on the Kona Coast a day or two later, forcing Kalani'ōpu'u's funeral flotilla to land at Hōnaunau, where it remained. Thus, it was there rather than at Kailua that Kiwala'ō made known his intentions regarding the lands of the Kona chiefs, whose fears would prove justified.

When Kamehameha reached Ka'ūpūlehu with Kekūhaupi'o and my father, he found Ke'eaumoku in a state of high dudgeon. "Your chiefly cousin Kiwala'ō would render us landless in our own country," Ke'eaumoku exclaimed after he and Kameha had hugged and wailed their greetings. "He means to give all of our lands to his uncle Keawema'uhili and the other chiefs of the rainy side. We must not abide this!" Ke'eaumoku's half-brothers, the twins Kame'iamoku and Kamanawa, scowled in agreement. It was common knowledge that the Hilo chief Keawema'uhili and the chieftains of the neighboring Puna and Hāmākua districts coveted the temperate and fertile uplands of the Kona and Kohala districts on Hawai'i's dry side. For the arid lands of the Ka'ū district, they cared little.

When Ke'eaumoku said "we," he meant to include Kameha. But in truth, my uncle's hold on his lands in Kohala was never threatened by Kiwala'ō, who respected his father's wish that Kameha's authority over Kohala should continue even after his own death. But as Hawai'i's new mō'ī, he meant to divide the rest of the Big Island's land as he saw fit. And as the reigning chieftains of Kona, Ke'eaumoku, his brothers, and even Kameha's own kahu, Kekūhaupi'o, felt threatened. They sought to draw Kamehameha into *their* quarrel with Kiwala'ō. Kameha was not quite ready for that.

"This is a time for mourning, not fighting," he said. "I wish only to go to Hōnaunau to join my cousin in grieving for my uncle. We will learn the truth of Kiwala'ō's intentions soon enough."

"But Pai'ea," Kekūhaupi'o demurred, "in the meantime, we would do well to be prepared for the truth at such time as we should learn it."

"Doubtless you are correct in that, Kekū," Kamehameha said. "Let us make the necessary preparations, then."

Following Kekūhaupi'o's counsel, Kamehameha and the Kona chiefs positioned their warriors around Kealakekua Bay. The twins Kamanawa and Kame'eiamoku invested Nāpo'opo'o. Their half-brother Ke'eaumoku settled with his warriors at Ka'awaloa. Kamehameha took his people to Ke'ei, Kekūhaupi'o's village.

"Kiwala'ō has more warriors than we do," Kekūhaupi'o said. "If we must fight, the ground between Ke'ei and Hōnaunau will be the most favorable for us. It is pitted and there is much sharp *'a'ā* lava. It does not favor large battle formations. And by occupying all the villages around Kealakekua in force now, we can compel Kiwala'ō's people to meet us there."

"Kamehameha chose Ke'ei because he wished to be closest to the battlefield when the fighting began," my father said.

Of all the Kona chieftains, Ke'eaumoku was the most enthusiastic for war. "Ke'eaumoku was certain that Keawema'uhili and his rainy-side allies coveted his lands below Hōnaunau, and he was convinced that Kiwala'ō would accede to their demands," my father said. "Moreover, he had not been in battle since Kalani'ōpu'u's Maui campaigns, and was anxious to blood his *pahoa* again. Ke'eaumoku loved a good fight."

Just as Kiwala'ō had honored his father's wish to entrust Kohala to Kamehameha, Kamehameha respected Kalani'ōpu'u's wish for peace between his son and his nephew. "I will go to Hōnaunau to grieve for my uncle Kalani'ōpu'u with my cousin Kiwala'ō before I will raise my spear against him," he told Ke'eaumoku and the others. "And I will appeal to him to divide the land fairly among all the chiefs." How Kamehameha could have expected Kiwala'ō to give his appeal a sympathetic hearing after his own impetuous action at the Pakini Heiau, I cannot say.

Canoes lined the lava-stone shelf from one side of the point at Hōnaunau to the other as ali'i came from throughout the Big Island to mourn Kalani'ōpu'u, whose bones had been laid to rest at last in the Hale o Keawe. All the rainy-side chieftains were there, as were the chieftains from the dry-side districts of Kona and Kohala. Now it was time for the ritual purification of Kalani'ōpu'u's bones, still kapu despite their cleansing in the imu. The kapu would be lifted by a ceremonial offering of 'awa to Kūkā'ilimoku and to Kiwala'ō, the new mō'ī.

The ceremony commenced with the arrival of Kiwala'ō and the island's principal chieftains, who took their seats around a large mat specially made for the occasion. My father looked on from a respectful distance. "It was Kameha's part as the keeper of Kūkā'ilimoku to prepare the 'awa—one portion for Kiwalaʻō, one for himself, and one as an offering to the god," he told me.

Kamehameha chewed the root of the pepper plant from which the ʻawa was derived. When he had reduced the root to a soft pulp, Kameha spat the pulp into a large, hollowed-out half gourd containing water mixed with *ōlena*—turmeric. After thoroughly combining the pulp and the water in this vessel, he strained the resulting mixture through grasses into three coconut-shell cups, one filled with water of the coconut, another with sugar cane juice, and the third with pure rainwater. This last had been collected *mauka* of Hōnaunau, high on the mountainside where Lono's clouds surrendered their moisture nearly every afternoon. The first cup was for Kiwalaʻō, the second for Kamehameha, and the third cup was for the god. This cup, Kamehameha, the keeper of Kūkāʻilimoku and his heiau, held high over his head and offered to the god with a prayer.

Here is the ʻawa O god,
Choicest ʻawa only,
Food for your child,
Drink of the prized leafed ʻawa,
Of the ʻawa of Kāne, planted
in Kahiki,
From him who chewed in his mouth,
It stands ready to be poured.
O heavenly being whose shadows fall upon the land of the living,
To the myriad gods,
To you, O Kū, who are life.

Kamehameha set this cup on the mat and then offered the first cup of ʻawa to his royal cousin Kiwalaʻō. "All expected Kiwalaʻō to accept this cup from Kameha and drink from it," my father said. "But instead, he turned to Keawemaʻuhili and handed the cup to him. Kameha was both surprised and angered." But Kamehameha said nothing. He only stared intensely at Kiwalaʻō.

Keawemaʻuhili lifted the cup to his own lips. But before he could drink from it, Kekūhaupiʻo leaped to his feet, and lunging past both Kamehameha and the new mōʻī, dashed the cup from Keawemaʻuhili's hands. As the spilled ʻawa spread across the mat in a darkening stain, an apprehensive murmur spread among the chieftains and the gathered onlookers.

Now Kekūhaupiʻo stood over the mōʻī, with no regard for the kapu that required all chieftains of Kekūhaupiʻo's rank to sit or squat in Kiwalaʻō's newly elevated presence. "You have wronged your royal cousin by this action," he thundered down into Kiwalaʻō's startled, upturned face. "The one whose bones lie there has decreed that you and Kamehameha are to be the keepers of the land and the god," Kekūhaupiʻo said, gesturing angrily at the Hale o Keawe where the earthly remains of Kalani'ōpu'u now reposed. "Each of you must respect the other. Yet now you show nothing but disrespect for Kamehameha, who, as was his obligation, has chewed the ʻawa for *you. And only for you!*" Kekūhaupiʻo jabbed a clenched fist with one outstretched finger at Keawemaʻuhili, who stared back at him without flinching.

Now the murmurs of the assembly turned to loud protests, which coalesced and hardened into threats. "This is rebellion! This is treason!" the chieftains allied with Keawemaʻuhili cried. They directed their angry shouts not at Kekūhaupiʻo, who had spoken so harshly to Kiwalaʻō, but at Kamehameha, who had said nothing.

"Paiʻea!" Kekūhaupiʻo said urgently. "We must go, *now*!" Kiwalaʻō and Keawemaʻuhili remained seated as Kamehameha clambered to his feet, but the other rainy-side chieftains rose nearly as one and made to block their way. Kekūhaupiʻo jumped between them and Kameha. "This is sacred ground and it is kapu to fight here," he cried. "Whoever would violate the kapu by attacking my chief will have to come through me!" No one moved.

"Though some of the chiefs may have carried pahoa or even ailonʻe daggers on their persons, none were carrying spears," said my father. "And no one was willing to risk being the first to close with Kekūhaupiʻo."

Now Kekūhaupiʻo stepped toward the opposing chieftains, with Kamehameha and my father following. The chieftains slowly made way for them.

"Show those chiefs no concern," said Kekūhaupiʻo, who led Kamehameha and my father at a rapid, yet controlled pace. "But we must move quickly now. The kapu of Hōnaunau ends at the water's edge and we must be well away to sea before Keawemaʻuhili and his people can follow us."

"I am not concerned about those rainy-side chiefs, Kekū," Kamehameha said, striding ahead of his kahu. "We will surely deal with them if it comes to fighting. And it may well come to fighting, for now I fear that there is little chance that my royal cousin will heed anything I have to say about a just land division." In fact, Kamehameha was to have one last chance to appeal to his *hoahānau aliʻi*, his royal cousin.

Kiwalaʻō's mother, Kalola, recently returned from Maui, was greatly distressed by the events at Hōnaunau. Fearful that enmity between her son and Kamehameha would erupt into war, she begged Kiwalaʻō to mollify his cousin. "You must go to Kamehameha at once," she urged. "Apologize and be reconciled with him." Thus, the next day, Kiwalaʻō traveled to Kaʻawaloa in an attempt to make amends with Kamehameha.

At once upon meeting, the two cousins fell into each other's arms and wailed loudly in greeting and then again for the late mōʻī. "Kiwalaʻō asked Kamehameha's forgiveness for the 'unwitting' insult he had visited upon him and said that he greatly regretted that his cousin had left the ʻawa ceremony so precipitously and had not yet had the opportunity to view Kalaniʼōpuʼu's sacred bones," my father said. "Kameha replied that he bore Kiwalaʻō no ill will and only wished to live in peace with him."

Then Kamehameha said to Kiwalaʻō, "Cousin, I appeal to you as my mōʻī to apportion the lands fairly among the chiefs. Then we will surely have peace."

Kiwalaʻō said something "strange" in reply, according to my father. "He spoke as if he had no control over events, even though he was now the mōʻī of all Hawaiʻi."

"*Auhea mai 'oe e kuu poki'i*," Kiwala'ō said. *Perhaps we two shall die.* "Our *makua kāne* insists upon a war between us and perhaps we shall both perish in this conflict," he said.

"The maukua kāne of whom Kiwala'ō spoke was his and Kamehameha's own uncle, Keawema'uhili," my father said. "He spoke as if Keawema'uhili was now the Big Island's mō'ī and not he. And Kiwala'ō said nothing about the lands in response to Kamehameha's appeal." As Kiwala'ō took his leave and returned to Hōnaunau, the unresolved issue of the lands hung in the air like the gray pall that clings to the mountainsides above Kailua in the afternoon.

The issue remained unresolved the following day when Kamehameha and the Kona chieftains returned to Honaunau to view Kalani'ōpu'u's remains. After the mourners' cacophonous wailing subsided, Kiwala'ō spoke to the assemblage. "*'Auhea 'oukou*," he said—*hear all.* "My father, your late mō'ī, gave two land bequests, one to my cousin Kamehameha and one to me. To Kamehameha, he gave the lands of Kohala, and I have no right to take this land, for it is his and his alone. To me, he gave all the other lands, and just as I have no right to take the lands of Kohala from Kamehameha, he has no authority to take the rest of the lands from me." Kiwala'ō said no more that day about his intentions for the balance of the island's lands under his domain. The Kona chieftains returned to their encampments around Kealakekua Bay more agitated than before.

"Kiwala'ō should have granted Kamehameha, the keeper of the war god and beloved nephew of Kalani'ōpu'u, lands beyond Kohala to divide among *us*," Ke'eaumoku exploded. "We must act, and the only way to secure our rights is through war." Then, pointing at Kamehameha, he concluded, "and the lands shall belong to the victor."

Even as Ke'eaumoku exhorted Kameha and his fellow Kona chieftains at Ka'awaloa, their worst fears were coming true at Hōnaunau. At the urging of Keawema'uhili, Kiwala'ō granted all the island's lands, save Kohala and Ka'ū, to Keawema'uhili and his rainy-side allies.

Kiwala'ō and Keawema'uhili disposed of the Big Island's lands in one night at Hōnaunau. "My lord," said Keawema'uhili, with the only the most pro forma of acknowledgments of Kiwala'ō's high chiefly station, "It is time to divide the lands among the chiefs, as is now your right as mō'ī. But this is a burdensome responsibility, for inevitably there will be some chiefs who will be displeased with you. Please, permit me to take the burden of their bitterness upon myself. Let me apportion the lands for you."

"Uncle," Kiwala'ō replied, "I will gladly let you undertake this task as my late father's beloved brother, my only reservation being that some of the Kona lands should be allocated to my cousin Kamehameha, so that he may dispose of them as he wishes among the Kona chiefs."

Had Keawema'uhili accepted this suggestion by Kiwala'ō—and it was no more than a suggestion, not a command—I believe war between Kiwala'ō and the Kona chiefs could have been avoided. But this was not to be, for Keawema'uhili scoffed at the very idea. "This was not your father's instruction," he said. "When Kalani'ōpu'u commanded that Kamehameha should be the keeper of Kūkā'ilimoku and all of his heiaus, he granted him his ancestral lands of Kohala and no more. He decreed that the remaining lands should be yours, to divide as you see fit. You must not transgress your beloved father's wishes now, and especially not here, so close by his own bones in the Hale o Keawe."

"But Uncle," Kiwala'ō responded, "how is giving all the lands to you to divide any different from giving some of the lands to Kamehameha to do with them as he wishes?"

"Kamehameha would be acting on his own authority, but it will be known to all that I am merely acting in your name, as your own agent," Keawema'uhili replied. "It will be as if you had divided the lands yourself."

Apparently perceiving no contradiction between Keawema'uhili's first assertion and his second—that he would absorb the displeasure of any slighted chiefs on one hand and that he would be acting in Kiwala'ō's own name on the other—Kiwala'ō pronounced himself satisfied with this explanation. "Uncle, I give you permission to apportion the lands in my name," he said, "save for the lands of Kohala, which are for Kamehameha, and the lands of Ka'ū, which shall be reserved for my brothers, Keōuape'e'ale and Keōua Kūahu'ula. I only command you to ensure that your dispositions will be fair to all the rest."

"They will be, my lord," Keawema'uhili said. "They will be."

Whether Kiwala'ō failed to perceive the guile in Keawema'uhili's proposal or merely chose to ignore it, I do not know. My father's explanation was simple and scathing. "Kiwala'ō was weak-minded," he said.

Keawema'uhili's land dispositions were announced several days later. They were more than "fair" to his rainy-side subalterns, among whom he divided all the lands of the Puna and Hāmākua districts—*and* the Kona lands. And of course, because Keawema'uhili announced *his* land division in the name of Kiwala'ō, the bitterness of the Kona chiefs fell upon the new mō'ī. Their course was now set for war.

Most immediately, Kiwala'ō felt the heated displeasure of his own brother, Keōua Red Cloak. He and his brother Keōuape'e'ale had not received any lands from Keawema'uhili beyond their ancestral lands in the Ka'ū District, which was the least prosperous of all the Big Island's districts. Its lower elevations were arid and windswept. For the people living in Ka'ū's coastal villages, it was a long trek mauka to the district's more fertile uplands, where Lono's clouds brought rain. The noxious fumes from the sulfuric caldera of Kilauea, where the fire goddess Pele dwelled, blighted the uplands, making them less desirable than the well-watered uplands of the Kona District to the north, a portion of which Keōua Red Cloak and his brother coveted.

After the uproar of the 'awa ceremony, Keōua Kūahu'ula and Keōuape'e'ale had decamped in haste from Kiwala'ō's court at Hōnaunau and taken up temporary residence at a village near the Ka'ū-Kona border. "They wanted no part in the fighting they were sure would follow," my father said. The brothers had left a few of their warriors behind. When one of these men arrived with news of Kiwala'ō's land division, they hurried back to their half-brother's side to remonstrate with him. Red Cloak spoke for both of them. First, he asked for part of the lower Kona lands.

"We have no lands in lower Kona," Kiwala'ō said. "For all those lands have been distributed."

Then Red Cloak asked for a portion of the Puna District lands, immediately adjacent to the Ka'ū district.

"Those lands, too, have all been distributed," Kiwala'ō said.

Next, Red Cloak asked for a portion of land in the Hilo district, near Kea'au. "Those lands are already spoken for," said Kiwala'ō. "Nothing remains for us there."

"Brother," protested Keōua Kū'ahu'ula, "you are the mō'ī of all Hawai'i. How is it that you—and we in turn—have no lands?"

"Keawema'uhili has distributed all the lands in my name, save for Kohala, which our father reserved for Kamehameha, and Ka'ū, which he set aside for you and Keōuape'e'ale," Kiwala'ō replied. "At least you have Ka'ū. I have no lands to my own name."

This was literally true, but meaningless in practice. As the Big Island's mō'ī, Kiwala'ō had no need of lands in his own name because he was entitled to abide wherever he would, whenever he would, and Keoua Red Cloak understood this.

Angered by their older brother's dissembling, Red Cloak and Keōuape'e'ale—who had said nothing throughout this exchange—took curt leave of Kiwala'ō and returned to their own people near Ka'ū.

Kalanimālokuloku, as my father was then still called, stumbled through the doorway of the dimly lit hale at Ka'awaloa, where Kamehameha and Kekūhaupi'o were conferring with the Kona chieftains. His appearance shocked the chiefs. Even in the weak light of the kukui-oil lamps they could see that his brow was laced with dark streaks of clotted blood. Kalanimālokuloku's hair was likewise caked with blood. A glancing club blow to his head had opened a deep gash.

"Pai'ea," he cried, "Keōua Red Cloak has attacked our people at Ke'ei and slain three of our men." Kalanimālokuloku swayed unsteadily as he spoke, still dazed from his injury hours after the blow.

Kamehameha rose from his mat and wrapped an arm around his brother's shoulders, to keep him from falling. "Come sit with us, brother," he said. "Drink some 'awa and tell us what has happened."

Kalanimālokuloku slumped to the hale's floor and accepted a cup of 'awa. He took a long drink. "We chiefs were at the shore, riding the waves," my father said. "When we first saw Keōua Red Cloak and his people approaching in the distance, we thought they were coming to join us in our sport." But Red Cloak and his men were not garbed for surf riding, which required no more than a simple malo, if that. Instead, they wore their finest feather cloaks and helmets and elaborate necklaces. They carried long pololū spears and clubs. "As they drew nearer," my father told Kamehameha and the Kona chiefs, "we saw that they were equipped for war. They set upon us suddenly, without provocation."

The melee that followed was decidedly one-sided, for only Red Cloak's people were armed. "They attacked us with their clubs and spears. We had nothing to defend ourselves with, other than our own hands," my father said. My father was fortunate. He was among the people who were farthest removed from the oncoming attackers. "When I saw Red Cloak's men fall upon our people," he said, "I ran toward the water. One of Red Cloak's warriors overtook me and struck me hard with his club, but still I did not stop."

Dazed and bloodied, my father staggered into the water and threw himself into an oncoming wave, out of his assailant's reach. A second and potentially fatal blow of the warrior's club met only water. "I forced myself to swim as far as I could under the water," said my father. His scalp was now bleeding copiously from the jagged club wound, staining the water red. When my father rose to the surface at last, his enemy was gone, but he was weak and struggling to keep his head above water. "I might have drowned then and there," he said, "had not one of my comrades seen me and pulled me onto his surf-riding board." My father and his rescuer waited beyond the surf line until Keōua Red Cloak and his people had slaked their bloodlust and quit the beach. Then they paddled back to shore and with another man secured the canoe that brought them to Ka'awaloa.

"Keōua Red Cloak and his men carried away the bodies of three of our people," my father said. "I do not know where they took them."

It not until much later that Kamehameha, my father, and the Kona chieftains learned of the events that preceded and followed Keōua Red Cloak's unprovoked attack at Ke'ei.

"After Kiwala'ō spurned his pleas for other lands in addition to Ka'ū, Red Cloak led his warriors to Keomo, on Kekūhaupi'o's lands between Hōnaunau and Ke'ei, where they chopped down many coconut trees," my father said. "This was a grave insult to Kekūhaupi'o and Kamehameha." In those days, our people looked upon coconut trees as sacred. They saw them as representations of men whose heads were in the ground as they offered their penises and testicles to the sky. It was kapu for any personage other than a nī'aupi'o chief to cut down a coconut tree, and then only on his own lands. To cut down the coconut trees on another chief's lands was an act of war.

"If Red Cloak's first quarrel was with his own brother, why did he seek instead to provoke Kamehameha?" I asked my father when he told me this story.

"He attacked us at Ke'ei because he wanted to curry favor with Kiwala'ō," my father replied.

Following the bloody attack at Ke'ei, Keōua Red Cloak took the slain men's corpses to Hōnaunau, where he offered the bodies to Kiwalaʻō to sacrifice to the war god. "It was a test of sorts," said my father. If Kiwalaʻō accepted Red Cloak's gift, it would mean that the new mōʻī still looked favorably upon him, he explained. "And if so, Red Cloak believed, he could still hope for a more favorable land settlement." But if his brother rejected his proffer, then Keōua Red Cloak could be certain that Kiwalaʻō would never grant him and his brother any lands beyond Kaʻū, in which case he would withdraw his own people from Hōnaunau forthwith and take no side in the pending conflict with Kamehameha and the Kona chieftains.

Kiwalaʻō accepted the bodies of Kamehameha's people and sacrificed them on the altar of the Heiau o Kūkāʻilimoku at Hōnaunau. "This was doubly insulting to Kamehameha," my father said, "for his royal cousin had offered the bodies of his own people to the war god, who was in Kameha's own keeping, and in a heiau for which he was responsible."

Moku'ōhai, 1782

Kamehameha was unwilling to provoke a battle with Kiwala'ō. "Let my cousin hurl the first spear," he said.

"Yes," said Kekūhaupi'o. "Let him come to us."

Keōua Red Cloak came to them first. Once Kiwala'ō had accepted the bodies of Keōua's victims for sacrifice, Red Cloak cast his lot with his older brother. Ever eager to prove his mettle as a warrior, and most especially against his cousin Kamehameha, it was he who instigated the battle of Moku'ōhai.

"The day after the sacrifices at Hōnaunau," my father told me, "Red Cloak's people sallied forth toward Ke'ei in search of another fight. But they did not find any of our people there because after the first bloodletting, Kamehameha, Kekūhaupi'o, and Ke'eaumoku had pulled them all back toward Nāpo'opo'o." Instead, Keōua's people found Kamehameha's men amid the 'a'ā lava rocks between Ke'ei and Nāpo'opo'o.

Sporadic fighting between small bands of warriors marked the next several days. These skirmishes were inconclusive, and Red Cloak's people did not fare as well as he had hoped. "Perhaps Red Cloak believed that having vanquished Kameha's people so easily at Ke'ei, his men would subdue them decisively now," said my father. "In this he was mistaken."

As Kamehameha and my father later learned, at the end of the third day of skirmishing, Keōua Red Cloak appealed to his older brother Kiwala'ō for help. Like Kamehameha, Kiwala'ō had remained reluctant to engage in battle. He yet hoped that Kamehameha would be satisfied with his own lands in Kohala, and ignore those who were pressing for war.

But Keōua Red Cloak persuaded Kiwala'ō that his cousin would never abandon the Kona chieftains and withdraw to Kohala. "Moreover," my father said, "Red Cloak convinced Kiwala'ō that if only he and his warriors would take the field alongside Keōua's men, they could easily overwhelm Kameha and our people, as we would be greatly outnumbered." Upon hearing this, Kiwala'ō agreed to join the fray. "Once Kiwala'ō was certain that the odds favored him, he was eager to fight," said my father. And thus did Kiwala'ō hasten into Kekūhaupi'o's trap.

The battle of Moku'ōhai was fought around Hauiki, a village below Kealakekua Bay. Hauiki was a small fishing village consisting of no more than a half-dozen humble hales. Its inhabitants were commoners and of no importance in those days, and the village no longer exists. For these reasons, the place is now known by the battle's name. The battle took its name from a grove of silvery-leaved *'ohai* trees that grew there. Today, those trees, like so much of our people's past, exist only in fading memories. But the day-long battle is legend.

Kamehameha did not take part in the fighting when it commenced in the morning. At Holo'ae's urging, he held all of his Kohala people back—my father included—when the serious fighting began. "The night before the battle, Holo'ae foretold that the morning's fighting would not go well for the chiefs of Kona," my father said. "Holo'ae told Kameha, 'Kiwala'ō and the rainy-side chieftains will prevail while Kāne's sun still favors Hawai'i's wet side. But later in the day, when the god's sun favors the island's dry side, the tide of battle will favor you. Therefore, hold yourself and your people in reserve until then.' Kamehameha readily assented to Holo'ae's counsel."

Kiwala'ō and his half-brother Keōua Red Cloak heard similar priestly divinations. "As we later learned, Kiwala'ō's kahuna nui warned him that while the battle would go well for his people in the morning, Kamehameha's people would be victorious if the fighting continued into the afternoon," said my father. "Kiwala'ō's high priest advised him therefore to break off fighting when the sun was still high in the sky—even if his foes were not yet vanquished—and to wait until the next morning to give battle again. Keōua Red Cloak's priestly adviser likewise foretold that should the fighting continue into the first day's 'dust of the evening,' Kamehameha's people would triumph." The two brothers would give the identical prophecies dissimilar credence.

The Kona chieftains and their people were badly outnumbered the next morning when Kiwala'ō and his warriors took the field against them amid the jagged 'a'ā lava of Moku'ōhai. Now arrayed against them, in addition to Red Cloak's people, were Keawema'uhili and the warriors of the Hilo district; the warriors of the Puna district, who fought under the leadership of their high chief, Ahia; and two other chiefs who had previously supported Kamehameha, but who suddenly changed sides, bringing their fighters with them. "Kameha's own uncles, Kānekoa of Hāmākua, and his brother, a lesser chief named Kahai, were the traitors," my father said. "Under Kalani'ōpu'u, they had held title to lands on the Hāmākua Coast. Though Kiwala'ō had left it to his uncle Keawema'uhili to distribute those lands, he had not yet apportioned them. When they saw how badly outnumbered the Kona and Kohala warriors were, Kānekoa and Kahai were sure Kiwala'ō's side would prevail. They deserted Kamehameha to ensure that they would not lose their Hāmākua lands."

In the morning, Ke'eaumoku and Kekūhaupi'o led the warriors of Kona while Kamehameha kept his men out of the battle. With the treacherous ground preventing the two sides from attacking each other in large formations, ranging bands of warriors engaged in scattered, uncoordinated clashes. In this way, the battle of Moku'ōhai resembled the clash between the forces of Kalani'ōpu'u and Keawe'ōpala nearly twenty years earlier. Kiwala'ō, Keawema'uhili, and Keōua Red Cloak exacted a heavy toll on the Kona warriors, but unable to bring their superior numbers fully to bear on their foes, could not vanquish them during the morning's fighting.

Kiwala'ō's warriors were merciless. Those enemy fighters whom they did not kill outright they slew later if they found them lying wounded and helpless on the battlefield. Kiwala'ō had not entered the morning's fray, keeping to the rear with his personal guard—just as his own father had done during his decisive battle with Keawe'ōpala. Kiwala'ō's people retrieved the bodies of the enemy warriors from the killing ground and delivered them to him. By midday, they had laid out several score corpses before their new mō'ī. Kiwala'ō was pleased, but he noted with some asperity that the bodies of Kamehameha and Ke'eaumoku were not among them. "If they are still at large," he said, "we have not yet won."

"Oh Lord, you now have many foes to sacrifice to the god Kūkā'ilimoku. It is enough for now," Kiwala'ō's kahuna nui implored. "Remember what is foretold: In the afternoon, the tide of battle will favor your enemy. Retire from fighting this day to give the god his due. Then tomorrow, victory will surely follow."

Keawema'uhili, who, like Kiwala'ō, had not fought that morning, would hear none of this. "Lord, you are right to say that we will have no peace until Kamehameha and Ke'eaumoku are dead and sacrificed to the god," he told his nephew, the mō'ī. "Our warriors punished their people severely this morning. They cannot have much fight left in them. We must not let them recover. Let us yet carry the fight to them this afternoon, when Kāne's hot sun beats hard upon the rocks and assaults their worn and weary bodies, and slay them—every one of them." The kahuna nui frowned at Keawema'uhili's words.

When Kiwala'ō heard the urging of his uncle he feared to accept his priest's counsel, lest he appear weak in the eyes of his own brother and the rest of his people. "Very well then, Uncle," he said. "We will continue, and I will lead our men to victory."

If Kiwala'ō had no thoughts of defeat at this time, Red Cloak, who witnessed this exchange between the priest, his uncle, and his brother, thought otherwise. "Keōua Kuahu'ula commanded some of his men to take canoes and maintain them offshore at Moku'ōhai," my father said. "He gave more weight than his elder brother to the priest's warning and he wanted to leave nothing to chance." Keōua Red Cloak ordered his mother to wait offshore, and Pauli as well. When Pauli objected, he said, "I am sorry, but you are still too young to fight, especially against your own father."

Neither Kiwalaʻō nor Keawemaʻuhili had fought that morning, and neither had yet spoken directly with the commanders who had. Thus, they did not know that Kamehameha had held his own people in reserve. Nor did they know that a new ally had joined him: Keawemaʻuhili's own son, Keaweokahikona.

Keaweokahikona was indebted to Kamehameha for saving his life years earlier on Maui. After he learned that his father intended to deny Kamehameha any portion of the new land distribution beyond Kohala, Keaweokahikona had taken a canoe and slipped away from Hōnaunau with one of his men. Finding Kamehameha at Kaʻawaloa the evening before the skirmishing began at Mokuʻōhai, Keaweokahikona said to him: "You risked your life to save mine on Maui. You are therefore like a brother to me. My father would treat you unjustly with regard to the lands and I cannot stand with him in this matter. If you must fight, I will fight with you."

Upon hearing this declaration, Kameha was nearly overcome with emotion and he enfolded Keaweokahikona in his arms. "Indeed, you a true brother to me," he cried. Keaweokahikona hugged Kamehameha in turn and the two chieftains wailed together. Then Keaweokahikona and his man returned to Hōnaunau.

"Keaweokahikona did not want to be missed by his father's people," my father said. "He planned to bring his people to Kamehameha's side later, amid the confusion of battle."

Ke'eaumoku, always an exuberant warrior, did not want to be overlooked by friend or foe in battle. At Moku'ōhai, he wore a vivid red malo, his yellow-and-red-feather cloak, and helmet. Around his neck, on a braided cord fashioned from his own hair, he wore a *lei niho palaoa*, a polished sperm whale tooth that glinted in the sunlight.

A lei niho palaoa was a prized possession among our nobles in those days. Our people did not hunt whales then, but they sometimes washed up on our shores. They were considered the property of the mō'ī and were kapu for everyone else. Only the king could take and cook their flesh. Only the mō'ī could distribute the seared whale meat among the people. And unless he chose to share them, only the king could possess the ornaments that our skilled artisans would fashion from a beached whale's teeth and bones. Accordingly, only a few ali'i of lower rank ever came to possess such ornaments.

My father said that Ke'eaumoku's lei niho palaoa was handed down to him by his father, who had received it from his own father, who in turn had received it from the hands of Keawe the Great himself. This particular lei niho palaoa was thus valued over all others extant on the Big Island at that time, and there was no ali'i who did not envy Ke'eaumoku for his possession of it. In combat, Ke'eaumoku's polished whale tooth often drew foes who hoped to slay him just to possess it themselves.

At Moku'ōhai, the gleam of Ke'eaumoku's whale tooth in the mid-afternoon sun caught the eye of Ahia, the high chief of Puna. Ahia was a large man, broad of shoulders and body, who could run faster than many warriors half his age and hurl a long pololū spear with such force that it would often pierce a foe through, impaling him to the ground as he fell.

When he saw Ke'eaumoku standing opposite him on the battlefield, Ahia hurled his spear at the Kona chieftain. Then, with the spear still in flight, he charged. Ke'eaumoku had just barely evaded the spear before the onrushing Ahia was upon him, thrusting at his midsection with a koa-wood dagger and reaching for the coveted whale tooth with his other hand. As Ahia stabbed at him, Ke'eaumoku brought his left forearm down hard on Ahia's right forearm, knocking the dagger from his grip. Shouting with pain, Ahia reached for Ke'eaumoku's throat. Ke'eaumoku was armed with a lei o manō, a shark-tooth slashing club. He struck Ahia in the forehead with the club's blunt handle, momentarily stunning him. Then he shoved Ahia's head down and wrapped his own powerful legs around Ahia's neck and squeezed them tight in an effort to strangle him. But the bigger man would not be subdued and with a howl he surged erect. He was unable to shake off Keʻeaumoku, who now hung over Ahia's shoulders with his face pressed into the larger man's back and his arms dangling below.

Keʻeaumoku still held his lei o manō and he slashed upward between Ahia's legs with the weapon. The club's sharp teeth bit into Ahia's thigh, but fell short of their intended target. Cursing more in anger than pain, Ahia wrenched Keʻeaumoku's legs from his neck and tossed the Kona chieftain onto the sharp lava rocks, which chewed into his back and knocked the air from his lungs. Retrieving his dagger, Ahia whirled on Keʻeaumoku and was about to strike when Kamehameha, Kekūhaupiʻo, my father, and Mulihele came upon them.

Kameha and Kekūhaupiʻo carried basalt-tipped war clubs. "Stay here, brother," Kamehameha shouted to my father. "Watch, and learn."

"Kameha's shout alerted Ahia and he turned to face my brother and Kekūhaupiʻo as they ran toward him," my father said. Forewarned, Ahia knocked the smaller Kekūhaupiʻo aside with one sweep of an arm and spun around to confront Kamehameha. Kameha raised his war club as if to strike, and when Ahia moved to block the expected blow, Kameha ducked under Ahia's raised arm and drove the stone head of his war club into his foe's stomach. Ahia grunted but was still able to reach down and grasp Kamehameha's head about the ears, intent on breaking his neck.

Now Kekūhaupiʻo leaped upon Ahia's back and grabbed the Puna chieftain's head in his own hands and abruptly twisted. "I heard the crack of breaking bones from where I stood," my father said. Ahia's hands fell from Kamehameha's ears and he slumped inert over Kameha's back.

Kamehameha struggled to his feet, casting off Ahia's dead weight with some difficulty. "Just now, brother, I could have made good use of a mūkʻe," Kameha said.

As they stood over Ahia's broken body, the group heard shouts and screams coming from the direction of the sea. "Look!" exclaimed Kekūhaupiʻo. "Keaweokahikona and his people have arrived!"

Kekūhaupiʻo, Kamehameha, Mulihele, and my father took off at a run. Still shaken by his struggle with Ahia, Keʻeaumoku was slow to regain his feet. Before he could catch up to his comrades, he was overtaken by one of Kiwalaʻō's roving warrior bands led by Kānekoa and Kahai, the same chieftains who had deserted Kamehameha's cause. Their spears fell round Keʻeaumoku like rain. He managed to evade nearly all of these missiles, dodging some and batting others aside with a spear he retrieved from the ground, all the while holding fast to his lei o manō with his other hand. But the Kona chieftain could not avoid every spear and one found its mark, striking him in his side. Still tightly gripping his lei o manō, he slumped to the ground, striking the back of his head on the cruel points of the ʻaʻā lava. Keʻeaumoku groaned and closed his eyes, still clutching his shark-tooth weapon.

Kiwalaʻō was ranging the battlefield at Mokuʻōhai with a small complement of personal guards, moving from one band of warriors to the next and urging them on, while avoiding the fighting himself. When he saw that Keaweokahikona and his Hilo warriors had suddenly changed sides, he began moving toward that skirmish to exhort his people to stand firm against the sudden traitors. As Kiwalaʻō started in that direction, he heard the exultant shouts of Kānekoa, Kahai, and their warriors: "Keʻeaumoku is slain! Keʻeaumoku is slain!" The mōʻī abruptly changed course, his guards following close behind him.

Kiwalaʻō found Keʻeaumoku supine upon the ground, his eyes shut, his body motionless. Kānekoa, Kahai, and two warriors stood over Keʻeaumoku's body, their spears raised, ready to plunge them into his bared torso and neck, if only for good measure. Kiwalaʻō's eyes were drawn to Keʻeaumoku's whale-tooth ornament, still fastened around his neck and resting at his throat. "Stop! Stop!" he shouted to the men as he ran toward them. "Do not strike, lest you defile the lei niho palaoa with a dead man's blood!" The two chieftains and their warriors stepped back to make room for their mōʻī.

Kiwala‘ō knelt, bent low over Ke‘eaumoku's inert form, and reached for the polished whale tooth. He had just grasped the braided hair necklace that held the whale tooth and was trying to pull it over Ke‘eaumoku's head when a rock struck him hard in the forehead. Kiwala‘ō toppled over and lay dazed next to the fallen Kona chieftain.

My father threw the rock.

"I was following Mulihele, Kamehameha, and Kekūhaupi‘o and had fallen a few paces behind them when I realized that Ke‘eaumoku was not with us," he said. "Then I heard shouting whence we had just come. I looked that way and saw that Ke‘eaumoku was down." With no thought for his own safety, my father ran back. "As I drew nearer, I saw that Kiwala‘ō and his guards were also running toward Ke‘eaumoku. Neither they nor the other warriors paid any attention to me.

"I heard Kiwala‘ō shout something and saw the other warriors around Ke‘eaumoku draw back. Then Kiwala‘ō knelt over Ke‘eaumoku and reached for his neck. I thought he meant to strangle him while he lay there as helpless as a newborn. I had no spear, only a dagger of haole ailon‘e. I saw a loose, ‘a‘ā rock, and I picked it up and threw it as hard as I could. It was a fortunate throw, for it struck Kiwala‘ō and he fell before he could do further harm to Ke‘eaumoku, who looked to be near death."

Ke‘eaumoku was not near death. Though grievously injured, he was only dazed. When Kiwala‘ō fell, his own people turned to see who had thrown the rock. They did not see Ke‘eaumoku tighten his grip on his lei o manō. They did not hear his soft groan as he rolled toward Kiwala‘ō's unconscious form. They did not see him slash his lei o manō across Kiwala‘ō's neck, nor did they see its shark teeth bite deep into their mōʻī's exposed throat. They only turned back to look when they heard the sound of Kiwalaʻō's unnatural gurgling, as he choked on the lifeblood that was now spurting from his mangled neck. And before they could truly comprehend what was happening, the new mōʻī of the Big Island was dead.

"Kiwalaʻō is dead! Kiwalaʻō is dead! Keʻeaumoku has slain Kiwalaʻō!" Commencing with the stunned warriors who now stood frozen in place, staring at their mōʻī's still-bleeding body, the wails of Kiwalaʻō's people spread across the battlefield at Mokuʻōhai. Their lamentations and exclamations propagated like the expanding ripples from a stone cast into a fishpond. Disbelief came first, followed by grief, and then confusion, and finally, panic.

Kekūhaupiʻo's prediction that Mokuʻōhai's unforgiving ground would rob Kiwalaʻō's people of their numerical advantage was now confirmed several times over. With their warriors divided into widely separated bands of skirmishers, Kiwalaʻō's allies could neither easily communicate nor coordinate a response to such a calamity. Moreover, because Kiwalaʻō's people were not fighting in formation, there was no single point on the disorganized battlefield from which his presumed successor, Keōua Kuahuʻula, could rally them. In any case, by the time Red Cloak learned of Kiwalaʻō's death, the mōʻī's warriors were already in retreat. With Kiwalaʻō dead, like the warriors of the slain Keaweʻōpala so many years before, they had no reason to continue fighting. Red Cloak joined the retreat, leading his own warriors to the canoe fleet that awaited them just offshore. Before any of the Kona chiefs could move to stop them, they waded through the surf, swam to their canoes, and made all haste for Kaʻū.

Kamehameha was distraught when he first learned of Kiwalaʻō's death. He wailed with grief for his cousin. "Kameha did not intend for Kiwalaʻō to die," my father recalled. "He merely wished to compel him to grant the Kona lands to him and his allies, or so he said."

When Kamehameha learned how Kiwalaʻō had died, he wailed again, this time with relief that his ally, Keʻeaumoku, though seriously wounded, still lived. And when Kamehameha learned that my father had saved Keʻeaumoku's life by felling Kiwalaʻō with a rock, he grasped both of his shoulders tightly and said, "Kalani, you were very bold to attack Kiwalaʻō and his people by yourself. Keʻeaumoku would not be alive but for your bravery."

After the deaths of Ahia and Kiwalaʻō and the withdrawal of Keōua Red Cloak and his people to Kaʻū, confusion ruled the chieftains and warriors of Puna, Hilo, and Hāmākua. Leaderless rank-and-file soldiers fled the battlefield, unwilling to hazard their lives for a lost cause. With precious few fighters left to command, any chieftains who had failed to decamp with their own men were soon subdued by their foes.

"Our people easily surrounded and captured Kānekoa, Kahai, and Keawemaʻuhili," my father said. "They offered no resistance, for they knew that any show of defiance would end in their own deaths. They hoped that Kamehameha and his Kona allies would show them the same mercy that the late Kalaniʻōpuʻu had shown his opponents after he defeated Keaweʻōpala so many years before."

Kamehameha was merciful to the turncoats Kānekoa and Kahai, for they were his own uncles, after all. But he ordered Keawemaʻuhili imprisoned to await execution and sacrifice to the war god, Kūkāʻilimoku. With the Kona chieftains' support, he now held presumed sway over all of the island of Hawaiʻi, save Kaʻū.

"The lands are all yours to divide now, Paiʻea," Kekūhaupiʻo told him. But it was not to be—not yet.

Pauoa, Oʻahu 1858

Esther and I are attending a gay celebration at the Hale Aliʻi, the official residence of His Majesty King Kamehameha IV, formerly Alexander Liholiho, and Her Majesty Queen Emma. It is by far the finest structure in Honolulu, boasting large rooms and an expansive portico and set back from the road amid well-manicured grounds. People sometimes call it "the palace," but in reality the structure is too modest to be called palatial. It was originally built as a private home. Today it houses a throne room, a reception room, and a state dining room, but that is the sum of it. *Hale Aliʻi*, house of the chiefs, is more apt, as that designation can apply to any house—even a small, one-room, grass-walled, thatched-roof dwelling—where a chief holds court. The king and queen in fact live in a separate building elsewhere on the grounds.

The royal couple enjoy entertaining and they have given many dinners and balls since their marriage two years ago. But this evening is special, for the king and queen have invited all of Honolulu society, Hawaiian and haole alike, to join them in celebrating the passage of three months' time since the birth of their son this past May.

Today it is no small thing for a Hawaiian child to survive his first thirteen weeks in the face of the constant onslaught of exotic haole diseases, and thus this night's festivity is as much an expression of all the company's profound relief as it is a cause for merriment. It is also an occasion for an outpouring of hope that the infant heir to our kingdom's throne will live to reach his majority. It is a hope shared by the king's cabinet ministers, almost all of whom are American émigrés. The king's personal secretary is an American, too. Kamehameha IV is surrounded by haoles.

Anglophiles and ardent admirers of Queen Victoria and her consort, the king and queen have named their little boy Albert Edward, after the Prince of Wales. His full name is Albert Edward Kauikeaouli, the last name being in honor of Kamehameha IV's predecessor, the late King Kamehameha III.

This evening, Emma pulls Esther aside to speak privately with her. Immediately thereafter, Esther runs to me. *Emma has just asked me to serve as nurse and governess for baby Albert,* Esther tells me breathlessly.

That is wonderful news, I say. Esther will at last have a baby to mother, albeit not her own. *Wonderful,* I say again.

It is just then that I notice the young man trailing in Esther's wake and the young woman who is a step behind him. They are her friends, David Kalākaua and his sister Lydia Kamakaʻeha. Kalākaua and Lydia are both close to Esther in age; Kalākaua is imposing, tall and broad-shouldered, but he is growing pudgy around his waist and his visage is softening. Lydia is attractive; she has intelligent eyes and an engaging smile and a delicate nose. Her glossy black hair is piled high on her head, which is all the style among aliʻi women these days.

Look who is here, Esther says. *You remember my friend David Kalākaua, don't you dear?* she asks. I can't help noticing how her hand lightly brushes Kalākaua's sleeve and his own hand as she speaks.

Of course, I say.

And you remember David's sister, my friend Lili, of course, Esther adds. The young woman comes forward; I smile and nod to both of them.

Kalākaua is politically ambitious, a member of the king's administration, and seems to be everywhere in Honolulu's tight aliʻi social circle these days. His sister is almost certain to be found at any social occasion Kalākaua attends. They are of high aliʻi birth, descended as they are from two of Kamehameha's most important chieftains and counselors, Keaweaheulu on their mother's side and Kameʻiamoku on their father's.

At Kalākaua's birth in 1836, his parents named him Laʻamea Kalākaua; his sister Liliʻu was born two years later. David and Lydia are their Christian names. Lydia, however, prefers to go by Lili. I take Lili's hand and squeeze it lightly. Then I shake Kalākaua's hand; his grip is firm.

How nice to see you both again, I say.

And you, sir, Kalākaua replies. He bows ever so slightly, according me the respect I am due as his elder and the nephew of Kamehameha I, whom our people nowadays most often call "Kamehameha the Great," or simply, "The Conqueror." Esther is still touching Kalākaua's hand without realizing it and gazing up at him with a look that reveals something more than mere friendship.

We are returning home in our carriage when Esther turns to me and asks, *What do you think of David and Lili, dear?*

Lili is quite pleasant and Kalākaua seems a most agreeable fellow, I say. Then I add, *You must have friends closer to your own age, of course.*

At this, Esther moves closer to me and rests her head on my shoulder. *Mahalo, Nāmākēha*, she whispers in my ear. Her warm breath caresses my cheek and I feel myself stiffening.

In our bedchamber later, we make love, Esther with the enthusiasm of youth and I with the gratitude of advanced age. I gasp as I find release, and with pride that I still can. Esther makes little mewling sounds. Then she is crying and clinging to me. She wants a child of her own. She wants to bear *our* child, a grandchild of my father, the good prince, Keli'imaika'i, and a great-grandson of her forebear, Kaumuali'i, the late mō'ī of Kaua'i. It could still happen.

I hold Esther close and pray silently to the god Kū to guard the potency of my seed and deliver it safely to her womb and I add a prayer to Lono to make Esther's womb fertile. I fall asleep listening to Esther's soft breathing and the nocturnal symphony of the mating calls of the countless small frogs beyond our bedroom window.

Early in the morning, while my young wife yet slumbers, I slip out of bed and throw on my robe, feeling rejuvenated and eager to return to my manuscript. It is still dark. I strike a match, light the wick of an oil lamp, and carry it to my desk on the lanai. Now, in the flame's wavering light, I begin to write once more.

Kamehameha

He niuhi ʻai holopapa o ka moku

The man-eating shark devours all on the island.

Hōnaunau, 1782

My earliest memories of Ka'ahumanu are of a large woman. Even seated or lying on a mat, she loomed over me like the uplands that rise above our islands' coasts. When I first became aware of her, at the age of two or three, she weighed several hundred pounds in the haole measure. And by the time I had turned five or six, she had become mountainous. When she stood over me, unless she bent toward me, the foothills of her bosom concealed the summit of her face from my view. But this is not the way she appeared to Kamehameha when he first saw her at Hōnaunau after the battle of Moku'ōhai.

Ke'eaumoku was taken to Hōnaunau after the battle to recover from his terrible wound. His wife, Nāmāhana, and his daughter, Ka'ahumanu, came to Hōnaunau to look after him while a *kahuna lā'au lapa'au*, a kahuna skilled in our peoples' medicinal arts, tended to him. Ke'eaumoku was resting on a sedge mat in the shade of a thatched-roofed, open-air canoe shed, a few paces back from Hōnaunau's small, sandy cove. Kameha and my father were sitting cross-legged in the sand next to Ke'eaumoku's mat when Nāmāhana and Ka'ahumanu arrived by canoe. Kamehameha had not seen Ka'ahumanu since the day she surprised him on the beach at Hana some seven years earlier. At first, he did not recognize the young woman who gracefully swung her long legs over the side of the canoe and drew herself to her full height. She was even then large-framed, but yet most pleasing to the eye: tall; pleasantly broad across her firm, ripening bosom; still slim in the waist; and suggestively lush in the hips. She was then about fifteen years old.

As she ran lightly across the sand to her father, her mother walking sedately behind her, my father heard Kamehameha suddenly suck in his breath.

"Your uncle could not take his eyes off Ka'ahumanu," my father said. "I had never seen Kameha so struck by a wahine before."

"Father!" Ka'ahumanu cried as she sank to her knees beside Ke'eaumoku. "Oh, father!" she cried again, weeping and pressing her face against his chest.

Weakly, Ke'eaumoku tried to reassure her. "Do not worry about me, daughter, I am not seriously wounded," he said. "Here, look who has come to visit me." Ke'eaumoku gestured at Kameha. "It is our late mō'ī Kalani'ōpu'u's beloved nephew, Kamehameha. Surely, you remember him."

Now Ka'ahumanu looked up and spied Kameha for the first time. She blushed. "Oh yes, dear father," she said. "I remember *that* one." Ka'ahumanu laughed, and Kamehameha laughed with her.

Nāmāhana and Ka'ahumanu remained at Hōnaunau with Ke'eaumoku until he was well enough to travel to his fiefdom at Honokua. Despite his interest in Ka'ahumanu, Kamehameha was too preoccupied with other matters at this time to follow her.

Most immediately, Kameha was pressed to decide what was to become of Kiwala'ō's body. Kekūhaupi'o argued for offering it to Kūkā'ilimoku. "It will greatly strengthen your mana to sacrifice the body of a mō'ī," Kekūhaupi'o said. "It is customary to sacrifice the body of a king slain in battle, just as Kalani'ōpu'u sacrificed Keawe'ōpala's body when he defeated him."

"That was different," Kamehameha replied. "Keawe'ōpala was no more than a distant cousin to Kalani'ōpu'u, whereas Kiwala'ō was my *ali'i hoa hānau.* I will not dishonor my first cousin by offering his body to the god."

Kamehameha decreed that Kiwala'ō's bones should be purified and laid in the Hale o Keawe with his father's. "Kiwala'ō will be laid to rest with Kalani'ōpu'u," he informed Kiwala'ō's mother, Kalola, who was both grief-stricken and angered by her son's death at the hands of Kamehameha's allies. If Kameha expected this boon to appease Kalola, he was disappointed.

"I will remain here only until my son's bones repose in the hale," she said. "Then I will go to live with my brother Kahekili on Maui, and I shall not return to Hawai'i as long as you live."

Her reproach stung Kameha, who had shared his first intimacies with Kalola and had always felt affection for her. He felt aggrieved because in his own mind, he had not sought war with Kiwala'ō and he had not wished him dead. But he said nothing.

Keawema'uhili still lived. Kamehameha meant to order his execution and offer his body to the god in a sacrifice marked by an elaborate ceremony. "Kameha wanted to teach a lesson to any would-be enemies that he was not to be trifled with," said my father. But Keawema'uhili's son Keaweokahikona pleaded for his father's life.

"I know that my father has done you a great wrong, Kamehameha," he said. "But he is a defeated man now. He has always been a loving father to me. I beg you, please spare him."

At these words, Kamehameha's heart softened. "You came to my aid even when your own father opposed me," he replied. "In gratitude, I will spare Keawema'uhili for your sake alone. Return him to Hilo, but he must remain there and not threaten my people or my allies in the future."

"Thank you. Your mercy will not be forgotten," Keaweokahikona said.

Kamehameha may have gained some stature among our people by showing mercy to Keawema'uhili, but he did not gain Keawema'uhili's allegiance. In the aftermath of Moku'ōhai, Hawai'i remained divided. Kamehameha's rule extended no farther than Kona, Kohala, and the northern portion of the Hāmākua Coast. Keawema'uhili still ruled in the Hilo District, southern

Hāmākua, and northern Puna, while the ever-belligerent Keōua Kū'ahu'ula remained defiant in Ka'ū.

Meanwhile, Kahekili, the mō'ī of Maui, who coveted O'ahu, Moloka'i, and Lanai, resolved to wrest them from their rightful ruler, Kahahana. But Kahekili needed more war canoes before he could invade O'ahu. His own people were unable to build new canoes fast enough to suit him, so he sent emissaries to Kamehameha in Kona to ask him for additional canoes.

"Kahekili, your father, asks you to send him fifty war canoes," they said.

Already husbanding his resources for likely war with either Keōua Red Cloak, Keawema'uhili, or both, Kamehameha was reluctant to relinquish any canoes. Moreover, he was angered by the emissaries' assertion that Kahekili was his true father. "Kahekili is *not* my father," he replied tartly. "And I have no canoes to spare for him." He sent the emissaries away.

Discouraged but undaunted, the emissaries from Maui continued on to Keawema'uhili's court in Hilo, where they met with more success.

Laupāhoehoe, Hāmākua Coast, 1783

After Moku'ōhai, the Big Island's three rival camps had made ready for eventual war. Kamehameha, Keōua Red Cloak, and Keawema'uhili increased their fighting forces, ordered the fabrication of more weapons, and sent their people to the uplands to fell koa trees for more war canoes. Yet even amidst these preparations, none of the three men was eager to commence the conflict.

"No one wanted to be accused of attacking the others unjustly," my father said.

"Then why couldn't they have agreed to share the island peacefully?" I asked.

"It was not in their natures," he replied.

Kamehameha attacked first. The death of his uncle, Kānekoa, at the hands of Red Cloak, provided him the pretext he sought.

"After Moku'ōhai," my father said, "our uncles, Kānekoa and his brother, Kahai, went to live at Hilo under the protection of Keawema'uhili. Kānekoa repeatedly pressed Keawema'uhili for permission to return to their lands in the Hāmākua district, but he would give no answer. Finally, Kānekoa and Kahai rose in revolt against him."

Keawema'uhili defeated the two brothers and they fled to Ka'ū, where Keōua Red Cloak welcomed them. Red Cloak granted them lands along Ka'ū's verdant north coast. "It was a generous grant," my father said, "because much of Ka'ū is desert. Red Cloak did it to spite Keawema'uhili."

Despite Red Cloak's generosity, Kānekoa and Kahai eventually raised arms against him as well, declaring their independence and asserting their rule over northeastern Ka'ū, from Wa'a Pele Bay to the Puna District border. Marshaling his own forces, Red Cloak struck back, forcing them to withdraw toward Hilo. He overtook them in the uplands between the Ōla'a forest and the Kīlauea crater and defeated them in a bloody battle that ended in Kānekoa's death. With nowhere else to turn, Kahai fled to Kona and his nephew, Kamehameha.

Kahai arrived at Kamehameha's court with a tale of betrayal. "We were living peaceably in Ka'ū when Red Cloak and his people suddenly fell upon us without provocation," Kahai said. "Red Cloak slew your uncle with his own hands."

"By this time, of course, we had heard that Kānekoa and Kahai had provoked Keawema'uhili," said my father. "And we had reason to assume they had likewise provoked our cousin Keōua Red Cloak."

Whatever the truth of the matter, Kānekoa's death at the hands of Keōua Red Cloak was sufficient excuse for Kamehameha to attack his cousin, whom he despised, and Keōua's then-ally, Keawema'uhili. He summoned his closest advisers for a council of war. "The time has come to finish what we started at Moku'ōhai," he said.

The council decided that Kamehameha and Kekūhaupi'o would lead an army overland from Kealakekua. Meanwhile, Ke'eaumoku would simultaneously sail from Kohala down the Hāmākua Coast to Hilo to attack the enemy from the sea.

"Kamehameha and Ke'eaumoku meant to trap Red Cloak and Keawema'uhili between them," my father said. "It was a good plan." My father and his kahu, Mulihele, marched with Kamehameha and his men, who were several thousand strong, from Kealakekua to the high plateau between Mauna Kea and Mauna Loa, a grueling ascent amid fog and rain. "We encountered no opposition along the way and though we were chilled and tired after our ascent from Kealakekua, we were in good spirits as we descended toward Kilauea," said my father. Certain that Red Cloak and Keawema'uhili would be watching for an attack by sea, Kamehameha intended to surprise his foes. "But it was we who were surprised," said my father.

Before Kamehameha's people could fall upon Hilo, they encountered a large enemy force south of the village. My father nearly lost his life in the ensuing debacle. "It was at Pana'ewa," my father said. "We were all at once surrounded by Keawema'uhili's people and the Maui warriors whom Kahekili had sent to Hilo in return for Keawema'uhili's canoes."

"Do you mean the canoes my uncle Kamehameha refused to lend him?" I asked.

"Yes, those canoes," my father said. "It was a terrible fight," he continued. "Pololu and ihe spears fell on us like a sudden rainstorm and many of our men died outright."

My father and his kahu were separated during the bloody hand-to-hand fighting that followed. "Suddenly, I was alone, and several Hilo and Maui warriors set upon me," he said.

One warrior launched a sling stone at my father's head. It missed. Simultaneously, another hurled a short ihe spear at his midsection. My father knocked it aside. A third warrior rushed at him swinging a club. That day, my father carried a crude sword he had fashioned from a haole iron dagger that Kameha had given to him. He slashed at his attacker with it. The sharp blade opened a deep, jagged gash in the man's raised arm. The assailant dropped his club, clutched his wounded limb, howled in pain, and fell away. Now the two remaining men closed warily on my father from opposite sides. One warrior brandished a shark-tooth club. The other, the sling carrier, wielded a long pololū spear. "I could not have fought them both off," my father told me. "In that moment, I prayed to Kūkā'ilimoku for protection."

I do not know if the god heard my father, but Mulihele saw that he was in mortal danger and rushed to his aid. "Mulihele and I were not far apart but we had lost sight of each other in the midst of the fray," said my father. "Now my kahu saw me and fought his way to me through several opposing Hilo men." My father ran at the man with the dagger, and advantaged by the longer reach of his haole weapon, stabbed him in the thigh. Mulihele brought down the other warrior and clubbed him in the head. Then he and my father fled.

Kamehameha's people—those who still could—ran headlong toward Hilo Bay with Keawema'uhili's and Kahekili's warriors close on their heels. Always in the vanguard of an attack, but now keeping to the rear of a disorderly general retreat, Kameha spurred his men on. "Ke'eaumoku is already at Hilo with the fleet!" he shouted. "Do not lose hope! Keep going! Keep going!" Despite his urging, a number of his fighters still faltered and the Hilo and Maui warriors cut them down without mercy. "Many more warriors of Kona and Kohala died during the retreat," my father said.

Ke'eaumoku's fleet was waiting offshore when Kameha's warriors reached Hilo Bay. "Kameha comes!" he shouted when he saw the first men emerge from the scrub and palm trees behind the beach. "Now we attack!"

"Ke'eaumoku believed at first that the men he saw were Keawema'uhili's people, fleeing from Kamehameha's warriors," my father said. "It was only when he neared the shore that he realized they were, in truth, Kamehameha's own people."

"What has happened?" Ke'eaumoku cried.

"We are defeated!" the warrior closest called back. "Keawema'uhili's people have overwhelmed us! Many of our comrades are slain! Save us!"

"What of Kamehameha? Does he yet live?" cried Ke'eaumoku.

"Kamehameha lives! He is coming behind us!"

Crying, "Save us! Save us! Keawema'uhili comes!" Kamehameha's people waded into the bay and crowded onto the double-hulled canoes' platforms. Ke'eaumoku's seaborne assault had become an evacuation. The canoes put to sea again as quickly as they filled with survivors, my father and Mulihele among them.

When at last Kamehameha and Kekūhaupi'o reached the beach, Kameha and Ke'eaumoku fell into each other's arms and wailed. Ke'eaumoku looked about in surprise. Only a few hundred of the several thousand men who had marched with Kamehameha had reached the beach before him. "Are these all who are left?" he asked.

"Yes," Kamehameha responded. "And the blood of our dead is on my hands, for I foolishly led my people into a trap."

Now from the palm grove beyond the beach came the triumphant howls of Keawema'uhili's warriors and Kahekili's men, still lusting for the blood of their foes.

"There will be sufficient time to assess blame later, Pai'ea," said Kekūhaupi'o. "Now we must go." He prodded Kamehameha into Ke'eaumoku's canoe and jumped in after him. Ke'eaumoku followed them.

The first of Keawema'uhili's people broke from the trees just as the canoe carrying Kameha, his kahu, and Ke'eaumoku pulled away from the shore. Even as its sail filled with wind, the warriors on the double-hulled canoe tore at the water with their paddle blades. Upon reaching the beach, the warriors of Hilo and Maui hurled sling stones and spears at the receding canoe, to no serious affect. When it was clear that their foes were beyond reach, they turned their backs on them as one, doubled over, and pulled down their malos, exposing their bare buttocks. "Here! This is what we think of you, mighty Kamehameha," one of the Hilo warriors jeered through his own legs. "Come and eat our excrement!" The warrior's insult stung Kamehameha, the mover of Hilo's own Naha Stone, and echoed in his mind all the way to Laupāhoehoe.

Kamehameha stumbled over the side of his canoe and staggered up the beach. He was bleeding profusely from a gash across his forehead. My father rushed to his side. "Kameha, what has happened?" he cried.

"I was attacked by some kānaka fishermen," Kamehameha said. "They struck me with their paddles."

My father was nearly dumbstruck. "*Commoners* attacked *you*?"

"Yes," said Kameha. "I barely escaped with my life."

"Why did they attack you?" my father asked.

"I cannot say," said Kamehameha.

In truth, Kameha could not at this time bear to tell my father what had transpired, because he was profoundly ashamed and embarrassed. He had assaulted innocent men, women, and children. It was a gratuitous act of violence born of frustration.

Seeking revenge for his ignominious defeat at the hands of Keawema'uhili, and without consulting his advisers, Kameha had set out in his war canoe from Laupāhoehoe early in the morning, taking only a few warriors with him. Kamehameha meant to attack and slay the first Hilo District people he came upon, regardless of their age, sex, or station in life.

Following a swift passage down the coast under paddle and sail, Kamehameha found his victims fishing on a pahoehoe lava reef at Papa'ī, below Leleiwi Point near Hilo. As his warriors quickened their strokes and dug their paddles deeper into the water, Kameha stood at the canoe's prow wielding a short ihe spear in one hand and a stone-tipped club in the other. At first, the people on the reef regarded the big war canoe with curiosity. When they realized that the intentions of the huge man in the bow were hostile, they clambered into their own small outrigger canoes and fled to the shore in panic, leaving two of their men behind. Kamehameha leaped from the platform of his canoe as it ran up on the reef and charged at the men, outdistancing his warriors. As he ran, he waved his club in one hand and readied to throw his ihe spear with the other. The fishermen cowered in fear. But just as Kameha was about to hurl his spear at the man closest to him, one of his own feet became wedged in a fissure in the reef. He tripped, and the two men set upon him immediately, beating him about the head and shoulders with their canoe paddles. One of them struck him so hard that his paddle broke.

"Kamehameha was garbed in a simple malo; he wore no badge of rank, no feather cloak or helmet. Those kānaka had no idea that my brother was a high-born chief," said my father, who learned the truth of the attack from Kameha later. "Had they known, they might have fled when he fell."

With the arrival of Kamehameha's own men, his assailants broke off their assault, diving into the water and swimming to shore. Two of the warriors made to follow them, but Kameha waved them off. "Let them go," he said, "and help me up."

For Kamehameha, this beating at the hands of mere commoners marked a dispiriting end to a season of increasing despair. He had gone to war sure of victory, but his foes had outmaneuvered and outfought him. Now, his reputation for invincibility was tarnished, and his self-confidence shaken for the first time in his life.

Kamehameha remained at Laupāhoehoe for some time after the unfortunate incident with the commoners at Papa'ī. Laupāhoehoe was nominally under Keawema'uhili's rule, but the Hilo chieftain's warriors had all been drawn away from the area to oppose Kamehameha's advance on Hilo, enabling him to bloodlessly annex it to his own lands. Kamehameha was in no hurry to return to Kohala. Laupāhoehoe was pleasant and boasted excellent surf riding. In the meantime, he would plan his next attack on Keawema'uhili and Keōua Red Cloak.

The battle just past had cost Kamehameha's cousin nothing, because instead of joining it, Red Cloak had held his own people well back at Kapāpala. "It is ever his way to let others bleed for him," Kamehameha scoffed. As for Keawema'uhili, my uncle told my father, "I should not have listened to Keaweokahikona and spared Keawema'uhili after Moku'ōhai. An enemy spared is an enemy who lives to fight you again."

Kamehameha regretted his attack on the commoner fishermen and their families, and not just because it ended poorly for him. "They were simple maka'āinana who had done nothing to provoke me," he said. "My own behavior was inexcusable." To atone for his actions, Kamehameha promulgated a law for the protection of the commoners throughout his domains. It was kapu, he decreed, for any ali'i to assault or in any other way molest the maka'āinana who were peacefully going about their ordinary, daily activities. Our people came to call this prohibition *mamala-hoe*, or the "law of the splintered paddle." The sanction for violating it was death.

Hāpu'u, Kohala, 1784

A grief-stricken keening rent the still evening air and brought my father running to Kamehameha's hale. He entered to find his brother on his knees, doubled over, holding his massive head in his hands. Holo'ae sat beside him. "Kamehameha," Kalanimālokuloku cried, "what has happened?"

Kameha looked up at my father through teary eyes and wailed again. "Oh, Kalani," he cried, "my beloved kahu is dead! Kekūhaupi'o is dead!"

"What!" my father gasped. "How?" Hawai'i was then enjoying a brief interlude of peace. The island's three contending factions were not fighting, not even skirmishing. That Kekūhaupi'o, one of our people's greatest warriors, could have perished at such a time was incomprehensible.

"Kekū was taking part in spear exercises at Nāpo'opo'o," Kamehameha said. "He failed to catch a thrown spear. It struck him in his stomach." Kameha wailed anew. My father sank to the floor next to him. The two brothers hugged and cried together.

Kekūhaupi'o had not died at once. Mortally wounded, he lingered for several days before succumbing. Holo'ae, Kekūhaupi'o's uncle, was the first at Kameha's court to learn of the great warrior's death. The high priest brought the news to Kamehameha. "His last thoughts were for you, Lord," Holo'ae said. Indeed, on his death mat, Kekūhaupi'o had asked Kamehameha's forgiveness for uselessly expending his own life. "Tell Kameha I should rather have been slain in his service," he said. "Now who will stand at the side of my beloved foster son, Pai'ea, and protect him?"

In truth, it had been a long time since Kamehameha needed Kekūhaupi'o's "protection." They had fought alongside each other with equal skill since

Kaupō, each saving the other on numerous occasions. Nevertheless, in the struggles of the years to come, Kameha would sorely miss his kahu, who had taught him so much.

While the Hawai'ians fought among themselves, Kahekili, the king of Maui, pursued his own ambitions for territorial expansion, overthrowing O'ahu's young king, Kahahana. To this end, he tricked Kahahana into turning against his own popular kahuna nui and killing the priest and his son. These murders shocked and angered a number of O'ahu's nobles, turning them against Kahahana. When Kahekili landed in force at Waikiki, his people easily overwhelmed Kahahana's demoralized forces. Kahahana survived the fierce battle and fled with his wife to the mountains, only to be slain two years later by his own brother-in-law.

Dispossessed of their lands by Kahekili, the O'ahu ali'i plotted to kill Kahekili and all of his people. But Kahekili's son, Kalanikūpule, discovered their conspiracy. In retribution, Kahekili ordered his warriors to slay all the O'ahu nobles and their families. Learning that some Maui nobles had plotted against him with the O'ahu ali'i, he ordered them killed as well. All of these traitors were slain, save one, who escaped to Kaua'i—a young chieftain named Ka'iana.

Honokua, Kona 1785

Kamehameha did not see the other surf rider angling toward him until the moment before their heavy surf-riding boards collided, sending Kameha headfirst into the water, where a large following roller at once overwhelmed him. As he struggled to regain the surface in the wave's roiling wake, his own board struck his head. Gasping for breath, dazed, and angry, Kameha cast about for the one who had the temerity to intrude on his course through the surf. He saw an indistinct form bobbing up and down amid the swells and silhouetted against the mid-afternoon sky—another surf rider kneeling on a board, laughing at him. It was a woman's laughter. Unable to find his own board, Kameha swam to her. Coming closer, he saw it was Keʻeaumoku's daughter, Kaʻahumanu, whom he had last seen at Hōnaunau three years earlier.

"You rode directly into my own line," Kamehameha sputtered, still angry.

"Your line? Your line?" Kaʻahumanu said, laughing anew. An oncoming swell lifted her board above Kameha's head and now she looked down at him over full, bared breasts. "I gained that wave before *you*!" she riposted. "That one was *my* line."

"*That one*? *That one*?" The next swell lifted Kamehameha above Kaʻahumanu and he scowled down at her. For her part, Kaʻahumanu continued to smile up at him.

Now Kaʻahumanu was higher than Kameha once more. Regarding him from above, she could see in the light refracted by the blue-green water that the wave had ripped away his malo when it tumbled him. "You had best join me on my surf-riding board," she said, "before the cold water shrivels *that one* beyond recognition."

Kamehameha looked down at himself and saw what Ka'ahumanu had seen. "Oh don't worry about *that one*," he said. "It can take care of itself." With three powerful strokes, he launched himself from a rising swell onto her board and sat astride it, pressing against her suddenly taut back.

"Oh yes," she said, laughing anew. "I am sure that it can."

"I will take Ka'ahumanu as my partner."

Kamehameha and Ke'eaumoku were sitting cross-legged on mats in Ke'eaumoku's hale. Late-afternoon sunlight streamed through the doorway. Ke'eaumoku cocked his head at Kameha, frowned, and pursed his lips. "And what if I say no?" he asked.

"Then as your mō'ī, I shall be sadly disappointed in you," Kameha replied. Given the island's continuing tripartite division, the title was more a conceit than a reality. But after Moku'ōhai, Ke'eaumoku and the other Kona chieftains had acknowledged Kamehameha as their sovereign, with the expectation that he would eventually become the mō'ī of all Hawai'i.

"Oh, I would not want my *mō'ī* to be disappointed in me," Ke'eaumoku said. "Of course, you shall have her."

Ka'ahumanu was not consulted in the matter, although if she had been, she would have readily agreed. "Ka'ahumanu was strongly drawn to Kameha, as he was to her," my father said. "He hungered for her body and she for his. She admired his strength and character. He loved her independent, adventurous spirit. His other wāhine were more conventional."

Ke'eaumoku called for his daughter. "Kameha has asked me to give you to him to be his partner, and I have agreed," he said.

"If that is your desire, Father, I will of course obey," she replied. In that moment, and without ceremony, the union was accomplished. The amorous couple wasted no time consummating it.

Soon thereafter, Kamehameha declared Ka'ahumanu kapu to all other men. This was unusual among our people in those days. Kamehameha had imposed no restrictions on his other wives' liaisons. "Ke'eaumoku had counseled him that if he wanted to reign supreme over all of our islands one day, he must keep Ka'ahumanu to himself," my father explained, "but, in any case, I believe that Kameha was simply unwilling to share her." While Kamehameha had forbidden Ka'ahumanu to take other partners, he expected her to share him with many other women, including her own younger sister, Kalakua Kaheiheimale.

My father took his first wife at this time. Her name was Ki'ilaweau. She was his own half-sister by his father, Keōua, and Alapa'i's daughter, Manono. Their first son was born within the year—my older half-brother, whom they named Kekuaokalani. By right of his bloodlines, Kekuaokalani was nī'aupi'o and had the *kapu moe*, the prostrating kapu. Also about this time, Ke'eaumoku's partner, Nāmāhana, gave him a son, whom they named after both the baby's uncle and his father. This younger brother of Ka'ahumanu was Kahekili Ke'eaumoku.

Hana, Maui 1786

Thwarted by Keōua Kū'ahu'ula and Keawema'uhili in his attempt to unify the Big Island under his own rule, Kamehameha turned to retaking the land on Maui that had earlier been won and then lost by his uncle, Kalani'ōpu'u. Kahekili was not at that time present on Maui to oppose him. After his conquest of O'ahu and the extermination of the O'ahu nobility, Kahekili had determined to remain on that island. He appointed his son, Kalanikūpule, regent of Maui. When he learned of this, Kamehameha saw an opportunity. "Kalanikūpule will not be expecting our people to attack him while Keōua Red Cloak and Keawema'uhili still oppose me here," he said. "Kalanikūpule is not experienced in warfare. With the advantage of surprise we can easily overwhelm him and his people." Kameha in fact knew little about Kalanikūpule and "his people" at this time.

Rather than risk absenting himself from Hawai'i at a time when his two rivals hungered for land in Kohala and Kona, he sent my father in his place. Kalanimālokuloku landed, unopposed, at Hana with a force of several thousand warriors early in 1786. Ki'ilaweau accompanied him, with their newborn son, Kekuaokalani, in her arms.

"As my brother had foretold, the people of Maui were not prepared for us," my father said. Indeed, no Maui warriors were at Hana to oppose the Hawai'ians when they landed. Only country people—maka'āinana men and women who had learned well to fear warriors of the Big Island—watched from hiding as Kalanimālokuloku led his men ashore. The only sounds that greeted the first wave of invaders were the sighing of the wind, the lapping of waves, and birds calling in the trees. The Hawai'ians were primed for battle and this peaceful scene unsettled them. My father's kahu, Mulihele, suspected an ambush. He scanned the slope that rose abruptly above the small bay at Hana, ringing it from end to end, in search of foes hiding amid the trees and brush, but he could see none.

"Kalani," he said, "do not let all of our people come ashore yet, lest we all become trapped on this beach. I fear our enemies have cunningly concealed themselves. I will lead some people mauka to see whether this is so. Meanwhile, it would be well for you to remain close to your own canoe." Gathering a dozen warriors, Mulihele ordered them to search the hillside for concealed enemies. Moving quietly with spears and clubs at the ready, the men soon disappeared from sight amid the thick foliage. On the beach, ringed protectively by his warriors, Kalanimālokuloku watched and waited.

Sometime later, two of the warriors returned, holding a frightened commoner between them. "This kanaka claims there are no Maui fighters here, Lord," said one of the warriors as they shoved the maka'āinana man toward Kalanimālokuloku. The man fell to the ground at Kalanimālokuloku's feet and pressed his forehead into the sand, not daring to look up. He shook with fear.

Kalanimālokuloku regarded the shivering commoner sadly. He recalled the depredations Kalani'ōpu'u had visited upon the people of Maui. "That man expected me to use him just as badly," he told me later. "And that I would not do."

Kalanimālokuloku spoke gently to the cowering Maui man, but loudly enough so that all his assembled warriors could hear. "Go back to your own people now," he said. Tell them that no harm will come to them from us." The man darted an astonished look at the ali'i chieftain who stood over him, then averted his eyes and began backing away on his hands and knees. When he had put a respectful distance between himself and Kalanimālokuloku, he stood and ran toward the hillside, rushing unseeing past more returning Hawai'ian warriors as he fled.

Now Kalanimālokuloku spoke to his own people. "My own brother, your lord, Kamehameha, has forbidden the nobles of Kona and Kohala to molest any commoners who are engaged in peaceful activities. As Kamehameha has ordered there, so let it be here," he said. "From this day forward, no warriors of Hawai'i shall beat, rob or otherwise assault any Maui kanaka who poses them no threat or harm. Nor shall any of our warriors cut their sugar cane, steal their pigs, destroy their taro fields, take their canoes, burn their hales, or in any other way interfere with their livelihoods. From this day forward, all such acts are kapu, on pain of death."

Word of Kalanimālokuloku's decree soon spread among the villagers of the occupied districts of Hana and Kipahulu. Some of Kalanimālokuloku's men, accustomed as they had become to despoiling the Maui people at will during Kalani'ōpu'u's time, greeted this kapu with consternation and resentment. It was not long before a warrior violated it. This man took some yams from a villager's larder. When the commoner objected, the warrior cuffed him about the head. The people of the village complained to Mulihele and the warrior was brought before Kalanimālokuloku at Kauwiki. His justice was swift. "You ignored the kapu which I proclaimed to all of our warriors. I said then that the penalty for violating this kapu would be death, and so die you shall. Mulihele, see to this at once, and be sure to make a spectacle of it."

Mulihele led the unfortunate man away. He was executed within the hour by Mulihele's own hand as Kalanimālokuloku and several hundred of his warriors looked on. From that day forward, no Hawai'ian dared lift a hand against the villagers.

Accustomed as they were to abuse and worse by the warriors of the Big Island, the maka'āinana of those districts were very grateful to Kalanimālokuloku. They began calling him by a new name: Keli'imaika'i, *the good chief.* My father was proud to be so regarded by the people of Maui, and thereafter took this name as his own. Word of my father's kindly treatment of the common people soon spread to Maui's other districts. This, of course, mattered not to the chieftains of Maui.

"Quick, conceal yourself among those *ka'e'e* vines and ti plants," Mulihele urged Keli'imaika'i. "Kamohomoho's people will soon be upon us." My father needed no urging and soon his yellow and red feather cloak was hidden behind the foliage. Satisfied, Mulihele crouched and gathered foliage around himself as well. Even as he watched for approaching enemy warriors, he hoped that in their hot-blooded haste the Maui people would pass them by.

Kamehameha's assessment of Kalanikūpule had been correct. He was young and not yet well versed in the ways of war, but his general, Kamohomoho, was battle-tested. Several years older than Kalanikūpule, he had fought against the Hawai'ians during Kalani'ōpu'u's invasions of Maui. Kalanikūpule was not so inexperienced as to place excessive confidence in himself and soon after he learned that Keli'imaika'i had invaded Hana, he sent Kamohomoho to push the Hawai'ians back into the sea. Kamohomoho set off from Wailuku with a few hundred warriors, gathering more to him as he and his men moved overland to Wailua. From there, Kamohomoho and his people, who now numbered some five thousand, struck out for Hana. Kamohomoho fully expected to find Keli'imaika'i and his warriors there, ensconced in the old fortress on Kauwiki Hill, where the Hawai'ians had taken refuge in years past. But he could not keep his movements secret from Keli'imaika'i. The country people of the Hana district warned their "good chief" of the threat soon after Kamohomoho and his men departed Wailua.

"Kamohomoho's people were more numerous than ours," my father said. "I knew that we could defend ourselves for a time at Kauwiki, but that in the end it would surely become a trap. So I ordered our people to withdraw down the coast." Keli'imaika'i and his warriors moved to Lelekea in the Kipahulu district, where they waited. "I should have withdrawn our people to Hawai'i then," my father told me ruefully. "But my pride would not allow it."

Encountering no Hawai'ians at Hana and learning from villagers there that Keli'imaika'i and his people had decamped down the coast, Kamohomoho marched his warriors overland from Hana, keeping well mauka of the ocean. "He thought to gain advantage over us by attacking from high ground," my father said, "but we prepared a surprise for him."

On Mulihele's advice, Keli'imaika'i arrayed his people along the sides of the lower reaches of the gully of the Alelele Stream that the Maui warriors would have to descend to reach Lelekea. "We turned their high ground into low ground and we gained the early advantage," said my father. When the first of Kamohomoho's fighters reached them, the Hawai'ian warriors rose from hiding places on both sides of the gully and attacked them with slings and spears, and many of the Maui warriors fell, injured or mortally wounded. Mauka of the initial skirmish, Kamohomoho saw what was transpiring below and ordered his people to scale the sides of the gully. With their greater numbers, they overwhelmed the Hawai'ians, pushing them off the heights and into the gully. The survivors fled to Lelekea and their canoes, but Keli'imaika'i was not among them.

Keli'imaika'i and Mulihele remained with the Hawai'ian rear guard in the thick of the fighting as their people withdrew. When at last they broke off the fight, they became separated from their comrades in the confusion of the general retreat, and now they were alone in the gully. Keli'imaika'i and Mulihele could hear enemy warriors calling to each other as they drew nearer. Now they heard a rustling in the thick vegetation behind them. Mulihele spun around on one knee and readied his spear. A villager emerged from the undergrowth and threw himself to the ground before Mulihele. Then he raised himself to a crouch, and pressing a finger to his lips, gestured at Mulihele and Keliʻimaikaʻi to follow him.

"That kanaka knew I was there all the time," my father told me. He chuckled as he said this. From the distant vantage point of many years, he found this amusing. There was, however, no amusement to be had in the moment.

The villager turned, and keeping low to the ground, pushed his way into the dense foliage and soon disappeared from sight. Mulihele and Keliʻimaikaʻi followed him. The man led them to a narrow trail, barely discernible amid the tangle of vines and bushes, just below the brow of the gully. "As we followed the commoner along the trail, we could hear the Maui warriors in the gully below us, but we could not see them, nor they us," my father said. "In any case, their eyes were not on the higher ground, intent as they were upon reaching Lelekea Bay before any of our people could make good their escape." The Maui fighters passed below, their voices fading as they went. Then there was only silence.

The trail led over the top of the gully and down into an adjacent ravine through which trickled a small stream. The villager, Keliʻimaikaʻi, and Mulihele followed this stream makai to the sea. From there, the man led my father and his kahu at a quick trot along a black-sand beach to his own fishing village at Waiuha Bay. Dusk was gathering as the three men reached the village, which consisted of little more than three or four hales and a canoe shed. No one emerged from their hales to greet them. Now the commoner prostrated himself before Keliʻimaikaʻi and Mulihele once again. "Lords, you must go, and quickly, before the lord, Kamohomoho, comes here with his people," he said. He was quaking in fear as he spoke to the earth without looking up at my father and his kahu. "We have several canoes, but only one with a sail. Please, take that one and go now." Without a word, or any gesture of thanks, Keliʻimaikaʻi and Mulihele turned away from the man who had just saved their lives. The canoe was a small one with a small sail. "It was fit for common fishing folk," my father recalled. Common though it may have been, this humble vessel was the only means of return to the Big Island for my father and Mulihele. They pushed it into the water, jumped in, and paddled away in the gathering darkness.

It took my father and Mulihele the better part of two days to cross the ʻAlenuihāhā Channel in the small sail canoe, which had never been intended for anything other than close-in coastal voyaging. By the time they reached Kohala, Kamehameha had every reason to believe they had been slain. None of the surviving warriors who reached the Big Island before the two men knew what had become of them during the fighting. My father had sent his wife, Kiʻilaweau, and my half-brother, the infant Kekuaokalani, back to Hawaiʻi before the battle. When there was no news of my father, she and Kameha wailed with grief over his presumed death. And when they learned that my father and Mulihele had landed at ʻUmiwai Bay in Northern Kohala, they wailed again with joy.

Kamehameha and my father were reunited at Hālawa, the ancestral village of Kameha's beloved first kahu, Naeʻole. "We suffered a grievous and shameful defeat on Maui, brother," my father cried as he fell into Kamehameha's arms. "I have dishonored you," he wailed.

"There is no shame for you in this defeat, brother, and any dishonor is mine," Kamehameha said to my father, hugging him close. "It is my fault; I did not send enough people to Maui with you."

"And yet the blood of so many of our men is on my hands," cried my father.

At this, Kamehameha—who was proud of the name that the people of Maui bestowed on my father—released him from his tight hold, held him by his shoulders, looked into his eyes, and said grimly, "Their blood will be avenged, Keliʻimaikaʻi. Rest assured: One day, their blood *will* be avenged."

Soon after his return from Maui, my father took a second wife, my mother, Kaliko‘okalani. Before the year was out, they had their first child: my sister, Ka‘ōanā‘eha.

Kailua, Kona, 1789

The ali'i Ka'iana sat cross-legged before Kamehameha, his head slightly bowed, at once a humble supplicant and a prideful prince. "Lord, I beseech you. Grant me refuge here in the land of my noble ancestors," he said.

Kamehameha narrowed his eyes and frowned. "Tell me why I should grant asylum to one such as you, an ally of our bitter enemy, Kahekili," he said.

"A *former* ally of Kahekili's," Ka'iana rejoined. His response was quick and curt, and lacking in appropriate respect.

"Ah, yes," said Kameha, with a teeth-baring smile. "A *former* ally." If he was offended by Ka'iana's tone, he did not show it. "Is it true that you joined the O'ahu nobles who rebelled against Kahekili's rule there and plotted to kill him?"

"Yes," said Ka'iana. "That is true, Lord." His voice softened again; he sensed that he had somehow offended Kamehameha, the undisputed ruler of Kona and Kohala and pretender to the throne of all Hawai'i.

"And why did you join with the O'ahu ali'i against whom you had previously fought?" Kamehameha inquired.

"I was offended by Kahekili's cruel treatment of Kahahana, who had served him so well," Ka'iana explained. "And I could no longer abide in his service."

This was in fact unlikely, as Kamehameha and my father had good reason to believe. "We had heard that Ka'iana boasted of the O'ahu lands he would gain once Kahekili was slain and the O'ahu ali'i were restored to power," my father said. "His was a rebellion of convenience."

Kameha glanced at my father. "Indeed," was all he said. Then he changed the subject. "Is it true that you have sailed to a far-off island and returned with mūk'e and other haole weapons?"

"Yes, Lord. They are on the haole great canoe, and I would place them at your disposal, and instruct your people in their use—for the benefit of the land of my forebears."

Kamehameha smiled again. This time, his smile was unforced. "Then welcome to the land of your forebears," he said.

Ka'iana had been born in the Hilo district. He was of high chiefly lineage. On his father's side, he was a great-grandson of Keawe the Great, as was Kamehameha. Through his mother, he was descended from Hilo's powerful Ī family. Ka'iana was physically arresting. He stood nearly as tall as Kamehameha, but was more sparingly built. His visage was handsome—angular and chiseled—whereas Kameha's broad, stern features, though powerfully imposing, might well have been considered homely but for his massive frame. Ka'iana was always quick to merriment and laughter, whereas Kamehameha was habitually solemn and frugal with his smiles. While people who were not close to him or did not know him well approached Kameha with fearful respect, Ka'iana's most casual acquaintances almost at once became ardent admirers and were thereafter drawn to him like moths to a flame. Well aware of his physical effect on others, Ka'iana instinctively sought advantage in it, affecting a regal bearing tempered with *noblesse oblige*. Others were uncommonly grateful to him for a favorable word or even just a nod and a wink.

Moreover, he could boast experiences unique in the islands. In 1787, two haole ships, the Nootka and the Iphigenia, had landed in Kaua'i, where he'd been living at the time. The ships' captains, John Meares and William

Douglas, had put in to trade haole manufactures and iron for the usual Hawai'ian provisions—pigs, produce, and fruit. The always-bold Ka'iana had appealed to Meares to allow him to accompany the Nootka's crew on their voyage—in this case, to China. His two-year voyage had taken him to the shores of Asia and back, and he'd returned with a substantial store of muskets and ammunition—and the knowledge of their use.

"No Lord, you must pour the *gun powder* into the *muzzle* first, and then insert the *cartridge*," said Ka'iana.

Ka'iana was instructing Kamehameha in the operation of the haole musket. Soon after the Iphigenia's crew had ferried his store of muskets, powder, and shot to shore, Ka'iana had gathered Kamehameha and his chieftains—my father among them—in the courtyard of Kameha's hale at Kailua to instruct them.

First, Ka'iana had affixed a breadfruit to a sharpened stick he had driven into the ground. He then proceeded to load a musket with an ease acquired through months of practice: extracting a paper cartridge from a metal box that he wore on a haole belt; biting off the cartridge's twisted end with his teeth; pulling the musket's hammer part way back; pouring some of the cartridge's gunpowder into the weapon's firing pan; closing the lid of the firing pan; pouring the cartridge's remaining powder down the musket's barrel, followed by the musket ball; inserting the remaining cartridge paper after it; drawing the ramrod from under the weapon's muzzle; reversing it; inserting its flat head into the musket barrel and thrusting it home, compacting the paper wad, musket ball, and powder. Then, he returned the ramrod to its place below the muzzle, cocked the hammer, raised the rifle's butt to his shoulder, took aim at the breadfruit, and squeezed the musket's trigger.

All this Ka'iana accomplished with a motion so fluid that it was difficult for his audience to follow in all of its intricacies. Moreover, whatever understanding they had achieved of this procedure was immediately shattered by the weapon's sharp report and the spectacle of the breadfruit suddenly exploding, fragments flying in all directions.

Kameha and his people regarded Kaʻiana in stunned silence as the gunfire's echo faded. "You see, that is how it is done," Kaʻiana said. He set the weapon down and impaled another breadfruit on the stick. Returning to the assembled chieftains, he asked, "Who will be the first among you to learn how to handle this *musket*?" He made a great show of slowly pronouncing the word in the haole fashion, having learned much of their language during his two years among them. "Lord?" Kaʻiana bowed slightly to Kamehameha. It was more of a challenge than an invitation.

Kamehameha did not hesitate. "Give *me* that mūkʻe," he said, seizing the weapon. Its barrel all but disappeared in his large hand. "I already have several of these that I took from Kāpena Kuke at Kealakekua," he said. "I have seen them used before against our own people and I have studied them. I know how they work." As he said this, Kameha gripped the haole weapon as he would a pololū javelin and waved it in Kaʻiana's face.

Kamehameha failed to impress Kaʻiana, who leisurely undid the cartridge belt at his own waist, took back the musket, and handed the belt to Kamehameha. "First, *Lord*," he said, "you must put this on." Kameha stared at Kaʻiana and then at the belt. Since Kekūhaupiʻo's death, he had become unused to taking direction from others. "Put it on now, Lord," Kaʻiana said, not at all intimidated. Now Kamehameha fumbled with the brass buckle as he struggled to fasten the belt around his thick waist. The cartridge belt fit, just barely. "Now, Lord," Kaʻiana said, "take the *cartridge* from the box." Once again, he gave the unfamiliar haole word extra emphasis. Kamehameha reached into the box, which was designed for smaller hands, and slowly extracted a cartridge. It slipped from his fingers. Kaʻiana knelt, retrieved it, and without standing again, handed it up to Kameha. "Here, Lord," he said, grinning.

When at last Kameha had rammed the powder, ball, and paper wad down the musket's barrel, returned the ramrod to its place, and raised the weapon to his shoulder, Kaʻiana instructed, "Now, Lord, take aim at the breadfruit and pull the trigger."

Narrowing his eyes and pointing the musket at the breadfruit, Kamehameha slowly pulled back the trigger. He was not yet ready when the hammer flew forward, and he flinched from the musket's recoil as it erupted. As the smoke cleared away, Kamehameha and his chieftains saw that the breadfruit was unscathed. Kameha scowled.

"It takes much practice, Lord," soothed Ka'iana. "Try again."

"No!" Kamehameha snapped. "I will be mōʻī of Hawaiʻi. It is not necessary for me to learn to use this mūkʻe." He thrust the weapon at Ka'iana. "It is for these others to learn this haole way of fighting," Kameha said. "You teach them, and teach them well, Ka'iana."

"Oh yes, Lord, I will," Ka'iana said. He spoke to Kamehameha's back, for the pretender to the Big Island's throne was already stalking from the courtyard.

Kamehameha's abrupt departure precipitated an awkward silence, broken only by a woman's soft laughter. Ka'ahumanu, standing outside the courtyard and unnoticed by Kameha and his chieftains, had witnessed her husband's humiliation.

After four years of marriage to Kamehameha, Ka'ahumanu was growing restive. Despite a vigorous physical relationship, she and Kameha as yet had no children together, and she had begun to chafe under his kapu forbidding other men to court her. Kamehameha's first wife, Pele'uli, was under no such restriction, and was free to enjoy congress with whomever she chose. This distinction between them incensed Ka'ahumanu, whose sexual appetites were as wide-ranging as any other Hawaiian woman's, and she had vigorously remonstrated about this with her husband.

"Why do you forbid other men to pay suit to me?" she had demanded one day, after they had been married for not quite two years. "Why is Pele'uli free to lie with other men and I am not?"

"Because it pleases me to so rule," was all Kamehameha would offer in way of explanation.

"That is an insufficient reason," Ka'ahumanu rejoined.

"As your mō'ī, that is the only reason I need give you," Kameha replied, and he turned away from her.

Kamehameha had not forbidden Ka'ahumanu from flirting with other men, but as all men of Kona, Kohala, and the rest of the Big Island knew, it was kapu to approach her with any but the most innocent of intentions. Thus, her occasional flirtations were for naught. Ka'ahumanu was immediately drawn to Ka'iana, who was so handsome, so easy-going, and closer to her in age than her stern husband. Moreover, his confident treatment of Kamehameha as an equal gave Ka'ahumanu reason to hope that Ka'iana might not respect the kapu.

"Despite my brother's stern admonition, it was not in Ka'ahumanu's nature to be intimate with only one kāne, no more than it was in the nature of any of our women, including our own mother," my father observed. Nor was it in Ka'iana's nature to concern himself much with a kapu that he considered unreasonable.

Kealakekua, 1790

The haole seaman was in grave condition when Kame'iamoku delivered him to Kamehameha. He was the sole survivor of the five-man crew of the Fair American, a small schooner that Kame'iamoku and his people had boarded and captured off Ka'ūpūlehu, in North Kona. Kame'iamoku had attacked the Fair American to avenge an indignity earlier visited upon him by the captain of another haole vessel.

This ship, the Eleanora, had stopped at Ka'ūpūlehu on her way to Maui. Its captain was Simon Metcalfe. As was their custom, the Hawai'ians paddled out to the ship in their canoes to trade. "Kame'iamoku began to board the ship to greet these haoles, which was his duty and right as the area's high chief," my father explained. "But *Kāpena Mekawe* beat him with a heavy rope and tumbled him into the sea. After that, Kame'iamoku resolved to attack the next haole ship to pass by."

Kame'iamoku's assault on the Fair American was brief and bloody. The small ship was beating up the Kona Coast, making toward Maui against an unfavorable wind. Kame'iamoku and his people went out to the schooner in two outrigger canoes. Thinking that these Hawai'ians had come to trade, the Fair American's crew made no effort to bar them from boarding. As soon as they gained the ship's deck, the Hawai'ians attacked the haoles with clubs and daggers, slaying all but one man and throwing the bodies overboard.

The one haole they did not kill was the ship's mate, whom they likewise threw into the sea, thinking that Kanaloa would take him. But unlike so many of the haole sailors, this man was a strong swimmer. He stroked to the nearest Hawai'ian canoe and tried to climb aboard, but the Hawai'ians beat him off with their paddles and clubs. Dazed and weakened, but still afloat, he swam to the other canoe. The men in that canoe were about to treat him just as roughly when he called out to them. "*Aloha! Aloha! Maikaʻi, maikaʻi!*"—Mercy, mercy! Good, good!—he pleaded in his limited Hawaiian. One of the paddlers in this second canoe took pity on the haole, who was now near to drowning. "*Aloha*," he said, as he hauled the struggling man out of the water.

"I do not know why that canoe paddler chose to spare the haole sailor," my father said. "But it was well that he did."

With their own canoes in tow, Kameʻiamoku and his men steered the Fair American to shore. "Though this boat was larger than our canoes, Kameʻiamoku's people had no difficulty sailing it, for wind and sail are the same everywhere," my father said. Sailing a vessel of unfamiliar design and larger than our people's canoes was one thing; bringing it close to shore safely was quite another. Accustomed to landing their shallow-draft canoes on beaches, Kameʻiamoku's men damaged the Fair American's hull when they ran the ship aground in the shallows at Kaʻūpūlehu.

The Fair American boasted a limited armory, with a half-dozen muskets, several pistols, and sufficient powder and musket balls to repel lightly armed attackers. Had the haoles been less trusting, Kameʻiamoku's attack would have ended differently. The schooner also carried a bronze cannon, several smaller swivel guns, slow-match cords and powder to fire them, cannon balls, and a small store of canister shot.

Ashore, the Hawaiʻians unloaded the Fair American's muskets, powder, and ammunition, and they stripped the schooner of its swivel guns and cannon. Leaving the ship to be dismantled for its iron, they loaded the weaponry and the wounded sailor into their canoes and set off down the coast to bring their trophies to Kamehameha at Kealakekua. Among the bodies left floating in the small bay that day was the corpse of the Fair American's nineteen-year-old captain, Thomas Metcalfe—Simon Metcalfe's son. Kameʻiamoku had unknowingly found his revenge.

Upon reaching Ka'awaloa, where Kamehameha was staying, Kame'iamoku had taken the grievously injured haole sailor straight away to a kahuna lā'au lapa'au. Now, with my father accompanying them, he led Kamehameha to the healer's hale, where the foreigner lay on a sedge mat. The kahuna lā'au lapa'au had applied poultices to his wounds and bound them with strips of kapa cloth. The man lay with his eyes closed and did not at first see the three Hawaiians as they entered the darkened interior of the hale through its single doorway.

"Ask him what his name is," Kameha said to my father.

My father had learned enough English from Burney during Cook's visit to put this simple question to the man. "*Yu'u…yu'u nā'ime*?" he said, struggling to pronounce the foreign words. The haole's eyes fluttered open and he regarded my father with surprise. "*Waka yu'u nā'ime*?" my father asked again.

"My name is Isaac…Isaac," the man groaned. He smiled wanly through his pain, relieved that someone in this strange place might understand him.

"His name is *'Aikake*," my father told Kameha.

"'Aikake," Kamehameha repeated. Smiling down at the captive haole from his great height, he said, "*E como mai oe iō Hawai'i nei.*" *Welcome to beloved Hawai'i.* The haole did not understand Kameha's words, but from his demeanor, he understood his meaning. The haole's full Christian name was Isaac Davis, but for the rest of his life among our people he would be known by the name my father gave him: 'Aikake.

Kamehameha was angry when he first learned that Kame'iamoku had attacked a haole ship and slain most of its crew. "What were you thinking?" he thundered, ignoring for the moment the captured haole weapons and munitions. "You know how angry Kāpena Kuke became when Palea took Kuke's small boat. If any haoles discover what you have done, they will be even more furious than Kuke and his people and they will retaliate more fiercely." Kame'iamoku bowed his head in embarrassment. Kamehameha softened. "What is done is done," he said. "You did well to bring the mūk'e and the kano'ono to me."

Upon learning that the Fair American was beached at Ka'ūpūlehu, damaged but still intact, Kamehameha ordered Kame'iamoku to return there and safeguard the vessel. "No one is allowed to break it up for its ailon'e. That is kapu," he said. "We must see to the repair of this great canoe. It must be returned to its owners, and in the meantime, it may prove useful to us."

When the Eleanora arrived at Kealakekua from Maui two days later, Kamehameha decreed a kapu on the bay. "These haoles must not learn that we are holding 'Aikake or that we have taken his great canoe," he said. "No one may approach their great canoe, either by canoe or by swimming to it. Moreover, no one may approach the haoles if they should come ashore."

After several days of isolation in the middle of Kealakekua Bay, and with the Eleanora running low on fresh produce, and his crew eager for trade—and, of course, women—Captain Metcalfe sent his boatswain ashore at Ka'awaloa to discover why the Hawai'ians were shunning his ship. Not immediately finding anyone to interrogate, this haole, whose name was John Young, shouldered his musket and went in search of fowl for the ship's larder. During his explorations, he passed several hales, but saw no one. "Many people saw him," my father told me, "but none allowed themselves to be seen." When Young returned to the beach, he discovered that his boat was missing. All at once, he was confronted by several young ali'i warriors, one of whom seized his musket. After disarming Young, they conducted him to Kamehameha.

Kameha was reclining on a mat in the courtyard of his hale when the newcomer was brought to him. Kamehameha looked up at him impassively and said nothing. Young looked down uneasily at the lounging ruler of Kona and Kohala, biting his lower lip and clasping his hands in front of him. Then he noticed that the warriors who had brought him to Kamehameha had all seated themselves on the ground, cross-legged. He sat down as well.

"Good," Kameha said to my father, who sat immediately to his right. "He shows me respect. Ask him his name."

Again, my father struggled with the English words, yet made himself understood. Young tapped his own chest and said, "My name, John Young."

Turning to Kamehameha, my father said in Hawaiian, "His name is *Ī'ona Ī'ona.*" My father could not say "John," nor could his ears distinguish the subtle difference between "John" and "Young."

"Now tell him my name," Kameha said.

My father gestured at Kamehameha and said to Young, "He nā'ime Kamehameha."

"*Tamaahamaah,*" repeated Young, who could not pronounce Kamehameha's name any better than my father could Young's name. Young would eventually learn to say *Kamehameha*, but he would never be known as "John Young" by the Hawai'ians, who called him *Ī'ona* for some time thereafter—or simply referred to him as "Kamehameha's haole."

Young would acquire a new Hawaiian name when Kamehameha charged him with teaching his warriors to sail the haoles' great canoes. Seeking to instill a sense of urgency in the Hawai'ian sailors while drilling them for battle, Young would shout, "All hands on deck!" Though the Hawai'ians did not understand his words, they grasped their import well enough through Young's tone and gestures, and soon began to call him *'Olohana*, for the way they heard the shouted order. But this would not be until later, after he'd earned Kamehameha's trust.

Now Kameha rose from his mat, looked down upon Young from his full height, and motioned him to stand. Young regained his feet and tilted his neck to meet Kamehameha's steady gaze. "Come with me," Kameha said, gesturing at the doorway to his hale. Young followed him, with my father trailing, to where Isaac Davis lay. Kameha had several days ago ordered the haole seaman moved from the kahuna's dwelling to his own house, to better see after his care.

"'Aikake was already somewhat improved and alert," my father said. "He and 'Olohana began conversing very rapidly in their own language. They seemed to know each other."

Young turned to Kamehameha, gestured first at Davis and then at himself, pointed in the direction of the bay, and pantomimed a paddling motion with his hands. "*Ship, ship,*" he said. "Tamaahamaah, please, *ship.*"

My father recognized the foreign word. "I think the haole is begging you to allow him and this 'Aikake to return to the haole great canoe," he said to Kameha.

"No doubt," Kamehameha replied. "Tell him they may return to their comrades tomorrow, but for tonight he and 'Aikake must rest here."

Through some words, but mostly through gestures, my father gave Young to understand that he and Davis were not free to go—yet. To Kamehameha he said, "But brother, if you release them, they will surely tell the haoles what Kame'iamoku has done."

"Doubtless they would, if I released them," Kameha replied. "But that will not happen."

The next morning, Young again asked Kamehameha for permission to return to his ship. "Tamaahamaah, me, him," he said, pointing first to Kamehameha, and then to himself and Davis, "go ship now?" Young gestured toward the bay, where the Eleanora's crew was commencing another day of kapu-imposed isolation. He made paddling motions again. My father was not there to interpret, but Kamehameha understood his meaning.

"*Yu'u...ko?*" Kameha replied. Then he shook his head and waggled his finger at Young. "*Yu'u...*" He shook his head again.

Young understood him. He looked dejectedly at Kamehameha. "Why we no can go?" he asked in English.

Kameha rose and left the hale in search of my father, abruptly ending his first attempt to speak the haole language. My father was at the shore with Ka'iana, regarding the Eleanora. Ka'iana had arrived just that morning from Kailua, where he had been drilling a number of Kamehameha's chieftains and warriors in the use of muskets. When he learned that Kame'iamoku had captured more haole weapons, including a cannon, he came straight away to Kealakekua. "Keli'imaika'i, Ka'iana, come with me," Kamehameha said, "now."

My father and Ka'iana followed Kamehameha to his hale. Entering his residence, Kameha said, "You can speak the haole talk, Ka'iana." Pointing at Young and then at Davis, Kameha said, "That one is called Ī'ona. The other one, the sick one, is called 'Aikake. They wish to return to the haole wa'a nui." Kamehameha explained to Ka'iana that he had no intention of allowing the two men to go back to the haoles' great canoe and reveal the fate of the Fair American to their comrades. But for the time being, and until the ships departed, he said, he wanted to put them at their ease.

"Please tell this Ī'ona that 'Aikake is not well enough to return to the great canoe yet. Tell him they must stay here for another day or two," he said. "Tell him that we will send word to their people that they are well and being cared for."

Ka'iana turned to Young and spoke to him in English. Young listened politely but still protested. "He says that 'Aikake has recovered enough to go with him to the great canoe," Ka'iana told Kamehameha.

"Tell Ī'ona that we are concerned for 'Aikake, nevertheless." Kameha said. "Tell him that we are very sorry for the harm our people have done to 'Aikake and that we desire Ī'ona and 'Aikake to stay with us for just another day or two as our honored guests. Tell him again that we will send word to the great canoe."

Ka'iana spoke to Young again. The haole seaman looked quizzically at Kamehameha and reluctantly nodded his assent. "'Olohana suspected all along that Kamehameha had no intention of allowing him and 'Aikake to leave," my father said. "He told me so many years later."

The next morning, Young looked expectantly at Kamehameha and again asked, "Tamaahamaah, we go ship?"

Kamehameha frowned and called for Ka'iana again. "Please tell Ī'ona that I cannot permit him to return to his great canoe. Tell him how Kāpena Kuke once killed many of our people because one of us stole a small canoe from him. Tell him I fear that if his chief learns that some of our people have taken a great canoe and slain all the haoles on it but 'Aikake, he will do the same, and that is why I cannot allow him to return to his great canoe. But I will allow him and 'Aikake to leave on the next haole great canoe that comes here. Tell him that."

Ka'iana told Young what Kameha had said. "'Olohana appeared very dejected," my father said. Young left the hale without a word and walked down to the shore. No one tried to stop him. He stood at the water's edge for a long time, watching his shipmates bustling about the Eleanora's decks and climbing in the rigging. They were unfurling the ship's sails. Young sat down in the sand and remained there for a long time after the Eleanora stood out to sea.

Kame'iamoku was pleased when he learned that the Fair American's slain captain was the son of the Eleanora's Simon Metcalfe—the same haole sea captain who had earlier assaulted him. Metcalfe departed Hawai'i unaware that Hawai'ians had taken the Fair American and slain his son.

Once Davis had healed sufficiently, he and Young tried to escape. "They went to the beach in the night and attempted to take a canoe," my father said. "But anticipating such a development, Kamehameha had posted guards there and they were quickly apprehended."

The two haoles were brought before Kameha again. The guards had handled them roughly and were now gripping them tightly about their necks.

"Release them, now!" Kamehameha ordered. He motioned to Young and Davis to sit and called for Ka'iana. Turning to my father, who had joined him at his hale, he said, "It is natural that these haoles should try to flee."

Ka'iana arrived to interpret. "Tell them that I understand why they would want to leave us," Kamehameha said. "Tell them also that if they remain here and serve us well, they will be richly rewarded. And tell them that if they try to flee again, they will be slain."

Young and Davis thereafter settled into life among us.

Some days later, Kamehameha commanded Young to accompany him, my father, Kameʻiamoku, and Kaʻiana to Kaʻūpūlehu, where the Fair American remained grounded in the offshore shallows. At his bidding, Young dove into the water to examine the damaged hull and pronounced the ship salvageable. "Give this haole whatever he needs and whatever assistance he may require to repair this great canoe," said Kameha. "Tell him I want him to teach our people how to paddle it and how to fight with the mūkʻe and kanoʻono. And tell the haoles that they must teach my brother and me how to speak the haole talk—this *Īʻiklī.*"

Kaʻiana saw to it that Young had as many craftsmen and laborers as he required to repair the Fair American. Under Young's supervision, the Hawaiʻians hauled the schooner onto the beach and set to work. "Fortunately," said my father, "the planking was still intact. The ship only needed some minor work to seal some cracks." The Fair American carried sufficient pitch and other materials required to make these repairs and the Hawaiʻians had the ship afloat again within a fortnight.

Davis soon joined Young at Kaʻūpūlehu and the pair set about training the Hawaiʻians to sail the Fair American properly. "As our people were already excellent sailors, they learned quickly," my father said. The Hawaiʻians were soon as adept at handling the schooner as any haole."

Leaving Young to continue training the Hawaiʻian sailors at Kaʻūpūlehu, Kaʻiana and Davis returned to Kealakekua to resume schooling Kamehameha's warriors in the use of haole weapons. The Hawaiʻians soon coined their own names for these new weapons, whose sound they mimicked by saying "*pū,*" the Hawaiian word for conch. They began calling muskets *pū poʻohiwi*—shoulder guns. Cannons they called *pū kuni ahi*—fire-kindler guns. Firearms in general soon became known throughout our islands as *pū.*

~

"You are too familiar with Ka'iana," Kamehameha snapped at Kaʻahumanu. "You must keep your distance from him."

"What? Is it now kapu for me to talk to other men?" Kaʻahumanu rejoined.

"No, it is not kapu," Kamehameha said. "But I do not like the way you talk to Ka'iana, or the way he talks to you."

"Then tell *him* it is kapu to talk to me."

"I have already decreed that it is kapu for other men to approach you familiarly," Kamehameha replied. "And Ka'iana well knows this."

"You decreed that it is kapu for other men to lie with me; you never said it is kapu for other men to talk with me, and Ka'iana well knows *that*," Kaʻahumanu retorted.

Kamehameha threw up his hands in frustration and stormed out of the hale he often shared at night with his youngest wife.

"She vexes me to no end," Kameha later complained to my father.

"Perhaps you should speak to Ka'iana," my father said.

"He is aware of the kapu," Kamehameha said. "There is no point in reminding him."

Kamehameha was caught in a dilemma; he could not tell Kaʻahumanu it was kapu for her to flirt with other men, else he would have to severely punish her, and he could not order Ka'iana to ignore Kaʻahumanu, lest he offend him at a time when he required the other man's help. Thus, he said nothing to either of them and Kaʻahumanu's flirtation with Ka'iana continued.

Eventually, Ka'iana responded; he could not help it. When Ka'iana and ʻOlohana drilled Kamehameha's warriors in the use of muskets, Kaʻahumanu was always a ready audience. She would cast coy smiles in Ka'iana's direction and make provocative comments. "You are so adept with that pū po'ohiwi," she said to Ka'iana one day. "Is there no end to your prowess?"

"My prowess extends to many matters," he said, grinning and flashing his teeth. "I have many skills I could teach you."

My father, whom Kamehameha had delegated to observe the drills in his place, overheard this exchange. "You should be more circumspect with Ka'ahumanu," he warned Ka'iana. "Kamehameha will brook no violation of his kapu, not even by you, Ka'iana."

"Can I help it if that wahine chooses to speak to me?" Ka'iana replied with a dismissive wave of his hand. "I cannot ignore her; it would be rude."

My father could only shake his head and walk away.

The arrival of Young and Davis so close together troubled Kamehameha. Thus, one morning, when his English had improved sufficiently to interrogate the Englishmen, Kamehameha summoned them to his hale. He also sent for Ka'iana.

"Ī'ona, 'Aikake, you say me: How many are your people?" Kamehameha asked the two haoles. "Are they many more than ours? Please, you speak true."

"You mean us English?" asked Young. They were all seated cross-legged on mats in Kamehameha's courtyard at Ka'awaloa. The day was still cool; a soft breeze played in the palm fronds overhead. A single dolphin broke the surface in the middle of the bay beyond and spun several times in mid-air before falling back to the water.

"No, not you Ī'iklī people only," replied Kamehameha. "All haole people. How many there are?"

"Many, many, Tamaahamaah," said Davis. "English people, French people, Spanish people, Portuguese, Italian, Dutch, Americans—many more people than be here." His voice trailed off.

"Where they all come from?" my father asked.

"Many come from England; many come from Europe and some others, like my captain, Simon Metcalf, come from America," said Young.

Kamehameha said nothing for a while. Then, in deliberate English, he asked, "All haoles, they have *mūk'e* and *kano'ono*?"

"Oh yes," Ka'iana interjected, losing patience with this tedious exchange. "They all have muskets and cannons—more than you have ever seen, bigger ships than you have ever seen. But *I* have seen them in *China* and other places."

Kamehameha turned to Ka'iana and narrowed his eyes as if to say, *I did not ask you.* But Ka'iana's intelligence had registered with him. Turning back to Young and Davis, he asked slowly in his ponderous English, "These haoles, who are so many, with so many great canoes and mūk'e and kano'ono, they come more here?"

"Aye," replied Davis. "Ye can count on that y'er highness. They be comin' here, an' more 'n more of 'em fer sure."

"Why they come?" my father asked.

Young made to reply, but before he could answer, Ka'iana broke in once more. "They will come for the same reason the others have already come," he said, again in Hawaiian. "Our islands are a convenient place for them to stop on their way to Kahiki, to *China*, where *I* have been."

Pointedly ignoring Ka'iana, Kamehameha turned to Young and asked, "You say me true now, Ī'ona, will these haoles want stay here?"

"Mayhap they will," Young said. "Y'er land is quite pleasant fer them."

"*La'ana*?" my father hazarded. This word was new to him.

"*Āina*!" snapped Ka'iana. "Our own islands! The haoles *like* our islands."

Kamehameha glowered at Ka'iana but said nothing. He signaled for him and the haoles to leave. When they had gone, Kameha turned to my father and said, "Keli'i, we must stop fighting among ourselves before more of these haoles come. Otherwise, I fear we will grow weak as they grow strong."

"But Kameha," my father said, "our people have fought each other for generations. Who will stop it?"

"*I* will," replied Kamehameha.

WAILUKU, MAUI, 1790

Kamehameha's warriors had pushed their foes deep into the narrow 'Īao Valley above Wailuku and hauled the Fair American's bronze cannon and swivel guns behind them. It had taken them several days of hard fighting to reach this point from Kahului. Every foot of ground gained by Kameha's warriors was soaked with the blood of Hawai'ian and Maui fighters alike. Now the cannon, named "Robert" by 'Olohana after his own father, and called *Lopaka* by the Hawai'ians, was in position, along with the other guns, cannon balls, canister shot, kapa-cloth wads, and powder.

Kamehameha and my father stood a short distance from the cannons. 'Olohana and 'Aikake stood directly behind the gunners, observing as they loaded the weapons with the practiced motions that the haoles had taught them. "Now!" Kamehameha shouted. The warriors holding smoldering kukui-oil-soaked cords lowered them to the weapons' touch holes. Lopaka and the smaller guns roared, and the slaughter of Kalanikūpule's people commenced.

With Kahekili away on O'ahu and his son still ruling Maui in his stead, Kameha had judged the time opportune for another invasion of the neighboring isle—especially now that he had secured muskets, cannons, a haole ship, and the aid of Young and Davis.

First, however, he sought to unite his Big Island rivals behind him. Kamehameha sent Holoʻae and my father to Kaʻū and Hilo to seek their support. "Go to Keōua Kūʻahuʻula and Keawemaʻuhili." he said, "Tell them that the time has come to avenge the eight hundred warriors of the ʻĀlapa and the Piʻipiʻi, including Keawemaʻuhili's own nephew, whom Kahekili's people slew on Maui. Tell them I request their assistance, as their *mōʻī*. Tell them that I have pū poʻohiwi and pū kuni ahi, and a haole great canoe. Tell them that I will be forever in their debt if they lend me the assistance that I ask, and tell them that there will be a reckoning if they should refuse. This I vow, *as their mōʻī*." Holoʻae and my father delivered Kameha's message as directed. "

Keōua Red Cloak scorned Kamehameha's request. "My cousin may call himself whatever he wishes," he said, "but he does not rule in Kaʻū; I do. You tell *him* that until the day comes when I no longer rule Kaʻū, he is not the mōʻī *here*. Tell him that I do not care about his haole weapons and I will not send him any of my people or canoes."

Keawemaʻuhili—distrustful of Red Cloak and seeking an alliance with Kamehameha against him—was more amenable. "I will help Kamehameha avenge the deaths of the ʻĀlapa and the Piʻipiʻi," he told my father and Holoʻae. "Tell *your* mōʻī that I will send him all the people and canoes I can spare, save for those I require to protect Hilo."

With the Fair American leading the way, Kamehameha's fleet had landed at Kahului Bay in a hail of musket and cannon fire. Kamohomoho, who had become Kalanikūpule's leading adviser after his victory over my father at Hana, had anticipated that the Hawaiʻians might attempt a landing at Kahului, with its wide sweep of sheltered beaches. Accordingly, he positioned several thousand of his warriors there to repulse them.

"Kalanikūpule's people rushed to the shore to oppose us," my father said, "but Lopaka and our pū poʻohiwi quickly drove them off."

Unopposed now, Kamehameha ordered the Hawai'ians to haul their double-hulled canoes high onto the shore. When some of his commanders protested that this would impede their people's escape should the enemy succeed in pressing them back to the bay, Kameha replied, "There will be no retreating from this battle. We conquer or we die."

Young and Davis supervised the offloading of the cannon and swivel guns from the Fair American. Using the ship's block and tackle, a device previously unfamiliar to them, Kamehameha's warriors lowered the weapons into canoes and ferried them to shore, where they placed them on wooden sleds designed by Davis.

Ka'iana's musket warriors loaded and primed their weapons. They were in the first rank, with Lopaka and the swivel guns, under the command of 'Olohana and 'Aikake, at the center. Fighters armed with slings came next. Behind them came the spear throwers. Warriors armed with clubs and daggers formed up behind them.

My father told me that 'Olohana had advised this order of battle. The musket warriors and gun crews would discharge their weapons; the sling bearers would then move forward to protect them while they reloaded their guns, whereupon the musket warriors would move to the front again, and the deadly cycle would repeat. "Throughout, we were to continue moving forward," my father explained. The warriors manning Lopaka and the swivel-guns were expected to keep pace with the rest of the army.

At a signal from Kamehameha, conch shells sounded from one end of the Hawai'ians' line to the other, and the army commenced its advance on the village of Wailuku, where Kalanikūpule's people waited for them. Spread across a wide front, the Hawai'ians advanced steadily and deliberately on both sides of the shallow stream that flowed to the sea from the 'Īao Valley, They moved forward in good order, though the gun crews lagged behind the rest. Kalanikūpule's people were drawn up in front of the village, also on both sides of the stream.

Now the two armies faced each other, unmoving. "We were separated by a distance of perhaps no more than the longest throw of a pololū spear," my father said. Silence reigned. There were none of the customary insults and taunts. The Hawai'ian artillery crews were just getting Lopaka and the swivel guns into position at the center of the front line when, with fearsome shrieks, the men of Maui charged.

Young's tactics worked, for a while. Ka'iana's musket warriors and gun crews discharged their weapons, killing many Maui fighters outright. Then sling stones flew from the Hawai'ians' ranks. With these missiles now falling among and all around them, the Maui warriors were slow to close with the Hawai'ians, giving Ka'iana's people time to unloose another volley of musket fire. But this time, Lopaka and the swivel guns did not join them.

Kamohomoho understood what was happening after the second volley. He exhorted his men to ignore the sling stones and spears and rush the Hawai'ians before they could reload and fire their muskets again. "Close the gap! Close the gap!" he cried. "The enemy cannot strike you with stones if you close with them!"

The warriors of Maui now released a volley of sling stones as they charged the Hawai'ians. Many of these missiles found their marks. Meanwhile, as Kamohomoho had anticipated, Ka'iana's musket fighters were unable to reload and fire their weapons in time to repel his warriors. Moreover, they made easy targets for their foes' stones and spears as they stood in place, struggling to reload and fire their guns.

Observing these developments from behind his own lines, Kamehameha ordered his commanders to direct their sling fighters to pull back and give way to the warriors with spears, clubs, and daggers. They rushed through the musket bearers' formation, scattering them in all directions. With their ranks dispersed and their own people now between them and the enemy, those musket bearers who had reloaded their weapons could not fire them. They were reduced to wielding their muskets like clubs.

A shower of spears from the Hawai'ians slowed the oncoming Maui warriors, who were soon engaged at close quarters by many more Hawai'ian fighters armed with clubs, daggers, and often no more than their own hands. Men on both sides were impaled, stabbed, and beaten to death. Many on both sides died at the hands of lua adepts. The bloodletting continued without resolution for the balance of the day, by which time the two sides remained where they had been at the battle's outset.

"What good are these haole weapons, these pū kuni ahi, these pū po'ohiwi?" Kamehameha demanded that night as he and his commanders assessed the day's fighting. "We made too little progress today, and we traded the lives of too many good warriors for it." Kameha addressed the entire group, but his eyes were fixed on 'Olohana, 'Aikake, and Ka'iana.

"We failed to take full advantage of our weapons because Lopaka and the other guns were silent," said 'Olohana.

"Why did they not speak?" Kamehameha asked.

"We had no more ammunition," 'Olohana replied. "This was our fault." He gestured at 'Aikake. Intent on supervising the cannon bearers, 'Olohana and 'Aikake had neglected the powder and cannon-shot bearers, who had fallen behind the rest of the army. "We will not repeat this mistake and our guns will speak loudly tomorrow," 'Olohana promised.

In the morning, the two armies took the field once more, forming their ranks opposite each other, this time separated by a distance greater than the range of spears, sling stones, and muskets. As on the previous day, neither side moved for some time. The Maui warriors thrust their spears at the Hawai'ians and hurled insults and jeers at them, thinking to provoke their foes into a headlong charge. They were met with silence. At length, Kalanikūpule ordered his own people to advance.

Kamehameha's commanders had ordered their front-line warriors to feign weariness. Some men even pretended to cower in fear. Mindful of the enemy's musketry, but less fearful of it than the previous day, Kalanikūpule's people came on warily but steadily, their confidence building with every step. They were about to unleash their sling stones and spears when Lopaka and the swivel guns spoke.

The Hawai'ians had drawn the guns close behind their front ranks and loaded them with canister shot. At the Hawai'ian center, and screened by the warriors in front of them, they were not visible to the advancing foe until, on command, the Hawai'ian fighters fell away. The warriors of Maui mistook this movement for the beginnings of a retreat and quickened their own pace. Now Lopaka roared and discharged a shell casing that disintegrated in mid-air just yards in front of the Maui warriors, spewing lethal iron balls and nails in all directions. The swivel guns fired next.

"The Maui warriors fell before our eyes like palm trees before a powerful wind," my father recalled. "Their blood flowed like mountain streams. It was a truly terrible sight."

Now the Hawai'ians advanced, and their panicked opponents fled before them. "Hold fast! Hold fast!" Kalanikūpule and Kamohomoho cried to their warriors. Overcoming their fear of Lopaka, the Maui fighters halted their flight and turned to face the Hawai'ians once again. But before they could reform their ranks, the Hawai'ians' muskets spoke. Scores more Maui warriors fell. Those who had somehow survived this volley unscathed milled about in shock. By now the Hawai'ians had reloaded Lopaka and the other guns, which bellowed anew, followed by more musket fire. Abruptly, the center of the Maui line collapsed and confusion reigned among its wings.

At this moment, the carefully laid plans of 'Olohana, 'Aikake, and Ka'iana collapsed as well. This day, Kamehameha had ordered his people not to close with their foes. They were to avoid hand-to-hand combat. Cannon fire was to follow musketry, followed again by sling stones, spears, musketry, and cannon in a continuous cycle of death and destruction. In this way, the Hawai'ians would take best advantage of their superiority in haole weaponry.

"We were not supposed to give chase," my father said, "but when Kalanikūpule's people began to run away, too many of our own people forgot about this and ran after them."

Whooping triumphantly and brandishing their spears and clubs, the warriors at the center of Kamehameha's lines surged through the breach in the Maui center, leaving the cannons and Ka'iana's musket corps behind. At the same time, the Hawai'ian fighters to each side collapsed on them, as their own commanders struggled to close the gaps between the Hawai'ian center and its right and left wings.

Seeing what was happening, Kalanikūpule, Kamohomoho, and their commanders shouted orders to their own fighters to attack the Hawai'ians on their flanks. The battle now descended into traditional close combat with spears, knives, and clubs as men fought each other on both sides and in the middle of the 'Īao Stream. Amid this struggle, the cannons and the Hawai'ians' muskets were rendered useless once more. Now it was the Hawai'ian commanders' turn to reform their lines. At last, with Ka'iana's help, they succeeded in repulsing the Maui left and right wings and restoring their center. "Ka'iana was very quick-thinking," my father said. "He divided his pū fighters into two groups and dispatched one group to support our warriors on the right and the other to support our people on the left." As Ka'iana's people reached their new positions with their weapons primed and ready, the commanders on the Hawai'ians' wings exhorted their warriors to disengage and fall back. The musket fighters stepped into the newly opened space between the two sides and opened fire, driving Kalanikūpule's people back.

Straightening their respective lines once more—Kamehameha's people by force of will and Kalanikūpule's in grudging withdrawal—the two armies' warriors now stood well apart, glaring at each other in silence. Neither the men of Hawai'i nor the warriors of Maui had any appetite for further fighting. Cautiously retreating from each other, they retired to salve their wounds and prepare for yet another day of combat. On balance, the Hawai'ians had won the day. They had pushed their enemies through and mauka of

Wailuku, and their camp was now hundreds of yards closer to the mouth of the ʻĪao Valley than it had been the night before.

In camp that night, Kamehameha upbraided his commanders once more. "Our people performed better today, but not well enough," he said. "We lost too many warriors yet again."

"This kind of fighting is new to all of us," Kaʻiana soothed. "We have made mistakes, but we are learning from them and we will not repeat them. Our people will do still better tomorrow."

Kamehameha was not so easily assuaged. He turned to his kahuna nui, Holoʻae. "What does Kūkāʻilimoku say?" The priest had just returned from a ridge of low hills where he had taken the god on its standard, there to learn whatever the breezes and the feathers atop the god's head could foretell.

"The god's feathers stood up brave and true in the wind," Holoʻae said. "You will have great success tomorrow, so long as one leg does not outrun the other."

In the morning, Kamehameha decreed a kapu: No man was to rush the enemy on his own initiative; all were to wait upon their commanders' orders to advance. Transgressors would be put to death, unless the enemy happened to slay them first. That day, the Hawaiʻians maintained good order throughout the fight, and steadily drove Kalanikūpule's people back before relentless cannon fire and musketry, and a steady rain of spears and stones.

Unable to advance, Kalanikūpule's people tried to stand their ground, but their ranks diminished steadily. At last the Hawaiʻian commanders ordered their warriors to charge, the enemy lines broke, and the Maui warriors, with nowhere else to turn, fled into the ʻĪao Valley. The women, children, and old men of Wailuku fled with them. Now the Hawaiʻians brought Lopaka forward and fired round after round of canister shot and cannon balls into the valley.

The ʻĪao Valley is narrow and its walls are steep. Since time immemorial, the valley had served as an unconquerable bastion against attackers armed with slings, spears, clubs, and daggers. Holding high ground from the outset, defenders enjoyed the tactical advantage of the valley's steadily rising, terraced floor, even in retreat. Moreover, as invaders advanced deeper into the valley, its narrowing walls would force them into ever-closer confines, making them vulnerable to sling stones and spears thrown from the terraces above and from perches still higher on the valley's walls. Furthermore, laying siege to the valley was fruitless, because its defenders could neither be starved out nor denied water. Intensively farmed in times of peace, the ʻĪao Valley was abundant with taro, yams, and sweet potatoes. And no enemy could dam the ʻĪao Stream, which flowed from the valley's nearly inaccessible heights.

But this day, with no easy way out and no cover from the Hawaiʻians' haole weaponry, the once-impregnable ʻĪao Valley became a trap for Kalanikūpule's warriors and the people of Wailuku. And on Kamehameha's orders, they were mercilessly slain.

As they ascended the terraces, the Hawaiʻians hauled Lopaka, the swivel guns, and their munitions with them and cut down their retreating foes with more rounds of cannon balls and canister shot. Sling stones and spears also took a fearsome toll. With increasingly accurate musket fire, the Hawaiʻians slew foes who tried to escape by climbing the valley's walls.

At last, the surviving warriors and the villagers whom they had tried to defend were forced into the valley's deepest reaches, where they became crowded together within a space no more than a few score yards wide. With ʻOlohana and ʻAikake supervising, the Hawaiʻians drew Lopaka into its final firing position and rammed powder, wadding, and the last round of canister shot down its barrel. Kaʻiana formed up his musket warriors in a line abreast of the cannon. The musket bearers loaded and primed their weapons. Kamehameha gave the signal to fire. Lopaka roared one last time amid the crackle of musket fire and the shrill screams of the dying and mortally wounded people of Wailuku. When at last the gunfire's echoes faded, there was only silence. Then, as the haze of powder smoke lifted, the Hawaiʻian warriors beheld a vision so terrible that even the most hard-bitten among them blanched to see it.

Shaking his head at the terrible memory, my father told me, "So many people had fallen and so thickly that the ʻĪao Stream was choked with bodies. The water ran red for days." Today, this battle is known among our people as *kaua i Kepaniwai o ʻĪao*—The Battle at the Dammed Waters of ʻĪao. The outcome of the battle convinced Kamehameha of the value of haole weapons. Surveying the killing ground, he turned to my father and Kaʻiana and said, "We must have more pū poʻohiwi and more pū kuni ahi."

Despite the widespread carnage, a few Maui people managed to escape. Kalanikūpule and his chieftains, my own father's vanquisher, Kamohomoho, among them, fled still deeper into the ʻĪao Valley ahead of their own retreating warriors. Ascending into the mountains along paths that followed steep, narrow gullies mostly unknown in those days, they crossed over to Lahaina and sailed to Oʻahu.

Molokaʻi, 1790

Having won a great victory on Maui, Kamehameha was eager to move on to Oʻahu, where Kahekili had moved his court. But first, he needed to secure the neutrality of the Molokaʻi chiefs, who had sworn allegiance to Kahekili. He also wanted to secure from Kalola guardianship of his sister, Kekuʻiapoiwa Liliha, and her daughter, Keopuolani.

Accompanied by my father and his other chieftains, he sailed to Molokaʻi, landing at Kaunakakai. "When we arrived there," said my father, "we learned that Kalola was dying."

Kalola, her daughter, and granddaughter were staying mauka of the coast at Kalamaʻula. The Molokaʻi chiefs had gathered there. Kamehameha sent a messenger to them requesting their permission to visit the dying chiefess. "The chiefs must understand that I come here in peace and in grief, and not as the vanquisher of Kalola's nephew, Kalanikūpule," he said.

Permission granted, Kameha hastened to Kalola's hale, where he found her lying on a sedge mat. A healer was administering to her. Kekuʻiapoiwa Liliha and Keopuolani sat nearby, crying. There was no mistaking Kalola's condition, even in the hale's shadows. Disease had laid waste to her body and her once-full face had collapsed. Her eyes were closed and her breathing was fast and shallow. Kamehameha knelt at her side and bent his head toward her. "I have come, Kalola, I have come," he whispered.

Kalola's eyes fluttered open. She turned her head toward Kamehameha. "You slew my son, and now you have come to watch me die?" she said.

"I have come out of love for you and full of grief to find you like this," said Kameha.

"It cannot be helped," Kalola said.

"Do not worry about my sister Lili and her daughter," said Kamehameha. "I will take them under my protection."

"They shall be yours to protect once I am dead," said Kalola. She turned her head away. These were her last words to Kamehameha, whom she had mothered when he was a little boy and later initiated into manhood so many years earlier.

Kamehameha's broad face was streaked with tears when he emerged from Kalola's hale. He clasped my father and wailed. The sight of this big, fearsome warrior weeping moved the Moloka'i chiefs gathered in the courtyard. "They saw that though Pai'ea's shell was hard, his heart was not," said my father. "This aroused their sympathy for him."

The Hawai'ians and the chiefs of Moloka'i kept vigil outside Kalola's hale for the next two days. During this time, Kamehameha told the Moloka'i chiefs that war between him and Kahekili was inevitable. "I have no quarrel you, and I wish you no harm," he said. "But if war comes here, all the people of Moloka'i will suffer. I would not have this, and I make you this pledge: Take no part in this coming fight, and I will not send my people here. And be assured that Kahekili's people will not come here either, for I will keep them well occupied on O'ahu."

"The Moloka'i chiefs believed Kameha was sincere," my father said. "They had chafed under Kahekili's rule in the past, and wished to be rid of him. They promised Kamehameha that they would take no sides in this fight between him and Kahekili."

When the keening of the women inside the hale signaled Kalola's passing, Kamehameha joined their wailing, picked up a lava stone, and struck one of his front teeth from his mouth. Now he fell into my father's arms again and the two cried together. Blood oozed from Kamehameha's mouth and ran down my father's arm. Many of the Moloka'i chiefs and some members of Kamehameha's party followed his example, knocking out their own front teeth. In those days, our people sometimes gave public expression to their profound inner grief over the death of a beloved chief or chiefess by injuring themselves in this or some other way. As I explained to my Esther, who was horrified when I first told her of this practice, "Inflicting such pain on oneself was the greatest homage the living could pay to the dead, and it was done only rarely."

"But still..." Esther sighed. Barely two generations removed from that time, Esther and her contemporaries find many of its aspects unfathomable.

Kamehameha and his people remained on Moloka'i for the next ten days, while Kalola's bones were purified in the imu.

While still on Moloka'i, Kamehameha sent two emissaries on simultaneous missions to O'ahu: one to ask a famous prophet what he must do to conquer all the islands; and the other to offer a peace of sorts to Kahekili.

The prophet was an old wise man from Kaua'i named Kapoukahi. "Tell your lord that he must build a great new heiau for his god," Kapoukahi told Kamehameha's emissary. "Its dimensions must be greater than any other temple he has previously built, greater than any other temple in our islands."

"Where should Kamehameha build this great heiau?" the emissary asked him.

"He must build it on the hill at Kawaihae," Kapoukahi replied. "Tell your lord that when he completes this heiau and consecrates it to his god, he shall gain all the islands without risk to his own person."

At Kahekili's court, Kamehameha's other emissary told the O'ahu ruler, "My mō'ī, Kamehameha, mover of the Naha Stone, has conquered Maui. He will come here next. But first, he wishes to know whether he should come in peace or in war." Then Kamehameha's emissary laid two stones, one white and one black, at Kahekili's feet. The white stone signified life-affirming pursuits: fishing, farming, and child-rearing. The black stone symbolized war and bloodletting. "My mō'ī asks which stone you would choose, Lord," the emissary said.

"I choose neither," Kahekili replied. "Tell my *son* Kamehameha that this is not the time to cast stones. Tell him that when the kapa cloth covers

Kahekili and the black pig rests at his nose—*that* will be the time to choose between war and peace. Tell him to come to Oʻahu and cast his stones *then.*"

Upon receiving Kahekili's reply, Kamehameha consulted with his advisers. "Should we wait until after Kahekili is dead to attack Oʻahu, or should we attack now?" he asked. Kamehameha and his chiefs had not yet resolved this question when word reached them that Keōua Kūʻahuʻula had attacked Hilo, slaying Keawemaʻuhili and his son Keaweokahikona, and was even then ravaging Kamehameha's own Kohala lands.

His hand forced by his fractious cousin, Kamehameha rushed back to the Big Island with his army, leaving a small garrison behind on Maui. When Kahekili learned of this, he appointed Kalanikūpule his regent on Oʻahu and led an expedition to retake Maui, relocating his court to Wailuku. Put to flight, the Hawaiʻians took refuge at Kauwiki once again.

"Our cousin Red Cloak has dishonored all the blood our people spilled to gain Maui," Kamehameha told his chiefs when word of this setback reached him. "We will make him bleed for this, and when we are done with him, we will finally settle with Kalanikūpule and Kahekili."

After taking Hilo, Keōua Kūʻahuʻula attacked Kamehameha's people first at Waipiʻo and then in northern Kohala. At Waipiʻo, Red Cloak and his people destroyed fish ponds, uprooted taro plants, and destroyed the taro patch embankments. Next, they raided and sacked coastal villages from Waipiʻo to Niuliʻi. Then they marched inland, attacking Hālawa, Halaʻula, Kapaʻau, and Hāwī. From Hāwī, they turned south, advancing under the spine of Mount Kohala to Waimea. There, they wreaked still more havoc.

"Red Cloak's warriors beat old men, women, and children, burned the people's hales, cut their fishing lines and nets, and robbed everyone they encountered, aliʻi and makaʻāinana alike," said my father. Red Cloak was in the forefront of all these activities. Observed my father: "He learned well from our uncle Kalaniʻōpuʻu's behavior on Maui."

Kamehameha landed at Kawaihae and led his warriors mauka to Waimea, where he intended to confront and defeat Keōua Kūʻahuʻula. "We will have the advantage of our pū, just as we did on Maui," he told his chiefs. But forewarned of Kamehameha's advance, Red Cloak and his forces retreated to the Hāmākua district, where they continued their rampage. Kamehameha overtook his cousin and rival at last at the village of Paʻauhau.

"Red Cloak's people have captured Lopaka! They have seized our *pū poʻohiwi*!"

The panicked warrior brought the news to Kamehameha behind Paʻauhau, where he had remained with a few guards at the outset of the battle, at ʻOlohana's insistence. "You are king," ʻOlohana had said in his rudimentary Hawaiʻian. "What if you killed? Who lead people then?"

Kamehameha, whose trust in Young had grown after the stunning victory at ʻĪao Valley, had readily complied. "What of ʻOlohana?" he demanded of the young warrior who was now on his knees, head bowed, before him. "What of ʻAikake?"

"They are unharmed, Lord," the warrior replied. "They fight with our people even now. *Aliʻi ʻai moku* Keʻeaumoku sent me to you."

"What? They have no pū poʻohiwi? No pū kuni ahi? With what do they fight? Spears, clubs, and daggers? Come, Keliʻi! We must go to them at once!" Kamehameha and my father, who had stayed behind with him, ran toward the fighting on the other side of the village, closely followed by the young warrior and Kameha's guards.

"When we got there, our people and Red Cloak's were mixed in with each other, fighting hand to hand," my father said. "Kaʻiana, Keʻeaumoku, Kameʻiamoku, Kamanawa, and the other chieftains were doing their best to rally our warriors. 'Olohana and 'Aikake were also in the thick of the fighting."

Young and Davis fought back-to-back, swinging muskets by the barrels, like long battle clubs. A dozen or more warriors had gone to their aid and were fighting alongside them, endeavoring to keep foes armed with spears away from the two haoles. Followed by my father and the others, Kamehameha waded into the battle, slashing about to devastating effect with his shark-tooth club. Now an enemy warrior rushed at Kameha, wielding a long pololū spear like a pike, thinking to impale him with it. The young warrior stepped in front of Kamehameha to parry the blow and took the enemy's spear in his chest. As he screamed and collapsed, Kameha reached out with his lei o manō and flayed open the opposing fighter's throat. The man dropped his spear and fell on top of Kamehameha's mortally wounded defender.

Kamehameha now saw Keōua Kū'ahu'ula nearby. Red Cloak had not yet seen him. Leaping over bodies, Kameha charged, shouting and throwing his lei o manō aside as he ran. "He meant to break Red Cloak's neck with his own hands," said my father. But alerted by Kameha's enraged shout, Keōua Kū'ahu'ula danced away. He was carrying an 'īkoi—a tripping club. Red Cloak lashed out with the 'īkoi as he dodged Kamehameha. The 'īkoi rope wrapped around Kameha's ankles, bringing him to his knees. All at once, Kameha was hobbled, unarmed, and alone. But Keōua Kū'ahu'ula, who also had a dagger, did not press his advantage. "Red Cloak still feared your uncle," my father told me. "He fled." Seeing their leader in retreat, Keōua Kū'ahu'ula's people fled with him, taking the captured muskets, but leaving Lopaka behind.

Kawaihae, 1791

After driving Keōua Kūʻahuʻula from the Hāmākua district, Kamehameha returned to Kohala, temporarily relocating his court to Waimea, and commenced planning for an invasion of Red Cloak's lands. "We will make Red Cloak and his people drink the water of Hilo Bay and swallow the dry earth of Kaʻū," he vowed.

To this end, he deputized ʻOlohana to help him acquire more muskets and cannons and increase his stores of powder and musket balls, and especially canister shot. Haole trading ships were now visiting our islands with increasing frequency. Thanks to ʻOlohana's assistance, Kamehameha was able to acquire many haole weapons and munitions from these traders. Mindful of the seer's prophecy, Kamehameha also directed Holoʻae to begin construction of the new temple at Kawaihae.

In addition to trading and preparing for his invasion of the Big Island's southern districts, Kamehameha was occupied at this time with the administration of his lands and the adjudication of the disputes that inevitably arose among his subordinates. As if commerce, day-to-day governance of his realm, and strife with his cousin Keōua Kūʻahuʻula were not enough, Kamehameha also had to contend with his wife, Kaʻahumanu.

"You forbid me to have relations with other men, yet you bring *that wahine* here to bed her!" Kaʻahumanu raged at Kamehameha.

"I have forbidden you nothing. It is kapu for *other men* to have relations with you," Kameha replied impassively.

Ka'ahumanu clenched her fists. "That is the same thing!" she exclaimed.

"In either case it is my right as mō'ī to impose any kapu I see fit," Kameha responded. "Be thankful that my kapu is not directed at *you*."

Ka'ahumanu was infuriated when Kamehameha returned from Moloka'i with his half-sister Keku'iapoiwa Liliha and her daughter Keopuolani. "From the start it was clear to Ka'ahumanu Kameha intended to partner with his niece Keopuolani and get children upon her," my father said. Ka'ahumanu had yet to bear Kameha a child.

"I can still give you keiki," Ka'ahumanu protested. "What need have you of Keopuolani?"

"For pleasure—none," Kameha replied. "But because Keopuolani is my own niece and because she and I are both descended from the great Keawe, a son of our union would be of the highest birth, and no one would dispute his right to rule after I am gone. Surely you can understand that as mō'ī, I must think of the future, Ka'ahumanu."

If Kameha thought that this explanation would appease his tempestuous wife, he was mistaken. "I can understand that as a kāne, you still think first of your own penis!" Ka'ahumanu cried, and she ran from Kamehameha's hale in tears, and into the arms of Ka'iana, who—kapu or no—was eager to console her.

Though 'Olohana and 'Aikake enjoyed Kamehameha's increasing confidence and were well treated by him, they were not yet reconciled to remaining among us for the rest of their lives. When a new opportunity presented itself, they sought to take their leave of our islands once more.

'Olohana, 'Aikake, Holo'ae, my father, and Ka'iana had accompanied Kamehameha to Kawaihae to inspect the work on the new heiau. When they arrived, they found a haole trading ship anchored in the small bay.

Kamehameha asked ʻOlohana to assist him in bargaining with the haoles. During negotiations with the ship's boatswain on shore, ʻOlohana let it be known that he and ʻAikake wished to leave with the ship.

Many years later, when I was old enough to ask him about such things, ʻOlohana explained why he and ʻAikake wanted to escape. "We were weary of the incessant warfare," he explained to me in fluent Hawaiian. "We had only just escaped death in the fight at Paʻauhau, and we feared no matter how pleasant our lives might be at the moment, we would not live much longer if we remained here."

Upon learning that the two seamen were desirous of leaving, the captain of the ship sent a crewman ashore with a letter to ʻOlohana and ʻAikake in which he offered them his protection in exchange for their help in effecting some repairs to his ship. ʻOlohana wrote back at once to accept this offer. But the youth to whom he entrusted his letter encountered Kaʻiana on his way to deliver it to the ship and showed the letter to him. Kaʻiana could not read ʻOlohana's letter, but under the circumstances, he intuited its meaning and he took the letter to Kamehameha.

"The haoles taught me to understand their markings when I sailed with them to far-off Kahiki," he said, and he proceeded to make a great show of translating ʻOlohana's letter, speaking slowly as he traced ʻOlohana's written words with an extended forefinger. The words Kaʻiana spoke were wholly his own and the story he told Kameha was kaao—an imaginative fabrication.

"Kaʻiana told Kamehameha that ʻOlohana and ʻAikake wanted the haole kāpena to lure Kameha aboard his own big canoe and hold Kameha hostage until he agreed to let them go," my father said.

Kaʻiana resented ʻOlohana and ʻAikake for displacing him in Kamehameha's favor and he wanted them out of the way. Knowing that Kamehameha already feared that if ʻOlohana and ʻAikake should ever gain the deck of a haole ship, they would reveal the fate of the Fair American's crew, Kaʻiana hoped that this lie would incite Kameha to put the two haoles to death for plotting against him.

When ʻOlohana and ʻAikake set out for the shore the next morning, they were immediately surrounded by a crowd of Hawaiʻians, orchestrated by Ka'iana. Though the two men were armed with muskets, they did not try to fire them. "We wanted to leave, but we did not want to hurt anyone," 'Olohana said.

'Olohana and 'Aikake submitted to the crowd and were conducted before Kamehameha by Ka'iana. "Ka'iana was quite pleased with himself, for all was proceeding as he had hoped," my father said. But to Ka'iana's chagrin, events now took a different turn.

Kamehameha had no intention of putting the two haoles to death, let alone of punishing them in any other way, for they had proved too useful to him. Instead of being angry with them, he was conciliatory. Speaking haltingly in their own language, Kamehameha begged the haoles to stay. "'Olohana, 'Aikake, why you still want go? You stay here. I give you all you want." Then he added sternly, "But you no leave. It is kapu for you to leave; to leave is death for you."

'Olohana and 'Aikake turned away from the shore without argument. They disowned their hopes of leaving Hawai'i to rejoin their haole comrades at sea. With an acceptance at first resigned but eventually enthusiastic, they settled on the Big Island and aspired to become more like us.

As he had promised, Kamehameha was generous with 'Olohana and 'Aikake, awarding them substantial land grants and elevating both men to chiefly status. To appease Ka'iana, Kameha granted him a small fiefdom of two ahupua'a in South Kona. Pleasant though these holdings were, with their fresh-water streams, good fishing, and productive uplands, they were not nearly so large as the holdings Kameha had granted to 'Olohana and 'Aikake, and Ka'iana was not placated. "Why does he favor these haoles and slight me?" he complained.

Even more to Ka'iana's displeasure, Kamehameha also invited 'Olohana and 'Aikake to join his innermost circle of advisers. 'Olohana soon became one of Kamehameha's closest counselors, delegated to negotiate transactions with the haole trading vessels that visited the Big Island with increasing frequency and in increasing numbers, and advise him on all matters pertaining to these foreigners.

After inspecting the heiau works at Kawaihae, Kamehameha moved on to Kailua to organize his latest assault on Keōua Kūʻahuʻula. Before Kamehameha departed, Holoʻae complained that he did not have enough workers to complete the temple's construction in timely fashion. "You must give me more people," he said.

"I cannot give you more people now, Holoʻae. I need every able-bodied man at my disposal to defeat Red Cloak."

"But the seer prophesied that to conquer all the islands, you must first build and consecrate this new heiau," Holoʻae objected.

"The other islands can wait," Kamehameha replied. "But Red Cloak will only grow stronger on *this island* the longer I delay. And if I cannot unify our own island, how can I subdue the others? No, Holoʻae, we will deal with Red Cloak first."

Kamehameha planned to break Keōua Kūʻahuʻula's hold on the Kaʻū, Puna, and Hilo districts with two simultaneous offensives, one overland from Waimea down the Hāmākua Coast to Hilo, and the other by sea from Kailua down the Kona Coast to Ka'ū. Ke'eaumoku was to lead the land attack, while Kaʻiana was to command the seaborne assault. ʻOlohana and 'Aikake were to remain with Kamehameha at Kawaihae.

Kamehameha's designation of Kaʻiana to command the assault on Kaʻū signaled his confidence in Kaʻiana's military ability, but there was more to it. "Kameha wanted to keep Kaʻiana away from Kaʻahumanu," my father said.

While Kamehameha was marshaling his forces, a disaster befell Keōua Red Cloak's army. Portents of this calamity reached Kameha and his people at Kailua days before the actual details. "One afternoon, we saw a thick cloud rising in the direction of Mauna Loa. It was black like the darkest night," my father said. Shot through with glowing streaks of fire and lightning, the cloud climbed into a clear sky, billowing in all directions and casting a spreading shadow. Its first sighting at Kailua was followed minutes later by a deep rumble that intensified into a continuous roar.

"It sounded like many pū kuni ahi, shooting all at once," said my father. "Then the ground began to shake under our feet. It was Pele, emerging angrily from her home at Kilauea."

Whether the wrath of the goddess or a natural event, the eruption wreaked havoc on Red Cloak's people. After he had been repulsed from the Hāmākua Coast, Keōua Kūʻahuʻula remained for some time at Hilo. Then, leaving a contingent of warriors behind to defend the village, he started for Kaʻū with the bulk of his army, which he had reorganized into two divisions, one under his own command. As was customary in those times, the warriors' wives and children accompanied them.

Keōua Kūʻahuʻula's division set off first. "Red Cloak led his people to Kaʻū by way of ʻŌlaʻa, mauka of Kilauea," said my father. At Kapāpala, Keōua halted to rest while he and his warriors awaited the arrival of the rest of the army. But the army's second division never reached Kapāpala. Seeking to ease their march by avoiding the ascent into the uplands of ʻŌlaʻa, the second group's commander led them south, across the caldera at Kilauea, where they were caught by the volcano's sudden eruption. Only a few women survived. Their account of what happened at Kilauea, told and retold from village to village, reached Kailua nearly a week after the event.

As Kamehameha, my father, and ʻOlohana heard the story, Red Cloak's second division was just makai of the Halemaʻumaʻu crater at Kilauea when the wrath of Pele fell upon them. One moment, they were marching in good spirits and making good time across the Kilauea caldera. In the next, the ground under their feet shook and fire suddenly erupted from the crater, searing them. Choking vapors smothered them, and ash and rocks fell from the sky, burying them. "We heard that these falling rocks were as large as hales," my father told me. "None of the people there could escape."

By some estimates, more than eight hundred men, women, and children perished. The few who were not killed survived only by chance. There were some women attached to the second division of Red Cloak's army who were menstruating. For this reason, they were kapu and not allowed to march with the rest of their party. This group was well behind the others when the volcano erupted and were thus spared. "They threw themselves to the ground as it shook and covered their ears," my father said. "They remained were they were for the rest of that day and through the night."

The next morning, they descended into the caldera. The air was still thick with hazy smoke and pervaded by a sulfuric stench. The women's eyes stung; they covered their noses and mouths with their hands as they walked. When they came upon the place where the others had died, they encountered a scene of horrific devastation. All around, the ground was covered with thick gray pumice, firm enough to walk on and still warm underfoot. As they picked their way across this desolate landscape, the women began to see odd shapes: an elongated form here and a rounded one there—a few at first and then more and more. To their horror, they realized that they were looking at the bodies of their husbands, sisters, brothers, and cousins, embalmed in the freshly laid lava stone. Some of them had fallen on their backs, while others were lying face down with their hands over their heads, as if they thought they could somehow shield themselves from Pele.

Many of our people believed the eruption was Pele's punishment of Keōua Red Cloak for his brutality and ambition. Kamehameha saw more in it. "The god Kūkā'ilimoku is with us," he said. "Victory over Red Cloak is assured." He dispatched his forces to Hilo and Ka'ū forthwith.

Ke'eaumoku marched unopposed into Hilo and pushed on to the upper Puna district, occupying it with ease. Ka'iana and his army, however, were rudely greeted by Red Cloak, who still had substantial forces at his disposal, despite the disaster at Kilauea.

Ka'iana's army had sailed south from Kailua in one hundred double-hulled war canoes. Holding a third of his forces offshore in reserve, Ka'iana led the rest of his men ashore at Pulehua in Ka'ū. They were unopposed at first. But as they advanced inland they found Red Cloak's people waiting for them mauka of the beach. Ka'ū skirmishers rained sling stones and spears down upon the invaders, and numerous Kona and Kohala warriors fell. They managed only one musket volley under this sudden onslaught.

Urging his people on, Ka'iana and his warriors continued to advance, bent over against the hail of stones and spears. When they gained the higher ground, they found Red Cloak's army drawn up in a long line, waiting for them. Before they could bring their firearms to bear on their enemies again, Red Cloak's fighters rushed Ka'iana's men, and in the pitched battle that followed, pushed them back to the beach.

As the warriors of Ka'ū jeered at them from the shore, Ka'iana and his people retreated to sea in their canoes. Ka'iana renewed his assault on Red Cloak the following day, but Red Cloak lured Ka'iana's people into a trap and inflicted such heavy casualties on his men that they broke and ran. Ka'iana was reduced to following them in their flight to safety. Red Cloak did not pursue him. "Ka'iana returned to Kailua bloodied and embarrassed," my father said.

Having failed to subdue Keōua Kū'ahu'ula, Kamehameha now turned his full attention to the construction of the new heiau. "You were right about the prophecy, Holo'ae," Kamehameha confessed to his kahuna nui.

Kameha now called upon all the able-bodied men of Kona, Kohala, Waimea, and the Hāmākua Coast to work on the new heiau. Thousands answered his call. Women came as well, with their young children in tow.

Ali'i and maka'āinana labored alongside each other, Kamehameha foremost among them. Thousands of men formed a human chain to transport lava rocks from the Pololu Valley to Kawaihae, a distance of fourteen miles. At the construction site overlooking the bay, hundreds of other workers received the rocks and labored to build the temple's massive lava-stone platform. From Pololu to Kawaihae, men worked in shifts, with time allotted for meals and rest. The work never ceased as long as there was daylight to guide the laborers' hands. Hour by hour, day by day, as the rocks continued to arrive from Pololu, the heiau rose from the hillside like a living thing.

Men and women settled in encampments along the way from the Pololu Valley to Kawaihae and near the temple site. Scores of men were assigned to gather food and cook. Women were set to such tasks as pounding bark into kapa cloth for new malos for the men, to replace the ones they tore while hauling stones. Others wove baskets for carrying smaller stones, or crafted articles such as drinking gourds. Older women who could no longer work watched keiki who were too young to work, shooing them away from the men who conveyed the lava rocks, and from the construction site.

None of Kamehameha's women were at Kawaihae at this time. Kameha had decreed the temple site kapu to them and ordered them all to remain at Waimea. "Kamehameha intended the kapu for Ka'ahumanu," my father said. "He wanted to keep her away from Ka'iana."

This kapu angered Ka'ahumanu. "If I cannot go to Kawaihae with you, then why should your brother's women be allowed to go?" she demanded.

"Fine!" Kamehameha replied. "It is kapu for them as well." Thus, my mother, then heavy with me, remained at Waimea with the others.

My father, Keli'imaika'i, was the only man in Kameha's domains who never added a stone to the new temple. Kamehameha forbade him from working on the heiau.

"When I saw my brother lift a heavy lava stone for the temple wall to his shoulders, I lifted one myself. I wanted to do my part," my father said. "But Kamehameha ordered me to set the stone down immediately. 'One of us must remain pure,' he told me. 'You are not to work on this heiau, Keli'i.' It was menial work, customarily unfitting for ali'i of any rank," my father explained. "Kamehameha insisted that one of us must remain untainted by it for the heiau's consecration."

Kameha ordered two maka'āinana workers to take away this stone that my father had touched and cast it into the sea well beyond the bay's confines, so that it would sink far out of sight. "Send it to Kanaloa," he said.

The heiau's foundation stones were laid under the close direction of kāhuna skilled in the arts of designing and building such structures. It was two hundred and twenty-four feet in length and one hundred feet wide, with walls twenty feet high. So expertly did the kāhuna choose the heiau's stones that even without mortar, its walls and foundation still stand today.

Once the heiau's foundation and walls were completed, Kamehameha set his people to work building the structures of the heiau itself: the *paehunu*, the image fence; the *anu'unu'u*, the oracle tower with its walls surrounding a deep hole for the bones of sacrificial victims; and the *hale malu*, the shelter house for the kāhuna. This last was built with wood of the *ohia* tree, which was sacred to the heiau's god, Kūkā'ilimoku. Kamehameha himself selected the tree for this purpose. With the help of his closest allies among the Big Island's chiefs, Kameha carried it from the forested uplands to the temple site. Again, my father had no hand in this work.

Finished at last, the massive new temple on the brow of the hill overlooking the bay awaited its consecration by human sacrifice. The heiau took its name from the place itself: *Pu'ukoholā*, the hill of the whale.

Despite his advisers' warnings, Keōua Kū'ahu'ula construed Kamehameha's invitation to attend the consecration of the new heiau at Kawaihae as a peace overture. So my cousin Pauli later told me. "Keōua would not believe that Kamehameha was conspiring against him," he said. "He was convinced that Kameha now understood that any further attempt to dislodge him from Ka'ū would be futile and wished to put their past enmity behind them."

My cousin Pauli was a forlorn figure. Though he was Kamehameha's son by Kaneikapolei, Kameha had ignored him during his youth. Kameha their part, Red Cloak's people looked on with dread, for they understood what must come next.

"After that, everything happened very quickly," my father said.

Though his men had ceased paddling, a light breeze still played in the sail of Red Cloak's canoe and the vessel had continued slowly toward shore during his exchange with Kamehameha. It was now within a few strides of the beach through thigh-deep water. Ke'eaumoku, Kame'iamoku, and the other chieftains around Kamehameha broke from their mō'ī and splashed through the water toward the canoe, brandishing spears, clubs, and daggers.

Keōua's paddlers made haste to turn the big canoe's double prows seaward again. They had brought the canoe around broadside to the shore just as the onrushing Hawai'ians reached it. The men in the closest hull tried to repel the assailants with their paddles, but the Hawai'ians easily parried their blows and clubbed the men aside. They clambered over the hull and onto the canoe's center platform, where Keōua still stood in front of his own chieftains. "Even then, Red Cloak was shouting and brandishing his bloody penis at us," said my father, who had remained on the beach with Kamehameha.

As Kame'iamoku, Keaweaheulu, and the others attacked Keōua's advisers, Ke'eaumoku and Ka'iana rushed at Red Cloak, who was still hurling imprecations at his cousin on the beach and did not see them. "Each wanted to be the one to slay Keōua," my father said. Ke'eaumoku, who was carrying a short ihe spear, reached him first and plunged the spear into his back. Keōua shrieked and fell to the deck face first. He lay there, both arms splayed out in a spreading pool of blood, quiet at last. Slain to a man, his chieftains and his brother Keōuape'e'ale lay sprawled about the deck behind him.

When the Hawai'ian chiefs had boarded Keōua's canoe, the paddlers riding in the hull on the opposite side of the vessel dove into the water and tried to swim to Pauli's canoe. "They were calling out to us to come to their aid, but already it was too late," Pauli said. Scores of warriors had gathered on the beach to witness the arrival of Keōua Kū'ahu'ula and the anticipated reconciliation between the two royal cousins. Now understanding their mō'ī's true intent, they swarmed into the water with their clubs and spears and haole daggers and axes. One by one, they hunted down the fleeing canoe paddlers and killed them. Throughout all this, Kamehameha remained at the shore's edge, his face impassive, his arms folded, as the water lapping at his bare feet turned red.

Other warriors had launched outrigger canoes and were now paddling hard toward Pauli's double-hulled canoe. "They were coming on very fast," said Pauli. "We had no time to escape and no weapons to defend ourselves with."

"When Kamehameha saw his people bent on slaying his own true son, who had done nothing wrong," said my father. "He called an end to it."

"Let live!" Kamehameha cried; his voice boomed across the bay. "Let live!"

'Olohana and 'Aikake, who by now had witnessed much bloodletting among our people and thought themselves inured to it, later professed their horror at the terrible events that had unfolded below them in Kawaihae Bay. Even more unsettling to them was my uncle's deception of his cousin. "We truly believed that Kamehameha intended to make peace with Keōua," 'Olohana said. "We were astonished when we realized that was not his intention."

Indeed, Kamehameha's true intention was a closely held secret, known only to his closest advisers. "I can never share Hawai'i with Keōua, for he will always scheme against me," Kameha told my father. "As soon as I turn away from him, he will attack us once more. Too many of our people have already died because of Red Cloak's aggressions. I will expend no more lives in battle with him."

"How can you be sure that Red Cloak will not divine your true purpose and refuse to come to Kawaihae?" my father asked.

"Yes," Vancouver replied. "They can give you much good meat. But first your people must allow them to make more cattle."

Kamehameha understood. He nodded. "Keiki," he said. "Keiki ka'ako."

"To be sure, little cattle," Vancouver said. "Find a place where there is much grass for them to eat, and water for them to drink, and do not permit anyone to kill them until they have made many more cattle."

"We have such a place for them," replied Kamehameha, "and they will be kapu." Later, these cattle were transported to the grasslands of Waimea, where they and others subsequently delivered by Vancouver were permitted to roam free and unmolested for many years.

The presentation of gifts now completed, Vancouver, who had not yet remarked on the surprising presence of two Englishmen among Kamehameha's entourage, asked Kamehameha, "Tamaahamaah, who are these two men with you?"

"This is 'Olohana and this is 'Aikake," Kameha replied, pointing in turn to each of the haoles. "They are my counselors."

Vancouver looked inquisitively at the two men, who nodded and smiled. "Well, well," said Vancouver. Turning to Kamehameha, he said, "Tamaahamaah, I invite you and your people to eat with me now."

"We will be happy to join you," Kameha replied. "Mahalo."

As Vancouver led the way to his quarters at the ship's stern, Kamehameha, his chieftains, 'Olohana, and 'Aikake fell in behind him. But the women hesitated. Seeing that they were hanging back, Vancouver beckoned to them. "Come," he said. "Everyone is invited—everyone."

Vancouver's intent was clear to all, but still the women remained where they were while Kameha and his chieftains conferred agitatedly among themselves. "This is not to be permitted," exclaimed Ke'eaumoku.

"It is kapu," said Kame'iamoku.

"We should decline, politely, and leave now," declared Keaweaheulu.

Vancouver stood to one side as this exchange took place, his arms folded across his chest and his head cocked toward the chieftains. He seemed genuinely puzzled.

Kamehameha looked at Vancouver, and then at the women. A panoply of bewilderment played across their faces, and they lowered their heads to avoid Kameha's eyes. All were unsure of what to do—all, save for Ka'ahumanu. She fixed her partner with an unwavering stare.

"We cannot decline," Kamehameha told his chieftains. "We are Kāpena Wankuwai's guests here, and it would be rude. Moreover, I would not have us insult this haole, for I hope to trade with him—for more pū po'ohiwi and pū kuni ahi especially."

"But the kapu," Ke'eaumoku protested anew.

Kamehameha looked again at Ka'ahumanu, whose gaze was still fixed on him. She said nothing, but defiance flashed in her eyes.

"The kapu is ours; it is not Wankuwai's. When he feasts with us at our mua, the women will not eat. But here, this day, we will all eat together." Kameha gestured to the women that they should enter Vancouver's cabin after the men. Directing the chiefs to precede him, he crossed the threshold just ahead of Ka'ahumanu, who led the women. "Do not make too much of this," he cautioned her.

Vancouver's crew had set up two tables in the captain's cabin to accommodate the large number of guests and once inside, Kamehameha directed the women to sit separately from the men. "Thus, although we were in close proximity to each other, we did not truly eat together," my father explained. The Hawai'ians had observed the kapu in spirit, at least.

As Kamehameha and his people took their leave that evening, Vancouver pulled 'Olohana and 'Aikake aside and spoke quietly to them. Kamehameha later asked 'Olohana what they had spoken about. "Captain Vancouver is a chieftain of King George, our people's mō'ī," 'Olohana said. "We asked for his permission to remain here with you and he granted it."

Kamehameha was well satisfied with this explanation. "This Wankuwai is a true friend of ours," he said.

Friend though he may have been, Vancouver was not agreeable with Kamehameha's subsequent request for weapons and munitions. "I cannot trade our weapons for your goods, Tamaahamaah, for I would not be the cause of worsened strife among your peoples," said Vancouver, who was aware of our penchant for bloody warfare. "I have already refused such a request from the mōʻī of *Woahoo*."

Indeed, Kamehameha had earlier heard that when he stopped at Waikiki the previous year, Vancouver had declined Kalanikūpule's offer to trade local goods for haole weapons. But whereas Kalanikūpule had been angered by Vancouver's rebuff, Kamehameha accepted it with equanimity. "Kāpena Wankuwai is even-handed," he told his chiefs. "I believe he wishes our people well."

During a feast at Kealakekua soon thereafter, the British captain proffered himself to Kamehameha as a peace emissary. "Tamaahamaah," he said, "it grieves me to see how much blood your own people have shed in fighting with your enemies. Please permit me to help negotiate a lasting peace between you and your adversaries."

Vancouver had ferried Kamehameha and his court to Kealakekua from Kawaihae aboard his own ship after Kameha expressed a desire to return there. This evening, Vancouver and his officers dined with the chiefs only; Kaʻahumanu and the other women of the court had been excluded.

"I would welcome peace, Wankuwai," Kameha replied. "And I would be content with Hawaiʻi alone if my enemies would promise to content themselves with their own domains. Go tell them this for me."

Vancouver conveyed Kamehameha's message to Kahekili, Kalanikūpule, and Kāʻeokūlani, the reigning king of Kauaʻi. They responded favorably despite their reservations about Kameha's sincerity and pressed Vancouver to remain in the islands until all parties could agree on an enduring peace treaty. But Vancouver would not be stayed from his mission to further explore the northwest coast of the vast continent to the east. He sailed for America soon after obtaining the assent of Kahekili and Kāʻeokūlani, and unfortunately, without his continued mediation, his efforts to promote lasting peace in our islands came to nothing.

Late that same year, word reached Kamehameha that Kahekili had died. His son, Kalanikūpule, now held sway over O'ahu, Moloka'i, Lanai, and Maui. Recalling Kahekili's admonishment to wait until after his death to move on O'ahu, Kamehameha asked his kahuna nui, Holo'ae, if the time was right to attack.

"It is not yet time," the old priest had responded. "You must wait for a clear sign from Kūkā'ilimoku."

"How will I know this sign?" asked Kameha.

"You will know it. It will be unmistakable," Holo'ae replied.

Mindful of his priest's counsel, Kamehameha resolved to wait.

Kawaihae, 1794

Ka'ahumanu was unhappy with Kamehameha, and he with her. This much I understood, even as a small boy scarcely three years old. I could not fail to notice that they hardly spoke to each other and never smiled when they were together, which was seldom at that time. "Why are Uncle Kameha and Aunt Ka'ahumanu upset with each other?" I asked my older brother, whom I looked upon as wise and all-knowing.

"Uncle Kameha is angry because Aunt Ka'ahumanu has not given him a keiki," Kekuaokalani said. "And Aunt Ka'ahumanu is angry with our uncle because she has been trying very hard to find one and cannot. She has even asked Uncle Ka'iana to help her find one. She thinks Uncle Kameha blames her unfairly." This intelligence Kekuaokalani had gleaned from overhearing snatches of our parents' conversations.

Kamehameha was no doubt disappointed that he had not yet gotten a child with Ka'ahumanu. But most immediately, he was distressed by her continued flirtation with "Uncle" Ka'iana, and suspected that their relationship encompassed more than flirtation. This suspicion aroused the otherwise phlegmatic Kamehameha to anger. "You continue to spend entirely too much time with Ka'iana," he snapped.

"Ka'iana seeks me out," Ka'ahumanu retorted. "He is your ally. Should I be rude to him? Tell him to keep his distance from me if you will; I do not care." Even as she said this, Ka'ahumanu knew it was unlikely that Kamehameha would speak to Ka'iana, because he still depended on him to train his warriors in the use of haole weaponry. For his part, Ka'iana mistook his usefulness to Kamehameha for indispensability, and mistook Kameha's silence on the question of Ka'ahumanu for tolerance.

Though Kamehameha still required Ka'iana's services, his importance to Hawai'i's mō'ī was in decline. The warriors whom Ka'iana had trained were now sufficiently proficient in loading and firing their muskets to teach these skills to others. Kameha now turned first to 'Olohana and 'Aikake, rather than Ka'iana, for advice regarding haole weapons and tactics. This alone should have alerted Ka'iana to his diminished standing in Kameha's eyes. Characteristically, he failed to notice, and his dalliances with Ka'ahumanu continued.

Once again, my father cautioned Ka'iana. "You would do well to turn your eyes away from Ka'ahumanu to other wāhine," he told him one day.

Once again, Ka'iana dismissed his warning. "I cannot help it if she will not turn her eyes from me," he scoffed.

My father could only shake his head at Ka'iana's foolhardiness.

As Ka'ahumanu and Ka'iana continued their flirtation—and perhaps more; my father could never be sure—relations between Ka'ahumanu and Kamehameha continued to worsen. In a final fit of pique, Ka'ahumanu refused to continue living with Kameha and removed herself to the compound of her father, Ke'eaumoku. When Vancouver returned to Kawaihae in the haole year 1794, he found Kamehameha despondent.

"What troubles you, Tamaahamaah?" he asked one afternoon as they sought relief from the sultry Kona heat in the shade of a palm grove close to the shore. Kamehameha lounged on his mat, while Vancouver, out of respect, sat cross-legged on his.

"Ka'ahumanu refuses to live with me. She has moved back to her father's household," Kamehameha replied.

"I am truly sorry about this," said Vancouver. "Please permit me to help heal this breach between you. Bring *Tahoomanoo* to my ship and we will discuss this together."

"She will not come," Kamehameha replied, "not so long as she knows I will be there."

"Then we need not tell her," said Vancouver. "I will invite her onboard to dine with me. You will come soon afterward to pay me an 'unannounced' visit. I will then extend my invitation to you. Tahoomanoo can hardly refuse me then."

Kamehameha sighed. "Wankuwei," he said, "I permitted the violation of our kapu against men and women eating together when last you were here, and you would have me do it again?"

"It is not *taboo* on my ship, Tamaahamaah, as I know you have already once acknowledged," Vancouver replied.

"Very well, Wankuwei," Kamehameha said. "You are welcome to try your scheme. I am more than willing to be reconciled. But do not expect much from *her*."

Ka'ahumanu came aboard Vancouver's ship the next evening, dressed in her finest kapa cloth, dyed with turmeric and imprinted in a complex black and red cross-hatched pattern with kukui-nut soot and red ochre pigment, and tied demurely over one shoulder. A lei of bright yellow *'ilima* flowers shown like the sun in her dark black hair. She wore a fine whale-tooth pendant around her neck.

Mt. Kohala was catching the last light of the setting sun as Ka'ahumanu gained the ship's deck, assisted from below by her own canoe paddlers and from above by the ship's officers. Vancouver awaited her, resplendent in his gold-braided dress uniform, its brass buttons gleaming. He wore a freshly powdered wig beneath his bi-cornered officer's hat. Vancouver bowed slightly to Kaʻahumanu. "My good queen," he said, "it is my pleasure to welcome you to my ship. Please come this way." Vancouver led Kaʻahumanu to his cabin, where a table had been set for them. It was covered with a linen cloth, reserved for special occasions and used only rarely. Two elaborate candelabra provided illumination in the gathering darkness; pewter plates, wine cups, and silver flatware glinted in the candle light. Kaʻahumanu paused to examine the candles, for she had never seen their like before.

Kamehameha arrived a short time later. Befitting the occasion, he wore a cloak woven of the brilliant, yellow feathers of Hawaiʻi's *mamo* bird and a matching feathered helmet. Kamehameha entered Vancouver's cabin without first announcing himself. He feigned surprise at seeing Kaʻahumanu there. "Wankuwai, I—" he said, breaking off abruptly.

Kaʻahumanu had just taken her seat. She bristled. "What are *you* doing here?" she demanded.

"I have merely come to pay my respects to Wankuwei," said Kamehameha. "I did not know you would be here."

"Well now," said Vancouver, who was enjoying this game. "You must join us for dinner, Tamaahamaah."

"I will gladly stay," Kamehameha said.

Kaʻahumanu looked away from Kameha and said nothing. She did not move from her chair. "She would not leave," Kamehameha told my father later, "determined as she was to enjoy Wankuwai's hospitality."

Vancouver called for his orderly to set another place for Kamehameha and indicated to Kameha that he should sit across the table from Kaʻahumanu. When Kamehameha had taken his seat, the captain rang a small bell and several young midshipmen entered the cabin carrying pewter platters. Kamehameha and Kaʻahumanu now saw arrayed before them a platter of traditional British Navy fare—salted beef, hard biscuits, and sauerkraut—and a second platter heaped with taro leaves, sweet potatoes, breadfruit, and yams from the Big Island. On a third platter, larger than the first two, was a roasted pig ringed by roasted bananas.

Vancouver's cook had come ashore earlier that day to roast the pig on a spit over a wood fire. This spectacle drew a crowd of curious onlookers, who had never seen a pig prepared in this fashion. Some of their number had shown the haole cook how to wrap bananas in ti leaves and roast them in the coals. Now, Ka'ahumanu delicately licked her lips as she eyed the pork and bananas. The aroma of these delicacies, otherwise forbidden to her, made her ache with desire.

As the midshipmen awaited his signal to serve him and his guests, Vancouver filled their cups with port wine and proposed a toast. "To my good friend, King Tamaahamaah, and to our own good King George," he said. "Long may you both rule and prosper, God willing, and long may our people grow in friendship with each other." Vancouver gestured with his cup to his guests, then lifted it to lips and drank deeply.

Vancouver had delivered his toast in English. Kamehameha had by now gained sufficient command of the language from 'Olohana and 'Aikake to understand much of it. Ka'ahumanu understood none of it. But she raised her cup in imitation of the captain. Now she looked to Kamehameha for guidance. Kamehameha looked to Vancouver, who was gesturing again with his cup, encouraging Kameha to drink. Kamehameha tasted the port. He frowned and spat the wine back into his cup. Ka'ahumanu set her own cup down on the table.

"The haole 'awa was much too sweet," Kamehameha later told my father. "It was like drinking sugar cane."

If Vancouver was offended, he gave no indication. "I am sorry our wine is not to your liking, Tamaahamaah," he said. "It is an acquired taste even among us." Then, with a nod to the midshipmen, Vancouver said, "Let us eat."

One of the midshipmen set to carving generous slices of meat from the pig. He served Kamehameha first. Then, as he began to serve pork and bananas to Ka'ahumanu, Kamehameha reached across the table with his long arm and stayed the midshipman's hand. Looking directly at Vancouver, he said, "No, Wankuwai, it is kapu for our women to eat this food, even on your great canoe."

Ka'ahumanu looked to Vancouver, silently beseeching him to intervene. Vancouver smiled at her and said to Kamehameha, "I would not risk our friendship by imposing upon your own customs, Tamaahamaah." Satisfied with this, Kamehameha released the startled midshipman's wrist. Vancouver gestured to the youth, who removed the offending dish. Ka'ahumanu tasted the salted beef and sauerkraut, but did not like them. Thus, as Kamehameha and Vancouver ate their fill of pork and bananas, she had to content herself with yams, sweet potatoes, and breadfruit.

After the midshipmen had cleared away the dishes and left the cabin, Vancouver said to Kamehameha and Ka'ahumanu, "It much pains me to see you angry with each other," he spoke slowly, in his rudimentary Hawaiian. "Tamaahamaah cares much for you, Ta'ahoomanoo," he said. "He has told me much times that you are his greatest woman."

Ka'ahumanu was not placated. "Kamehameha does not honor me as his *wahine nui*," she said.

Vancouver looked to Kamehameha. "What you say to this, Tamaahamaah?" he asked.

"Ka'ahumanu has always been my wahine nui," Kamehameha said. Turning to her, he said, "You know that I do not feel this way about my other partners, Ka'ahumanu. You are special to me. That is why I will not allow other men to sleep with you, and why you make me unhappy when you flirt with them. You will be my wahine nui for as long as I shall live."

"Am I more special to you than Keopuolani, on whom you will no doubt get a child some day?" she asked.

"Yes, of course," Kamehameha replied.

"If I am more special to you than Keopuolani, will you give me her own son in hanai to raise?"

"Yes," said Kameha, "I will."

"Then I will forgive you," said Ka'ahumanu, who rose from her chair, and crossed the cabin to Kamehameha on the other side of the table. The two threw themselves into each other's arms, rubbed noses, and wailed loudly. Vancouver kept his seat at the head of the table and smiled beatifically throughout this display, so characteristic of our own people in those days and so foreign to his.

Kaʻahumanu ignored our "Uncle Kaʻiana" from that day forward.

Reconciliation or no, Kaʻahumanu was still upset that Kamehameha had denied her the pleasure of eating forbidden foods. "By what right did you tell Wankuwai not to serve the pig and roasted bananas to me?" she challenged Kamehameha that night as they lay side by side. "He is haole; his ways are different, and we were away from own people."

"Is it not enough for you that we have eaten at the same table on Wankuwai's great canoe this night?" Kamehameha demanded. "I can never allow you or any other wahine to eat pig and roasted bananas because the god Kāne has reserved these foods for men, who are his direct descendants. He would punish me for it. So never speak to me of this again, and do not expect to eat with me or any other kāne again. It is best that you forget it ever happened."

Of course, as is the way of women, Kaʻahumanu forgot nothing.

Relishing Kamehameha's company, Vancouver extended his stay at Kawaihae by several weeks beyond his original departure date. During this time, Kamehameha offered anew to trade any goods Vancouver might desire for haole weapons, an offer the British naval captain once more declined. But in token of his friendship, Vancouver offered to direct his ship's carpenter to help Kameha's people build a small schooner like the Fair American. Kamehameha readily accepted.

As work on the vessel progressed, Kameha and Vancouver passed the days and evenings discussing all manner of subjects. Vancouver, whose command of our language was improving daily, was especially interested in learning more about our people's religious practices; Kamehameha, with a likewise improving grasp of English, craved more knowledge of the people of Vancouver's far-off island, and of the mōʻī who ruled it.

"Are there many more people on your island, Wankuwei, many more haoles such as you?" Kamehameha asked one day.

"Yes, and they are beyond counting," Vancouver replied.

"And your mōʻī. is *Kiʻine Keoke*?" Kameha asked.

"Yes, King George," Vancouver affirmed.

"Is this Kiʻine Keoke powerful? Does he have many great canoes such as yours—and many warriors and pū kuni ahi and pū poʻohiwi?" Vancouver looked quizzically at Kamehameha. "*Kanoʻono* and *mūkʻe*," he clarified.

"Yes, he does," Vancouver replied. "King George is very powerful. He must be strong to defend us against our enemies."

"Do your people have many enemies?"

"Not many, but our enemies are also powerful—the French, for example, and the Spanish."

"Will these enemies of yours come here?"

"They may well do so," Vancouver responded. Kamehameha pondered this, but said nothing more.

Another day, as he was admiring the great heiau of the god Kūkāʻilimoku at Kawaihae, Vancouver asked Kameha, "Why do your people worship so many gods? There is but one God, who made the heavens and the earth and all living things upon the earth."

So far as Kamehameha was concerned, the Englishman might as well have asked why our people breathed. He was amused by Vancouver's ignorance. "The night and daytime skies are not the same," Kameha said. "The sea is different from the air and the clouds. The land is not the same as the sea. The volcano is different from the rest of the land. No two plants are alike. How could one god have made all these things? It is not possible."

When Vancouver persisted, Kamehameha challenged him. "Come with me to the pali at Kealakekua, Wankuwei," he said. "We will stand on the edge. If you jump off and your god saves you, then I will believe in him, and I will jump too."

"God does not intervene in that fashion," Vancouver replied.

"Then your god is not of much use," said Kamehameha. "Our gods are better." And there the subject rested.

Vancouver's confidence that other haoles would inevitably follow the British to Hawaiʻi increased Kamehameha's concern about his people's future. Already, he and his chieftains had witnessed the coming of armed trading ships from America, Spain, and Portugal.

"A few haole great canoes at a time we can deal with, as we dealt with Kāpena Kuke and his people," he mused to my father and his other advisers. "But what if many more come here at once, with their pū kuni ahi and pū poʻohiwi, and what if they should come with hostile intent? Even if all our people are united against them, we will still need a powerful haole ally to safeguard us."

Already favorably disposed to the British by virtue of his trust in his two English advisers and his growing friendship with Vancouver, Kamehameha thus approached the English sea captain to request the protection of the most powerful haole monarch known to him: King George III of England.

"If you would give King George dominion over Ohwyhee and any others of these islands that may come into your possession in the future," Vancouver said, "he would gladly extend his protection to you."

"Would your king come here to rule us?" asked Kamehameha.

"No, he would not," Vancouver replied.

"Then I would do this, Wankuwei, but how shall I?"

"You must advise King George of your offer in a letter," said Vancouver. Knowing that Kamehameha could neither read nor write, he added, "Tell John Young—ʻOlohana—what you wish to say; he will write it and I will deliver it."

Thus, on the deck of Vancouver's ship a few days later, and in the presence of his chiefs, Vancouver, and the ship's crew, Kamehameha dictated a letter to 'Olohana "ceding" our islands—Vancouver's word—to the king of England. When 'Olohana had finished writing the letter, Kameha took the quill pen from him, and with the haole's assistance, made his mark on it. Kamehameha wielded the quill awkwardly in his large hand and his "signature" was no more than an illegible scrawl. 'Olohana and Vancouver signed the letter underneath Kameha's mark.

"By signing our names, we are swearing that your mark is true," Vancouver explained to Kamehameha. He then turned to the ship's company and announced, "Tamaahamaah, king of Ohwyhee, has just granted this island and all his future domains to his sovereign majesty, King George. From this day forth, Ohwyhee is English soil!" The crew cheered this proclamation lustily. The Discovery's three-pound guns roared a salute that echoed round the bay. On shore, one of Vancouver's officers ran the Union Jack up a pole erected for the occasion just below the great heiau. There followed a boisterous celebration, during which much rum was consumed by the haoles and a few of Kamehameha's chieftains, to their later regret.

Vancouver had lately learned from his ship's carpenter that the Hawai'ian canoe builders working under him were now sufficiently skilled to complete Kamehameha's great canoe with 'Olohana's help. "Your people are building you a fine ship," he told Kameha as he inspected their work the next morning. "They can build you many more, I am certain."

Vancouver departed Hawai'i a few days later, never to return. He carried with him Kameha's letter to King George III. In anticipation of his alliance with Britain, Kamehameha named his new ship the "*Pelekane*"—"Britannia"—in honor of King George, and proudly flew the British Union Jack from its mast. The English monarch never answered his letter.

As the year of Vancouver's last visit to our islands drew to a close, Kalanikūpule and his uncle, Kāʻeokūlani, the ruler of Kauaʻi, had a falling out. Kāʻeokūlani had attacked Oʻahu intending to depose Kalanikūpule and seize the island for himself. During several days of bloody fighting, the advantage shifted back and forth between the two sides until a British sea captain, one William Brown, turned the tide in Kalanikūpule's favor by cannonading Kāʻeokūlani's people from offshore. Kāʻeokūlani and his warriors took shelter from the bombardment in a ravine, where they were trapped by Kalanikūpule's people and slain to a man. Now the undisputed ruler of Oʻahu, Maui, Molokaʻi, Lanai, Kauaʻi, and Niʻihau, Kalanikūpule set his sights on the Big Island.

Thinking to gain a tactical advantage over Kamehameha by seizing all the muskets, cannons, and munitions on Brown's ship, Kalanikūpule turned on his erstwhile English ally. Brown had earlier agreed to aid Kalanikūpule in exchange for some four hundred hogs. Kalanikūpule and his chieftains delivered these animals to Brown's ship, the Jackal, on the last day of 1794, whereupon Brown invited them to remain on board to celebrate the haole New Year. Accepting Brown's invitation, Kalanikūpule's people killed him and most of the Jackal's crew during the ensuing festivities, sparing a few of the Englishmen to help them sail the ship.

The Jackal now set sail for the Big Island, its deck crowded with scores of cheering Oʻahu warriors and its hold full of squealing pigs. But the British sailors thwarted Kalanikūpule with trickery. ʻOlohana told me the story. "Once away from Honolulu and abreast of Waikiki," he said, "they made a great show of climbing the ship's rigging, while at the same time smearing it with noxious oil." The oil's fumes so sickened Kalanikūpule, his chieftains, and their warriors that they demanded to return to Honolulu at once. Sometime later the Jackal again sortied for Hawaiʻi, with Kalanikūpule, his general, Kamohomoho, and a few of their retainers on board. Kalanikūpule's warriors, meanwhile, followed the ship in their sail canoes.

"The ship soon outdistanced the canoes," ʻOlohana said. "And once they were well away, the sailors forced Kalanikūpule and the others into a boat and sent them ashore. In this, they showed more mercy to Kalanikūpule than he deserved."

The British seamen had heard that Kamehameha was a great friend to Britain. Now they sailed directly for the Big Island just as Kalanikūpule had intended, albeit without him. "Kameha was delighted to receive them, and their weapons," my father said. "He held a great feast for those haoles and gave them all manner of trade goods and produce."

The next day the Jackal again set sail, escorted by the Fair American and a flotilla of double-hulled canoes. After waving farewell to the British sailors from the Fair American's quarter deck, Kamehameha turned to his kahuna nui, who was standing next to him. "Holoʻae, I believe that Kūkāʻilimoku has spoken now," he said. "Do you agree?"

"He has indeed spoken," the priest replied.

Waikiki, 1795

Kamehameha landed on O'ahu unopposed. His war canoes—more than five hundred—were drawn up along the beaches from Waikiki to Wai'alae. Kameha and his closest advisers had sailed from Hawai'i to O'ahu in his new schooner, the Pelekane, which now lay at anchor offshore with the Fair American. The ships' Hawai'ian crews, now as adept as all but the most experienced haole mariners, had handled them smartly. Transferring with his chieftains from the Pelekane to his great double-hulled war canoe, Kamehameha came ashore in full battle regalia, standing at the forefront of the canoe's central platform. My father stood directly behind him bearing the royal kahili. The vivid red and yellow feathers of Kamehameha's new cloak and helmet, made expressly for this occasion by Ka'ahumanu herself, fluttered in the morning's light breeze. The feathers topping the kahili standard matched his helmet and cloak. Kameha held a long pololū spear in one hand and a musket in the other.

Kamehameha leaped from the canoe as its hulls fetched up on the narrow beach at Waikiki. More than ten thousand warriors awaited him, mustered for battle below *Le'ahi*, which the haoles now call "Diamond Head." They roared as Kameha and his chiefs, water lapping around their ankles, walked the full length of their ranks. Their shouts raced around the volcanic mount rising above them, rushing from the far end of Waikiki to the farthest reach of Wai'alae like a rip current.

Hawai'i's mō'ī had devoted much of the year since Vancouver's departure to acquiring more weapons from visiting haole trading ships and drilling his warriors for the battle to come. Kameha's people were armed with all manner of spears, clubs, and iron daggers. Also among their number were a thousand well-trained and well-provisioned musket bearers and more scores of men bearing extra powder and musket balls. Another one hundred warriors constituted a light artillery corps—bearing swivel guns and canister shot that Kamehameha had acquired in trade.

Upon landing, Kamehameha's commanders had learned from the few people of Waikiki who had not fled from the invaders that Kalanikūpule and his warriors had withdrawn to the Nuʻuanu Valley. This valley climbs into the Koʻolau Range, which straddles Oʻahu like a spine between its southern and northern shores. Rather than oppose Kameha's formidable invasion force along the beaches' broad front, Kalanikūpule sought to lure him into battle within the valley's narrower confines, where, he hoped, he and his people could gain a tactical advantage. To this end, Kamehameha's commanders learned, Kalanikūpule and his people had invested a village situated about a third of the way up the valley, on the heights overlooking the Nuʻuanu Stream.

My father and some of the other chiefs were disturbed by this news. "Kalanikūpule will have the advantage of high ground," Kamanawa warned.

"It is of no concern," Kameha said. "Kūkāʻilimoku is with us." Turning to his waiting soldiers, he shouted, "Warriors of *Hawaiʻi nei*, we will not be denied the fruits of victory this day! Let us march!"

With Kamehameha at their forefront, ten thousand Hawaiʻian fighting men commenced their advance on the Nuʻuanu Valley, where Kalanikūpule and his people waited. Also waiting with Kalanikūpule was Kaʻiana.

Relations between Kamehameha and Kaʻiana, never truly amicable, had frayed considerably since Vancouver's departure. For his part, Kaʻiana was angry that Kaʻahumanu would no longer speak to him. He rightly blamed Kamehameha for this, but dared not say so openly. Instead, he complained to anyone who would listen, including my father, that Kamehameha was not sufficiently grateful for his services. "Who first brought him muskets? Who first showed our people how to use them?" he demanded. "I did, and yet he raises these haoles, ʻOlohana and ʻAikake, above me, and he trusts the Kona chiefs before me—I who am also a direct descendant of the noble Keawe."

When Kaʻiana's latest complaints reached Kamehameha's ears, as Kaʻiana may have intended, they only served to harden Kameha against him.

Unbeknownst to Kaʻiana at this time, Keʻeaumoku and Kameʻiamoku were urging their mōʻī to cast him out, even to kill him. "He is a troublemaker," they said. "Better to be done with him."

Kamehameha would not hear of this. "He has offended me, certainly, but he has done nothing to warrant such treatment," he said. "I will not turn him aside as long as he is willing to stand with me against Kalanikūpule."

In truth, Kamehameha had no further need of Kaʻiana or his services. His musket warriors were well trained and training others. He had gained sufficient command of English, and ʻOlohana and ʻAikake had learned enough Hawaiian that they no longer needed Kaʻiana to interpret. Moreover, after Kaʻiana's defeat at the hands of Keōua Kūʻahuʻula, Kamehameha had lost respect for his military acumen, and no longer counted him among his most trusted commanders. Thus, this proud aliʻi found himself increasingly isolated, unappreciated, and diminished in Kamehameha's camp.

Before his assault on Oʻahu, Kamehameha's armada made first for Maui. I was four at the time, and remember standing atop the wall of the Puʻukoholā Heiau, along with my brother, Kekuaokalani, and Kaʻahumanu's brother, Kahekili Keʻeaumoku, who were still too young to fight. From our vantage point above the bay we watched the grand spectacle of Kamehameha's fleet as it set sail.

Kamehameha had amassed so many canoes that the bay could not accommodate them all. Drawn up on the sand side by side, they spanned the entire curve of beach at Kawaihae and spilled out of sight around both of the bay's points. The canoes' prows bowed in an arc toward the Fair American and the Pelekane, which lay at anchor in the middle of the bay.

Earlier that morning, Kamehameha and his chieftains had assembled at the heiau, where Holoʻae once again sought the guidance of Kūkāʻilimoku. The feather atop the war god's head had stood erect. The god was with Kameha.

Now a tumultuous cheer arose from the multitudes below as Kamehameha and his entourage filed down the hill to the beach. Waving their spears, clubs, and muskets, the warriors acclaimed their mōʻī as he made his way through their ranks to his double-hulled war canoe. The men in the first ranks on either side of Kameha dropped to their knees and lowered their foreheads to the sand in observance of the prostrating kapu. They rose again, cheered, and waved their weapons with the rest of their comrades as Kamehameha boarded his canoe with his chieftains and crossed the water to the waiting Pelekane. Kaʻahumanu had boarded the ship earlier. The other chiefesses, Kaʻahumanu's mother, Nāmāhana, among them, were already on board the Fair American.

"Kaʻahumanu was the only wahine permitted to sail with Kamehameha," said my father. "It was Kameha's way of demonstrating to Kaʻahumanu that he valued her above all of other women."

Kamehameha had not invited Kaʻiana to sail with him and the other chieftains. He had allowed, however, that Kaʻiana could make the voyage to Oʻahu on the Fair American if he liked. But Kaʻiana was too proud for that. He perceived Kamehameha's offer as an insult. "I am descended from Keawe the Great; I am higher born than Keʻeaumoku, Kameʻiamoku, Kamanawa, and the others who sail with him and yet I am excluded from their company," he foolishly complained to my father. "He would have me travel with the chiefesses. It is not right."

Kamehameha's purpose, of course, was to deny Ka'iana proximity to Ka'ahumanu. My father could have reminded him of this, but he kept such thoughts to himself. Ka'iana sailed separately with his own contingent of retainers and warriors, drawn from his holdings in South Kona.

When Kamehameha, his kahuna nui, and his chieftains were at last aboard the Pelekane, the two ships weighed their anchors and unfurled their sails. Cannons roared from the deck of each ship as their bows swung round toward the open ocean. Conch shells sounded up and down the beach as Kamehameha's army launched their canoes and followed their mō'ī to sea.

My brother, Kahekili Ke'eaumoku, and I sat on the temple wall and watched until the fleet had disappeared from view, the warriors' exuberant cheers, the reverberating cannon fire, and the calls of the conch shells still echoing in our ears.

The fleet's passage from the Big Island to Maui was much swifter than heretofore, as all of Kamehameha's sail canoes were by now rigged in the haole fashion. The fleet landed at Lahaina unopposed, Kalanikūpule having diverted most of his warriors for the defense of O'ahu.

The landing at Lahaina was for provisioning, and a simple requisition of the Lahaina people's stores would have been sufficient for this purpose. Kamehameha nevertheless ordered his men to plunder the village, but to avoid inflicting physical harm on its inhabitants or molesting their women. He also forbade them from destroying the villagers' dwellings.

"As we cannot spare enough warriors to hold Maui at this time, we must ensure that its people submit to us by demonstrating to them that Kalanikūpule can no longer protect them," Kameha explained to his council. "And by sparing their lives and dwellings now, we will also give them to understand that worse things might have befallen them, and most surely will if they should oppose us while we are away at O'ahu."

Kamehameha left one hundred warriors on Maui. He also left among the people there a certainty that Kalanikūpule was destined for defeat. This, along with the rapid spread of stories among the islanders about the size of Kamehameha's fleet and army and of his many haole weapons, not to mention the people's still-fresh memories of the slaughter at 'Īao Valley, ensured that no one dared to rise up against Kameha's small garrison in his absence.

Next, Kamehameha moved on to Moloka'i. Though nominally under Kalanikūpule's rule, the Moloka'i chieftains were unfriendly to him and still sympathetic to Kameha, who had grieved so deeply over Kalola's death. They eagerly allied themselves with him, especially after seeing the size of the Hawai'ian fleet and the strength of Kamehameha's army.

At Moloka'i, Kamehameha called his chiefly intimates together for a final council before the invasion of O'ahu. Once again, he excluded Ka'iana. "Ke'eaumoku, Kame'iamoku, and Kamanawa strongly objected to Ka'iana's inclusion in the council," said my father. "Moreover, Kamehameha deemed Ka'iana's presence unimportant, since his only role in the battle to come would be to lead his own small contingent of warriors."

When my father suggested to Kamehameha that he invite Ka'iana rather than needlessly offending him, Kameha replied brusquely, "I will speak privately to Ka'iana after the council. That should be sufficient for him."

Unadvised of the council beforehand, Ka'iana assumed the others were plotting against him when he learned of it. Afterward, Kamehameha dispatched my father to summon him, to discuss tactics for the forthcoming assault. He had decided to ask Ka'iana to lead the musket corps. "I searched everywhere for Ka'iana, but I could not find him," my father said.

Ka'iana was still nowhere to be found when the Hawai'ian fleet made ready to sail for O'ahu the next morning. He had put to sea under cover of night with about one hundred of his men. "Well, it is of no matter," Kameha said when apprised of this. "I will lead the pū warriors."

Preceding Kamehameha's fleet to Waikiki, Ka'iana warned Kalanikūpule of the invasion. When the fleet announced its presence with a thundering fusillade of cannon fire from the Fair American and the Pelekane, he had already withdrawn his people to the Nu'uanu Valley.

Nu'uanu Valley, 1795

As I have said, Kalanikūpule chose to confront Kamehameha's army in the Nu'uanu Valley because he believed the ground there favored his fighters. The meandering Nu'uanu Stream divides the valley's floor. In the lower half of the valley, this stream flows through a gully of varying width and steepness. Kalanikūpule and his general, Kamohomoho, elected to make a stand at the village of Pu'iwa, on the eastern side of the valley, where the gulley's banks are the highest and steepest. They hoped to lure the Hawai'ians into attacking them across the gully, wherein they would inevitably become bunched together and vulnerable to the defenders above. Moreover, once into the ravine, Kamehameha's warriors would be compelled to fight their way up a slope rising nearly one hundred and thirty feet from the bottom of the gully to the village itself. Even in the event of withdrawal, the ground would favor Kalanikūpule. This would have been a sound plan in other days, but Kalanikūpule and Kamohomoho unaccountably failed to reckon with Kamehameha's artillery, despite the debacle at 'Īao Valley.

Kamehameha gathered his army at the foot of the valley and encamped there for the night. Early the next morning, with some local villagers pressed into service to lead the way, the army marched up the valley and swung around to face Pu'iwa, just as Kalanikūpule had anticipated. Kalanikūpule's people also had muskets, though not nearly as many as Kamehameha's forces. Kalanikūpule had positioned these soldiers, under Ka'iana's command, at intervals in concealed positions along the length of the gully in front of the village.

As the Hawai'ians arranged themselves on the opposite side of the gully, Kalanikūpule taunted them. "Do not wait over there," he called. "Come across to us! We will make it worth your while!"

Ke'eaumoku answered him from the Hawai'ians' front line. "You are welcome to stay over there, Kalanikūpule, while Kamehameha rules the rest of the island!" he shouted, brandishing a pololū spear. "Our priests will come to collect your tribute at Makahiki time."

"Here is our tribute!" Kalanikūpule shouted. Ragged musket fire erupted from his side of the gully. Though the Hawai'ians in the front line were fully exposed, Kalanikūpule's people were poor marksmen, and it was to no effect. A musket ball did, however, pass through the crest of Ke'eaumoku's helmet, showering feathers all around him.

"Is that the best tribute you can offer?" Ke'eaumoku demanded. "Here is ours!"

Now, the Hawai'ian front-line warriors parted ranks to reveal a dozen swivel guns. At signal from Kame'iamoku, the guns roared in unison, sending a hail of lethal canister shot into the hidden positions of the musket troops on the gully's opposite bank. Shrieks erupted as mortally wounded men tumbled into the gully and others jumped up and ran for their lives toward the village. The Hawai'ians elevated their guns as they had been taught by 'Olohana and 'Aikake, reloaded them, and sent a salvo of canister shot into Pu'iwa itself. The canister shot tore through the village, felling men, women, and children alike. The air filled with the screams of the wounded and the dying. Kamehameha's people reloaded again and this time fired a volley of small-caliber round shot; and then yet another volley. The cannon balls sent up geysers of dirt, dust, and thatch as they thudded into the earth and into the roofs and walls of people's hales. Pu'iwa was now hidden in a dirty cloud.

Kalanikūpule tried to rally his men amid the growing confusion. "Warriors of O'ahu, stand with me!" he cried. "They must still come across to us! They cannot use their pū kuni ahi against us then. Hold fast here and wait for them!"

Somehow, his warriors managed to regroup in the pall and form a ragged line in front of the village. They were still several thousand strong, carrying spears, clubs, and iron axes and knives. They still had many muskets among them. Ka'iana had survived the cannon barrages and now stood with them. "All you men!" he called out. "Look at me!" Ka'iana dropped to one knee and gestured at the warriors to do likewise. "Crouch low so that you will not be easy targets for the enemy's pū kuni ahi!"

As they faced the Hawai'ians massed on the other side of the gap, Kalanikūpule, Kamohomoho, and Ka'iana failed to see Kamehameha approaching under the cover of the gloom on *their* side of the gully, leading several hundred warriors armed with muskets.

"Kamehameha had sent scouts to spy out Kalanikūpule's position," my father said. "When they reported that Kalanikūpule and his people were waiting for us at Pu'iwa, Kameha led his pū warriors across the stream well below the village and advanced along the opposite bank. Then he and his men waited for the rest of our people to form up across the gully. Our pū kuni ahi attack was a diversion."

The diversion continued, now with taunts and insults instead of cannon rounds. "Is that pig Ka'iana hiding with you over there, Kalanikūpule?" Ke'eaumoku shouted. "Are you so afraid that you crouch like a wahine taking a piss, Ka'iana? Stand like a man so that I can see you!"

"Stand like men! Stand like men!" the Hawai'ians chanted, brandishing their weapons at their enemies. "Do not crouch and pee like women! Stand like men! Pee like men!" This taunt rippled across the Hawai'ians' front rank, and then rolled to the rear through successive echelons until ten thousand warriors were screaming, waving their spears and clubs, and shaking their fists. As the Hawai'ian host chanted, the cannon corps reloaded their guns.

Amid this commotion, Kamehameha and his people emerged like apparitions from the settling haze, alongside and behind Kalanikūpule's men, whose attention was still fixed on the jeering enemy across the ravine. They leveled their muskets. Kamehameha waved at Ke'eaumoku, who signaled in turn to Kame'iamoku and the warriors at the cannons. Now the Hawai'ians' guns and muskets spoke as one. The cannon rounds flew over the heads of Kalanikūpule's men, crashing harmlessly into the village behind them, but musket fire from Kamehameha's men tore into their ranks from the flank and rear.

Kalanikūpule and most of his fighters did not understand what was happening at first. They ascribed the screams of their comrades to the cannon fire. They did not flinch as men toppled over beside them. "Hold! Hold!" Kalanikūpule shouted again. His men waited obediently for the frontal assault that would not come.

It was Ka'iana who first comprehended what was happening. "Kamehameha attacks us on the flank with *muskets*!" he shouted. The O'ahu men looked at him in bewilderment. They did not understand him. "Pū! Pū!" Ka'iana shouted now.

At last, Kalanikūpule understood. Now recalling the first days of fighting at 'Īao Valley, he cried, "Form up on me! Charge them before they can feed their pū again!" He and some of his men wheeled around to face Kamehameha and his warriors, but it was too late. Another musket volley lashed the O'ahu ranks, felling a score of warriors and igniting panic in all the rest. They broke and fled for their lives. Kalanikūpule and Kamohomoho fled with them. Only Ka'iana remained, disbelieving and momentarily transfixed in place.

A moment was all Kamehameha required. Kameha, who had never deigned to master the musket, carried an iron-tipped pololū spear. Now he stepped forward. "Ka'iana!" he shouted. "I am here!" As Ka'iana turned to look his way, Kamehameha hurled the spear. Ka'iana's eyes widened in astonishment as Kamehameha's spear struck him in his chest. For a moment he stood there, regarding the spear's shaft and the blood spilling from the surrounding wound in bewilderment. Then his eyes glazed over and he crumpled to the ground.

Kamehameha jerked the spear from Ka'iana's chest as he rushed by in pursuit of Kalanikūpule and his warriors. He did not spare so much as a glance at the dying turncoat.

Blocked from escaping to the coast, Kalanikūpule and his people retreated deeper into the Nuʻuanu Valley, and Kamehameha gave chase. Seeing the enemy fleeing, Keʻeaumoku ordered the Hawaiʻian army massed on his side of the gully to pursue and outrun the Oʻahu warriors.

"Just up the valley from Puʻiwa, the ravine becomes shallower," said my father, "and then it deepens again. Keʻeaumoku had only just learned of this. Now he wanted to get there before Kalanikūpule could cross the stream at that place, and block his escape."

"Follow them! Follow them! Quickly!" he shouted. "We must not let them cross!"

But an army the size of Kamehameha's does not move all at once on its general's command. By the time Keʻeaumoku's order had filtered through the ranks and the army had begun its pursuit, the Oʻahu warriors had reached the stream crossing. Keʻeaumoku and the few score of his warriors who reached the crossing with him could only stand and watch as Kalanikūpule and his men fled up the valley.

Once across the ravine, Kalanikūpule's people gained a narrow stretch of land along the valley's western wall. Kamehameha and his commanders could not deploy their army in breadth here, nor could they outflank Kalanikūpule's men. Here, Kalanikūpule stood and fought.

"Kalanikūpule's warriors were a match for us at this place because we could not bring up all of our men at once," my father said. "The fighting was bitter and hand to hand." In this close-quarter combat, with spears, clubs, and knives, Kamehameha's muskets and artillery were of no use. By mid-afternoon, hundreds of warriors on both sides had fallen.

Kamehameha, Keʻeaumoku, Kameʻiamoku, my father, and the other Hawaiʻian chieftains were everywhere during this fighting, urging men forward to take the places of fallen warriors. Kalanikūpule and Kamohomoho were similarly pressing their people into the fray. The Oʻahu forces slowly gave ground, but they made the Hawai'ians pay in blood for every yard they gained. Unable at last to replenish his front ranks in sufficient force to counter the Hawai'ians' offensive, Kalanikūpule was compelled to order a general retreat. Once again, he and his people turned and fled. The Hawai'ians were by then exhausted and reluctant to follow them, but Kamehameha spurred them on.

"We have them now!" he shouted. "Do not let the enemy rest; do not let them regain their strength. Our fallen brothers have already paid dearly for this moment! Let us finish this today!"

The advance continued. Now, where the valley floor broadened, Kamehameha's forces had room to maneuver again.

Kalanikūpule and his men were making for the very end of the valley, where a high pali overlooks the distant coastal village of Kailua. A narrow footpath descends from this cliff to the plain hundreds of feet below—a path that promised the O'ahu fighters escape if they could gain it in time.

With Kamehameha leading them, the Hawai'ians picked up their pace and lengthened their line as they sought to overtake, flank, and encircle Kalanikūpule's warriors.

Seeing Kameha and his people drawing closer, Kamohomoho rallied nearby warriors to his side. "We must stand here and fight so that our mō'ī and our brothers can live!" he cried. "Stand here with me!" While Kalanikūpule and the rest of his men continued their headlong flight up the valley, these brave warriors turned about to face the enemy. But even as the O'ahu men turned, the Hawai'ians brought their muskets and cannons into play again, and cut them down. Kamohomoho was one of the first to fall. No doubt, the last sounds he heard were the screams of his men, intermingled with the booming of cannon fire and the crack of the muskets echoing off the walls of the Nu'uanu Valley. Shouting and waving their spears, clubs, and muskets in the air, Kamehameha's people now leaped over the bodies of the dead and dying warriors as they pursued their remaining foes toward the precipice.

The Waikiki villagers who had led the Hawai'ians to Pu'iwa had earlier told Kamehameha of the footpath to which Kalanikūpule and his men now fled. Now he urged his warriors to run faster. "Cut them off! Cut them off!" he shouted as he ran. "Do not let them escape from this valley!" My father and Kame'iamoku were just behind him. "Keli'i!" he called over his shoulder, pointing to the right, "You and Kame'iamoku take some people over there and stop Kalanikūpule's people from reaching the footpath!"

"We gathered a few score warriors and ran in the direction Kamehameha had indicated," said my father. "Kameha continued on with the rest of the army."

Kamehameha set a torrid pace for his men, who were hard put to keep up with him. The warriors armed with spears and clubs were closest behind him; those with heavier muskets and awkward ammunition boxes slung over their shoulders or around their waists followed. The artillery corps fell farther and farther behind as they struggled to bring their guns along. Finally, they abandoned them and ran to catch up with the rest.

A number of enemy warriors were already escaping down the footpath by the time my father and his men reached it. Several of the Hawai'ians hurled spears at the fleeing men, but the missiles fell short, ricocheting off the hardened footpath and falling away down the mountainside. Just then, one of the O'ahu warriors turned round, looked up at Kame'iamoku and my father, and shook his fist. It was Kalanikūpule. Several of the Hawai'ian warriors, including Kame'iamoku's son, Ulumaheihei Hoapili, made to pursue him, but Kame'iamoku called them back. "Forget about Kalanikūpule," he said. "We must stand here and prevent the rest of his people from following him." The Hawai'ians turned to face the scores of enemy warriors running toward them.

Led by Kamehameha and Ke'eaumoku and propelled by bloodlust, the warriors of Hawai'i raced headlong up the Nu'uanu Valley in pursuit of their fleeing foes. They cut down stragglers without mercy. The broken bodies of wounded and slain warriors littered the ground in their wake.

At last, within a score of yards of the precipice, the O'ahu warriors turned to face the oncoming main force of the Hawai'ian army, still some seven thousand strong. "Hold! Hold!" Kamehameha shouted to his people. "Form a line on me! Spears and pū to the front!"

"Hold! Hold! Spears and pū to the front!" The shouts echoed up and down the ranks as Ke'eaumoku, Kamanawa, and the other chieftains repeated Kamehameha's commands. The Hawai'ians' surging advance ground to an uneven halt just a few pololū spear lengths from the O'ahu fighters' defensive line. Some warriors at the front of the Hawai'ians' ranks, now many scores of men deep, all crowding upon each other, were armed with spears, others with clubs and knives. The musket warriors, having come up last, were still to the rear.

"Spears and pū to the front!" Kamehameha's chieftains shouted again. Men in the rear ranks parted to allow the musket bearers to come forward; fighters holding only clubs and knives gave way to comrades armed with spears. An army which only moments earlier had verged on becoming a disorganized mob rearranged itself into an orderly battle formation, its front rank bristling with spears and haole firearms. Now Kamehameha's people awaited further orders. Opposite them, the exhausted men of O'ahu also waited, their chests heaving, their eyes wild with fear.

To the rear of the compressed O'ahu ranks, fighters began slipping away and fleeing toward the footpath. Leaderless now, their only thoughts were for escape. They threatened to overwhelm my father, Kame'iamoku, Hoapili, and the other men who still blocked the way out of the valley. Kamehameha saw this and called out to Ke'eaumoku. "Ke'eau! Quickly!" he shouted, pointing in my father's direction. "Keli'i and Kame'iamoku will need help! Take some men and go to them now!"

Ke'eaumoku set off at a run, at the head of several dozen warriors. One of them was his nephew, a young man named Kalanimoku, who was about the same age as his cousin Ka'ahumanu.

"Spears ready! Load pū!" Kamehameha cried now, clasping his long pololū spear tight against his side and pointing it at the enemy. As his commanders repeated his orders up and down the ranks, the Hawai'ian front line rippled with motion from one end to the other. Hundreds of warriors leveled their spears at the foe as Kamehameha had done. Others hurriedly rammed powder, balls, and wads down their musket barrels, filled the firing pans, pulled back the weapons' hammers, and took aim. For a brief moment—save for the shifting of bodies, the commanders' muted encouragement to their men, and the rustle of foliage in the afternoon breeze—silence reigned.

At the head of the footpath, my father, Kame'iamoku, Hoapili, and their men braced for the onslaught of the fleeing O'ahu warriors who now ran toward them. More interested in escape than doing battle, these men ran in a ragged line, singly and in pairs, and paid little heed to the Hawai'ians blocking their way.

"Many of them had thrown away their weapons in their haste to get away," my father said. "We were more concerned that they would overcome us with their sheer numbers and carry us down the trail with them than we were with any harm they might want to do us."

The Hawai'ians tightened their grips on their weapons as the O'ahu warriors drew closer. Men cocked their arms back, ready to hurl their spears. But before any of them could throw, a piercing cry came from the middle of the onrushing throng, and one of their number staggered and fell to the ground, a pololu spear protruding from his back. The O'ahu men were thrown into greater confusion, some stopping suddenly to look about while others stumbled into them. Ke'eaumoku had arrived with his warriors.

Thus reinforced, my father's group now advanced on the men of O'ahu. Ke'eaumoku's men meanwhile pressed in upon them from the side. To the O'ahu warriors' other side was the head of the valley and empty space where the ground fell away. Halting their flight, they crowded together and made ready to fight.

"Now!" Kamehameha shouted. "All pū! Fire!"

In an instant, the whole length of the Hawai'ian front line erupted with muzzle flashes. The O'ahu men were packed so tightly together by now that nearly all of the musket balls struck home. Scores of enemy warriors collapsed to the ground.

"Advance!" Kamehameha cried. From his position at the center of the Hawai'ian line, Kameha stepped forward, his spear still locked against his side. His army moved with him, the men in the front ranks holding their spears level and stepping over their fallen foes, while the warriors following immediately behind plunged their spears and iron daggers into still-writhing bodies. Behind them, the musket soldiers halted briefly to reload. Some O'ahu warriors threw their spears at the Hawai'ians, who easily deflected them as they continued to advance. The men of O'ahu could only retreat.

At the footpath, a desperate struggle raged. "We had no pū, no space to throw spears. We fought hand to hand," my father said. The O'ahu warriors were outnumbered by the Hawai'ians, but only slightly, and their perilous position between their foes and the edge of the pali infused them with strength beyond their numbers. "They fought fiercely and we suffered more than a few dead and wounded," said my father.

Ke'eaumoku sent Kalanimoku running for additional reinforcements. Within a short time, he returned with scores more of Hawai'ian warriors, drawn from the rear of Kamehameha's army. Now the numerical advantage shifted decisively. Swinging their clubs and jabbing with their spears, they relentlessly pressed their foes back upon the ranks of their comrades, who were themselves slowly giving way before the massed Hawai'ian army.

Disorder took hold among the O'ahu warriors, the remnants of their army now reduced to a densely packed crowd of men stumbling over each other in confusion. In this moment, Kamehameha and his commanders shouted once again, "Pū warriors! Forward!" Again, the Hawai'ians made way for their musket soldiers. Their front ranks, which now extended from one side of the pali to the other, bristled with long dark barrels.

"Fire!" shouted Kamehameha and his chieftains. Hundreds of muskets sounded as one, spitting death amid fire and smoke. Scores more of O'ahu warriors now sagged against their comrades, there being no open ground to receive their suddenly limp bodies. Men looked about in wild despair for any avenue of escape, but there was only the Hawai'ian army in front of them and behind them, the abyss.

"Warriors of Hawai'i!" Kamehameha roared. "Kūkā'ilimoku is with us! Forward!"

His commanders echoed the cry and thousands of Hawai'ian warriors now advanced as a single being, pressing their foes back upon each other. First singly, then in pairs, then in threes and fours and larger groups, O'ahu fighters pushed to the very edge of the pali by the crush of bodies in front of them tumbled over the cliff, screaming as they fell. Others who still had a purchase on solid ground fell to their knees mere yards from oblivion and begged for mercy.

"Let none live!" Kamehameha now cried. "Slay them all!"

"Slay them all!" his commanders shouted.

Step by step, the Hawai'ians forced their enemies' diminishing ranks to the cliff's brink and over it, spearing, clubbing, and shooting men who clawed at the earth to avoid tumbling into the void at their backs. The warriors of Hawai'i continued to advance until they were the only ones standing at the pali's edge. The battle of Nu'uanu Valley was won. For a moment, there was silence. Then a raucous cheer swept through the Hawai'ian ranks as warriors shook their clubs, spears, and muskets above their heads in a joyous salute to their mō'ī.

Hawai'i, Maui, Lanai, Moloka'i, and O'ahu now all belonged to Kamehameha.

To give thanks to the war god Kūkā'ilimoku for his victory at Nu'uanu Valley, Kamehameha ordered a new heiau built in the crater of Le'ahi. Kalanikūpule and his few surviving followers had meanwhile fled to the coast at Kailua, east of Kaneohe. It was their intention to seek asylum on Kaua'i, as yet unconquered by Kamehameha. Kaua'i and Ni'ihau were now ruled by Kaumuali'i, the only son of the late Kā'eokūlani. "Why Kalanikūpule believed that Kaumuali'i, whose own father he had slain, would give him refuge, I do not know," my father said.

In any case, the Kailua people, bearing no love for Kalanikūpule, betrayed his presence among them to the warriors whom Kamehameha had dispatched to search for him. Slaying all of his companions, Kalanikūpule's captors bound him and took him by canoe to Waikiki. There, they force-marched him with whips through a gantlet of jeering Hawai'ians to the new heiau at Le'ahi, where Kamehameha waited with Holo'ae and his chiefs.

Kalanikūpule's hands were still tied behind him and he was breathing hard from his rushed ascent to the volcanic mount's crater when he was brought before Kamehameha. It was midday; the sky was clear, and in the caldera, the heat of the unforgiving sun was intense. Kalanikūpule looked up at the terrible visage of Kūkā'ilimoku, mocking him from beyond the new heiau's altar, and then at Kamehameha, who was holding a length of haole rope. Bound but unbowed, he met his conqueror's eyes. He said nothing, waiting for Kamehameha to speak. But Kamehameha, impassive, merely nodded to a warrior behind Kalanikūpule. The warrior clubbed him and knocked him to his knees. Stepping around Kalanikūpule and leaning over his back, Kamehameha looped the rope around his enemy's throat, tightened it, hauled Kalanikūpule to his feet, and then lifted him higher still. He betrayed no emotion as Kalanikūpule kicked at empty air and struggled for breath. When it was done, Kamehameha laid Kalanikūpule's body at the god's altar, and Holo'ae chanted thanks to Kūkā'ilimoku for bringing Kamehameha victory at Nu'uanu Valley.

"Kūkā'ilimoku has been served," Holo'ae concluded, "and this heiau is sanctified."

There was much feasting at Waikiki that night.

The sanctification of the Le'ahi Heiau was Holo'ae's last service to Kamehameha. Several days later, the old priest fell ill and died. Though he had reached an age when death had lost its power to surprise, Kamehameha was desolate. "Holo'ae was like a father to me," he wailed, "and his counsel was ever wise."

"Holo'ae will become your 'aumakua," my father consoled him, "and surely, he will always be with you."

Kamehameha insisted on tending the imu that rendered the kahuna nui's flesh, and when the fire had purified Holo'ae's long bones, he would not permit anyone else to touch them.

"Kamehameha hid Holo'ae's bones, as he had Keoua's," my father said. "It was the greatest honor he could pay him."

Kailua, Kona 1796

My brother was excited and I was dejected, for he was to march in Ka'ahumanu's procession and I was not. "Your brother is almost a man, but you are too young, Nāmākēha," our father told me. My brother Kekuaokalani was about eleven, then four years short of the threshold of manhood. I was still a keiki of five. I cried.

Kamehameha had sworn to Ka'ahumanu that she was first among his wives. He had ordered this procession to demonstrate to his subjects that Ka'ahumanu was his wahine nui. A great feast in her honor was to follow the spectacle.

"Stop crying, Nāmākēha," my father said. He placed a hand on my shoulder and bent toward me, smiling. "Though you will not march in the procession, you will see it all, for you will stand with your uncle and me in the place of honor."

Thus it was that on the day of this grand pageant, I stood with my father, Kamehameha, and the other chieftains to receive Ka'ahumanu at the 'Ahu'ena Heiau. In truth, I stood immediately behind my father and Kamehameha, peering between them at the unfolding spectacle. As a mere boy, of course, I was not permitted to stand *with* the chiefs.

The procession commenced at the southernmost end of Kailua and progressed through the village to the edge of Kailua Bay opposite the temple. There, Ka'ahumanu and her party were to board double-hulled canoes to cross the water to the heiau. Kamehameha, his chieftains, and I stood on the temple's great stone platform awaiting Ka'ahumanu's arrival.

I wore a new malo, dyed in a muted red and yellow pattern. It was my first garment of any kind. Heretofore, I had gone everywhere naked, like all children of my age, ali'i and commoner alike. My father had given the malo to me. "You are not yet a man, but you are no longer a *little* keiki," he said. This made me feel very proud.

Kekuaokalani was prouder still. He received a new malo *and* a feather cloak to wear in Ka'ahumanu's procession. It was red and yellow, like the cloaks of Kamehameha's chiefs. It was a present from Kamehameha himself. "You must wear this in Ka'ahumanu's procession because you will be an important chief someday, Kekua," Kamehameha told him.

"You see, Nāmākēha," Kekua said to me. "Uncle Kameha has said that I will become a great chief like him."

Greatness would have to wait. Today, Kekuaokalani marched far behind Ka'ahumanu at the rear of the procession with a score or more of ali'i boys about his age, Kahekili Ke'eaumoku among them. Moreover, all the boys were similarly garbed, though Kekuaokalani's feather cloak was finer than the other boys' were.

Nāmāhana walked directly behind Ka'ahumanu, bearing the kahili standard that signified her daughter's high rank. Kamehameha's first wife, Pele'uli, followed them. Beside her walked Keku'iapoiwa Liliha, half-sister of Kamehameha, widow of Kiwala'ō, and mother of Kamehameha's nī'aupi'o wife, Keopuolani. Keopuolani herself could not walk in the procession. She had grown into womanhood and now she had the burning kapu and was restricted from walking abroad in the daytime, lest her shadow fall on a commoner or lower-born ali'i, condemning that person to death. Thus, her mother walked in her place. Behind them came the wives of two score lesser chieftains. These women carried gourd rattles, which they shook as they walked.

"Kapu moe! Kapu moe!" Nāmāhana called out as the procession moved through Kailua. Upon hearing these words, the ali'i along the footpath knelt and remained in this posture until Ka'ahumanu had passed. Commoners, who stood well behind the kneeling ali'i, prostrated themselves, their foreheads to the ground. They did not look up until all of Ka'ahumanu's company had moved on.

No aspect of our people's domestic industry escaped his attention, and no aspect was overlooked by his tax collectors. At Kamehameha's direction, Kalanimoku appointed tax gatherers for every district of Hawai'i, Maui, Moloka'i, Lanai, and O'ahu. Tribute was collected once a year, during the Makahiki time, as of old, but with a difference. "Kamehameha's tax gatherers are not kāhuna," my father once noted. "They do not travel from ahupua'a to ahupua'a collecting taxes for the god Lono as the kāhuna once did." Instead, on the appointed day, the district chiefs and their retainers came to a designated village to pay the tax. The goods thus gathered went first of all to Kamehameha.

Each ahupua'a was taxed proportionally, according to its size. Kalanimoku watched the tax collectors closely to ensure that Kameha received a tenth of everything his people produced. It was kapu to shortchange the mō'ī, and few tried. Kamehameha would distribute these goods to his household and his principal chieftains, whom he kept close to him at all times.

Kamehameha restored the old heiaus of our people's gods and built new ones. These were many and widely dispersed throughout the islands: temples dedicated to Lono; temples dedicated to Kanaloa, god of the sea; temples dedicated to Pele, the god of the volcano; and to Papa, the deity of women. Kameha restored or constructed heiaus dedicated to many more gods and goddesses, for as I have said, our people saw gods in everything around them and worshiped them as needed. Kameha was most attentive to the maintenance of the temples of his war god, Kūkā'ilimoku, and was adamant that no new temple should eclipse in size the great Pu'ukoholā Heiau at Kawaihae.

Kamehameha restored or built so many temples that many more priests were required to serve them, so he appointed many new kāhuna. In this way, and by example of his own piety, Kameha maintained our people's religious traditions.

Kamehameha was especially anxious to encourage his subjects' devotion to our generations-old religion and laws in the face of the haoles' increasing presence among them. Our benign climate, and, to their minds, our easy way of life, attracted foreigners in ever-greater numbers. Kamehameha welcomed them because he found them useful.

But as much as he valued the haoles' skills and services, Kamehameha worried about their influence among our people. "They do not worship our gods," he told my father. "They do not prostrate themselves before our chieftains. They do not understand our laws. I am loath to apply our kapus to them, but I am concerned about the example this sets for ali'i and maka'āinana alike." Requiring their services, Kameha could not isolate the haoles from our people, and especially not from our women. Thus he was at pains to ensure that people never mistook the haoles' license for their own. To this end, he charged Kalanimoku with strictly enforcing the kapus.

Amid his immersion in trade, law-giving, religion, and the daily affairs of his people, Kamehameha found time for his wives, now numbering five, among them his own niece, Keopuolani. About eighteen at this time, she was yet a virgin—which was then almost unheard of for women of her age.

As I have said, Keopuolani had the burning kapu and could not walk about in daylight. Thus, she spent her days sequestered in her own hale. She could receive visitors there, of course, but only other women, for Kamehameha had forbidden other men from visiting her, on pain of death. He was determined to get a nī'aupi'o son from her and the child's parentage must be beyond question.

Keopuolani's belly began to swell with child within a few months of Kamehameha's return to Kailua. Her first son, the sacred nī'aupi'o chief, Liholiho, was born in 1796. Ka'ahumanu presided at the delivery. The very day my cousin was born, Kamehameha gave him in hanai to Ka'ahumanu, as he had promised.

Liholiho's lower lip quivered. "But I have always eaten with Ka'ahumanu," he cried. "I want to eat with her."

The chieftains seated near Kamehameha and Liholiho scowled. The older boys within earshot began to laugh among themselves, my brother among them. I felt sorry for my little cousin. I was not so long away from the women's eating-house that I had forgotten how intimidating it was to leave my mother's side and join the men. My father cast a stern look at Kekuaokalani, who composed himself.

Kamehameha ignored his son's crying and paid no attention to his chieftains' disapproval or the other boys' muted mockery. "It is kapu for men to eat with women, my son," he said again, evenly. "It has *always* been kapu for men to eat with women. As much as I care for Ka'ahumanu, I may not eat with her. You will be mōʻī of all Hawaii one day, and it will be your duty to uphold the kapus."

For many months immediately thereafter, Kamehameha spent time with Liholiho every day, schooling him in the kapus and teaching him about our people's gods. Most often, he would summon the boy to his hale early in the morning before the press of the day's business began. Respecting his son's higher kapu, Kamehameha would recline on his mat, seat Liholiho on his stomach, and speak to him of Kāne, Ku, Lono, and Kanaloa. He would tell him stories of Pele, the goddess of the volcano, of the trickster god, Maui, and other such tales. At other times Kamehameha would take Liholiho to a heiau, where together they would sacrifice a goat or a hog to the temple's god.

Liholiho's introduction to the men's house commenced my companionship with him. It fell to me to intercede for him with the other boys, and especially with my older brother. Kekuaokalani did not much care for Liholiho and made no effort to hide it.

"Kekuaokalani says my mana is weak," Liholiho complained to me one day. "He says I will never be a great warrior like my father." Liholiho screwed up his face as he fought back tears.

"Liholiho whines too much," Kekuaokalani said when I asked him about this. "If a few harsh words can reduce him to tears, how can he become a warrior? He needs toughening."

"Kekua, Liholiho is still a keiki," I said, doing my best to defend my little "brother," as my duty demanded. "Remember how easily I cried when I was his age?" I was thinking of the day not so many years before, when I could not march in Ka'ahumanu's procession.

"Yes, but when you came from the women's house, you did not complain, and you did not run back to your mother's hale when you were teased," Kekuaokalani said. "Liholiho is always running off to Ka'ahumanu at the slightest excuse."

There was nothing I could say in response to this, for it was true.

My father cautioned Kekuaokalani against teasing or in any other way distressing his royal cousin. "Liholiho is nī'aupi'o. He will succeed Kamehameha as your mō'ī someday, and you must respect him," he said. Kekuaokalani thereafter refrained from mocking Liholiho, but he treated our young cousin coolly and had as little to do with him as possible.

Other boys gave him a wide berth. "Cousin, why do the other boys avoid me?" Liholiho asked me one day.

"Because you are nī'aupi'o and they fear your kapu," I said. "It is not your fault." There was some truth to this. Liholiho had the burning kapu and other boys claimed to be fearful that their own houses would be burned down or that they themselves would be put to death if they somehow violated his person or otherwise offended him in the course of their often rough-and-tumble games. This was in fact unlikely within the precincts of the royal court, but still they mostly kept their distance from him. Thus, Liholiho often found himself quite alone amidst the throng of contemporaries at the men's house, save for my companionship. And when this proved to me. "Your brother thinks only of the coming battle, Nāmākēha," he said. "But what will he do after Kamehameha subdues Kaua'i?"

Every day while we were at Kailua, Liholiho and I would accompany Kalanimoku as he made the rounds of the war-canoe builders and weapons makers and conferred with Kamehameha's generals. And every evening, Kekuaokalani would ask me what I knew of Kamehameha's growing armada. "How goes the fleet? Did you see many more war canoes today?" he would demand.

"Yes, brother, many more," I would always respond.

The fleet's size was expanding by the day, and not only at Kailua. Hundreds of laborers were denuding whole hillsides of koa trees on the Big Island, Maui, and O'ahu, and hauling the trunks down to the coasts. Kamehameha had ordered every canoe builder on the three islands to work from sunrise to sunset turning them into hulls for his war canoes. These new double-hulled canoes, called *peleleu*, had commodious central platforms and sails rigged with booms, in the haole fashion. They could carry at least ten men in each of their hulls and another twenty or more on their decks.

At Kailua, a dozen haoles and scores of Hawai'ian craftsmen labored to build eight more schooners like the Fair American and the Pelekane. 'Aikake supervised their work. Many more haoles had settled in our islands by then, seafaring adventurers drawn here from America and Europe by the pleasant weather, the promise of an easier life, and the encouragement of Kamehameha, who was ever eager to exploit their knowledge and skills to his advantage. And the promise of a warm welcome by our women was just as alluring as the embrace of our king.

As his new war fleet grew, Kamehameha continued to accumulate haole weapons and munitions—cutlasses, swords, muskets, small cannons, powder, musket balls, cannon balls, and canister shot—from the American and European ships that visited the Big Island with increasing frequency. In the two decades since Cook "discovered" our islands, the Americans in particular had come to rely on our people for provisions, trade goods, and their own renewal in the midst of the long sea voyage to faraway China. Determined to control all commerce with the haoles, Kamehameha had of late barred foreign ships from trading at any island other than where he happened to reside—for the present on the Big Island, either at Kailua or at Kealakekua. "They must all come to me," he said.

'Olohana and Kalanimoku were Kamehameha's agents in transactions with the haole sea captains. Acting in his behalf, they drove hard bargains for haole goods in exchange for provisions like livestock, fruit, vegetables, and wood, and even for watering rights, which the haole merchantmen sorely needed. The visiting captains complained bitterly about the latter, accustomed as they had become over the years to freely collecting as much fresh water as they wished from our streams. "Lono sent this water to us," Kamehameha admonished them, "and it is not yours to take." Left no choice, the haole captains paid for the water.

Kamehameha's invasion commenced in May of 1803. The fleet's first stop was Maui. Liholiho, Kekuaokalani, Kahekili Ke'eaumoku, and I sailed with Kamehameha, my father, and the rest of Kameha's most trusted counselors on the Fair American. 'Olohana was not among them—as governor of the Big Island, he remained at his home in Kawaihae.

Our passage across the Alenuihāhā Channel was swift and especially rough. The same strong winds that filled the ship's sails and sped our passage roiled the sea and whipped up high swells. From Upolu Point to Hana, our first port of call on Maui, the Fair American's prow rose and fell, rose and fell without relief. Kekuaokalani reveled in the channel's turbulent rhythm. I endured. Liholiho became deathly ill.

"Ho! Little brother!" Kekua called to me from the schooner's bowsprit, upon which he had ventured out as far as he dared. "Have you ever seen such a thing?"

Indeed I had not. Rising and falling amid the swells to each side of the Fair American were the Pelekane and Kameha's newest schooners. Scores of the newly launched peleleu war canoes trailed the haole ships, spread out in all directions. Unlike the schooners, whose bows bit into the sea, the double-hulled canoes rode high in the water, cresting the swells and then all but disappearing into the deep troughs between them, then reappearing atop the swells moments later. A few of the more adventurous peleleu crews thought to race our haole ships and trimmed their sails tightly against the strong reaching wind. But they were forced to fall off the wind when their canoes heeled over so far as to raise one of their twin hulls entirely out of the water, straining the crafts' lashings and threatening to break them in two.

Kekuaokalani laughed at this spectacle. "Nāmākēha!" he shouted. "See how those warriors are lifted so high that their paddles strike nothing but air!"

I looked where my brother pointed and saw one double-hulled canoe tipped over so far that the warriors riding in the high hull to windward had stowed their paddles and were gripping the hull's side to avoid being tumbled. The men riding on the deck had fallen to their hands and knees to keep from being spilled into the lower hull. Their alarmed cries carried to us over the sounds of the wind and the water slapping against the Fair American's hull.

I turned back to Kekua again. The island of Maui, ever closer, seemed to rise and fall in front of him. My stomach churned and I returned my gaze to the more stable far horizon. At mid-deck, where Kamehameha was conferring with his chieftains, Liholiho clutched his stomach and vomited.

At Hana, the schooners anchored in the bay and the war canoes covered its beach from one end to the other, and the shore beyond its southern point to the cove at Hāmoa. Kamehameha lingered at Hana for several days, relaxing and feasting nightly with his chieftains. After this brief respite, the war fleet moved on to Lahaina, where it grew larger still, with additions from Maui and Lanai. We remained at Lahaina for several months while Kamehameha's chieftains drilled their warriors in the use of muskets.

The bay at Lahaina echoed with gunfire from dawn until dusk, periodically punctuated by the cannons' roars. Kamehameha was unconcerned about the profligate expenditure of munitions. The haole merchants who had sailed to Lahaina in the wake of his fleet were happy to replenish his stores of powder, shot, and musket balls in exchange for food and water.

When he was not drilling with the other warriors, Kekuaokalani shadowed Kamehameha. As the fleet's stay at Lahaina stretched on, he became ever more impatient to set sail for O'ahu and the invasion of Kaua'i. "Why are we staying so long on Maui, Uncle?" he asked Kamehameha one day. "We are only giving Kaumuali'i' and his people more time to prepare for our invasion."

"Kaumuali'i has been preparing for this since the day our fleet was wrecked between O'ahu and Kaua'i, nephew," Kamehameha replied. "I want his people to hear of *our* preparations. I want them to fear our arrival. I want them to quake at the sight of our army and flee for their lives."

My brother pondered this. "Then you hope not to give battle, Uncle?" he asked at last, his voice infused with disappointment.

"Kekua, I know you thirst for battle and glory," Kamehameha said. "But I have seen enough battles and had enough glory. We will fight for Kaua'i if we must, but I hope we will not have to. Men are always fighting. There will no doubt be other battles, and you will prove yourself as a warrior one day."

Our uncle's assurances did not mollify Kekuaokalani. He was impatient to prove himself. He would have to wait.

The plague that decimated Kamehameha's people on O'ahu, carrying away his oldest and most trusted advisers and nearly killing Kamehameha himself, put an end to his campaign to take Kaua'i. Kameha was many days recovering from his illness.

One afternoon, loud cries outside his hale awakened Kamehameha from a fitful sleep. My father, who had been tending to him, was not at his side.

Kamehameha was struggling to his feet when my father rushed into the hale, weeping.

"What has happened?" Kamehameha demanded.

"Kameha!" my father wailed, "Ke'eaumoku has died!"

"No!" Kamehameha cried. "Not Ke'eaumoku too!" His legs gave out from under him and he collapsed onto his sleeping mat. My father knelt beside him and the two men clasped each other tightly and wailed.

The grief of my father and uncle for their old friend and ally was eclipsed only by the sorrow of Ke'eaumoku's wife, daughter, and son—Nāmāhana, Ka'ahumanu, and Kahekili Ke'eaumoku. They were still aboard the Fair American when he died and were overcome when word of his death reached the ship. Ignoring the danger of contagion, Nāmāhana insisted on going ashore where she could grieve properly. Her children begged her not to go.

"Stay with us, Mother," Ka'ahumanu pleaded. "It is too late to go to Father's side, and he would not want you to risk your life only to mourn his death."

Kalanimoku refused Nāmāhana's request to leave the ship. "Kamehameha set me over all the women and children here," he said. "And you shall not go."

"And *you* shall not stop me, nephew," Nāmāhana rejoined. Then, before either Kalanimoku, her son, or daughter could intercept her, she tore off her short skirt, ran to the ship's railing, climbed over, and dropped into the water below.

"Mother!" Ka'ahumanu and Kahekili Ke'eaumoku cried. "Come back!"

Already stroking toward the beach, Nāmāhana ignored her children's cries. Ashore, she grieved for her husband, took ill, and died within ten days.

Profoundly shaken by the loss of Ke'eaumoku and so many of his other old friends and advisers, Kamehameha emerged from his convalescence convinced that divine will had thwarted his ambition to subdue Kaua'i.

"Kūkāʻilimoku has forsaken me," he said. "First he sent a storm to scatter my ships and canoes and then he sent a plague to destroy my army. He protects Kaumualiʻi now. My priests should have foreseen this. Holoʻae would have. I will stay here on Oʻahu and rebuild my army until the god favors me once more."

Kamehameha remained on Oʻahu for another six years.

Waikiki, 1810

The plague forced Kamehameha to rebuild his government. He instinctively turned to the sons of his late comrades-in-arms to replace their fathers. Thus he appointed to his innermost council Ke'eaumoku's son, Kahekili Ke'eaumoku; Koahou, son of Kamanawa; Ulumaheihei Hoapili, son of Kame'iamoku; and Haiha Naihe, the son of Keaweaheulu. Kamehameha set Ke'eaumoku's nephew, Kalanimoku, above them all as leader of the council and, in effect, as his prime minister. With the exception of Keaweaheulu's son, Naihe, and of course my own brother, Kekuaokalani, Kamehameha was almost entirely surrounded by Ka'ahumanu's relatives.

In an unprecedented move, Kamehameha also invited Ka'ahumanu to join his council. No chiefess had ever before sat as an equal among men in a mō'ī's innermost circle. My brother and I were surprised by this news, but 'Olohana, then at O'ahu to confer with our uncle, was not. "Don't you see?" he said to us. "Your uncle binds all those young chiefs and their families more firmly to him through their blood ties to Ka'ahumanu and her marriage to him. He could not have subdued all the other islands without their fathers' support and he cannot hold them without the support of their sons. Your uncle ensures their support by keeping Ka'ahumanu close by him."

Kamehameha and Kalanimoku devoted the years after the pestilential decimation to rebuilding the fighting forces and acquiring more muskets, cannons, and munitions. By the middle of 1809, Kamehameha had further increased his arsenal of intimidating haole arms, and gathered and trained hundreds more warriors to bear them. He had also employed haole shipwrights to build more schooners on which he mounted many cannons. Kameha was determined that no storm would scuttle his fleet when next he assaulted Kaua'i. Haole ships were more reliable in heavy seas than traditional war canoes. As much as he was counting on Kūkā'ilimoku to bless this endeavor, he would not rely on his god for protection from the weather.

With our uncle once more bent on war, Kekuaokalani's spirits lifted. Because so many of Kamehameha's contemporaries had been carried away by the pestilence, Kekuaokalani counted on being one of his senior commanders when the time came. "I will be in the battle's forefront, brother," he said. "I will make our father and Uncle Kameha proud of me." Toward this end, Kekuaokalani trained harder than ever in all the arts of combat, Hawaiian and haole.

Our cousin, Liholiho, meanwhile, held himself aloof from such pursuits. He claimed he saw no purpose in joining other youths in their mock battles. "If war comes, my place will be at my father's side," he said to us. "And my father will not lead the fight this time."

Kamehameha shrugged when his son's words reached him. "Liholiho is ill-fitted to be a warrior," he told my father. "But that is no matter, for there will be no more fighting after we defeat Kaumuali'i."

Early in 1809, Kamehameha dispatched messengers to his chieftains on Maui, Moloka'i, and the Big Island with orders to muster their warriors and bring them to O'ahu. As Kamehameha's army grew and training continued, the younger, untested warriors' impatience for battle became more palpable with every passing day. And as the nervous tension among Kamehameha's warriors escalated, their mock battles grew in ferocity and a number were seriously injured. This continued until several warriors suffered mortal wounds from thrown spears in a single afternoon.

Recalling the senseless death of his own kahu, Kekūhaupi'o, in mock fighting years earlier, Kamehameha ordered a halt to these contests. He told his commanders to conduct light musket practice and close-combat drills only. "But do not allow them to relax overmuch," he cautioned. "They must be ready for battle."

The warriors continued to drill—and wait.

Kekuaokalani became so frustrated that he dared confront Kamehameha directly. "Uncle," he blurted out one evening, "my people want to fight. The entire army longs to fight. Why do we still delay here?"

My father sharply reproved my brother. "Kamehameha may be your uncle, but he is also your lord, and you must show him more respect," he snapped.

Yet Kameha took no offense. "Brother," he said, "do not rebuke Kekuaokalani for his eagerness to fight." Still, Kamehameha could not let my brother's outburst pass entirely. Turning to Kekuaokalani, he said, "I delay because the time is not yet right to attack." At this, my brother made as if to protest again. Kamehameha silenced him with a brusque wave of his hand. "I have my reasons," he said, "and they do not concern you, Kekuaokalani. You should return to your own men now. Your proper place is with them." Kameha gestured next at me and said, "You go with him, Nāmākēha. And in the future, *boys*, leave such matters to your elders and me."

Thus chastened, we left Kamehameha's hale.

"Pay your elder son's poor manners no mind, Keli'i," Kamehameha told my father later. "Our army is now full of young men who have yet to blood their spears. But if all of Kekuaokalani's contemporaries are of like mind when the battle begins, they will fall upon the enemy with no hesitation and no thoughts for themselves. They are more than ready for combat now, and I *will* order them into battle soon, while they still seethe with impatience. This has always been my intention."

Kamehameha's order to invade Kaua'i never came. Fate intervened. My father died. Keli'imaika'i's death was sudden. Kekuaokalani and I were sitting with our father in the courtyard of his hale at Waikiki. One minute he was talking with us, and in the next he gasped, clutched at his chest, and collapsed as if struck by a spear. He still breathed but he did not respond to our cries. His eyes were open, but he did not appear to see us as we hovered over him. His gaze was fixed on the sky, which was filled now with fluffy white clouds blowing in from the sea and piling up against the mountains behind us. Keli'imaika'i blinked as if in surprise and spoke at last. "Kāne calls," he said. "Lono must be served." Then he sighed, his eyelids fluttered closed, and his chest ceased to move.

Our anguished cries soon drew scores of people—men, women, and some frightened children—who encircled us at a respectful distance and joined in our wailing. Some moments later, the crowd parted like waters before a canoe prow as Kamehameha came upon us. Without a word, he fell to his knees, enfolded Kekuaokalani and me in his long arms, and cried with us.

Exhausted from crying at long last, we lapsed into silence. Now I heard sobbing nearby and looking up I saw that Kalanimoku, Ka'ahumanu, Kahekili Ke'eaumoku, and Liholiho had arrived. They were standing to one side. Ka'ahumanu's and Kalanimoku's eyes glistened with tears and Kahekili Ke'eaumoku was downcast. But Liholiho's eyes were clear and he regarded this tableau with only mild interest. When Liholiho saw me looking at him, he lowered his own gaze and twisted his mouth into a frown, but he did not cry for his own uncle, my father.

Grief-stricken, Kamehameha suspended all martial drilling for the duration of the funeral rituals for Keli'imaika'i. Thus all military activity at the Waikiki encampment of some eight to ten thousand men was halted for a fortnight—for the ten days during which the hot stones of the imu slowly seared our father's flesh from his long bones, and for several more days while the priests prayed over my father's cleansed bones for his departed spirit.

When the priests were done, they gave my brother two bags of kapa cloth bound with twine, one containing our father's charred flesh and the other his long bones. As Keli'imaika'i's oldest son, it was Kekuaokalani's sad task to offer our father's flesh to Kanaloa and to hide his bones. Joined by our Uncle Kameha, my brother and I wailed over our father's remains late into the night. Early the next morning, as Kāne's light was just breaking over Le'ahi, Kamehameha and I helped Kekuaokalani carry an outrigger canoe to the water and step its mast. My brother and I hugged each other tightly and wailed one more time. Then Kamehameha grasped Kekuaokalani by his shoulders, drew him close, and said, "Your father was sacred to me, Kekua. Hide his bones well."

Kekuaokalani set off in the direction of Le'ahi. Kamehameha left me to consult with his advisers and priests. I remained alone on the shore at Waikiki, watching my brother's canoe until it slipped from sight behind Kupikiki'o point, just below Le'ahi. Kekuaokalani was gone for a night and two days. To this day, I do not know where he hid Keli'imaika'i's long bones.

During this time, Kamehameha asked his priests to divine the import of our father's last words: *Lono must be served.* Led by the reigning kahuna nui, Hewahewa, the priests of Kāne and Lono agreed that Kāne, speaking through Keli'imaika'i, was calling upon our people to foreswear war and the ways of the fearsome god Kūkā'ilimoku in favor of peaceful pursuits blessed by the god Lono.

"A long Makahiki time is coming, when the god Lono will be ascendant and the war god Kū will be retired," they said. But they could not, or would not, say whether this time was to come immediately or only after Kaua'i was subdued by force.

In council with Kamehameha and his chieftains, Kalanimoku contended that our father's last words could only be interpreted to mean that the time of war in our islands was already at an end.

"Lord," he said, "you have gathered and equipped the most powerful army our people have ever seen, all in plain sight of Kaumuali'i and his people. You have spoken of your hope to subdue Kaua'i by presence of arms in place of actual force of arms. The god, speaking through Keli'imaika'i, has now affirmed your purpose. You can achieve your ends without resort to more bloodshed."

Kalanimoku proposed that Kamehameha send an embassy to Kaumuali'i with an offer: His envoys were to tell Kaumuali'i that though Kamehameha was fully prepared to subjugate Kaua'i by force if necessary, he wished to spare Kaumuali'i and his people the suffering he had visited upon O'ahu fourteen years earlier—suffering well known on Kaua'i. Therefore, if Kaumuali'i would recognize Kamehameha as his lord and swear obedience to him, Kamehameha and his people would not invade his island. And of course, Kamehameha would leave the continued governance of Kaua'i to Kaumuali'i as Kamehameha's royal representative there.

But others argued that Keli'imaika'i's last words could only be interpreted as a call for one last conquest. Among these were two young chieftains named Kauiwa and Holo'ialena, comrades of my brother who had fought at his side many times in war games. They spoke for a faction of untested younger chiefs still eager to blood their spears.

"Lord, what else could the god who spoke with your brother's voice have meant," Kauiwa asked Kamehameha, "other than to say that you must conquer Kaua'i to put an end to war among your people?"

"What of the god Kūkā'ilimoku ?" asked Holo'ialena. "What has the war god said?"

Seated between my brother and Liholiho, Kamehameha listened thoughtfully as the debate raged around him. Liholiho appeared bored. He yawned, scratched his chest, and occasionally fidgeted with his malo. Kekuaokalani, however, sat ramrod straight, his eyes fixed on each speaker in turn. He said nothing. I knew of course that my brother sympathized with the council's war faction, and his peers assumed they were speaking for him as well.

At this meeting, Kahekili Ke'eaumoku spoke in the council for the first time. "Lord," he said, "I want to see all of our islands united under your own rule as much as anyone else here, but if there is hope that we can gain the same ends without any more of our brave men dying, should we not try?"

His comments drew a puzzled look from my brother. Later he said to me, "It is curious that Kahekili Keʻeaumoku made no mention of Lono or Kāne, whom the kahuna said spoke through our father."

Kalanimoku and Kahekili Keʻeaumoku had spoken for themselves and Kaʻahumanu. Though Kaʻahumanu kept her silence during this council, she had no confidence in Liholiho's prowess as a warrior and feared that he would be at risk in a battle. Kalanimoku, likewise, thought Liholiho would fare poorly if Kamehameha decided on war.

When all had spoken their minds, Kamehameha raised one broad hand and signaled for silence. Turning to Kekuaokalani, he asked, "Kekua, my brother's last words were to you, yet you have said nothing. Have you no opinion as to their meaning?"

"What I may think does not matter, Uncle," Kekuaokalani replied. "Only your opinion matters here."

"Then here is what *I* think," Kamehameha said to the assembly. "My brother Keliʻimaikaʻi was as courageous in battle as any aliʻi. Even so, he preferred peace to war and he was magnanimous toward those he governed, even former foes. Hence his name, The Good Prince. I think that the god Kāne was telling me through my brother's dying words that it is past time for fighting. Therefore, we will set aside the war god now and serve Lono."

Now Kamehameha again turned to my brother. "Kekuaokalani," he said, "you will go to Kaumualiʻi as my emissary to offer him governance of Kauaʻi, provided he first comes to me here at Waikiki to pledge his fealty. You will be assisted in this by Kalanimoku and your own brother. This is my decision. Kaumualiʻi willing, we will be done at last with war among our own people."

Kaumuali'i was willing; eager even, though he camouflaged his eagerness in royal hauteur. We, Kamehameha's envoys, were careful not to puncture this conceit, representing ourselves as supplicants. This, after arriving at Lihue, close to where Kaumuali'i now conducted his court, in one of Kamehameha's newest haole schooners, bristling with cannons.

During the voyage from Honolulu, Kalanimoku instructed my brother and me on the importance of humbling ourselves before the ruler of Kaua'i. "Kaumuali'i is a proud man and he must be allowed to keep his pride before his own people," he said. "You must never lose sight of this." Nor did we. Kaumuali'i had the kneeling kapu and thus when his guards bid us to enter his hale we at once fell to our knees before him and bowed our heads.

Kaumuali'i was sitting cross-legged on a mat on a raised platform. Now he rose so that he could look down upon us from his full height, which in fact was not considerable for an ali'i. He stood with his arms crossed just below his chest.

"So," he said, "my royal cousin Kamehameha has sent you here to sue for peace?"

Kalanimoku and I were kneeling just behind my brother, and I saw his neck and shoulders tense at these words. Kalanimoku leaned forward and whispered to Kekuaokalani. I could not hear what the royal counselor said, but I could see his words' effect because my brother soon relaxed.

Now Kekuaokalani looked up from the hale's floor, still taking care not to meet Kaumuali'i's eyes. "Oh Lord," he began, "the god Kāne spoke to my uncle, Kamehameha, through the dying words of my father, Keli'imaika'i. The god said Lord Kamehameha must put aside Kūkā'ilimoku and serve Lono. Only Lono. The god bid Kamehameha to send us here."

"The god Kāne has ordered Kamehameha to send peace emissaries to me?"

"Yes, Lord," said my brother.

"Kāne now favors me, then?"

"Kāne favors peace over war, Lord," my brother replied. The cords of his neck muscles tightened again as he spoke. He steadied himself and continued. "The god has told Kamehameha that he must allow you to continue to rule Kaua'i, Lord."

"This is truly what the god Kāne has decreed?"

"It is, Lord," my brother said. "And the god has decreed another thing."

Now it was Kaumuali'i who tensed. He frowned, thrust his shoulders forward, and tightened his grip on his own elbows. "And what is that other thing?" he asked.

"The god bids you to come to Waikiki to accept Kamehameha's request that you continue to rule Kaua'i in his stead, Lord."

"Kamehameha is *asking me* to rule Kaua'i *for him*?" Kaumuali'i's voice grew cold. Out of the corner of my still-lowered eyes I could see Kalanimoku stiffen.

"Oh no, Lord," my brother quickly said. "The *god* asks it of you."

Kaumuali'i relaxed again. "The god asks it?" he said.

"Yes, Lord. The god desires this."

"Well we must certainly appease the god Kāne in this regard," said Kaumuali'i. "Tell me," he continued, "how shall I come to Waikiki? Has the god also decreed that I must come in your *haole* vessel?" Now an edge crept into his voice again.

Kekuaokalani responded without hesitation. "No, Lord," he said. "The god wishes you to come with your war fleet and as many of your fighting men as you choose."

"And the god said all this in your father's voice as he lay dying?" Kaumuali'i asked.

"The god did not need so many words to make his wishes known to the kāhuna, Lord," my brother replied.

Kaumuali'i stared intently at my brother, who now returned his gaze just as steadily. No more was spoken in that hale for what seemed to me the longest time as Kaua'i's mō'ī weighed the sincerity of my brother's words and our uncle's offer of peace.

"No," Kaumuali'i said, at last. "Of course not. Tell your Uncle Kamehameha that I will meet him at Waikiki to secure peace between us, as the god wishes. Now come with me to the Heiau o Lono to offer a sacrifice to the god of peace. Then we will feast together."

It is said that when Kaumuali'i's great fleet of double-hulled war canoes rounded Keana Point, the rhythmic chanting of his thousands of warriors could be heard the length of O'ahu's west coast to the beach at Waikiki. The spectacle drew thousands of villagers to the shore. By bringing so many warriors to O'ahu with him, Kaumuali'i meant to demonstrate that he was Kamehameha's equal as a sovereign ruler. And yet, Kaumuali'i's pageantry proved no match for the martial display that awaited him at Waikiki.

My brother and I stood at the water's verge with Kamehameha, Liholiho, Kalanimoku, Kahekili Ke'eaumoku, and the rest of Kameha's council, wearing our finest feather cloaks and helmets. All but Kamehameha carried spears. Ka'ahumanu stood apart at the head of the chiefesses. They wore fine feather robes like the men's, and elaborate flower leis.

Thousands of spear-carrying warriors stood behind us in ranks that extended the full length of Waikiki from Ala Wai to Le'ahi. Their feather cloaks and helmets were new, though none were as fine and bright as ours. And among our company, the yellow feathers of Kamehameha's ceremonial cloak and helmet shone brightest under a clear, blue sky. Standing at the center of this host and towering over everyone else, our uncle Kamehameha seemed like Kāne's sun come to earth. At least, that is how I saw him, and I could only imagine how he and the rest of our assemblage must have appeared to Kaumuali'i and his people as their canoes came into view.

Kaumuali'i would doubtless have expected nothing less from Kamehameha. No doubt, he would have been impressed but unsurprised by the one hundred double-hulled canoes drawn up in two lines stretching from the beach to the edge of the shallow waters of Waikiki. Between them they defined a broad, watery avenue for Kaumuali'i's fleet.

A dozen haole schooners with Hawai'ian crews also awaited Kaumuali'i in the deeper waters off Waikiki. Like the canoes, these ships were anchored in two lines. They were each fitted out with small cannons, three-pounders and six-pounders. The Hawai'ians had loaded the guns with powder charges and wadding only, and at 'Aikake's command, they fired a salute in unison as the Kaua'i fleet drew near.

On shore, we saw the guns' flames and smoke well before we heard their report. But we saw the cannons' effect on Kaumuali'i's people at once, as here and there startled men threw away their paddles and dove into the water. Kaumuali'i did not flinch, however. He stood without moving at the center of his double-hulled canoe's platform, seemingly unperturbed, with his arms folded across his chest. Then, as the thunderclap of the ships' cannons reached the beach and echoed off the hills behind us, clouds of white smoke settled over the water and Kaumuali'i's great fleet momentarily disappeared from view.

Kamehameha and Kaumuali'i had never met before, but now they called each other "brother." At the elaborate feasts that Kamehameha held in Kaumuali'i's honor during the several days the two men spent together, they shared a mat, served each other food, and chewed pepper root for each other's 'awa. They spent many hours huddled together in quiet conversation, most often in the courtyard of a hale especially constructed for the occasion. They continued their discussions during leisurely strolls along the beach, and each night after the feasting ended, the two men retired to the same hale to speak further.

To all who saw them during those days, Kamehameha and Kaumuali'i appeared as equals. But from the moment Kaumuali'i's proud figure had disappeared amid the haze of Kamehameha's cannon smoke to the moment of their parting—when Kamehameha enveloped the king of Kaua'i in a clenching hug—there was no question as to who was the master.

Some days after Kaumuali'i's departure, Kamehameha summoned Liholiho and my brother to the courtyard of his hale. It was midday; Kāne's sun was high in the sky. Kameha was taking his ease on a mat in the shade of a palm tree. He beckoned his visitors to sit beside him.

My brother and Liholiho were a study in contrasts at this time. Like many ali'i both of them were of imposing height, but any similarity ended there. Where Kekuaokalani was broad-shouldered and well-muscled, Liholiho was of slender build and finely featured. Kekuaokalani exuded the confidence of the natural leader he had become. Liholiho, meanwhile, often seemed timid and unsure of himself, a disposition born of the isolation that his own severe kapu had imposed. Nevertheless, it was Liholiho who was destined to rule.

When Kekuaokalani and Liholiho were comfortably seated, Kameha said, "Fighting amongst us is at last at an end. Now that our islands are united, it is time to think about the future. More haoles are coming here every day. 'Aikake and 'Olohana have told me that many more will come in the years ahead, and many more will wish to settle among us. 'Olohana and 'Aikake understand our kapus and honor them when they are among us, but they have lived here for many years. We cannot expect haoles newly arrived here to understand and do likewise." Kamehameha paused while Liholiho and my brother considered this. Then he continued, "Haole ways are easier than our ways, and some of our people may be tempted to follow them. This cannot be allowed. After I am gone, it will fall to you, and you, to see that this does not happen," said Kamehameha, gesturing at Liholiho and Kekuaokalani in turn. "Liholiho, you are young yet, but you are high-born, a nīʻaupiʻo chief and my chosen successor. You will one day rule all of our islands, and you must begin preparing now. You will make yourself known to all the chiefs and chiefesses of each island, those who would succeed them, and their people. And you must come to know them well in turn. No one must doubt your right to rule after I am gone."

At this, Liholiho, who was then fourteen, became agitated. "Will you die soon, father?" he asked. His voice trembled. My brother cast him a disdainful sidelong glance.

Kamehameha frowned and said nothing for a moment. Then he replied, coolly, "No, Liholiho, I will not die soon, but I will die, as all people do, and you must be ready."

Now Kamehameha turned to my brother. "Kekuaokalani, I know that under different circumstances, you would be a great warrior and a great leader of warriors," he said. "You have prepared all your life for this. But what will you do, now that there are no more battles to fight?"

Kekuaokalani shrugged. "I am unsure, Uncle," he said.

"Have you thought about entering the priesthood?" Kamehameha asked.

Kekuaokalani frowned at this suggestion. "And become a simple kahuna?" he protested.

"Oh no, not simple by any means, nephew," Kamehameha replied. "To *you*, I will entrust Kūkāʻilimoku, the same god who has raised up our family to rule over all our islands. You will be the god's keeper and high priest, just as I have been. I will set you over all of the god's heiaus, on every island. The task of enforcing our most sacred kapus will fall to you. Can you do this?"

Without hesitation, Kekuaokalani replied, "Yes, Lord, I can."

Now Kamehameha said, "Kekua, as the keeper of our most fearsome god and the enforcer of his kapus, you will be as important to the life of our people as your royal cousin, Liholiho." And turning to Liholiho, he asked, "Do you understand this, my son?" This was not so much an inquiry as a command.

"Yes, Father," Liholiho replied.

"Good," said Kamehameha. "It shall be done."

As the seasons unfolded, Kekuaokalani assumed the mantle of Kūkāʻilimoku's high priest and gained much stature throughout the islands, just as Kamehameha had foreseen. And all of Kamehameha's chieftains abided by his wish and acknowledged Liholiho as his successor. But Kamehameha was mistaken about one thing: Our peace would prove fragile, for there was yet one more battle to be fought.

Kawaihae and Kailua, 1810-1817

His rule over all our islands secured, Kamehameha returned to his beloved Hawai'i. At this time, he sent me to live with 'Olohana at Kawaihae, with instructions to improve my facility in the haole language. I was an apt student and I enjoyed it. 'Olohana also had much to teach me about the haoles and the world beyond our islands, most particularly about England and America and their people. I attended to all of it.

Kamehameha had granted 'Olohana extensive property holdings at Kawaihae and the Englishman had begun making a home for himself there in 1793. After Kamehameha subdued O'ahu in 1795, 'Olohana took his first Hawaiian wife and brought her to Kawaihae to live with him. She was at that time fifteen years old. 'Olohana was fifty-one. By 1798, 'Olohana had expanded his homestead to some seven structures. These buildings were the first on the Big Island constructed with stone walls in the haole style, albeit with thatched roofs. By this time, well accustomed to our ways and respectful of our kapus, 'Olohana reserved one of these buildings as a residence for his young wife, who bore him two sons before a haole disease carried her away in 1804, at the age of twenty-four. In 1805, when I was about ten years old, 'Olohana took a new wife, our own older sister, Ka'ōanā'eha, who was then eighteen. By the time I went to live with them at Kawaihae in 1812, Ka'ōanā'eha had borne 'Olohana four more children.

At 'Olohana's side, I became fluent in the coarse English of sailors, for that is what he was and that is what he spoke. It was only later, at the missionary school in Kailua, that I learned to speak English as better-educated haoles did, and to read and write it properly as well. Nevertheless, I sometimes lapse unthinkingly into sailors' argot when conversing with lettered haoles, which invariably surprises and often confuses them.

The haole presence in our islands grew steadily in the years of peace after 1810, as more foreign sailors and adventurers came to live among us. French explorers and Spanish and American merchant ships, en route to the Philippines and China, stopped regularly at Kailua, Kawaihae, and at Honolulu. It was quite common for a few sailors from each vessel to find our gentle climate and even gentler women so beguiling that they elected to remain among us.

Inevitably, many of our people found some of their ways enticing as well, despite Kekuaokalani's best efforts to encourage them to follow all the ways of our ancestors. For example, there was the aforementioned rum. It was a more convenient drink than our traditional ʻawa, and it was more intoxicating besides. Many of our people soon learned how to distill it from the sugarcane that grew in abundance in our islands. Kamehameha frowned on this but did not forbid it. Some people have claimed that he made his own rum and drank it liberally, but I never observed this.

Then there was the matter of haole dress. In this regard, it was Kamehameha himself who set a new fashion for our men folk. For years now, he had often taken to wearing the coat Vancouver had given him over his malo, in place of his feathered cloak. Now he oftimes appeared in haole breeches, shirt, vest, and cravat instead of his malo and kapa-cloth robe, though occasionally he would wear his feather cloak over them.

Among the haoles who arrived on our shores in those days was an American sailor named John Parker. When his vessel put in at Kailua in 1809, Parker "jumped ship," in the haole parlance. He soon gained the favor of Hawaiʻi's governor, ʻOlohana, who appointed him superintendent of our uncle's fish ponds. Parker stayed on the Big Island for several years, sailing away again in 1812 and returning in about 1815. When he came back, Parker had a new American musket. He soon found work for it.

Some twenty-two years had passed since Kamehameha sent George Vancouver's cattle to the Waimea uplands and declared that no harm must come to them for ten years. And in that time, as Vancouver had predicted, these unmolested creatures had thrived and their numbers had multiplied. Now they seemed to be everywhere, not only in Waimea but farther afield, having found their way into the lowlands of northern Kohala and even down the foot trails that threaded back and forth across the sheer walls of Waipiʻo Valley. The roaming herds of wild cattle devoured every edible thing in sight, including sweet potato and taro plants, the grass thatching of houses, and even kapa-cloth garments left to dry in the sun. These cattle, bulls and cows alike, had long, fearsome horns and people were afraid to approach them because they were known to charge and gore when challenged. The people had come to call this too-prolific haole gift *ili o Wankuwai*—Vancouver's curse.

Pestered with complaints and at a loss for other solutions, Kamehameha gave Parker leave to shoot as many cattle as he could with his new musket. He was the first person ever granted permission to kill the beasts. Parker wasted no time in this, and soon a new trade—preserving and trading the meat of slaughtered cattle to merchant ship captains for haole goods—was born. Parker married one of Kamehameha's granddaughters and they settled in Waimea.

Kailua was always the first port of call for all haole merchant ships, for their captains were not permitted to visit other ports without Kamehameha's leave. In exchange for trading and watering rights, Kamehameha would exact goods from them such as iron and copper pots, pewter mugs and metal cooking implements, and, whenever he could, weapons and munitions.

Kamehameha formalized these trading rights with papers which haole ship captains were required to present in turn to each island's governor. They were signed by Kamehameha with his own bold "X" and countersigned and dated by ʻOlohana. This was ʻOlohana's idea. "Your permission costs you nothing, but it means everything to them, Lord," ʻOlohana had explained. "Why give away something you can sell?"

Because of the prevalence of American and English merchant ships in our waters, English was the language most commonly used in trade. Though Kamehameha's command of the haole tongue was by now fluent enough for negotiating with the merchant captains, he preferred to remain mostly silent behind a remote, forbidding countenance during these bargaining sessions, with ‘Olohana at his side to speak for him. I was at ‘Olohana's side during many of these negotiations.

One day, Kamehameha admired a haole merchant captain's pocket watch. "Get that for me, Nāmākēha," he said.

"Truly, Uncle?" I asked.

"You can do it, nephew. Go on; get it," Kamehameha said.

The trader, who did not understand a word of our language, looked from one to the other of us.

"The king hankers to have y'er…" Here I hesitated, seeking the word.

"*Pocket watch*," ‘Olohana whispered to me.

"'Y'er watch," I finished. The haole seemed startled to hear a Hawaiian speak to him with such a pronounced English accent.

"But 'tis not for trade, *boy*," he protested.

I translated this for Kamehameha, who had in fact understood the haole perfectly. Maintaining his sternest expression, Kamehameha looked first at the haole and then at me. "Tell him that he smells bad and looks worse," he said.

"The king, my uncle, says 'ta tell ye that he will understand if ye'll not part with y'er watch," I told the haole, "an' that he hopes ye'll understand if he don't give you leave to trade with his own people." Then with a bravado that I truly did not feel, I added, "An' truth be tol' *sir*, I ain't no *boy*. I am King Kamehameha's royal nephew and m'self a grown man. An' I would thank ye to remember that ye be in these islands by my uncle's grace." By the time I had concluded this admonition, both Kamehameha and ‘Olohana were hard put to suppress their smiles.

There was a moment of silence as the merchant captain considered this. Then, extracting the pocket watch from his jacket and handing it to me, he said, "But a'course, I meant no disrespect to ye, *sir*. Please ask y'er uncle the king ta accept this gift with m'compliments."

"Thank ye, sir," I said, and gave the watch to Kamehameha.

After the haole sea captain had left, Kamehameha and ‘Olohana burst into laughter.

"Here, Nāmākēha," my uncle said, returning the watch to me. "This is yours now; you most certainly earned it today." When I left him, Kamehameha was still smiling at the joke he'd played on the haole. I have that haole pocket watch to this day.

As much as Kamehameha enjoyed bargaining with the haole sea captains, he enjoyed fishing more. Kāne's morning light would find him at the shore in Kailua, casting and hauling in fishnets. And as the sun rose from behind the mist-shrouded summit of Mauna Kea, an unusual spectacle was revealed: common fishermen laboring alongside the great Kamehameha.

These same men worked alongside Kamehameha every morning. When he first appeared among them, they were terrified and prostrated themselves in the sand, not daring to look at him. "Rise," Kamehameha said to them. "It is not kapu to help your mōʻī cast his fishnets."

Of course, this was not true. The kapu forbade commoners from standing in the presence of the king, and required them to immediately lie face down upon his approach. Kamehameha had in fact made an exception for these fishermen, although he was careful not to put it that way. "It is kapu *not to help* your lord when he comes to the shore to fish," he told them. "Now, rise!"

In this way, Kamehameha sought to preserve the prostrating kapu of the king, even as he waived it. Kekuaokalani was horrified when he learned of this. "Uncle, the common folk will come to disrespect all aliʻi and all the kapus when they see these men helping you," he exclaimed. "And as *kahuna nui o Kūkāʻilimoku,* I must counsel against this."

"*Nephew,*" Kamehameha replied, "if *I* say that the kapu requires these fishermen to assist me as their mōʻī, then it must be so. And as *my* kahuna nui of Kūkāʻilimoku, you will tell your own people and anyone else who asks that these men help *your* mōʻī because *he has ordered them to,* and that it is kapu to mistake their behavior for anything other than obedience to their king."

"Yes, Lord," Kekuaokalani said. I was present at this exchange, and as Kekuaokalani left Kamehameha's courtyard, he muttered to me, "No good will come of this. You'll see, Nāmākēha."

"Our *cousin*, Liholiho, has disappointed our uncle," Kekuaokalani exclaimed. "He is not applying himself to serious matters, as Kamehameha instructed."

To speed Liholiho's diplomatic voyaging from island to island, Kamehameha had given him the Fair American. But Liholiho, who was as willful as he was irresponsible, had abused our uncle's trust and now Kekuaokalani was incensed.

"He does not confer with the high chiefs and chiefesses of the other islands," Kekuaokalani said, his voice rising in agitation with every word. "Instead he spends all his time feasting with the young nobles and in dissolute carousing with the younger ali'i, kāne and wāhine alike. And he prefers the haole rum to our own 'awa." My brother fairly spat this last, most bitter indictment.

Kekuaokalani had brought his complaints about Liholiho to 'Olohana and me at Kawaihae. We were seated on a mat in the central courtyard of 'Olohana's hillside compound mauka of the Pu'ukoholā Heiau, overlooking the bay.

'Olohana had listened impassively to my brother's outburst. Now he said, "Mind ya tend to y'er own affairs, Kekua. Buttin' heads with that 'un'll do ya no good." 'Olohana spoke in English. Though he looked to my brother as he spoke, he directed his words to me, bidding me to translate them for Kekuaokalani.

'Olohana's counsel did not sit well with my brother. "But what Liholiho does *is* my concern," my brother protested, after I'd translated 'Olohana's words, "because by ignoring Kamehameha's instructions, he has transgressed the most basic of kapus—obedience to his ruler. Moreover, he never visits the heiaus, never consults with my priests. Liholiho is nīʻaupiʻo. He should be setting an example for aliʻi and makaʻāinana alike, but he does not. And as the high priest of Kūkāʻilimoku, that *is* my affair."

Though ʻOlohana understood every word my brother had said in Hawaiian, he waited for me to translate them.

"Kekuaokalani says that 'tis so his business how Liholiho conducts himself, because he ain't observin' our ways as he should, and he's settin' a bad example for others," I explained.

ʻOlohana nodded. "Well, tell y'er brother to belay that an' attend to bein' the most worthy high priest of Kūkāʻilimoku he can be. He does that, an' betimes others will see the difference 'twixt the right of his own ways an' how Liholiho has been behavin' an' most likely come t'agree with Kekua's opinion of 'yer cousin," he said.

"ʻOlohana counsels you to have patience and let matters rest as they are," I told my brother. "He says time is on your side."

In this, ʻOlohana was wrong.

During these years, my brother recruited many young men to join him in the priestly order of Kūkāʻilimoku. They were contemporaries who had trained with him for the aborted invasion of Kauaʻi. Had the invasion proceeded, they would have fought under his command. With the islands united, and facing the unexpected prospect of peace, they had followed Kekuaokalani into the service of the war god. Several hundred of their friends eventually followed them as well.

My brother urged Kahekili Keʻeaumoku to join him, but he politely declined. Though wishing Kekuaokalani well, he said that the priesthood of Kūkāʻilimoku was not for him. Kekuaokalani was disappointed. He had always liked and respected Kahekili Keʻeaumoku and wanted him at his side. "He says the time of the war god has passed," my brother told me.

Foremost in the circle around Kekuaokalani were his two closest friends and followers, Kauiwa and Holo'ialena. They and many of the other young men who had trained with them were already skilled in the use of muskets. Kekuaokalani named Kauiwa and Holo'ialena his principal lieutenants, and lieutenants they became in truth, for the priesthood of Kūkā'ilimoku subsequently took a decidedly martial turn.

With Kekuaokalani's encouragement, mock battles and musket drills became part of the daily regimen of Kūkā'ilimoku's priests. Traveling throughout the islands, Kauiwa and Holo'ialena visited every heiau of the god to supervise the military training of Kekuaokalani's growing corps of kāhuna. The war god's time was not past for them.

I watched this with growing concern, especially after I learned that several members of Kamehameha's council, Ka'ahumanu among them, disapproved of this development. "Why do you train your priests to be soldiers?" I asked my brother one day.

"I train them to fight because they are the war god's kāhuna, and though we face no threats today, Nāmākēha, no one knows what tomorrow may bring," he replied. "Our uncle or Liholiho may yet have need of spirited young warriors to defend all that Kamehameha has gained for us. I do it out of love for Kamehameha, our cousin, and all of our people."

I still had my doubts about the wisdom of turning the war god's priests into warriors, but I did not want to argue with Kekuaokalani about it that day, so I let the matter rest.

Others questioned Kekuaokalani's actions, however—Ka'ahumanu and her relatives on Kamehameha's council. Kalanimoku raised the issue before Kamehameha in council one day.

"Lord, your nephew Kekuaokalani schools his kāhuna as soldiers," Kalanimoku complained. "They fight regularly in mock battles and even drill with pū."

"I am here, Kalanimoku," Kekuaokalani interjected, "and since I am, why don't you speak of this to me?"

"I serve our lord, Kamehameha, and it is only natural that I speak of you to him, *Kekuaokalani*," Kalanimoku replied.

Kamehameha ignored this exchange. He turned to my brother. "This is the first I have heard of this, nephew," he said. "Please explain to me why you train these kāhuna to fight." That our uncle was unaware of this was, I think, due to his interests in fishing and other domestic pursuits, to the exclusion of the daily details of governance, which he was content to leave to Kalanimoku.

"They are spirited young men, Uncle," my brother replied. "And as priests of your war god Kūkā'ilimoku, they should be ready to serve you and the kingdom as soldiers as well," he said. "It is *only natural*, after all." He turned toward Kalanimoku as he said this last; he could not help himself. Kalanimoku frowned, but more worrisome to me was the angry expression that passed across Ka'ahumanu's face.

"Very well, nephew," Kamehameha said, continuing to ignore the tension between his nephew, his prime minister, and his consort. "I see no harm in this, and, as you say, your priests are young and spirited." Now he turned to his prime minister and said, "They may continue to train, Kalanimoku. It will do them some good, and perhaps we will again need trained fighters someday."

"And what of these priests' drills with pū po'ohiwi, Lord?" Kalanimoku asked.

"Let Kekuaokalani's priests train with haole arms as well," Kamehameha said. "Let them keep the pū po'ohiwi they now have."

"Yes, Lord," Kalanimoku said; his mō'ī had spoken and that was the end of it.

Now Kamehameha turned to my brother and said, "Kekuaokalani, it is good that these young priests train in the old way, but these are not the old days, when too many of our people were slain in mock battles, as was my own kahu, Kekūhaupi'o." Kamehameha paused before continuing. "You must take care to ensure that this does not happen now."

"I will, Uncle," my brother replied.

"Good enough," said Kameha. "I think we have considered enough matters for today. You may all go; I am going fishing now."

By 1817, Kamehameha's days had settled into a comfortable routine. Most afternoons, after he was done fishing with his nets and bargaining with visiting haole merchantmen, Kamehameha would swim or resume fishing from a canoe with a line and bone hook, or, when Kanaloa and Lono stirred up the sea in Kailua bay sufficiently, he would ride the waves. At those times, he was often joined by many other people—women, men, boys, and girls, ali'i and even maka'āinana, whom Kamehameha allowed to ride the waves with him in contravention of our traditional kapu against commoners sharing waves with ali'i.

My brother complained about this as well, but not directly to Kamehameha. "Nāmākēha, our uncle is becoming too familiar with the kānaka," he said to me. "Why does he allow them to ride the waves with him now?"

I put the question to Kamehameha, and though I was diplomatic about it, Kameha still discerned the source of the misgiving.

"It gives me pleasure to ride the waves with my people, Nāmākēha," he replied. "Thus, I have decreed that when the gods roil the sea, the kapu is freed for all at the water's edge, and only there. And you can remind your brother that I have decreed that ali'i and maka'āinana alike must always respect *my* line through the waves, as their mō'ī."

Kekuaokalani was not consoled. "If our uncle continues to suspend kapus as it pleases him, what will become of our laws when he is gone? And what will become of our people without our laws?" I had no answer.

When he was not engaged in fishing or surf riding, Kamehameha would inquire about such matters as the progress of the season's harvests, the construction and maintenance of fishponds, the manufacture of kapa cloth, and the other industries of our people. Though his hair had turned gray, Kamehameha was still robust in body and his appetite for life was yet unquenched. In 1814, he fathered a second child by his sacred wife Keopuolani—a boy whom they named Kauikeaouli.

Though Kamehameha had already taken many wives and fathered many children by them, he took two more partners during this time, young chiefesses whom he invited to warm his sleeping mat in his advanced age. One of these wāhine was Kalanimoku's own sister, Manono. My brother was often in Kamehameha's company at Kailua, and thus also frequently around Manono. Kekuaokalani and Manono were close in age, and he was soon attracted to her.

One evening, Manono danced a hula for Kamehameha, several of his advisers, my brother, and me. This hula was very sensual. Even though she was dancing for Kamehameha that night, it seemed to Kekuaokalani that she meant every provocative gesture for him. And as she danced, Kekuaokalani said to me, "She is a beautiful wahine, perhaps the most striking I have ever laid eyes upon." From that moment, my brother was smitten.

Manono had already noticed Kekuaokalani, but whenever the two were together in Kamehameha's presence, she averted her eyes for fear of offending our uncle. Kekuaokalani, however, could not keep his eyes off her and when she felt his gaze upon her, she would respond with a shy smile. Kamehameha was bound to notice.

One day he called the pair to him and said, "I see how you look at each other. You need not withhold your affections on my account. I will not be offended if you want to lie together. And Kekua, it is past time you had a partner."

And so it was that Manono became, as the haoles say, my "sister-in-law." Unlike his contemporaries, Kekuaokalani never took another partner. "Manono is more than enough wahine for me," he told me one day when I teased him about this.

"And your brother Kekuaokalani is more than enough kāne for me," said Manono, who overheard our exchange. She swayed her hips seductively and grinned at Kekuaokalani as she spoke. She never sought another partner either.

Our cousin Liholiho also took the first of four wives around this time. Her name was Kamehamalu, and she was Liholiho's own half-sister by Ka'ahumanu's sister Kalakua Kaheiheimale, one of more than twenty wives Kamehameha had taken by this time. Both Kamehameha and Ka'ahumanu encouraged this match; Kamehameha because any child of their union would be a high-born nī'aupi'o ali'i, and Ka'ahumanu because marriage to her own niece would bind Liholiho even closer to her.

The pleasant cadence of Kamehameha's life in these years stood in marked contrast to the nearly constant strife of the decades that had preceded them. And as he turned his attention more and more to domestic pursuits, Kamehameha remained content to leave the more taxing matters of the islands' governance to Kalanimoku.

I questioned Kamehameha about this one day after he, 'Olohana, and I had completed another bargaining session with a China-bound haole merchant captain at Kailua. "Uncle, does it ever concern you that Kalanimoku has gathered so much authority to himself?" I asked.

"Nāmākēha, Kalanimoku has only the authority that *I* have given him," he said. "And I trust him not to abuse it. But if he ever should, *I* can just as easily take it back. For now," he concluded, "I am at ease with him."

In truth, I had not put this question to Kamehameha for myself. As I had in the matter of surf riding, I raised it on behalf of my brother. Ever since Kamehameha had so thoroughly upbraided Kekuaokalani for counseling him against fishing with commoners, my brother had been reluctant to question our uncle about anything related to enforcement of the kapus and now, affairs of state. Kamehameha's seeming indifference to Kalanimoku's growing influence troubled Kekuaokalani, and he was not reassured when I told him what Kamehameha had said.

"Certainly, Kalanimoku has no more authority than Kamehameha himself allows," Kekuaokalani said, "but I worry that Kalanimoku's influence grows too much while our uncle devotes his days to fishing and surf riding. And does Kamehameha notice how much time Kalanimoku spends with Ka'ahumanu? Does he know that Ka'ahumanu is always present when Kalanimoku confers with Liholiho? I think not."

Though he could not prove it, Kekuaokalani was convinced that Kalanimoku never decided any important matter without first consulting Ka'ahumanu. He also believed that when Liholiho was present at these deliberations, he was no more than a passive bystander. "Our cousin has ever been Ka'ahumanu's keiki," he said. "And he always will be."

Was Kamehameha, now in his seventh decade, so distracted by his own pursuits that he was truly unaware of Kalanimoku's and Ka'ahumanu's relationship and Liholiho's feckless behavior? Or did he know and simply wish to avoid strife over the former while having abandoned hope of altering the latter? I have no answer to these questions.

In any case, Kamehameha continued to fish, inspect his fish ponds, swim, ride the waves, and bargain with haole merchantmen, as all the while Ka'ahumanu met daily with his prime minister, his royal son and heir abjured his princely responsibilities, and his favorite nephew, my brother, the high priest of Kūkā'ilimoku, fumed in silence.

Pauoa, Oʻahu 1858

The king, queen, and most of the court have gone to Maui, where the king seeks relief from his terrible asthma. Esther, who is little Prince Albert's nurse and governess, has gone with them. I would have gone as well, but not feeling well again, I chose to stay home.

Are you sure you will be alright staying here without me? Esther asks before she departs for the harbor in Honolulu, where a ship awaits the royal party.

Do not trouble yourself about me. I will manage tolerably well, I say. *Perhaps I shall join you in Maui later.*

David is also going, Esther says. *And his sister Lili is going as well.* Esther adds this a bit too quickly; almost parenthetically. I already know this, of course. Kalākaua, I suspect, is more than just a good friend of Esther's; Lili has become their companion and chaperon in public.

Outwardly, Esther and Kalākaua are behaving as proper Victorians. But I believe Esther understands that I see past this façade and she wants reassuring that I have no objection. I smile. *Of course, they are both going,* I say. *It will be nice for you to have them along.* I leave it at that, in part from necessity and in part because I still appreciate the old ways in such matters.

I am not entirely alone here. Our servants, Gideon and his wife, Sarah, live on the property with their son, Ezra. They have been with us since 1851. Gideon and Sarah are about forty, I think. They are uncertain of their birth dates because their parents, being commoners, knew nothing of the haole calendar. Their parents told them, however, that my uncle, the great Kamehameha, was yet living when they were born, hence my estimate of their ages. Their son Ezra is fifteen; a minister noted his birth date in a church baptismal record.

Ezra is a handsome youth. His eyes reflect intelligence; his face is lean with even and well-defined features and yet he is only of middling height, in the way of our common people. Ezra is the youngest and the only one of Gideon's and Sarah's four children still living. Successive epidemics carried away two brothers and a sister.

The family lives together in a three-room, thatched-roof dwelling at the rear of our property, opposite the main house among our guava, passion fruit, and banana trees. I can see their dwelling from our lanai.

Gideon and Sarah are from Wai'anae, on the coast northwest of Honolulu. For generations, their forebears farmed the land there as tenants of successive chieftains, who held the land at the pleasure of a succession of O'ahu rulers, and later by leave of successive Kamehamehas and their ministers. Chieftains and rulers came and went, but Gideon's and Sarah's people stayed, true maka'āinana, people of the land. They are people of the land no longer.

Eight years ago, after generations of tenancy, Gideon and Sarah became landowners in their own right, thanks to an undertaking by the legislature known as the *Great Mahele*—the great division of the royal lands. The ali'i were the first to receive titles to land, after the king, of course. The king then gave a portion of his lands to the government, for division among the maka'āinana. Gideon and Sarah were among some ten thousand commoners throughout the islands who gained permanent titles to their own small parcels through this division. Unfortunately for them, haoles also gained the right to own land here at the same time. Previously permitted only to lease, they were eager to offer cash in exchange for the commoners' new landholdings and thousands eagerly accepted, Gideon and Sarah among them.

My father and mother thought they could sell their property, use the money to buy some haole goods they so much wanted, and continue to farm the land as tenants, as they had always done, Ezra says. *They thought that the haole who bought their land would accept vegetables and hogs as rent payment, as the king and chiefs had done,* he tells me. But Ezra's parents had been evicted from their home by the new landowner, a scion of American missionaries who cared nothing for taro, sweet potatoes, or pigs, and was buying up and consolidating the commoners' small parcels for sugar production. Forced off the land, Gideon and Sarah moved to Honolulu with their son in search of employment as wage laborers. That is how they came to work for us.

My parents do not understand that the land does not mean the same thing to the haoles as it means to them, says Ezra, who does understand, with a wisdom perhaps beyond his years. *For my parents,* he says, *the land is nourishment.*

When Ezra speaks of the land as "nourishment" he speaks of a deep attachment to the ʻāina that has always fed, clothed, and sheltered us. He speaks of how our people worked the land to grow enough produce and raise enough livestock to provide for themselves after paying their "taxes" at Makahiki time, with no further thought beyond their daily sustenance and happiness. *The haoles think differently,* Ezra says. *For them the land is only good for one thing—money, and they never have enough of that.*

I have seen this for myself. Soon after I obtained title in the Mahele to a portion of my father's ancestral lands in Kohala, and well before the haoles were permitted to buy land here, an American came to me, eager lease my property. He approached other aliʻi landholders as well. He had no thought of farming the land for his own family; he wanted to grow sugar cane for export and he has remained ever-avid for more land. Lately, this American has been pestering me to sell him my land outright. Unlike Ezra's parents, I have refused. I would rather share in his profits through steady lease income than give up my land for a one-time windfall.

We are sitting on my lanai as we speak. Ezra has come to bring me tea and I have invited him to stay and talk with me for a while before I turn in. The day's light is fading; the evening's first stars are coming out overhead, and across from where we sit, the wavering light of an oil lamp appears in the window of the servants' quarters.

Ezra gestures at the small cottage. *They do not understand,* he says again.

Neither of us speaks for a time. Then I say to Ezra, *Tell me, what do you want for yourself?*

I want more than that, he replies, gesturing at the small house he shares with Gideon and Sarah. *I do not want to be just a kanaka.*

To become more than a kanaka, you must learn to speak with the haoles in their own language, I say. *You must learn to speak English like a white man, to read it and write it as well as any white man.*

I already read and write Hawaiian, says Ezra, who has attended a free public school where the children of the maka'āinana are taught in our own language. *I can learn to speak, read, and write English too.*

Recalling how I learned to speak English with 'Olohana's help and how I later learned to speak, read, and write proper English from the early missionaries, I tell Ezra, *I believe you can.*

In another time, I would not have condescended to associate so easily with a commoner, a "kanaka" such as Ezra. It shames me to think of this, and I am all at once saddened for Sarah, Gideon, and Ezra, and all the Hawaiians who have been, or will soon be separated from the land and estranged from their heritage.

It is for Ezra, as well as for Esther and her friends, that I write.

Ka'ahumanu

E iho ana o luna
E pi'i ana o lalo
E huiana nāmoku
E kūana ka paia

That which is above will come down
That which is down will rise up
The islands shall unite
The walls shall stand firm

-- The Hawaiian prophet Kapihe

Kailua-Kona, May 1819

Kāne's sun, touching the edge of the sea, had turned Lono's clouds ominous blood red by the time the summons reached Kawaihae. I was watching the sunset from the courtyard of 'Olohana's compound above the great heiau when a large double-hulled canoe entered the bay. It was one of Kamehameha's peleleu canoes, built for war but now reserved for coastal voyaging. It carried two haole-rigged sails on tall masts stepped on a wide central deck. The afternoon winds had diminished with the failing light and the canoe's sails were by this time more decorative than functional. There were more than a dozen men on board—six paddlers in each hull and two others on the central platform, one steering and another who was chanting and beating a drum. I could see the deep orange glint of the setting sun through the water that spilled from twelve paddle blades as they rose and fell as one to the cadence of the chant and drum beat.

Ia wa'a nui
That large canoe
Ia wa'a kioloa
That long canoe
Ia wa'a peleleu
That broad canoe
A lele mamala
Let chips fly
A manu a uka
The bird of the upland

A manu a kai
The bird of the lowland
'I'wi polena
The red honeycreeper
A kau ka hoku
The stars hang above
A kau ka malama
The daylight arrives
A pae i kula
Bring the canoe ashore
'Amama ua noa
The kapu is lifted

The chanting and drumming were slow at first, but their tempo intensified as the canoe neared the beach. The singer's urgency communicated to the broad backs, powerful shoulders, and strong arms of the paddlers, who drove the canoe forward with ever-increasing force. The chanting and drumming crescendoed and climaxed as the canoe, propelled by a final stroke of twelve paddle blades, came to rest half out of the water on the damp, sandy shore.

"'Olohana! Nāmākēha!" You must come to Kailua with us at once!" the helmsman cried. "Our lord, Kamehameha, has taken gravely ill!"

'Olohana and I hurriedly made ready to go. Darkness had fallen by the time we set off, but the night was clear and the coastline was illuminated, albeit dimly, by a full moon. There was no more chanting or drumming and very little talking, and for some time there was no wind. We journeyed on in silence, save for the splashing of a dozen paddle blades and water slapping against the canoe hulls.

'Olohana steered the canoe while the other two men and I relieved the paddlers at intervals as they tired, and we made good progress, even with empty sails. We continued to paddle when Lono's wind filled our sails again, and we reached Kailua just as Kāne's dawn was breaking behind the darkened uplands. We were exhausted, but there was no time for resting.

When Kamehameha returned to the Big Island, he had taken up residence with Ka'ahumanu and Keopuolani at Kamakahonu, just to the north of Kailua proper. There, he had directed his people to build a new royal compound for him and his wives, opposite the 'Ahu'ena Heiau, where Kameha had honored Ka'ahumanu following the conquest of O'ahu twenty-three years earlier. Fish were abundant in the small inlet at Kamakahonu, which also boasted excellent surf riding. Certainly, it was the prospect of big waves on windy days and plentiful fishing on still days that had drawn Kamehameha to the site.

This morning, the waters of Kailua Bay were calm, ruffled only by a light breeze. Silence enveloped the village. We saw no one about, though this was at a time when the fishermen of the area, Kamehameha often among them, would usually be preparing for their day's work. It was as if the place were holding its breath.

A lone figure on the beach beckoned to us as we neared the shore. It was Kekuaokalani. "Hurry!" he called. "You are only just in time. I fear that Kamehameha is near death."

Kamehameha had taken ill several days previously. He had gone fishing by himself early in the morning in a small outrigger canoe, as he would do occasionally. He had only just returned when he was stricken.

"Kamehameha was pulling his canoe onto the beach when all at once he clutched his head and sank to his knees," my brother recounted. "I was just then coming to greet him and I ran to help, but he would not have it."

Instead, Kamehameha waved my brother away and struggled to his feet. Then he said to him, "Fishing has fatigued me this morning, Kekua. I must rest now."

"Our uncle was breathing poorly and he did not look well," Kekuaokalani told me. "He was unsteady on his feet and unable to take more than two steps without my help."

There were other people about and Kamehameha did not want them to see that he was indisposed. "Come, walk with me, Kekuaokalani," he said in a voice that was sure to be overheard. Then he laid an arm around my brother's shoulders as if in a fatherly gesture, lowered his voice, and said, "And I will lean on you as we go."

Despite my brother's forewarning, I was shaken by the sight of Kamehameha's still form as I entered his hale. I had seen my uncle at rest before, but now he seemed inert. In that moment, I thought that his mana had already fled. I was on the verge of wailing my profound grief when Kamehameha weakly raised one hand and beckoned us to approach him. Kalanimoku, several priests and chieftains, Ka'ahumanu, Kahekili Ke'eaumoku, and Hoapili were gathered around Kamehameha. Keopuolani was conspicuous by her absence. Her kapu had kept her away. It was so strong that the others would have been required to partially or fully disrobe in her presence.

"Kekuaokalani, Nāmākēha, 'Olohana—is that you? Come closer so that I can see you better," Kamehameha said. His voice was weak and I strained to hear him. "It has grown so dark in here."

Indeed, the interior of Kamehameha's hale was deep in shadows, but I could see the entire tableau clearly: my uncle supine on a mat, covered to mid-chest with several kapa cloths; his prime minister and his chieftains to one side; Ka'ahumanu, Kahekili Ke'eaumoku, and Hoapili to the other; and the priests between them. I could make out their worried expressions and the tears in their eyes. And even in the weak light, I could see that my uncle's color was poor, almost gray, and his face was drawn. But more disturbing to me than any of these sights was the sound of Kamehameha's labored breathing.

'Olohana, Kekuaokalani, and I bent over Kamehameha and gently rubbed noses with him. "Kekuaokalani, Nāmākēha, my beloved nephews, and 'Olohana, my dear friend and brother, I am so glad you are here with me now," Kamehameha said. He struggled to speak amid ragged breaths and the effort tired him. When he caught his breath he spoke to each of us in turn.

To my brother, Kamehameha said, "Kekuaokalani, preserve the kapus after I am gone. Our people must continue to observe them, lest they become no better than the haoles."

"I will, Uncle," Kekuaokalani replied, fighting back tears.

"And one more thing, nephew," Kamehameha continued. "The kāhuna must not sacrifice anyone to the gods for me. You will see to this?"

"Yes, Uncle," my brother replied. He was sobbing now.

"'Olohana," Kamehameha said, "you have long been a loyal adviser and friend to me. My son, Liholiho, will likewise need your advice and steady friendship. Promise me that you will serve him as you have always served me."

'Olohana grasped my uncle's hand firmly and said, "I could do no less, Lord."

To me, Kamehameha said, "Nāmākēha, tell me you will continue to be a good friend and companion to Liholiho as you have always been."

My voice close to breaking, I answered, "Uncle, I will ever be Liholiho's aikāne."

"Good," Kamehameha said. Then he motioned to Hoapili to come close. 'Olohana, Kekuaokalani, and I stepped away so that Ka'ahumanu's cousin, Hoapili, could approach. Kamehameha spoke so softly to him that we could not hear what he said. Next, Kamehameha asked to speak to Kalanimoku and Ka'ahumanu. Again, we could not make out his words to them. At length, Kamehameha asked, "Where is my son, Liholiho? Why is he not here yet? I would speak to him before I die."

"He has been at Keauhou, Lord," Kalanimoku replied. "He is coming now."

"Good," said Kamehameha. "I can wait." Then he sighed, closed his eyes, and slept.

Long hours passed as we kept a quiet vigil around Kamehameha's still form. The sun was lowering toward the ocean when Kamehameha opened his eyes and spoke to us again. "Where is Liholiho?" he asked, his voice breathy and faint. "Has he not come yet?"

"No, Lord," Kalanimoku replied, "he has not yet arrived."

"But he is coming?"

"Yes, Lord," Kalanimoku said, adding, "I *know* he is coming." Then, perhaps discomfited by his own uncertainty, Kalanimoku changed the subject. "You have not eaten all day, Lord," he said. "Will you take something now?"

"No, thank you, Kalanimoku," Kamehameha replied after a long pause. "I am not hungry now; I will wait for the boy."

"*The boy.*" All those gathered exchanged knowing glances. Those two words spoke volumes to us. They hung in the air as night fell and Kamehameha slipped away from us, deep in sleep once more.

Throughout the night, while we kept silent watch, Kamehameha slumbered, his shallow breathing the hale's only sound. There was no need to waken Kamehameha that night, for Liholiho did not come.

Kamehameha did not stir again until early morning. Kailua was still slumbering in the shadow of Mauna Kea when he opened his eyes and grunted as he struggled to raise himself from his mat. He had no need to ask after Liholiho this morning; he could see that his son was not among those gathered close around him. Instead, he inquired after Liholiho's little brother. "Where is my keiki?" he asked. "Where is Kauikeaouli? Why is he not here?"

"Kauikeaouli is yet at the mua, Lord," replied Kalanimoku. "We did not want to fetch him at this hour; we feared that he would cry and disturb you."

"Please bring him to me now," said Kamehameha.

My other royal cousin, then just five years old, was brought into Kamehameha's presence. When he saw his father lying there and our sad faces, the little boy understood that something was dreadfully wrong. He began to whimper.

Kamehameha tried to console him. "Come to me, my beloved keiki," he said, in a voice barely above a whisper. Now, Kauikeaouli's sobs came closer and closer together until they fused into a high-pitched wail. "Don't be afraid," Kamehameha implored. "Come closer to me."

Still crying, Kauikeaouli slowly edged closer until at last Kamehameha reached out with one long arm and gathered the little boy to his chest. This effort cost him dearly and his breaths came in quick, shallow progression as Kauikeaouli settled against him. But as Kamehameha's arm enfolded my cousin, Kauikeaouli must have sensed that his father's strength was failing and wailed even louder.

"Hush, hush," Kamehameha soothed. "Soon I will join my ancestors. But I will always watch over you, Kauikeaouli. I will become your own ʻaumakua." These words quieted Kauikeaouli at last. Now Kamehameha drew the little boy closer and said so softly that we could hardly hear him, "Kiss me, my beloved son." Kauikeaouli bent his little face low over his father's broad visage and gently rubbed the tip of his small nose against Kamehameha's.

At this moment, Liholiho burst through the door of the hale and rushed to Kamehameha's side, weeping and wailing. "Father!" he cried, "Do not leave us!"

Kamehameha sighed. He rubbed noses with Liholiho and whispered something to him. Then he looked from his two high-born sons to the others gathered around him. Willing himself to speak loudly enough for all to hear him clearly, he said to us, "E oni wale no ʻoukou i kuʻu pono ʻaʻole e pau." *Endless is the good I have given you to enjoy.*

Now Kamehameha closed his eyes and took his last breath. As his mana departed, his arms went slack, and Kauikeaouli commenced to wail again, even louder than before, his cries almost immediately submerged in the chorus of our own grief.

It was Saturday, May 8, 1819.

Liholiho did not remain long at Kailua. No sooner had he arrived than he was required to leave, lest proximity to his father's corpse defile his own person. He fled north to Kawaihae with his retinue of young nobles, where he remained for the next ten days, drinking haole rum and disporting with women while in Kailua the heat of the imu melted Kamehameha's flesh from his bones. During this time, in fact, the whole of the Hawaiian archipelago plunged into licentiousness as the kapus against men and women eating together and against women eating pork, roasted bananas, and other foods were suspended. Kekuaokalani and I had heard of this traditional way of mourning a great and beloved mōʻī, but we ourselves had never before witnessed it. Kamehameha, after all, was the only mōʻī we had ever known.

I was astonished by the spectacle of men and women eating together. My brother was profoundly disturbed. "Why should our mōʻī's death give people license to violate the kapus he held sacred?" Kekuaokalani asked. "Our people's misbehavior now dishonors his life, and you can be sure that no good will come of it, Nāmākēha."

"But surely, brother, this is a passing thing," I said. "Our people have ever mourned the death of beloved rulers in this way and the kapus have always been restored when the people have finished grieving."

"And when was the last time this happened?" rejoined my brother. He did not wait for an answer. "It was when Alapaʻi died, before you and I were born. It didn't happen when Kalaniʻōpuʻu died because war broke out so soon after his death. And of course, no one mourned for Kiwalaʻō in this fashion, for he was never a true mōʻī. Do you think anyone alive remembers this now?"

"Does it matter?" I asked. "Everyone knows about it. We have all heard the stories."

"Oh yes, Nāmākēha, everyone has heard the stories. But I fear that for most of our people today, they are just stories," Kekuaokalani said. "And think of how much has changed since the days of Alapaʻi. Haoles were unknown to us then. Now they live among us. They do not observe our kapus, and nothing ill has befallen them because of this. This is not just a story to our people, Nāmākēha; they *see* it."

"But Kekua, Kamehameha ruled that the haole ways were not our ways," I protested. "Our people still understand this. Liholiho understands this—he will honor his father and restore the kapus when he returns."

"You are right; it all depends upon Liholiho," Kekuaokalani said. Now his tone turned bitter. "And that, little brother," he spat, "*that* is what worries me."

I did not share my brother's unease at this time. Liholiho's inner circle was composed of the sons and nephews of the chieftains who had fought with Kamehameha to unite the islands, and who had raised their sons to respect the kapus. Moreover, as high-born aliʻi themselves, Liholiho's advisers enjoyed all the benefits the kapus conferred upon the nobility: status, land, and wealth without effort. What chance was there that they would ever counsel Liholiho to do anything other than uphold the kapus, as his own father and their fathers had done? Little to none, or so it seemed to me.

But I had not reckoned with Kaʻahumanu or Keopuolani, for where they were concerned, our royal cousin proved as malleable as he was feckless.

Kawaihae, May 1819

Liholiho was lounging with some of his friends in a palm grove near the beach when Kekuaokalani and I reached Kawaihae. Though it was not yet midday, he and his companions were already drinking rum. Liholiho greeted us with a desultory wave when he saw us approaching.

"My cousin, the kahuna nui of my father's god Kūkāʻilimoku, comes to see me, with his brother and dear companion of my childhood, Nāmākēha," he said, to no one in particular. "Welcome, cousins."

I could smell the liquor on Liholiho's breath as we knelt next to him. My brother had journeyed to Kawaihae to urge our cousin to restore the kapus before returning to Kailua. Kekuaokalani had entreated me to accompany him. "I believe Liholiho has some affection for you yet, Nāmākēha," he said. "He may be more easily persuaded if you are with me when I speak with him."

Kekuaokalani hoped that my presence would help dispel the chill that had settled over his own relations with our royal cousin since Kamehameha's death. My brother had only himself to blame for this state of affairs, for he had always been distant toward Liholiho when he was a boy, and had made no effort to befriend him in later years. I had remained cordial with him.

"*Lord*," Kekuaokalani began, and then paused. I could tell that it had cost my brother some effort to use the honorific, and perhaps Liholiho sensed it as well. "Lord," he resumed, "your father's bones have been purified, and Kailua is no longer a place of defilement for you. Your people await your return, but you must first restore the kapus."

"But cousin, my foster mother Ka'ahumanu has not yet summoned me to Kailua," Liholiho replied. "I must await word from her. Do you bring word from Ka'ahumanu?"

"Lord...my brother and I have come to bring you this word from Kailua which you have been awaiting," Kekuaokalani said. "The time has come for you to restore the kapus and return."

Indeed, Kekuaokalani's decision to travel to Kawaihae had been precipitated by news that Ka'ahumanu was about to recall Liholiho to Kailua while the people still flouted the kapus. This intelligence had come from my brother's closest advisers in the priesthood, Kauiwa and Holo'ialena, who also reported that Ka'ahumanu had secretly eaten kapu foods while Kamehameha yet lived.

"Do you see what this means, Nāmākēha?" Kekuaokalani asked me when he heard this news. Then he answered his own question. "It means that Ka'ahumanu does not want the kapus restored! She wants to end them. I think she has long wanted to end them. If Liholiho returns to Kailua without first restoring the kapus, Ka'ahumanu will see to it that he never does. We cannot allow this to happen. We must speak to Liholiho first."

Having considered my brother's words, Liholiho now turned to me. "So my foster-mother and *kahu*, Ka'ahumanu, wishes me to restore the kapus now, Nāmākēha?" he asked.

I was surprised to hear Liholiho speak of Ka'ahumanu as his kahu. When had Ka'ahumanu supplanted Kalanimoku in this role? And what did it mean that a wahine had become kahu to a kāne? I carefully weighed each word of my response.

"As Kekuaokalani, the kahuna nui of your father's god, Kūkā'ilimoku, has said, the time of mourning for your father is past and it is time to restore the old ways," I replied. "You will be our mō'ī, Liholiho, and it falls to you to restore the kapus, as your own father would have wished and as he would advise you now."

Liholiho pondered this for a moment, and then said, "It is true, Nāmākēha. My father would wish the kapus restored, and so I shall restore them—when I return to Kailua. But I must remain here until Ka'ahumanu summons me." Liholiho addressed these remarks to me as if my brother was not present.

Kekuaokalani could no longer contain himself. "Liholiho—*Lord*," he exclaimed, "*you are the mō'ī.* You may go where you will and act as you will. You need not wait for anyone's summons. But I beg you: Do not countenance men and women eating together. Likewise, do not look away while women yet eat kapu foods and enter the heiaus at will, as they do now at Kailua and elsewhere. Right order must be restored; you, our mō'ī, must restore it *now*."

"Kekuaokalani," Liholiho said, turning to my brother at last, "my father left you the god, but he left the kingdom to me, and it is not for you to tell me what I must do or not do. As mō'ī, I choose to remain at Kawaihae until Ka'ahumanu summons me to Kailua. Now would you care to join my friends and me? The haole rum is *very* good."

I had never seriously questioned the kapus that ordered our peoples' lives in those days. After all, why would I? I was *ali'i*; I was a member of the great King Kamehameha's immediate family; and I was male. I had been born to benefit from the kapus. The entire world—such as I knew of it—seemed open to me. I never considered the inequities our kapus visited upon the maka'āinana at large and upon our ali'i women in particular. Indeed, the concept was foreign to me.

Yet I had also come of age at a time when haoles were living alongside us, and anyone could see that there were other ways of living. It was common knowledge, for example, that haole men thought it odd that we Hawai'ian men would neither eat with our women nor allow our women to cook for us. In the recesses of my own mind, I had begun to wonder if the haoles might be right.

One day I discovered that Ka'ahumanu's younger brother, Kahekili Ke'eaumoku, had turned his back on our gods and our kapus. "Kahekili," I had said to him, “Kekuaokalani told me that you believe the time of the war god is past. Do you feel the same way about our other gods?”

“Look to the haoles,” he replied. “They do not follow our gods. I believe they have shown us that the time of our gods is past, Nāmākēha.”

“Then what of our kapus?” I asked.

“If the gods’ time is past, then it is past time to end *their* kapus,” he said.

I was shaken by Kahekili Ke‘eaumoku’s certainty on these questions, and doubly shaken by my own certainty that his sister, Ka‘ahumanu, shared his rejection of the gods and the kapus. Thus, even as I accompanied Kekuaokalani to Kawaihae to convince Liholiho to restore the kapus, I doubted we would succeed. I nevertheless suppressed my doubts in hopes of avoiding a clash that, looking back now, I must already have known was coming.

Kailua-Kona, May 1819

Liholiho's sacred mother Keopuolani had emerged from her hale to walk abroad in the daytime. No one preceded her to warn others of her coming, so those who had the misfortune to be in her path had no time to flee to avoid her approaching shadow. With the sun already well seaward on this cloudless, late afternoon, Keopuolani cast a long shadow as she walked along the beach at Kailua. The best anyone could do was to fall to the ground as she approached. The beach was crowded with fishermen cleaning their catches or mending their nets, women beating bark into kapa cloth, and keiki playing amid their elders. Keopuolani's shadow brushed the still, prone forms of dozens of people just mauka as she walked along the water's edge. Yet she of the unforgiving burning kapu seemed to neither notice nor care. Looking straight ahead, Keopuolani smiled and sang to herself as she walked. She was on her way to Ka'ahumanu's hale.

To the onlookers, it was as if the ground had trembled in advance of an angry eruption by Pele, the goddess of the volcano.

Kekuaokalani and I had just returned from Kawaihae, where Liholiho still remained with his entourage. Already disturbed by our cousin's refusal to restore the kapus at once, my brother was dismayed when he learned what Keopuolani had done.

E ka lalani o ke ʻkua,
E ka pukui akua,
E ka mano o ke ʻkua,
E kaikuaana o ke ʻkua,
E ke ʻkua muki,
E ke ʻkua hawananawana,
E ke ʻkua kiai o ka po,
E keʼkua alaalawa oke aumoe,
E ihio, e ala, e oni, e eu,
Eia ka mea ai a oukou la, he hale.

It is no simple thing to translate our language into the haoles' rough tongue, but I will do my best:

Ye forty thousand gods,
Ye four hundred thousand gods,
Ye rows of gods,
Ye collection of gods,
Ye older brothers of the gods,
Ye gods who smack your lips,
Ye gods who whisper,
Ye gods who watch by night,
Ye gods who show your gleaming eyes by night,
Come down, awake, make a move, stir yourselves,
Here is your food, the house.

"Now," said the chief priest, "let us sacrifice a pig to Kūkāʻilimoku and tonight we will feast and share ʻawa together. The gods will surely answer you then, Lord."

The priests slaughtered a pig and laid it on the altar. They commanded villagers from Kawaihae to fetch another pig, which they slaughtered, gutted, and deposited in an imu just makai of the temple. Bananas, sweet potatoes, and yams, all wrapped in ti leaves, joined the animal in the fire. The priests roasted fish and coconuts on a separate bed of coals.

The heiau boasted an ample store of pepper root and after the feast, we returned to the temple, where the priests chewed the roots for us and spit the intoxicating ʻawa juice into gourd bowls. Kekuaokalani, the kahuna nui of Kūkāʻilimoku, himself prepared the ʻawa for Liholiho.

"Drink this, Lord," he said, passing a half-full bowl to Liholiho, who sipped from it. The taste was not quite to his liking and he made a face. Kekuaokalani chuckled. "It is not like the haole rum, is it, Lord? But it is better still," he continued, "for it is the drink of Hawaiian kings. Drink, Lord, drink. The ʻawa will help you receive the gods' wisdom." Eager for this counsel, Liholiho drank it down. Kekuaokalani served our cousin many bowls of ʻawa that night.

I never much cared for ʻawa and I drank little of it that night—just enough to show my respect for the kahuna who chewed the plant root for me. Thus, my head was still clear hours later when Liholiho and Kekuaokalani fell into each other's arms, hugged, and wailed. All around us lay the inert, shadowy forms of the great temple's kāhuna, deep in their ʻawa-induced slumber. None of them so much as stirred, despite the loud cries of my brother and our royal cousin.

"Have the gods spoken to you yet, cousin?" Kekuaokalani asked at last.

"Cousin, the gods say I have slighted you," Liholiho cried. "They remind me that my father, Kamehameha, entrusted our people's well-being to both of us: you through the keeping of the god and me through the keeping of the kingdom. One is just as important as the other. But I forgot this in my grief for my father and I did not give you proper respect. Please forgive me."

The kahuna nui Hewahewa was not at Kailua when we arrived there. We learned from Kauiwa and Holo'ialena that he was at the Heiau o Lono at Honokōhau, a short distance up the coast. We set out by canoe once again and found him later that day at the heiau.

Now well advanced in years, Hewahewa was frail, his sight was dimming, and he was hard of hearing. My brother looked forward to the day, soon he hoped, when he would succeed the old man as kahuna nui.

Hewahewa and a young assistant were sacrificing a goat to the god as we entered the heiau. As the high priest chanted, the two men bowed and swayed before an altar that in late afternoon was deep in shadows. The goat, just recently slain, lay atop the altar; its blood still ran freely, collecting at the two men's feet in a dark, congealing pool that spread slowly across the heiau's lava-stone floor.

Kekuaokalani and I waited patiently while the two priests chanted their prayer to Lono:

E Lono-i-ka-po,
O Lono in the night,
E Lono-i-ke-ao.
O Lono in the day.
E Lono-ke-ka'ina o mua
O Lono of the leading forward
E Lono-nui-a Hina
O great Lono given birth by Hina
Mai 'aniha mai 'oe iau e Lono
Do not be unfriendly to me, o Lono.

The two men continued chanting in this manner for some time before concluding:

Eia ka 'ai,
Here is the food
E Ku, e Lono, e Kāne.
O Ku, o Lono, o Kāne.

E Lono I ke ao uli e,
O Lono in the firmament
Eia ka ʻai.
Here is the food.

Hewahewa turned from the altar at last to acknowledge us with a slight nod of his head and said to my brother, "Kekuaokalani, welcome. Do you come to greet your cousin Liholiho when he passes this way?"

"Liholiho is coming here now?" My brother and I were both surprised by this news. After all, Liholiho had only just pledged to restore the kapus before returning, and to our knowledge, had yet to do so.

"Oh yes," the old priest replied. "Kaʻahumanu and Kalanimoku have sent for him now that Kamehameha's long bones have been purified."

"But Kailua is still a place of defilement for him," Kekuaokalani protested. "Liholiho has promised me that he will not set foot in Kailua before the kapus are restored—before *he* restores them."

"I cannot say what Liholiho will do, only that he is coming this way," said Hewahewa. "It is already late in the day; perhaps he means to rest here for a bit."

"Hewahewa, you must help me persuade Liholiho to stay on here until the kapus are restored in Kailua."

"I will speak to him if you wish, Kekuaokalani," Hewahewa replied.

"Tell Liholiho you agree with me that he must restore the kapus."

"Is this truly necessary?" Hewahewa asked. "Surely, Kalanimoku will tell him?"

"Kalanimoku will be of no help to *us*," said my brother. "He has abandoned Kāne, Kū, and Lono, and no doubt their kapus; he worships the haoles' god now."

"Truly? Oh this is very troublesome," Hewahewa said, wringing his hands, "very troublesome indeed. To be sure, when Liholiho comes, I will tell him to be mindful of his duty."

Liholiho reached Honokōhau near sunset. Ka'ahumanu expected him in Kailua the same evening, and he meant to continue to the village after a brief respite ashore. When Hewahewa reminded him, albeit humbly, of his duty to the gods, and my brother warned him once more not to return to Kailua while the people there flouted the kapus, Liholiho decided to stop at Honokōhau. He sent one of his friends ahead to tell Ka'ahumanu and Kalanimoku that he would not come to Kailua until men and women no longer ate together there. Having thus resolved matters for the moment, Liholiho settled in for the night at a hale near the beach. My brother made sure that he and his friends had ample food and plenty of rum.

The next day, Ka'ahumanu and Kalanimoku dispatched Kahekili Ke'eaumoku and Hoapili to Honokōhau to conduct Liholiho to Kailua forthwith. They found us at the heiau, but they were soon frustrated in their mission because no amount of pleading on their part would persuade Liholiho to return with them.

"Kekuaokalani says Kailua is kapu to me; he says the kapus must be restored before I can return," he said.

"Who is Kekuaokalani to say what is kapu for the mō'ī?" demanded Kahekili Ke'eaumoku. My brother tensed at this but held his tongue.

"Kalanimoku does not say Kailua is kapu for you," said Hoapili. "Your foster mother Ka'ahumanu does not say it is kapu for you. In any case," he continued, "they have said that the kapus will be observed and obeyed wherever you reside."

"And they have said that anyone at Kailua or elsewhere who wishes to continue observing the kapus may do so," added Kahekili Ke'eaumoku.

Kekuaokalani could no longer hold his tongue. "In other words, Kahekili," he said, "any others who wish to disregard the kapus may do so now?" Turning to Liholiho, he said, "Lord, your father charged you to uphold the kapus; he would tell you that it is not for anyone to choose whether they will obey them. All must obey the kapus or surely, none will." Kekuaokalani now turned to the high priest for confirmation. "Is this not so, Hewahewa?" he asked.

"One would most assuredly say that," Hewahewa replied.

The kahuna nui's response was hardly the definitive answer my brother had expected, but he tried to make the best of it. "You see, Lord?" he said to Liholiho. "Your own kahuna nui agrees."

"Ka'ahumanu has said otherwise," Kahekili Ke'eaumoku snapped, "and *she* is Liholiho's co-ruler."

"So Ka'ahumanu is now to rule with Liholiho?" asked my brother. "By whose authority?"

"Liholiho is to share rule with Ka'ahumanu by the authority of our lord's late father, Kamehameha!" Kahekili Ke'eaumoku rejoined.

"When did Kamehameha ever say this?" Kekuaokalani pressed, and feigning surprise, exclaimed, "I have never heard such a thing before!"

"Kamehameha told Ka'ahumanu and Kalanimoku just before he died that Ka'ahumanu was to rule with Liholiho," said Hoapili. "You and your brother were both there when he said this."

"We were there, but nevertheless, neither my brother nor I heard Kamehameha say any such thing," said Kekuaokalani, and he looked to me for confirmation.

"We saw Kamehameha speak to Ka'ahumanu and Kalanimoku, but our uncle's voice was so weak that we could not hear him," I said.

Hoapili turned to Hewahewa. "Old one," he said, "you were also there when Kamehameha spoke to Ka'ahumanu and Kalanimoku. What did you hear?"

Hewahewa spread his wrinkled hands open in front of him and said, "Truthfully, I regret to say that I could not hear his words either. It would have been better had he spoken loudly enough for everyone to hear."

Now my brother turned to Liholiho. "Cousin," he said, "do you truly believe that Kamehameha, with his dying breath, said you should share *your* government with your foster-mother, Ka'ahumanu?"

"I do not know what my father said at the time, cousin," Liholiho replied. "For as you know, I was regretfully not there." He looked unhappily at Kekuaokalani, as if pleading with my brother not to press him further.

But Kekuaokalani would not relent. "Well, then," he continued, "did Kamehameha *ever at any time* give you reason to believe this? Did he *ever tell you* that Ka'ahumanu should rule with you?"

"He only told me that I would be mō'ī and rule after him."

"And this he proclaimed to all of the chiefs, did he not?" Kekuaokalani asked.

"Yes, cousin, that is so," Liholiho said. Now he looked resolutely at Hoapili and Kahekili Ke'eaumoku and declared, "It is true. *I* never heard my father say that I should share the government with Ka'ahumanu."

"So you see?" Kekuaokalani said to Kahekili Ke'eaumoku and Hoapili, "Even Liholiho, our mō'ī, is unaware that Ka'ahumanu is to rule with him. He does not acknowledge her authority to release anyone from the kapus. Go tell this to her and Kalanimoku. Tell them that Liholiho will not set foot Kailua again until the kapus are restored for all."

"Is this truly your will, Lord?" asked Hoapili.

Liholiho seemed relieved to let my brother speak for him. "It is my will to remain here for now," he replied. Then, apparently hoping to appease Hoapili and Kahekili Ke'eaumoku, he added, "You both have given me much to think about today. Please tell my kahu, Ka'ahumanu, and Kalanimoku that I am considering all you have said."

Thus thwarted, Hoapili and Kahekili Ke'eaumoku made ready to leave. Ignoring Liholiho and me, Kahekili Ke'eaumoku turned to my brother and said, "This is not finished yet." Then he spun around and stalked off.

As Liholiho watched them go, he said to us, "Kahekili Ke'eaumoku is very angry. I hope Ka'ahumanu will not be angry with me."

Later, after Liholiho had returned to his friends, my brother reflected, "Kahekili Ke'eaumoku is right of course. We prevailed today, Nāmākēha, but Liholiho is like a feather on Lono's wind. The wind was with us today and so was Liholiho, but tomorrow, who knows?"

The wind indeed changed direction the next day, but it was not Lono's doing.

Ka'ahumanu descended upon Honokōhau the next morning like a storm off the ocean, sweeping all before her. Kalanimoku, Hoapili, and Kahekili Ke'eaumoku trailed in her lee.

"Where is my foster son? Where is Liholiho?" Ka'ahumanu demanded of the first person she encountered at the shore—a maka'āinana fisherman who had immediately thrown himself to the ground upon seeing her approach. "I—I do not know," the man said. He addressed his words to the dirt because he did not dare look up at the famous ali'i chiefess who towered over him. Ka'ahumanu was so much greater in stature than the three ali'i men accompanying her that he hardly noticed them. "I have not seen Liholiho today."

Failing to find Liholiho near the shore, Ka'ahumanu continued mauka to the heiau, where she found my brother and me with Hewahewa just outside the temple.

"Liholiho—where is he?" she asked us.

"He was here earlier, Aunt," I replied, "but we do not know where he is now." This was the truth, although we did know that our cousin and a few of his friends had earlier gone to see some nearby fishponds that his father had built.

Now Ka'ahumanu turned to Hewahewa. "Old one, did you tell Liholiho that Kailua is kapu for him?"

"I merely reminded him of his duty to the gods—" Hewahewa replied, his voice trembling, "—of his duty to uphold the kapus."

"And you, Kekuaokalani, did you tell Liholiho not to return to Kailua?"

Unlike the meek kahuna nui, my brother, the keeper of the war god Kūkā'ilimoku, was resolute. "Kailua must be kapu to our new mō'ī as long as men and women eat together there and women eat foods forbidden to them by Kāne," he declared. "Liholiho would be defiled if he returned there now. You know this to be true, *Aunt*."

Ka'ahumanu scowled at my brother. "I only *know* that Liholiho may return and yet keep the kapus, *nephew*," she retorted. "My foster-son is nī'aupi'o, like his mother, and therefore his very person is kapu. Any ground on which he stands is kapu. It does not matter where he is. I sent my brother and cousin to tell him so. I have no doubt that he would have returned to Kailua with them yesterday had you not stood in his way."

"I have no doubt you wish that were true," Kekuaokalani snapped. "In truth, I did not stand in Liholiho's way. He is the mōʻī now, and like his father before him, he makes his own way!"

I felt my heart sink as this argument between my brother and Kaʻahumanu became more heated. I feared that if it continued a moment longer, the two would trade words so regretful that neither could take them back, with awful consequences for all of us. In desperation, I tried to redirect their attention to Hewahewa. "Our high priest is here, after all," I said. "Does he not have the final word on what is kapu?"

My brother and Kaʻahumanu had been arguing in front of the kahuna nui as if the old man were not there. Now as I had hoped, they both turned to him. But Hewahewa, who had for two days now cautiously parsed his every word to avoid giving offense to anyone, merely fidgeted with his hands as his eyes darted from Kaʻahumanu to Kekuaokalani and back again. Neither of them spoke, and my brother shook his head at me, willing me to keep silent. Nevertheless, I was determined to press the question with Hewahewa, if only to stop this alarming confrontation for the time being.

"Hewahewa, is it so that Liholiho can return—" I began, but I never finished my question, for at that moment, there was a flurry of movement behind Kaʻahumanu. Kalanimoku, Hoapili, and Kahekili Keʻeaumoku abruptly stepped aside to make way for Liholiho.

Upon seeing him, Kaʻahumanu began wailing and shedding copious tears. To me it seemed as if a powerful wind gust had passed, replaced by a drenching downpour. Kaʻahumanu opened her arms, widening her already formidable girth, rushed to Liholiho, and enveloped him in a tight hug. For a moment, his face was almost lost to sight in her ample bosom.

"Liholiho, my foster son, why are you so angry with me?" Kaʻahumanu cried. "Why have you refused to come to me in Kailua?"

At this, Liholiho also began to wail. "Oh, my kahu, forgive me," he pleaded. "I have never been angry with you. My only desire was to honor my father's wishes and uphold the kapus. Please forgive me if I hurt you." At this, Liholiho's remorse overcame him, and he sobbed uncontrollably.

"Oh, how could I not forgive you, my heavenly son?" said Ka'ahumanu, still weeping. "But tell me why you have not come to me in Kailua as I begged?"

Through his continuing sobs, Liholiho said, "I wanted to come to you, Mother, but I feared to come to Kailua. I feared I would be defiled."

Ka'ahumanu released Liholiho from her embrace. "You can never be defiled, my son," she said. "You are nī'aupi'o. Your kapu is so strong that wherever you go, the dirt under your feet and the ground around you become kapu. Men and women will obey the kapus wherever you are, wherever you will them to obey. You are the mō'ī now. Kailua cannot be kapu for you. Return with me. Once more, I beg you." All through this, Ka'ahumanu continued to sob. Liholiho could not help but embrace her and wail anew.

"Mother," he cried, "I will return to Kailua."

Kekuaokalani and I looked at each other. My brother slowly shook his head as if to say, "*See how she bends Liholiho to her will like a thin wili-wili branch.*"

Ka'ahumanu abruptly ceased her crying. Disengaging herself from her foster son's arms, she said, "Good. Then we shall leave at once." Grasping Hewahewa by an elbow, she added, "The kahuna nui shall come with us." Then without another word to my brother or me, Ka'ahumanu marched back to the shore, with Hewahewa, Kalanimoku, Hoapili, and Kahekili Ke'eaumoku close behind her.

Liholiho lagged behind them. Realizing that he was not in step with the others, Ka'ahumanu stopped and called out to him, "Come my foster-son, Kailua is waiting for you."

Liholiho turned and looked at us apologetically. Then, turning back to Ka'ahumanu, he called out, "I will be only a short distance behind you in my own canoe." This seemed to satisfy Ka'ahumanu, who continued to the shore without another backward glance.

As we watched them go, Kekuaokalani turned to me and said, "The ground where Liholiho stands may be kapu, brother, but wherever Ka'ahumanu walks, it is not."

Kailua Kona, May 1819

My brother and Hoapili nearly came to blows over which of them would hide Kamehameha's long bones. The priests had wrapped our uncle's sacred remains in kapa cloth and were holding them at the 'Ahu'ena Heiau. Soon after Liholiho left for Kailua, Kekuaokalani went to retrieve them. I went with him.

Discounting Liholiho's claim on his father's bones, Kekuaokalani had always presumed that as Kamehameha's favorite nephew, the high priest of his war god, Kūkā'ilimoku, and the future kahuna nui of the Hawaiian kingdom, the honor of hiding them was his. But when we reached the heiau, we found Hoapili had just received them from the priests.

Kekuaokalani was furious and demanded, "Why have you given my uncle's long bones to this one?"

Before the priest could reply, Hoapili answered for him. "Do not berate the kahuna, Kekuaokalani," he said. "He is only complying with Lord Kamehameha's wishes."

My brother ignored Hoapili and once more addressed the priest. "Did Lord Kamehameha tell you to deliver his long bones to this man?"

His eyes wide in the face of my brother's anger, the priest shook his head, and stammered, "No, he did n-not speak t-to me of th-this."

"Well, then," Kekuaokalani continued, "Why have you given the bones to *him*?"

Again, Hoapili spoke before the priest could answer. "Kamehameha asked me as he was dying to carry away his bones," he said. "You were there; you saw, Kekuaokalani."

"Yes, I saw him speak to you, but I did not hear what he said," my brother replied, advancing on Hoapili. "Moreover, I do not believe you." He lunged for the precious kapa-cloth bundle.

As Hoapili tried to push him away, the bundle slipped from his hands and clattered to the heiau's stone floor. The two thin strands of bark twine around the bundle snapped and the cloth came undone, spilling the long bones of Kamehameha's legs and arms at the two men's feet.

"Stop!" I shouted at them. "Look what you have done! This is desecration! For the sake of our beloved Kamehameha's spirit, I beg you; leave off at once!"

My brother and Hoapili looked aghast at the floor, and backed away from each other. At once, the kahuna rushed between them, knelt, gathered up Kamehameha's bones, and wrapped and tied them in the cloth once more. Rising to his feet, he looked from one man to the other. So ashamed were Kekuaokalani and Hoapili that neither moved to take it from him.

At length I said, "Give Hoapili *my Uncle* Kamehameha's long bones." My brother looked at me in surprise, but did not object when the priest handed the bundle to Hoapili. Hoapili thanked the priest, and without another word to either of us, left the heiau.

"Why did you do that?" Kekuaokalani asked me.

I had no ready answer, for I had surprised even myself. "Our uncle's spirit will thank you for this," was all I could think to say.

Some believe that Hoapili hid Kamehameha's long bones at Kawaihae; others say he hid them farther up the Kohala Coast, near Kamehameha's birthplace at Kokoiki. No one will ever know the truth. It died with Hoapili in 1840.

Though the period of mourning for Kamehameha was now past, Liholiho had yet to decree that all people must obey the kapus once more. Moreover, despite his promise to Ka'ahumanu to return forthwith, he lingered for days at sea. In his absence, his subjects were left to sort out matters for themselves.

Free to choose, people at Kailua and elsewhere on the Big Island now divided. Led by Kekuaokalani, a number of chiefs and their adherents contended that it was time to restore all the kapus, most especially the strictures forbidding men and women from eating together and barring women from eating certain foods—kapu eating. A substantially larger group persisted in ignoring these restrictions, a practice that came to be called "free eating." The free eaters were leaderless at this time, though it was widely believed that Kaʻahumanu, Kahekili Keʻeaumoku, and Kalanimoku sympathized with them. Hewahewa kept his thoughts on the controversy to himself.

Kekuaokalani railed against free eating. "The gods will surely strike down all who defy the kapus," he warned. The free eaters ignored him, and the gods refrained from striking them down.

It was in the midst of this turmoil that Liholiho finally returned to Kailua—where the conflict between the free eaters and the kapu eaters raged the hottest—to be formally invested as mōʻī. Kekuaokalani stayed away from the ceremonies. It was just as well that he did.

Still hesitant to return to Kailua while free eating continued, Liholiho had remained offshore, his double-hulled canoe aimlessly sailing this way and that at the outer edge of Kailua Bay. A dozen or more young chiefesses joined them, paddling out from shore in small outrigger canoes. Liholiho and his comrades had brought an ample supply of rum from Honokōhau and they consumed it freely along the way. Now the young king sent word to shore for more of the haole liquor. Liholiho and his friends became ever more boisterous as they continued drinking. They were close enough to shore that we in the village could hear the royal party's rhythmic drumming, rattling calabashes, and wild chanting, which continued at all hours.

Liholiho's brazen display of debauchery offended my brother. "Our cousin may profess respect for the kapus and the gods," he said, "but he does not practice it." Moreover, Kekuaokalani worried that Liholiho might be wavering in his resolve to restore the kapus. And so, he dispatched me once again to remind our cousin of his duty to his father and his father's gods.

Liholiho greeted me effusively when I boarded his large, double-hulled canoe later that same day. Pulling me close to him, he hugged me and wailed, "Nāmākēha, my cousin and dear companion of my childhood! Welcome, welcome!" Liholiho's words were slurred, he smelled of rum, and he was unsteady on his feet. If not for the fact that he was hugging me, he might have fallen over. When Liholiho released me, he straightened with effort and called out to his friends, "See who has come to join us! It is my aikāne, Nāmākēha!" Then he staggered away.

Liholiho and his companions did not remain long at Kailua Bay. Soon after I joined them, they resumed sailing slowly in the direction of Keauhou. They took more than a day to complete a journey that should have taken no more than an afternoon. During this time, I tried to remind my cousin of his promise.

"Yes, yes, of course, Nāmākēha," he said, still slurring his words. "When I am invested as mōʻī, I will decree that free eating must end wherever I am and I will restore all the other kapus."

I could not help but notice Liholiho's stipulation. "Do you mean to say that you will not end free eating everywhere?" I asked him. Liholiho ignored my question and I was unable to gain any further assurances from him.

The rum had run low, as had the food, by the time we reached Keauhou. When Liholiho sent word ashore for more food and liquor, he was dismayed to learn that while food was available aplenty, no rum was to be had there. For as soon as Kaʻahumanu had learned that her foster son was sailing toward Keauhou, she sent people ahead to confiscate whatever supplies of rum remained at the royal retreat. His hunger appeased, but his thirst for haole liquor unslaked, Liholiho ordered his people to return him to Kailua.

If Ka'ahumanu was angry with Liholiho for loitering at sea for days instead of immediately returning to Kailua as he had promised, she did not show it. Instead, she greeted her errant foster son with a welcome befitting a king.

We had just rounded Kalaepa'akai Point at the southernmost reaches of Kailua when a great double-hulled canoe raced out to meet us. It was Ka'ahumanu's own. She stood at the front of the platform, wearing a bright yellow bosom-to-ankle gown of fine haole linen that shimmered in the bright sun and billowed about her as the vessel surged forward, propelled by some forty paddlers. Behind her were Kalanimoku and Kahekili Ke'eaumoku, and ranks of chiefs and chiefesses, filling the length of the platform, wearing their finest cloaks of brilliant red and yellow feathers, which fluttered in the gentle breeze and flashed in the sunlight. Ka'ahumanu's flowing gown contrasted with the fluttering of the many feathered cloaks behind her and drew our eyes back to her.

Her canoe turned and slipped alongside ours; men in the vessels' adjacent hulls reached out to keep the two canoes together. Now, Ka'ahumanu stood opposite Liholiho.

"Lord," she cried, "you have returned to us at last! How your people have yearned for this day! Come across and join me here and we will greet them together."

Liholiho made to reply but his words were lost amid a thunderous salute of cannon fire. Anchored in the bay were Kamehameha's two favorite haole ships, the old Fair American and the Pelekane, their guns' barrels smoking.

"Will you come with me, Lord?" Ka'ahumanu called anew.

After continuing in this fashion at some length, the priest paused again. Now Ka'ahumanu stepped forward once more, raising her hands more quickly this time. But at this, Hewahewa commenced a third prayer, this time to Lono, calling upon the god to make the land fertile.

E Loni-i-a-po,
O Lono in the night,
E Lono-i-ke-ao.
O Lono in the day.
E Lono-i-ke ka'ina o mua
O Lono of the leading forward
E Lono-nui-a-Hina
O great Lono given birth by Hina
Mai 'aniha mai 'oe ia, e Lono.
Do not be unfriendly to me, o Lono.

This prayer-chant was longer than the last, and when Hewahewa's old lungs forced him to pause several beats for breath, Ka'ahumanu stepped forward and took the leis from the kahuna's assistants. The priest and Liholiho looked at her with surprise; the multitude of onlookers, quiet until now, began to murmur, as if to protest. Before the crowd's murmuring could grow to something more consequential, Ka'ahumanu whirled around and brandished the leis at them. The assemblage quieted at once.

"My beloved people," Ka'ahumanu cried, "see how we are blessed with a great mō'ī! This is a new day for our *Hawaii nei*!" At this, she turned to Liholiho and held out the leis. He stepped toward her and she placed one of them around his neck, handed him the other one, bent close, and whispered to him. Not even those standing closest to Ka'ahumanu could hear what she said. Liholiho nodded. Now Ka'ahumanu bent before her king, and Liholiho placed the other lei around her neck, though not easily, for it briefly caught on the high crest of Kamehameha's great feathered helmet. Ka'ahumanu stood straight again and swept Liholiho into her arms. Save for his own feathered cloak and helmet, my cousin all but disappeared in Ka'ahumanu's embrace as the two wailed together.

When she released him at last, Liholiho faced the onlookers again and cried, "Hear me! As our lord, my father, Kamehameha the Great, willed, I proclaim that my foster-mother and kahu, Ka'ahumanu, shall be your *kuhina nui*! Together, she and I will bring peace and prosperity to all the islands!"

The crowd cheered. The dual reign of Ka'ahumanu and Liholiho had begun.

Contrary to his promise to Kekuaokalani that he would restore the kapus and end free eating upon his formal installation as king—a pledge he had just recently confirmed to me—Liholiho issued no such decree before the assemblage at Kailua. I questioned him about this when he greeted me immediately after the ceremony. "My lord, you said nothing of the kapus. Why?" I asked, as we hugged each other.

Releasing me abruptly and frowning, Liholiho replied, "It seemed untimely to me, Nāmākēha." I did not need to ask him why, for I knew the reason. Liholiho was reluctant to make such a decree while standing next to Ka'ahumanu.

"Kekuaokalani will surely ask me about this," I pressed, ever my brother's intermediary. "What shall I tell him? Will you restore the kapus at the luau this evening, then?"

"That would be a more appropriate time," he answered. His reply was noncommittal, but I was reluctant to press him further, especially when he suddenly embraced me again and joyously exclaimed, "Come celebrate with my friends and me, Nāmākēha! We have more rum."

make himself heard, he called out to them, "All who still honor the gods and the kapus follow me!"

One of the chiefs who had been sitting with Liholiho had not immediately followed him and the others to sit with the women. This was Naihe, son of Kamehameha's old ally Keaweaheulu, and the only member of Liholiho's inner council other than my brother who was not related to Ka'ahumanu. Now Naihe stood, touched Kekuaokalani on his shoulder to gain his attention, and spoke quietly to him. "I had best not leave with you at this time, brother, even as my own 'aumakua bids me to follow you," he said. "I hope you will understand."

"Yes, I understand indeed," Kekuaokalani replied. Then, with his entourage of priests in tow, he marched down the avenue of open space that had formerly divided the men's and women's eating mats. I followed.

Others followed as well. Kekuaokalani's beloved partner, Manono, who had been sitting with the chiefesses, rose and left them without a word. Here and there throughout the large crowd, scores of men and women, ali'i all, abandoned their places to join Kekuaokalani and his priests in their protest.

As we were leaving, Naihe joined Liholiho. I noticed that he was careful to avoid sitting next to any of the women who were now feasting with his mō'ī.

Upon leaving the feast, we withdrew to the high ground immediately above Kailua. The luau revelers had kindled fires atop the still-hot stones in the imu pits, illuminating the field below us. We could make out the shadowy forms of people cavorting in the wavering firelight. Even muffled by distance, we could hear their raucous cries as they rejoiced in the end of kapu eating.

Now we saw a new light flare opposite the luau grounds. As the flames shot upward, Kekuaokalani comprehended to his horror that they were rapidly consuming a thatched structure, and there was only once such structure at that place.

"They are burning down the Ahu'ena Heiau," Kekuaokalani cried. "There is no longer any place for us here!"

"It would be a place of refuge for those who still observe the kapus?" asked Liholiho. "Like Honaunau?"

"Yes, exactly," I said. "But if Kekuaokalani comes there at your invitation, he implicitly acknowledges your authority and accepts free eating here, even if he never says so."

Liholiho brightened at this. "What do you think?" he asked Ka'ahumanu.

"I think that is a wonderful idea, Lord," Ka'ahumanu said, smiling now. "Thank you, Nāmākēha. I believe you have just solved all our problems."

Ka'ahumanu decided that Keopuolani should go to Ka'awaloa to speak with Kekuaokalani and that Hoapili and I should go with her. Naihe, whom Ka'ahumanu also decided to send with us, explained her reasoning to me. "Ka'ahumanu said neither she nor her brother should approach Kekuaokalani on this matter because of the present enmity between them," he said, and went on to explain that Kalanimoku would not go either—as Liholiho's new military commander, his presence would likely be seen as a threat. "Ka'ahumanu said Kekuaokalani would receive Keopuolani more kindly than the others because he has had so little to do with her in the past," Naihe continued. "She is sending me to represent the council because I have never quarreled with your brother. Keopuolani is to present the council's terms and you are to convince your brother to accept them. Hoapili is coming to keep an eye on me and to make sure you succeed."

"I will indeed succeed, and gladly," I said. Again, I was hopeful that a clash between my brother and Liholiho over the kapus could be avoided. Unfortunately, my hopes were dashed by the time we departed for Ka'awaloa two days later.

Just before we were to sail, Naihe came to me with alarming news. "Ka'ahumanu and Kalanimoku have no intention of allowing Kekuaokalani and his people to settle at Keauhou and keep the kapus there," he said. "They will not even allow them to reach Keauhou. They are setting a trap for them." Naihe said he had learned that at Ka'ahumanu's instruction, Keopuolani was to ask Kekuaokalani to return the canoes he and his people had previously taken from Oneo Bay, "as a personal favor" to Liholiho.

"Ka'ahumanu and Kalanimoku do not care about the canoes," Naihe said. "They only want to lure your brother to sea, and once he and his people are at sea, Kalanimoku will attack them."

"We must warn my brother!" I said.

"You must warn him, Nāmākēha. I cannot because Hoapili will surely be watching me closely. Tell Kekuaokalani to go overland to Keauhou, if he goes at all."

"Does Liholiho know about this?" I asked.

"No, of course not," replied Naihe, "nor does Keopuolani. But I believe Hoapili does."

Naihe told me that if Kekuaokalani and his people put to sea, they would be attacked on two sides—by Kalanimoku with haole schooners armed with cannons and musket-bearing warriors on one side, and by Kahekili Ke'eaumoku with many war canoes, carrying swivel guns and more men armed with muskets on the other. "Whether your brother fights or flees will make no difference," Naihe said. "Either way, he will be trapped. It will be a slaughter."

We entered the bay at Kealakekua at sunset. The high cliff face was dull red in the day's fading light. No one had preceded us to herald our coming, and we were not expected. Thus, the beach at Ka'awaloa, the very same beach where James Cook had died some forty years earlier, was deserted. Naihe blew on a conch shell to signal our arrival. Echoing off the cliff face, the shell's deep call soon drew people to the shore.

Keopuolani stood at the center of the canoe's platform. She wore a gown of white linen that fell from her bosom to her ankles and over this a yellow and red feather cloak. On her head she wore a lei of white flowers, tinged pink by the setting sun. I stood behind Keopuolani, holding a kahili with white feathers.

As we neared the beach, the people gathering there began to point at Keopuolani and talk among themselves. When she stepped lightly from the canoe to the land, some of the people fled while others knelt in the sand and still others removed articles of clothing. Kekuaokalani's people still observed the kapus, but since the recent events at Kailua, many of these ali'i were now unsure how to behave in her presence.

Keopuolani promptly relieved them of their uncertainty. Approaching the closest kneeling figure, she stood over the man and said gently, "Please rise. You need not demean yourself before me in this way anymore."

Curious now, people gathered around this once-remote royal personage. Now Kekuaokalani pushed his way through the crowd and confronted Keopuolani. My brother made no show of respect for her high-born lineage.

"Why have *you* come here?" he demanded.

When Kekuaokalani and his people had first arrived at Ka'awaloa, the former royal retreat of Kalani'ōpu'u, they found the place shabby and in disrepair. There were large gaps in all of the hales' roof thatching and many of the structures' supporting poles and beams were cracked, rotting, or in otherwise precarious condition. The grounds were covered with decaying palm fronds and other detritus. My brother immediately set his people to repairing the damage of years of neglect.

By the time Keopuolani's party arrived, the hales were habitable again. The houses' wooden frames had been strengthened; failing corner posts and beams were replaced and the supporting structures freshly lashed together. Fresh pili grass thatching now securely sealed walls and roofs against rain and wind. The mua and the *hale aina*, the eating houses for men and women, were the first repaired; the *hale moe*, the family dwelling and sleeping houses, were next. Kekuaokalani built a new hale moe for himself and Manono upon the lava stone floor laid decades earlier for the hale of Kalaniʻōpu'u. All these structures were clustered together as they had been in Kalaniʻōpu'u's day. My brother ordered an additional building constructed well away from the others: the armory, where the muskets, powder, and shot Kauiwa and Holoʻialena had secretly taken from Kailua were kept.

"I have come with a proposal from my sacred son, the king, who desires only peace between you and himself," Keopuolani said to Kekuaokalani.

"What proposal is this?" asked Manono, who had followed closely behind Kekuaokalani as people made way for him. In contrast to Keopuolani's full-length, haole-cloth gown, Manono wore a short skirt of kapa cloth. Her breasts were bare.

"As I have said, my royal son wishes for peace," Keopuolani began in reply. "But *we two*," she continued, and then paused to indicate that she was speaking of herself and Kekuaokalani, "we two should discuss the details of his proposal together."

"Anything you have to say to me you can say also to Manono," my brother replied curtly. "And to Kauiwa and Holoʻialena, who are my trusted advisers," he added.

"That is just as well, nephew," Keopuolani said. "Naihe, Hoapili, and your own brother, who have come with me, should also attend."

Engaged as he was with Keopuolani, my brother had not heretofore noticed me standing just behind her, holding the kahili. "Nāmākēha!"

he cried and stepped past Keopuolani to hug me. I could not hug him in return because I was still holding the royal standard. When we finished wailing our greetings to each other, my brother greeted Naihe but pointedly ignored Hoapili. Of course, I had no opportunity to warn Kekuaokalani of the plot against him while Hoapili and Keopuolani stood there.

His mood now improved, my brother turned back to Keopuolani. "You must be hungry," he said. "Let us meet at my hale and speak of my cousin's proposal after we eat. Manono will show you to the hale aina."

At this, Hoapili stepped forward. "There is no need for Keopuolani to eat at the women's house," he snapped. "We are free eaters now."

"*You* may be free eaters at Kailua," my brother growled, "but we are all kapu eaters here."

Both men tensed; I feared they would come to blows. Ever the intermediary, I stepped between them, being careful not to drop Keopuolani's kahili. "Perhaps you and Keopuolani can eat together here while the others eat at the mua and the hale aina," I said to Hoapili. "Would this be acceptable, Kekua?"

"Whom Keopuolani and Hoapili choose to eat with is of no concern of mine," my brother replied, "but I cannot eat with a wahine."

Hoapili now had a change of heart. "Very well," he said. "Because we are your guests here, Keopuolani and I will abide by *your* kapus. I will join the men. Keopuolani will join the women; I am sure that she and Manono will have much to talk about."

Keopuolani made no objection as Manono and the other women led her to the hale aina. Meanwhile, we men repaired to the mua. I understood why Hoapili had changed his mind. He had been charged with keeping watch on Naihe and me and did not want to leave either of us alone with Kekuaokalani.

The meal was sparse: yams, sweet potatoes, breadfruit, poi, and some fish, but no pig meat, coconut, or bananas. Kekuaokalani saw that we were still hungry as we licked the last of the food from our fingers. "I apologize if your hunger is not appeased," he said. "The common people here will not share their produce and pigs with us except in exchange for haole goods, and we have few of those to trade now."

Looking directly at Hoapili, my brother continued, "They have heard about what has transpired at Kailua of late. This is what happens when the kānaka learn that certain aliʻi do not respect the kapus." Hoapili scowled at my brother, but said nothing.

"My son, the mōʻī, offers all of Keauhou to you and your people," Keopuolani said to Kekuaokalani. "He promises that you may live there and observe the kapus, unmolested."

We had assembled at my brother's hale after the meal. We sat on sedge mats around a kukui-oil lamp, our shadows wavering on the hale's grass walls.

"Will Liholiho permit others to come to us?" my brother asked.

"Yes. Any who desire to live according to the kapus may join you there," Keopuolani replied.

"What of our landholdings? Will they extend from the sea to the mountains?"

"My son says you shall have all the lands at Keauhou, makai to mauka."

"Liholiho offers us an entire ahupuaʻa? What does he want in return?"

"My son asks only that you live peacefully within your own lands and refrain from opposing the rights of those who reside in *his* lands," Keopuolani replied.

"In other words, they may indulge in free eating if they choose?"

"They have *already* chosen," retorted Hoapili, who had said nothing since my brother's earlier reprimand.

Kekuaokalani would have responded in kind had Manono not spoken first. "Liholiho has made a reasonable and generous offer," she said. "You will consider it, won't you Kekua?" Manono hungered for peace between the two cousins as much as I did. Moreover, the promise of an ahupua'a that included some of the Kona District's most productive lands was indeed a reasonable offer on its face.

Before Kekuaokalani could reply, Keopuolani spoke again. "My son asks only one favor of you, nephew," she said.

"What favor is that, Aunt?" my brother asked.

"He asks only that you bring back the canoes you took when first you came here."

Now Manono spoke again. "That seems only fair, does it not, Kekua?"

"Yes," said my brother, "it does." Now Kekuaokalani turned to me. "What do you think, Nāmākēha?"

I glanced at Hoapili who was staring hard at me now. "I think you should consider it, brother," I replied. Hoapili frowned, for my answer was less affirmative than he expected, and I quickly amended it. "Our cousin *is* the mōʻī," I said. "I think he wishes only peace with you and he has made you a generous offer in good faith." All this, at least, was true.

Kekuaokalani stared at the single kukui-oil lamp, as if seeking an answer in its flame. "I will consider it this night, Aunt," he said at last. "You will have my answer in the morning."

"You should have spoken to Kekuaokalani more forcefully," Hoapili said to me as he, Naihe, and I left Kekuaokalani's hale. Keopuolani had parted with us to pass the night alone at the hale aina. "Ka'ahumanu sent you here to persuade your brother to accept our Lord Liholiho's proposal."

"I well know why I was sent here," I rejoined, "and who sent me. I have already vouched for the sincerity of Liholiho's proposal. What else would you have me do?"

"Talk to your brother again and see that he accepts it," he snapped.

I offered to return to Kekuaokalani's hale to speak to him again, but Hoapili would not allow me to go alone and said he was too weary to accompany me. "We will speak to him again the morning," he said.

Hoapili, Naihe, and I slept that night in the mua, there being no other accommodations for us in Ka'awaloa. I lay on my mat, fighting sleep and listening to the other men's breathing until I was certain both slept. Then I stole out of the hale. Lono's moon was no more than a shard of silver and the night was deep in darkness as I crossed the settlement to the hale of Kekuaokalani and Manono. It was darker still within the hale. Remaining at the threshold, I called softly to the slumbering couple.

"Kekua, Manono, wake up, wake up." I called out several times before either of them stirred. Manono was the first to reply.

"Who is there? Nāmākēha, is that you?"

"Yes. Please, rouse my brother; I have something I must tell both of you," I said.

"Nāmākēha?" Kekuaokalani was awake now. "Why are you here, brother?"

"Listen to me," I said. "Do not go to Keauhou by sea. It's a trap."

"A trap? What sort of trap, Nāmākēha?" Kekuaokalani demanded. "You told us that Liholiho's proposal was sincere."

"Liholiho is sincere," I said, "but Ka'ahumanu, Kahekili Ke'eaumoku, and Kalanimoku are not. They are plotting to destroy all of you as you sail to Keauhou. Our cousin does not know of this, nor does Keopuolani."

"How is it that *you* know about this, brother?" Manono asked.

"Naihe told me and I trust him," I said.

"How and when will they attack us?" my brother said.

"I do not have time to explain, Kekua. Just trust me. Now I must get back lest Hoapili awakens and misses me. He is part of this conspiracy against you as well." With that, I turned away and retreated into the night.

I had almost regained the mua when an indistinct form separated itself from a palm tree directly in front of the hale. To avoid being seen, I kept to the deep shadows of the trees, working my way to the rear of the eating house, whence I approached the front. Rounding a corner, I encountered Hoapili. He had been urinating on the tree, a mark of extreme disrespect for my brother and his people.

"Where have you gone?" Hoapili demanded of me.

"I went to relieve myself," I replied, "the same as you. But, unlike you, Hoapili, I had the decency not to foul this eating house!" I pushed past him into the mua and lay down on my sleeping mat without another word.

My sleeping mat was near Naihe's. "Well done, Nāmākēha," he whispered, "well done."

Kekuaokalani seemed in good spirits as we said our farewells the next morning. Turning to Keopuolani, he said, "Please tell your son, my royal cousin, that we will return his canoes to Keauhou."

"Thank you, nephew, I am sure my son, the king, will be most happy to hear this," Keopuolani replied.

"When will you sail?" Hoapili asked. His question conveyed an urgency that he no doubt had not intended. "Your mōʻī will surely want to know when to expect you," he added.

Kekuaokalani smiled broadly at Hoapili. "Please understand that we have much to prepare before we depart. Tell the mōʻī that we will sail for Keauhou in four days' time," he said.

As my brother and I hugged and wailed goodbye, Kekuaokalani whispered into my ear, "Take care, little brother. I will see you in Kailua in three days."

"This is pointless!" Hoapili exclaimed. "What difference does it make now what Nāmākēha knew or did not know? Kekuaokalani's people are already on the march. What if they do not intend to stop at Keauhou? What if Kekuaokalani means to attack Kailua while we are looking for him and his people at sea? We must get word to Kahekili Ke'eaumoku that Nāmākēha's brother marches overland. His people must keep them from reaching Kailua!"

I struggled to conceal my emotions as Hoapili spoke.

Kahekili Ke'eaumoku and his fighters were at this time just north of Kealakekua at Keawakāheka, waiting in ambush. With their head start, my brother and his people were already no doubt well beyond Keawakāheka in their drive up the coast toward Kailua. Kalanimoku understood the danger at once.

"You are right to be alarmed about Kekuaokalani's purpose, Hoapili," he said. Now he looked up at the Pelekane's foremast, where a small pennant was flapping in a stiff northerly wind. "This wind is unfavorable for us," he said. "It may already be too late for us to overtake Kekuaokalani in our great canoes. But Kahekili Ke'eaumoku and his people can still beat them to Keauhou if they start soon. We must get word to them now!

Hoapili, take Keopuolani's canoe and as many paddlers as it can hold and go at once," Kalanimoku said. Then he gestured at me and added, "And take this one with you. I want him to be there when we crush his brother."

As Hoapili grabbed me roughly by my arm and led me away, I heard Kalanimoku mutter, "I would also march on Kailua if I were in *his* place."

The unfavorable wind slowed Hoapili's progress, and we did not reach Keawakāheka until late afternoon. Kahekili Ke'eaumoku was surprised to see Hoapili. "Cousin, what brings you here now?" he asked, when Hoapili found him on the shore among his men. "Why are you not with

Kalanimoku? And what is *he* doing here?" he demanded, just then noticing me.

"Kekuaokalani and his people have already left Ka'awaloa and are marching overland to attack Kailua! You must overtake them and stop them, else our mō'ī's life may be forfeit. As for *this one*," Hoapili said, gesturing at me, "Kalanimoku has sent him along to witness his own brother's defeat."

"Then he comes with us," Kahekili Ke'eaumoku replied, adding, "and if he is to watch us crush Kekuaokalani, we must go at once."

With hundreds of men to organize and scores of canoes to launch, Kahekili Ke'eaumoku did not get away from Keawakāheka until early evening. The wind still blew from an unfavorable quarter, and he ordered his people to furl their sails and paddle through the night, resting only in shifts.

My brother had by then gained two days on his foes. I knew it would not be enough.

Kekuaokalani pushed his own people as hard as he could. They marched without rest or complaint throughout the first night of their advance northward along the coastal trail from Ka'awaloa, taking advantage of the cover of darkness to conceal their movement from their enemies. In this way, they avoided early detection by Kahekili Ke'eaumoku's people and were already well north of them by morning. But with dawn came exhaustion and Kekuaokalani was forced to call a halt for several hours before moving on. Several more hours of steady marching in mounting heat under a cloudless sky found his people weary again. They had little to eat and less to drink. Few freshwater streams ran down from the uplands in this area and they perforce relied on scattered pools of brackish water to relieve their thirst. By mid-afternoon of the first day, Kekuaokalani called another halt, resolving to rest his people until nightfall, when cooler temperatures would favor the resumption of their march. The second night, he and his people moved more slowly and made less progress than they had the first night,

Manono ran forward and threw herself upon my brother's body. She gestured frantically at Hoapili's men and called out to them. I could not make out her cries. Later, some said that Manono had begged to die with my brother; others claimed she pleaded for her life. A final, ragged volley from Hoapili's line decided the issue. There was some further scattered musket fire intermixed with the cries of the wounded and the dying. Then, all the birds having fled, there was only the sound of the wind in the trees.

No bodies were sacrificed to the gods after the battle. The dead were buried where they fell, a'a lava piled over their bodies. I do not know which cairn conceals my brother's bones.

I returned to Kailua with Kahekili Keʻeaumoku's people, but I did not remain there long. Liholiho was as affectionate toward me as ever and urged me to reside with him at his court. I could not bear to live in daily contact with my brother's killers, so I declined his offer and withdrew to Kawaihae to live for a time with ʻOlohana, my older sister, Kaʻōanāʻeha, and their children.

At Kawaihae, Kaʻōanāʻeha and I fell into each other's arms and wailed over our brother's death. When he could bear no more of this spectacle, ʻOlohana sought to console us, saying, "You can be proud of your brother. He lived as he wished and died for what he believed in. He would not have had it any other way, and you can take some comfort in that." At the time, ʻOlohana's words were cold comfort.

As days became weeks and weeks became months, I eventually found comfort in the gentle rhythms of daily life there. Surrounded by my sister and her children John, Jane, Grace, and Fanny, and soothed by the calm presence of ʻOlohana himself, I was able to set aside the horror of Kuamoʻo. And when I looked upon the great, denuded foundation of the Puʻukoholā Heiau below us, and the bay beyond, I no longer dwelled on the day Kekuaokalani and I had visited the temple together with our cousin Liholiho, when I still hoped that conflict between them could be avoided. Instead, I would recall another day, some twenty-five years earlier, when my big brother and I capered on the beach below the heiau, so excited to see George Vancouver's ship anchored offshore. I would remember how Kamehameha stood so regally on that beach awaiting the haole explorer, the yellow feathers of his cloak and helmet shimmering in the morning sun and enveloping him in a nimbus of Kāne's light.

I would smile at the memory of my big brother gleefully proclaiming that one day, he too would be a great warrior like our uncle. My brother, Kekuaokalani, the last kahuna nui of the war god Kūkāʻilimoku, became a great warrior at the end—even though his and the god's cause was already lost.

Kailua-Kona, 1859

Ha'ina 'ia mai ana ka puana. The story is told.

Esther and I are sitting on the lanai. It is late afternoon. The weather has been hot and muggy of late, and we are making the most of the slight breeze that stirs as the day wanes. Ezra and Gideon are repairing the roof thatching of their quarters among our fruit trees across the lawn. Ezra looks up and waves to us. I wave back.

Ezra is a conscientious young man, I say. *He wants to make something of himself. He must learn English first, and I would like to help him.* I would like to make amends for the way my people treated his people from time immemorial, I think to myself. For the way *I* treated his people, for that matter.

Perhaps you can arrange a scholarship for him to attend the school at Punahou, Esther suggests. *They are teaching Hawaiians there, are they not?* Esther has never learned English herself, but then she has little need of it. She is speaking of the school the missionaries started eighteen years ago for their own children on land my uncle, Kamehameha, originally wrested from Kalanikūpule in 1795. These days, it is known as O'ahu College. Some ali'i now attend as well as haoles, and I see no reason why a thoughtful, young maka'āinana like Ezra should not be welcome among them. He would do well there.

I may have some influence in that quarter, I say. *I will speak to Beckwith about Ezra.* Griffin Beckwith, whom I have met at palace affairs, is the school's second principal.

For a while, there is a comfortable silence between us. Then, taking Esther's hand, I ask, *Will you go to Hawai'i with me? We shall invite Kalākaua and Lili to come with us. What do you say?*

Oh yes, replies Esther. *But first, I must obtain Emma's leave to go.*

Of that, there is little doubt. The king and queen are in seclusion. The royal couple's sojourn on Maui last year ended tragically when the king, thinking his queen had taken up with his own personal secretary, shot the poor man and grievously wounded him. Now the king is tormented by guilt and distraught with grief for his secretary—an American who is a close friend and who has served him honorably. When he is not at his friend's sickbed, the king keeps to his residence and Emma remains there with him, keeping their little son, Albert, close to them. She has no need of Esther's assistance with the boy for now.

And so it is that several weeks later the four of us take passage on the *Frances Palmer,* a three-masted clipper bark out of San Francisco. The *Frances Palmer* carries passengers, cargo, and mail between San Francisco and Honolulu on a regular schedule. She is normally prohibited from plying inter-island trade because she is of foreign registry, but the authorities have made an exception in this instance at the urging of a haole attorney with urgent business on Maui. We were fortunate to obtain passage on the *Frances Palmer,* as she is much preferable to our Hawaiian-registry ships, crowded as they are with maka'āinana and their pigs, chickens, and goats.

We have booked passage on this ship from Honolulu to Kailua. The *Frances Palmer* will stop briefly at Molokai then sail to Maui, stopping at Kahului, and then, at our request, continue to Kailua on the Big Island. We are among the ship's complement of fourteen passengers, the other ten of whom are haoles. As luck would have it, Griffin Beckwith, the principal of O'ahu College, is among them. He is also going to Maui.

Settling into our small cabins, Esther and I in one and Kalākaua and his sister Lili in another, we hear the clamor of sailors shouting to one another and the sounds of heavy ropes groaning as sails are hauled aloft and trimmed. Stepping outside again, we watch Honolulu fall away behind us as the sails overhead snap in the wind and our bodies sway to the gentle rolling of the *Frances Palmer's* deck.

As the ship works its way down the island chain from Honolulu, I use the occasions of each port visit to tell my stories about personages and events of days long past. It is mainly for Kalākaua's and Lili's benefit. Esther, of course, has heard all my stories by now. Yet she listens as if she's hearing them for the first time.

The first day's sail brings us by late afternoon to the small village of Kaunakakai on Moloka'i. Here, I tell them how Kamehameha came to Moloka'i to see Kalola, collect his half-sister and niece, and take them back to Hawai'i with him, and how my uncle knocked out one of his own teeth in grief over Kalola's death. Kalākaua shakes his head in disbelief as he reflexively raises one hand to his lips. *I had not heard of this before,* he says.

We remain in the small harbor at Kaunakakai overnight, the captain preferring to sail among the islands in the daytime. At dinner, I take the opportunity to speak to Beckwith about Ezra. He is noncommittal. Nevertheless says Beckwith, *Send the young man to me.* Perhaps there will be more to my legacy than a memoir.

In the morning after breakfast, the first mate barks his orders, crewmen haul up the anchor and scramble into the rigging to unfurl the ship's sails, and the *Frances Palmer* is all at once under way for Kahului. It is mid-afternoon when we reach Kahului, where our ship is to remain until the next morning. After bidding farewell to Beckwith, I see a young man at the dock, a Hawaiian with a horse and cart, and ask him if he can take us the few miles mauka to the ʻĪao Valley. *Why would you want to go up there, old man?* he asks.

I am Nāmākehaʻokalani, I say. *My father was Keliʻimaikaʻi, and the Conqueror was my own uncle.*

The young man's eyes widen. He understands and requires no further explanation.

About twenty minutes later we are standing at the mouth of the ʻĪao Valley. I recount the story of that horrible battle, of how bodies of the fallen choked the stream and the water ran red with their blood. Lili cringes to hear about it; Esther bites her lip and shakes her head, truly seeing the battle for the first time. Kalākaua is fascinated, eagerly asking many questions about tactics and weapons, which I try to answer as best I can.

Esther has told me about your memoir, sir, Kalākaua says. *I would like to read it, and help you publish it if you wish.*

The next evening finds us at anchor in the bay at Hana. From the ship's deck, I point out Kauwiki Hill, where the old fort stood and where Kaʻahumanu was born. To the women's further dismay and Kalākaua's unflagging interest, I speak of yet more battles and suffering. I am compelled, for everywhere we touch land, I see soil soaked in blood.

Departing Hana the next morning, we are graced by a strong following wind. The *Frances Palmer* is under full sail and positively surfing the swells, which are rolling in the same direction. Dolphins leap in and out of the foam that boils around the ship's rising and falling bow. The air is full of salt spray. We are exhilarated and laughing now, all the sad thoughts of the previous day expunged. We cross the forty miles of the ʻAlenuihāhā Channel to ʻUpolu Point in northern Kohala in less than three-and-a-half hours.

As the *Frances Palmer* stands in to land and sails southward, I point out Kokoiki, Kamehameha's birthplace, which I can make out through the early-afternoon haze. Perhaps an hour and a half later, we come abreast of

Kawaihae and I call out in excitement, *Look up there on that long hill, do you see the old temple?* The Puʻukoholā heiau's lava-stone walls still proudly grace the Hill of the Whale. Beyond it we can see ʻOlohana's old compound. *And look above the temple,* I cry. *That is where my old friend John Young once lived.*

Queen Emma's grandfather! Lili exclaims.

Yes, I say. Now I am subdued, seeing my younger self on that hillside, watching the sun set over the bay. Can it really have been so long ago?

Esther notices. *What is it, my love?* she asks, taking my arm gently in hers.

Oh, it is nothing important, I say. I am thinking of ʻOlohana's daughter, my niece Fanny, who is Queen Emma's mother. At fifty-three, fifteen years my junior, Fanny is in ill health. I may well outlive her. Already, I have unaccountably outlived so many of my contemporaries: Liholiho and his wife Kamehamalu, who traveled to London in 1824 to call upon King George, only to succumb to measles there; his younger brother, Kauikeaouli, who reigned as Kamehameha III until his own death five years ago; and Kaʻahumanu, Keopuolani, Kalanimoku, Kahekili Keʻeaumoku, and the rest. The future calls to Esther and her friends, but it is the past that beckons me now. I keep these thoughts to myself as the *Frances Palmer* continues down the Kohala Coast toward Kailua.

We reach Kailua at sunset. The *Frances Palmer* drops anchor in the bay, and one of the crew rows us ashore in the ship's dinghy. The small craft rides low in the water, burdened as it is with our assorted valises and travel chests as well as us. Fortunately, the bay is calm at this hour.

At Kailua, we have been invited to stay at the Huliheʻe Palace by its young master, John Pitt Kīnaʻu, who greets us effusively. *Welcome! Welcome! Come in at once,* he exclaims, as we stand at the threshold, shaking the sand from our boots.

Kīna'u is my uncle Kamehameha's great-great grandson. Now in his seventeenth year, he was only five when he inherited the palace from his father, who died in the measles epidemic of 1848. He is an engaging young man—outgoing, friendly, and immediately likeable. Alexander Liholiho—Kamehameha IV—is not well, and has already named his brother, Lot Kapuāiwa, as his heir. As a lineal descendant of Kamehameha I, young Kīna'u is eligible to succeed Lot on the throne. Kīna'u bustles cheerfully here and there, directing household servants to see us and our luggage to our rooms, while others go about preparing a simple meal for us. I am very tired after our daylong sail, and excusing myself, I retire soon after dinner. Hours later, I awake briefly as Esther slips into bed beside me.

Mother has agreed to join us for dinner! Kīna'u exclaims.

We have just returned to the Hulihe'e Palace after a pleasant morning walking about Kailua village. I have taken Esther, Lili, Kalākaua, and Kīna'u to see the nearby site of the long-since vanished Ahu'ena Heiau. This place, I explained to them, is where Kamehameha honored Ka'ahumanu as his most important partner, and where, years later, Ka'ahumanu invested Liholiho, better known these days Kamehameha II, as king, and proclaimed herself as his co-regent. Now, with the day growing sultry, we have returned to the palace to rest and to take advantage of the cooling breezes off the bay.

When he is not attending school in Honolulu, Kīna'u lives at the palace with the Big Island's governor, his mother, Ruth Ke'elikōlani. She is Kamehameha's great-granddaughter—her grandfather was Pauli Ka'ōleiokū, Kamehameha's son by Kaneikapolei, so she and I are distant cousins. Ruth is a tall woman of thirty-three, who in the way of many ali'i women, already weighs several hundred pounds or more. Her broad, mostly dour countenance is only occasionally relieved by a smile.

Ruth is a traditionalist. She refuses to reside in the palace, preferring to live in a large, stone-floor, thatched-roof, pili-grass hale on the spacious grounds. Ruth patronizes dancers of the hula and singers of the old meles and will not attend worship services at the Congregationalist church directly across the road. I believe the structure itself offends her because it is built in part with stones taken from the Ahu'ena Heiau's lava-rock foundation. Villagers say that in the privacy of her hale, Ruth Ke'elikōlani worships the old gods.

Much like the *Hale Ali'i* in Honolulu, the palace that Ruth abjures is a pleasant, unpretentious structure with large, comfortable rooms. It boasts two floors, with rooms for entertaining on the first floor and private rooms for its occupants on the second. The Hulihe'e Palace presents an unadorned façade to the road just mauka. But makai it is graced by a lanai that runs the length of the building's second story and affords a view of the bay.

Kīna'u tells me that it is most unusual for Ruth to dine at the palace. *Mother prefers to eat at her hale,* he says. *She will not come to the house to eat with me; I must always go to her. I think she has made an exception in this instance for you, sir.*

Later, Ruth takes her seat at the head of the long koa-wood table in the palace's dining room. As the five of us join her, Ruth insists that I sit next to her. *I want to hear about the old days from one who was there,* she explains. Ruth withholds her questions, however, until we have finished dinner, a splendid meal of Hawaiian fare: succulent kalua pork baked all day in an imu; yam, roasted bananas, and coconut; and, of course, poi—plenty of poi. For all her insistence on observing the old traditions, Ruth thinks nothing of men and women eating together, or of women eating food once kapu to them. In this respect she is a thoroughly modern wahine.

After dinner, Kīna'u begins to interrogate me about Kamehameha's old battles, but Ruth silences him with a wave of her hand. *You were there the night Ka'ahumanu and Keopuolani ended the kapu eating, were you not?* she asks me. *You saw the burning of the heiau?*

Yes, I respond.

Tell us about that, Ruth says. *Tell us about Kuamo'o.*

Much later, Ruth thanks me, bids us good evening, and returns to her grass house. We all go upstairs to sit on the lanai. The unclouded, moonless sky is alive with the light of untold thousands of dancing stars. Looking up in this moment, I imagine our ancestors gazing heavenward in awe of the gods who set them there. For some time we sit in companionable silence, listening to the sound of the waves striking the lava shelf that lies between the house's lawn and the bay.

At last, Lili asks me, *Benjamin, what was the purpose of all the fighting? What was gained?*

I take some time to respond. Then I say, *Alapa'i, Kalani'ōpu'u, Kahekili, and those other old chiefs gained nothing enduring, but my uncle, Kamehameha, gained a nation.*

Later in our room, I am about to join Esther in our elegant, four-poster haole bed when I glance out our window toward Ruth's grass house, enveloped in the shadows between the palace and the road. I see a pale light through Ruth's window. Kīna'u has told me that his mother refuses to use whale-oil lamps and persists in lighting her hale with kukui-oil lamps. As I watch, Ruth's light flutters and winks out.

In the morning, we go by carriage to Keauhou and then to Kuamo'o, where my brother Kekuaokalani fought his only battle. The five of us—young Kīna'u has come, too—stand at the edge of the barren, rocky field, near the place where Hoapili and his men waited with their muskets for my brother and Manono forty years ago.

Kalākaua surveys the field and says, *There is nothing to mark this place. It is all a confusion of rocks. Who would know that an important battle was waged here?*

Keep looking, Kalākaua, I say.

Kīna'u sees the cairns first. *Look!* he cries. *Graves!*

Yes, burial mounds, I say. *Keep looking.*

Now they all see them. *There are hundreds of them!* Lili exclaims. *The longer I look, the more I see.* Lili turns to her brother. *Can you see them now, David? They extend all the way to that long, low hill over there.*

Yes, I see them, Kalākaua replies. Turning to me, he asks, *Benjamin, where is your brother's grave, do you know?*

No, I say.

As I watch the cairns reveal themselves in ever-increasing numbers, my mind's eye has turned elsewhere, toward Ruth Ke'elikōlani's hale, where the light fades as her kukui-oil lamp's flame dies. I think of Gideon and Sarah, Ezra's dispossessed, maka'āinana parents, and how our people are like Ruth's lamp. As we lose our connection to the land, and our numbers continue to decline, our flame is also dying, our light is growing dim. *We are drowning in a sea of foreigners*, I murmur.

What did you say, Nāmākēha? Esther asks. She sees that I am upset and draws closer to me as the others gather around us. I hardly take notice, for my eyes are still fixed on the cairns and I am listening to other voices, whispering to me on the afternoon breeze.

Do you hear them? I ask Esther and the others. *Do you hear spirits of this place calling to us?* They cannot, of course.

What are they saying? Kalākaua asks.

Turning to him, I reply, *'Remember, once there was fire.'*

— Kailua-Kona, July 18, 1859

Afterward

Nearly all the persons portrayed in *Once There Was Fire* are historical figures, and accounts by near-contemporaneous, 19th century historians inform many of the events described in the novel. While I have strived to keep faith with the history of the Hawaiian people, *Once There Was Fire* is fiction. History is its armature, but dramatic license propels it.

For example, the battle at ʻĪao Valley on Maui is described only in the most general terms by the 19th century historians S.M. Kamakau and Abraham Fornander. Kamakau devotes a third of a page to this battle in his 430-page work, *Ruling Chiefs of Hawaii*, and Fornander, about one of 350 pages in his *Ancient History of the Hawaiian People.* Both men write that Kamehameha won a decisive victory thanks to his superiority in haole weaponry and the assistance of his English advisers, John Young and Isaac Davis. Kamakau and Fornander, however, leave the battle's details to the imagination, and I felt free to imagine how this fierce fight waged with clubs and spears on one side and muskets and cannons on the other might have unfolded.

Similarly, Kalanimoku's and Kaʻahumanu's plot against Kekuaokalani prior to the battle at Kuamoʻo is my invention. Kamakau recounts that Kekuaokalani refused a request to go by sea to Kailua — not to Keauhou, as in the novel — electing instead to travel overland with his people, and that his decision precipitated the battle. I spun the scheme against him from this bit of historical detail. I imagined the way the battle developed, but not the way Kekuaokalani and Manono died. Today the Kuamoʻo battlefield is a historical site, and the cairns of the dead are still there. The first time I visited the site, I initially saw a jumble of rocks, and perceived the graves only gradually, cairn by cairn, just as Nāmākēha's companions do. I do not believe in spirits, but in that moment, I felt a chill.

The ancestry of Benjamin Nāmākēha, the narrator of *Once There Was Fire*, is conjectural. Nāmākēha was a contemporary of Kamehameha's who lived until 1859. Early in my research, I came across Benjamin in a genealogy of Big Island aliʻi posted on Ancestry.com. I wanted to tell the story of Kamehameha and his times from the perspective of a Hawaiian noble who could have been close to him, and Nāmākēha, identified in the online genealogy as the son of Kamehameha's favorite brother Keliʻimaikaʻi and the half-brother of Kekuaokalani, seemed ideal for my purpose. According to other sources, however, Benjamin was neither Keliʻimaikaʻi's son, nor Kamehameha's nephew, nor Kekuaokalani's brother. Whatever the truth of the matter, Benjamin (or Bennett) Nāmākēha did in fact marry the much younger Esther Kapiʻolani, who married David Kalākaua after Benjamin died. Esther became the Hawaiian Kingdom's queen when Kalākaua ascended to the islands' throne in 1874.

During the more than ten years I spent researching and writing *Once There Was Fire*, my appreciation for the Hawaiian people and their culture deepened considerably. The Hawaiians of old were resourceful and industrious. Inhabitants of volcanic islands with no access to metals and thus no opportunity to develop metallurgy, they made the most of the resources at hand — stone, wood, and all manner of plant material — to make their clothing, build their temples, construct their houses and sailing vessels, and to farm, fish, and conduct warfare.

Preliterate 18th century Hawaiians had a rich oral tradition handed down through generations in genealogies, chants, and dance. Spiritually, they were animists who saw manifold gods and goddesses invested in the physical world and the natural forces that surrounded them. Their religious beliefs are exemplified in the *Kumulipo*, the complex Hawaiian creation myth whose metaphysics eerily anticipate modern cosmology's "big bang."

The old Hawaiians have been portrayed elsewhere in fiction as simple, childish people. I found them to be anything but.

The Hawaiians lived in a Garden of Eden, but it was by no means paradisiacal. Their society was rigidly stratified and their *kapus*—laws—were unbending and often unmercifully harsh on transgressors. Warfare among the Hawaiians of old was constant and prosecuted with bloody enthusiasm. The Hawaiians propitiated their gods with human sacrifice and they decorated their heiaus with human skulls.

Benjamin Nāmākēha touches on good and unfortunate aspects of this milieu without judgment. I have endeavored throughout the novel to treat the old Hawaiians and their culture with respect through his voice. Readers will have noted that commoners, the *maka'āinana*, receive little notice or respect from Nāmākēha. This was perhaps inevitable, since the story of this period as told by Kamakau and Fornander, two of its most prominent exponents, is the story of the ali'i, in which commoners hardly register, and Nāmākēha, himself a proud ali'i, reflects this ethos.

Though I do not speak Hawaiian, I have sought to infuse *Once There Was Fire* with a sense of the old Hawaiians and their world by incorporating Hawaiian words, phrases, and sentences (of my own questionable construction) in the novel. In doing so, I have no doubt subjected this beautiful, lyrical language to a certain amount of abuse and for this, I can only say to native Hawaiian speakers, *E mihi au.* I apologize. Finally, to readers who have persisted to this point, *mahalo.*

Stephen Shender
Santa Cruz, California

Bibliography

Beaglehole, J.C. *The Life of Captain James Cook*. Stanford University Press, 1974

Beckwith, Martha. *Hawaiian Mythology*. University of Hawaii Press, 1970.

Bushnell, O.A. *Hygiene and Sanitation among the Ancient Hawaiians*. Hawaii Historical Review, 1966

Bushnell, O.A. *The Return of Lono*. University of Hawaii Press, 1971.

Cahill, Emmett. *The Life and Times of John Young*. Island Heritage Publishing, 1999

Cook, Capt. James. *The Journals*. Penguin Books, 2003.

Cordy, Ross. *Exalted Sits the Chief*. Mutual Publishing, 2000.

Desha, Stephen L. *Kamehameha and his Warrior Kekūhaupi'o*. Kamehameha Schools Press, 2000.

Emerson, Nathaniel. *Unwritten Literature of Hawaii*, The sacred Songs of the Hula. Government Printing Office/Forgotten Books, 1909/2008.

Fornander, Abraham. *Fornander's Ancient History of the Hawaiian People*. Mutual Publishing, 1996.

Gutmanis, June. *Na Pule Kahiko Ancient Hawaiian Prayers*. Editions Limited, 1983.

Haley, James L. *Captive Paradise, A History of Hawaii*. St. Martins Press, 2014.

Hough, Richard. *Captain James Cook*. W.W. Norton, 1995.

Kalākaua, King David. *The Legends and Myths of Hawaii*. Mutual Publishing, 1990.

Kamakau, S.M. *Ruling Chiefs of Hawaii*. Kamehameha Schools Press, 1991.

Kāne, Herb Kawainui. *Ancient Hawaii*. The Kawainui Press, 1997.

King, Capt. James. *Voyage to the Pacific Ocean, Volume III, Book V*. Lords Commissioners of the Admiralty, 1784. https://ia601405.us.archive.org/5/items/voyagetopacifico03cook/voyagetopacifico03cook.pdf

Krauss, Beatrice H. *Plants in Hawaiian Culture*. University of Hawaii Press, 1993.

Kukendall, R.S. *The Hawaiian Kingdom, 1778-1854*. University of Hawaii Press, 1938.

Malo, David. *Hawaiian Antiquities, Mo'olelo Hawai'i*. Bishop Museum, 1951.

Pukui, Mary Kawena. *'Ōlelo No 'Eau, Hawaiian Proverbs and Poetical Sayings*. Bishop Museum Press, 1983.

Silverman, Jane L. *Kaahumanu, Molder of Change*. Friends of the Judiciary History Center, 1987.

Tregaskis, Richard. *The Warrior King, Hawaii's Kamehameha the Great*. Falmouth Press, 1973.

CPSIA information can be obtained
at www.ICGtesting.com
Printed in the USA
LVOW13s0907070517
533591LV00010B/794/P